The past is never truly buried . . .

Generations of Jillian Cley's family have been tasked with a strange duty—tending the burial plot of Gabriel Vane, whose body was the first to be interred in the Hode's Hill cemetery. Jillian faithfully continues the long-standing tradition—until one October night, Vane's body is stolen from its resting place. Is it a Halloween prank? Or something more sinister?

As the descendants of those buried in the church yard begin to experience bizarre "accidents," Jillian tries to uncover the cause. Deeply empathic, she does not make friends easily, or lightly. But to fend off the terror taking over her town, she must join forces with artist Dante DeLuca, whose sensitivity to the spirit world has been both a blessing and a curse. The two soon realize Jillian's murky family history is entwined with a tragic legacy tracing back to the founding of Hode's Hill. To set matters right, an ancient wrong must be avenged...or Jillian, Dante, and everyone in town will forever be at the mercy of a vengeful spirit.

Visit us at www.kensingtonbooks.com

Books by Mae Clair

Weathering Rock
Twelfth Sun
Myth and Magic

The Point Pleasant Series
A Thousand Yesteryears (Book 1)
A Cold Tomorrow (Book 2)
A Desolate Hour (Book 3)

The Hode's Hill Novels
Cusp of Night (Book 1)
End of Day (Book 2)

Published by Kensington Publishing Corporation

End of Day

The Hode's Hill Novels

Mae Clair

LYRICAL PRESS
Kensington Publishing Corp.
www.kensingtonbooks.com

LYRICAL UNDERGROUND BOOKS are published by
Kensington Publishing Corp.
119 West 40th Street
New York, NY 10018

All Kensington titles, imprints, and distributed lines are available at special quantity discounts for bulk purchases for sales promotion, premiums, fund-raising, educational, or institutional use.

Special book excerpts or customized printings can also be created to fit specific needs. For details, write or phone the office of the Kensington Sales Manager: Kensington Publishing Corp., 119 West 40th Street, New York, NY 10018. Attn. Sales Department. Phone: 1-800-221-2647.

Lyrical Underground and Lyrical Underground logo Reg. US Pat. & TM Off.

First Electronic Edition: January 2019
eISBN-13: 978-1-5161-0728-5
eISBN-10: 1-5161-0728-4

First Print Edition: January 2019
ISBN-13: 978-1-5161-0731-5
ISBN-10: 1-5161-0731-4

Printed in the United States of America

To Carmen Stefanescu
for treasured friendship across miles, countries, and languages.

Chapter 1

They were coming.

Men with dogs and guns. Men he'd once called friends and neighbors.

Gabriel Vane wiped sweat from his face and zigzagged deeper into the woods. A sliver of moon shadowed him, ghost-white behind the frantic scuttle of spider clouds. The limited light helped him weave unnoticed through dense pillars of trees, but not without cost. He'd lost count of how many times branches nicked his skin or tore his clothing. On another night he would have dodged the obstacles with ease, but the fever made him clumsy. He tried to vault an overturned tree but misjudged the leap in the darkness. His leg buckled on landing, and his ankle twisted beneath him. Sprawling to his hands and knees, he inhaled the mold of decayed leaves, the peat of hard-packed soil.

Get up!

He forced himself to move, slipped on the leaf-strewn ground, and climbed unsteadily to his feet. The wind carried the sound of baying.

The dogs were closer, gaining on him. If only he could think. Clear his mind of the fever. Convince Atticus he wasn't responsible for the deaths in the village. Couldn't they see he was sick—that the fever would claim him as it had the others, including his beloved Dinah? Her eyes, green as the emerald she'd folded into his hand, still had the power to haunt.

"It will protect you," she'd said, closing his fingers over the stone.

But it hadn't. It wouldn't.

He hobbled forward, lurching faster despite the pain splintering from his ankle. The sound of crashing exploded behind him, men and animals trampling through the woodland. Someone shouted, commanding him to stop. A musket ball winged past his ear and blew the bark from a tree five feet away.

"Don't shoot!" Atticus Crowe's order resounded from the shadows. "We need him alive."

For how long? He was slated to die—if not by gunfire or the scourge of sickness, then by sacrifice.

"They will kill you," Dinah had said as he'd cradled her in his arms. *"My father has convinced the men of the village you are possessed by a demon. He has lost all sanity to grief. Do not let him have the emerald. I fear how he might use its power."*

Gabriel slowed, his energy ebbing, body wracked by chills. He could no longer see for the sweat in his eyes. Perhaps the illness was fey, as Atticus proclaimed, but killing him would not end the disease.

"Gabriel!" Atticus sounded close.

He heaved a breath, knowing his strength had reached its end.

I will be with you soon, Dinah, my love.

Undone by the fever, he swayed. Behind him, Atticus and the others spread in an arc, torches blazing, blocking his escape. Gabriel turned slowly, the flickering light illuminating the faces of his pursuers—Thaddeus Keel with three coon hounds. Andrew Whitley, who restrained two ragged mutts by their collars. Only last month, Gabriel had helped Cyrus Herman shore up his porch, and now the man hunted him like a criminal.

There were others, too. Everett Donner, who he'd called friend. Farley, the tanner. Ira Blake. And of course, Atticus. Whipcord lean, stern-faced, unforgiving. A man Gabriel had once believed would be his father-in-law.

Breaking from the others, Atticus stepped forward. "I want my daughter's pledge."

The emerald.

"She gave it to me."

"She should have given it to her brother. He might be alive if not for her foolishness." He extended his hand, palm up. "I will have the gem, Gabriel."

"I do not have it." He'd taken steps to ensure no one would.

Atticus motioned curtly to Cyrus and Farley. "Search him."

Gabriel withstood their pawing in silence, pain radiating from his ankle, cold sweat matting his hair to his brow.

"He speaks the truth," Farley said. "He does not have the jewel."

Atticus passed his torch to the man beside him. He stepped close to Gabriel. "What have you done with it?"

"I have hidden it."

"Where?"

"Where you will never find it."

"You fool!" Atticus cracked him across the face, the blow hard enough to make Gabriel stumble. The men beside him held him upright, rigidly locking his arms behind his back when he would have fallen.

"We did not come for a jewel," Keel said. "Your emerald means nothing to us, Atticus. The demon must die. We will have the sacrifice, and we will have it now."

"Very well." Atticus's mouth thinned in a sneer. "Perhaps my daughter's pledge is lost, but it matters little, given she will never bestow it on another. When you are dead and buried, Gabriel Vane, I will raze your house to the ground and find where you have hidden the stone." Reaching beneath his frock coat, Atticus spat on the ground, then withdrew a long knife. The blade was crudely hammered but gleamed with a rim of silver in the pale moonlight. He edged nearer. "You understand what is required of you."

Gabriel's mouth had gone dry. Even with the fever blurring his vision, his body burning with cold and heat, fear curdled his stomach. "If you do this thing—you will curse the spot upon which we stand for all eternity. No good will ever come from this place."

"What do I care for these wretched woods, when people die on our farms and in our village? My own daughter and son have been taken from me. And for what? For this!" Grabbing a fistful of Gabriel's shirt, Atticus ripped it from his shoulder. The scratches from the wolf were only partially healed, red with pinpricks of blood where skin had broken open.

Gabriel shivered as the air struck his exposed flesh. "I hunted the beast to *protect* the people of our village."

"And so you shall protect them—in the next life. As these men bear witness…" Atticus edged in a circle, letting his gaze rest briefly on each of those gathered. "Yours will be the first body set in the ground." He shifted to face Gabriel. "You know what is expected of you."

Anger shot through Gabriel. "I am not a dog to be treated this way. Nor a demon."

"Say what you will. Possessed or not, you will protect us from the demons to come." Atticus plunged the dagger into his chest.

* * * *

Present Day

"Come on, Blizzard. Time for a walk." Jillian Cley hooked the leash to the collar of her two-year-old husky, then opened the front door and stepped outside. A gust of air, tainted by the chill of autumn, cleared her head of a day spent hunched over the computer. Eli Yancy wanted a website to reflect his personality, but she was having a hard time pinning down the character of a man who'd spent his previous career cloaked in an ambiguous role at Wickham.

No surprise he'd chosen the nondescript brick building for his new enterprise. After an initial meeting to discuss design, she'd pegged him as too withdrawn to be a successful life coach. But a paying customer was a paying customer, and she needed the work. Business had been slow. She'd even toyed with the idea of taking a part-time job at the library where her neighbor, Maya Sinclair, worked. Three weeks ago there'd been a general services opening that didn't require a degree. Jillian had dragged her feet, hemming and hawing until the position was filled. Too many people. Too many stray emotions.

Blizzard whined impatiently.

"Okay, I get it." She let the husky lead her down the steps, away from the six brownstones tucked into the south end of Hode's Hill. Following her usual route, she crossed the road and picked a path running parallel to the Chinkwe River. The water carried a slate gray cast this late in the day. In another few weeks it would be Halloween, followed by the end of Daylight Saving. Her evening walks would be blanketed in darkness rather than the diffused twilight creeping from the horizon.

She was fond of autumn—vivid colors and smoky scents—but could do without the hasty onslaught of night. It would mean earlier trips to Hickory Chapel Cemetery to keep up her duties as promised.

Blizzard stopped to poke around a clump of dry ferns. Nose to the ground, he pattered into the grass, snuffling as he roamed ahead. Jillian kept his leash looped around her wrist, hands in the pockets of her black pea coat. Across the narrow trail, the wind sang through maples and oaks, scattering rust-red leaves from knobby branches. If she walked far enough, she'd pass the North Bridge. Farther still, the remains of the Old Orchard Truss Bridge.

Last June, a drifter who suffered from an abnormality that made his skin blue committed suicide by leaping from the crumbling central pylon. At least, that was the official version, but Jillian had always suspected there was more to the story. Rumors hinted Eli Yancy had been involved, but she'd never been able to pin down his connection. If she dwelled on the association, she'd end up questioning whether she wanted him as a client. Technically, he'd done nothing illegal. Ethically, he made her skin crawl.

The sad reality was that she needed the money. Especially with the cost of Madison's treatments skyrocketing and insurance only stretching so far. There was still hope for her sister, no matter what traditional medicine said. If Jillian was forced to live on peanut butter sandwiches between clients, it would be worth every scrimped penny if Madison would only smile.

"Hi, Jillian. Hi, Blizzard."

She swiveled in time to see a thin boy with straw-colored hair extend his hand to the husky. Blizzard happily nosed his palm, then bumped closer, tail wagging in greeting.

"Hi, Elliott." Jillian smiled as the boy knelt to rough Blizzard's fur. She knew his mother, Tessa, well enough to pass pleasantries—a casual hello or comment about the weather—but kept her new neighbor at arm's length. If Tessa was offended, she'd never allowed her resentment to show.

"No schoolwork tonight?" Jillian asked.

At twelve, Elliott was small for his age. Tessa once absently confessed she hoped he'd make friends in his new school. Even without her empathic nature, Jillian would have pigeonholed him as awkward and shy. He'd since come to trust her, but it was Blizzard who'd created a safe buffer between them.

"I did it in school." Standing, Elliott swept his bangs to the side. "Think I'm gonna drag my telescope out when it gets dark." Behind the thick frames of his glasses, his eyes were the color of coffee beans, often worried, always serious. How many nights had he spent looking up at the sky? Jillian didn't doubt he liked stargazing, but any activity was better with friends. There had to be kids in school he could connect with.

Maybe she should talk to Tessa, suggest that Elliott join an astronomy or science club. Find a way to fit in. She understood the stigma of being a loner, could sense the familiar pain of isolation seeping from him and reawakening—

No!

Mentally, Jillian clamped the conduit shut.

"Hey, are you all right?" Elliott's mouth fell open as he stared up at her. "You look...you look kind of—"

"I'm fine." She forced a smile, ignoring the cold sweat on the back of her neck. Always in tune with her emotions, Blizzard whined and pulled on the leash. "Just a little tired from all the work I did today. I should probably get going. Blizzard needs his walk."

"Yeah, okay." Elliott stuffed his hands in the pockets of his sweatshirt and scuffed a sneaker against the ground.

Poor kid was bored, but it wasn't her problem. *He* couldn't be her problem. She had enough of her own. And yet—

"Want to walk with us?"

The smile that blazed across his face made the invitation worthwhile. "That'd be great. Mom said dinner won't be ready for fifteen minutes. Our cousin is coming over for meatloaf." Another flash of a smile. "Maybe you could join us sometime. Mom doesn't have many friends since we moved."

"I'm usually tied up." A lie. "And that's not true about your mom." Jillian started walking, letting Blizzard lead the way. The husky trotted ahead, tail in the air, tongue lolling from his mouth. "Your mom has become friendly with Maya Sinclair."

"I guess." Elliott shrugged as he fell in at her side. "But she seems lonely. Ever since Dad left—" His face twisted as if he'd stumbled over something ugly. His despondency oozed into the air and tugged at Jillian's heart.

Divorce wasn't easy, children often the ones who suffered the most, but Elliott had a mother who loved him, a grandmother who lived two doors away and doted on him, and the potential—from what Jillian could see—to be a top student. Maybe his lack of friends made the divorce a harder pill to swallow. Given he was lonely, he probably imagined his mother harboring that same emotion.

"You know what?" Jillian tried to steer the conversation elsewhere. "Your mom is doing just fine. It takes a while to get settled into a new town, but you've got family here. I think it's great your mom was able to rent a place so close to your grandmother."

"Yeah." Elliott's voice was soft. "It's just hard adjusting, you know?"

Jillian wasn't sure if he referred to his parents' divorce or the move. She shifted to the side as a jogger passed by. Up ahead, Blizzard had wandered off the path to nose in the grass again. Cars kept up a steady pace on River Road, the traffic signal at the entrance to the North Bridge holding on green. The soft ripple of the Chinkwe underscored the hum of tires, the chatter of walkers passing on the trail, the hiss of a bus braking two stops down—familiar sounds. City sounds.

"Hode's Hill is a good place." She didn't know if Elliott believed her, or if perhaps he fit more comfortably into the small beach town that had been his home for twelve years. What boy wouldn't want to live where the shoreline stretched to the Atlantic and the bay offered long summers filled with fishing and boating? "The Chinkwe isn't saltwater, but you can still boat and fish. Some of the bigger islands are great for docking, too."

"I don't have a boat." He sounded glum. "Dad always took care of stuff like that. Mom doesn't know the first thing about boats. Or fishing."

"Maybe she'll learn."

"Do you fish?" He glanced at her hopefully.

"No." It had been years. She had no intention of taking him fishing, or of getting involved and becoming friends with his mother. Getting involved was how people got hurt. How Madison ended up with a shattered mind and a life spent staring at four walls.

Jillian's heart ratcheted faster, the sights and sounds of the city fading. Her hands grew clammy, her breath hissing quick and short through her lips. She tightened her fingers on Blizzard's leash, barely aware when the dog whined and nudged against her.

Somehow, she managed to pull the city back into focus—the smell of bus exhaust, the raucous blare of a car horn. She blinked, the sting of light a telltale sign her pupils had dilated. She reached for the cord around her neck, but her glasses were missing. Foolishly, she'd left the tinted lenses at home.

"We should go back now."

"Oh. Okay." Elliott studied her queerly, but she couldn't blame him. She had to be a sight—long blond hair hanging in a thick, waist-length braid, face pinched and pale, pupils obliterating the green of her eyes. He probably thought she was a freak.

She didn't have the guts to tell him he was right.

"This way." She gave Blizzard the lead, letting the husky guide her home.

* * * *

"How's that?" Dante DeLuca darkened the pupils of the creature's eyes then slid the drawing across the table. Far from his best work, especially when jotted on a paper napkin, but it should impress a twelve-year-old.

"Wow, I wish I could draw like that." Elliott held the sketch closer. "You draw better than anyone I know, Dante."

"He paints, too." Tessa held out her hand. "Can I see?"

Dante watched as his cousin examined his work. She still had the same smattering of freckles across her nose as she'd had when they were kids, but her eyes—black as India ink—showed the wear of starting over after thirteen years of marriage. Tightening his fingers around his pencil, he tried not to think of the dickhead who'd left her for a fling with a twenty-year-old.

"I see you still like monsters." Tessa's mouth curved with the hint of a smile.

Dante traded the pencil for a fork and speared a piece of meatloaf. "It's an alien. You know—outer space? E.T.?"

"Yeah, Mom. It's got antennas."

"I'm teasing, Elliott." Tessa passed the napkin to her son. "Dante used to like to draw monsters when he was a little older than you."

"Really?" Elliott's eyes grew wide behind his glasses. "Would you draw me a monster sometime, Dante?"

"Sure. Any reason why?"

"I don't know." Squirming slightly, Elliott dropped his gaze to his plate.

They'd all but finished with dinner when Elliott started talking about space creatures and Dante got it in his head to do a sketch on the fly. Tessa had served dinner in the breakfast area off the kitchen, so it had been easy to snatch a pencil from the junk drawer by the refrigerator and reward her son—his cousin by blood—with a bug-eyed alien. Weird how family ties fit together.

Sucking on his bottom lip, Elliott pushed a clump of corn kernels into his mashed potatoes. "Monsters aren't always bad. If they know you're friendly, maybe they won't spook you."

"Do you get spooked?" Dante sensed something left unsaid.

Before Elliott could answer, Tessa stood, gathering her plate and silverware. "I don't think you need to worry about monsters, but you need to finish eating if you want Dante to help set up your telescope." She nodded toward Elliott. "It's a school night. I don't want you out late, even if it is for stargazing."

"Yeah. Okay." Elliott exhaled, the sound morose.

Dante waited until Tessa had crossed to the sink, then lowered his voice. "You can tell me about the monsters while we set up your telescope. After dinner."

"Okay." As if suddenly eager to finish, Elliott scooped corn and mashed potatoes into his mouth.

* * * *

"What's its name again?" Dante stepped back from the telescope and gazed up at the moon with his naked eye. He could still see the crater, but without the beefed-up magnification that had made it seem inches away.

"Copernicus." Elliott fiddled with the focusing knobs. "It's called the Monarch of the Moon. Once you know where to look, it's easy to find even without a telescope."

After dinner, Dante had carried the telescope several blocks away, while Elliott had talked his ear off about impact craters, maria, rilles, and other lunar features Dante was clueless about. Elliott normally did his stargazing across the street, just off the walking trail, but Dante suggested the empty field below Hickory Chapel. There were fewer city lights at the south end of town, not to mention less traffic.

"The science teacher at my old school used to make drawings of what he saw on the moon." Elliott continued fiddling with the magnification.

"You mean little green men?"

Elliott poked his head up long enough to roll his eyes.

At least the kid had a sense of humor. Dante hadn't seen much of his cousin or her son since Tessa had followed her ex-husband to Maryland shortly after Elliott was born. Sure, there were holidays and visits when she came home, but he wasn't exactly on speaking terms with his Aunt Imelda—Tessa's mom—so even those occasions had been limited.

When Aunt Imelda was feeling kind, she referred to him as "a hippie nonconformist." When she was in a snit—her standard attitude for most of his life—he became "a no-account bohemian living off a trust fund." It probably didn't help that he favored ragged jeans and usually wore his long hair tied in a ponytail. She'd been on the outs with his father for most of his life. No surprise she'd transferred the same ridiculous grudge to his son. Top that off with the stupid mistake he'd made about her late husband and there was no common ground between them.

Dante tilted his head to study the sky. "At least it's not too cold, and we have a good viewing spot, huh?"

"I guess so." Elliott glanced nervously over his shoulder.

Dante followed his gaze, looking past the steeple of Hickory Chapel to the hulking shapes jutting from the ground behind the old church. Many of the tombstones—thin black slabs in the darkness—dated back to the late 1700s when Hode's Hill was a rustic village with a pinwheel of outlying farms. The chapel wasn't used anymore, a boarded-up shell that encroaching weeds and ivy gradually claimed as their own. Many of the graves were untended, the descendants of those buried long ago passed from the Earth. Occasionally, there was talk of trying to preserve the place, but progress had been stalled for years. Several folktales had sprung up over the decades, all spooky stuff kids liked to tell at Halloween. Most of the stories were harmless campfire stuff.

Unless you happened to be the rare soul who'd inherited an affinity for the spirit world.

Dante recalled an old sketchbook filled with drawings he rarely examined. The memory of a long-ago Halloween night danced in his head, conjuring images of hideous creatures lurking behind trees and gravestones. He jerked his chin in the direction of the cemetery. "Is that where the monsters are?"

Elliott swallowed audibly. "I heard kids talking at school. Finn Carrigan said some boy cut through the cemetery when he was walking home. It was after dark, and he was never seen again. A monster got him."

"Is Finn a friend of yours?"

Elliott shook his head. "I just overheard him talking about it."

"Hmm." He tried to appear neutral. Kids had no clue what really lurked in the cemetery, just made up stories because that had been the way of it for generations. "Did he know who the boy was? The one who disappeared?"

Another shake of the head. "Rodney Townsend said it was a bad place, and not to go there. That monsters creep out of the graves after dark."

"Not ghosts? Monsters?"

"Maybe both."

"And maybe these boys knew you were listening and decided to put you on."

Elliott flushed, the heightened color on his cheeks evident even in the dark. He jiggled the focusing knob but didn't bend to look through the eyepiece. "Hickory Chapel is close to where Mom and I live. What if the monsters leave the graveyard? Our house and Jillian's would be the first they'd find."

"Jillian?"

"She lives next door, on the corner. She's got a husky named Blizzard."

"Oh." Dante remembered seeing a blond-haired woman with a dog earlier that night. "I don't think you have to worry about monsters or ghosts." *Just the jerk kids at school who are making it rough for you.* "When I was a kid, I cut through the cemetery all the time."

"Really?" Elliott gazed up, moonlight reflecting off his glasses.

"Sure. Sometimes even at night."

Especially one Halloween night that had gone horribly wrong. He thought of the medallion beneath his shirt. A medal with an etching of the Archangel Michael that had once belonged to his father.

"Is that why you drew monsters?"

Dante gave a short laugh. It was amazing how the kid had glommed onto that bit of information from dinner. Time to change the subject and lock the memories in the past where they belonged.

"Hey." He pointed to the moon. "What happened to the lunar mountain ranges you were going to show me? We can't stay out long. Your mom will be waiting."

"Yeah. Okay." The reminder seemed to energize Elliott. He began fiddling with the magnification knobs, chattering about declination angles and optimum viewing time.

Dante only half heard, the boy's earlier question pinging around inside his head.

"Is that why you drew monsters?"

Hunching his shoulders against the chill air, he recalled his father's sudden death and the awakening of his spiritual sight.

No. I drew them because my monsters were real.

* * * *

The house was empty, too big. Dante should have stayed at his apartment in town, the small unit he rented near the senior center where his grandmother lived. But the sprawling two-story, inherited from his father, had been his home growing up. Most of his memories were bottled in these walls, not all of them good.

Visiting with Tessa and Elliott—especially Elliott—had him dredging awake memories of the days and months after his father had been killed. Salvador DeLuca's death had been accidental, a mishap while on the job at Wickham, but the details had never been clear. Dante's medical scientist father had enjoyed a lucrative career, the specifics of his work clouded in secrecy. After his death, Dante and his grandmother received a large wrongful death settlement, the bulk of it put in trust for him until he turned twenty-one.

Eight years later, he was still living off those funds and the wealth inherited from his father. Most of his time was spent painting or working at the gallery he'd established in the center of town, a place to showcase his work and that of other local artists. He freelanced on the side, most recently doing some conceptual drawings for Hode Development's new senior living project. He had plenty to keep him occupied, but every now and then his mind drifted to the unseen creatures that lurked in Hickory Chapel Cemetery.

Like tonight.

Monsters.

There had been a moment when he'd thought Elliott had inherited his family's spiritual sensitivity. Other than Dante, several of his ancestors had possessed the trait, including Dante's father. Salvador once told him he had memories of his great-grandfather communicating with the dead through flickering lights and table rappings.

Despite the DeLuca affinity for the supernatural, Tessa's mother, Imelda, wanted nothing to do with it. Part of the reason she and Dante didn't speak. She hadn't liked when her brother, Salvador, dabbled in otherworldly things, and had taken offense when Dante continued in that vein. He'd committed the cardinal sin by making the mistake of telling her he'd inadvertently once communicated with her dead husband. From that point on, she'd wanted nothing to do with him.

At least Tessa hadn't written him off, but by then she'd been married, living elsewhere. It was best her son stayed neutral, having nothing to do with spirits, wraiths, and the nightmarish things that hovered out of eyesight.

Dante jogged up the staircase to the second floor, then down the hall past the master suite and the southern-facing room he'd converted to a studio. His old bedroom, the place he'd spent numerous nights scratching in a sketchbook as a teenager, was tucked at the end of the hall. He'd changed it up not long ago—fresh paint, new carpet and furniture—but a lot of his old drawing supplies were still stored in the walk-in closet.

Switching on the light and stepping inside, he eyed the arrangement of boxes stacked on the shelves. Some were labeled with dates, others stuffed wherever they would fit. An open box, shorter than the rest, contained a smattering of loose drawings and a sketchbook. Dante carried the box into the bedroom then dropped to a seat on the mattress. He settled the carton on his lap and shuffled the papers aside. Tucked underneath, the sketchbook kindled a stockpile of memories.

Halloween night. He, Spencer Wright, and Alex Price chucked hickory nuts at the old chapel just for something stupid to do. See who could pockmark the siding or loosen the boards on the windows. When they grew bored with the game, they smoked cigarettes. Guzzled a few beers and tried to psych each other out by pretending to hear noises in the dark.

Dante was effed up, his dad just a few months dead. Maybe that's why he saw what the others didn't. It was after midnight when they heard the eerie tolling of the church bell, all three freezing in place, wide-eyed stares sweeping to the bell tower.

The empty *bell tower.*

Nothing there, but the invisible bell continued to toll, a keening shrill almost human.

"Let's get the hell out of here." Spencer was the first to find his voice. Tossing his beer, he raced toward the hill that would spill him onto the street and safety. Alex stood rooted, jaw hanging open as he gaped at the derelict church.

The feeling of something malevolent swept through Dante. He pivoted, spurring Alex into motion. It was obvious his friend didn't see the creatures, but they couldn't have been more apparent to him.

Nightmarish things that lurked behind trees and gravestones, hideous abominations without name. Conglomerations of scales, bulging eyes, and fangs soiled with blood. Chains spooled behind them, each lumbering movement sending a rattling clank through yokes of corroded iron. Fetid breath scorched Dante's face. Hot, reeking of brimstone.

The bell tolled again, warning of something horrible to come. In that split second, frozen with the creatures creeping among the tombstones, he understood what the knell signaled. Would never forget.

It was too late by the time headlights splintered the darkness. The squeal of tires and the tar-like stench of burning rubber filled the air. If Spencer had been a second earlier, a half second later, he wouldn't have blundered into the street at that precise moment.

The sickening sound of three thousand-plus pounds of metal impacting flesh ripped through Dante. Alex barreled down the hillside, racing to the scene of the accident, but Dante couldn't move.

The bell ceased its death knell. Creatures slithered into the Aether from which they'd come. Only a dog remained, a massive beast with red eyes and a coat as black as the grave. Unlike the monsters, the shadowy animal was not tethered by a chain.

The canine met Dante's gaze briefly, then padded away, vanishing under the hickory tree at the rear of the church.

Dante didn't need to walk down the hill to know Spencer was dead.

He flattened his hand on the cover of the sketchbook, all too familiar with what the book contained.

The monsters of Hickory Chapel Cemetery.

* * * *

"We coulda picked a better night for this." Clive Porter tossed a fresh shovelful of dirt over his head, wincing when pain boomeranged across his lower back. "Moon's too bright, and I'm spent. How deep do you think this mother's buried? We gotta be over seven feet by now."

"Quit whining." Clive's brother Warren sank his spade into the soil with a vengeful stab. "We got a hefty payday coming. That's all that matters."

"I don't care about the cash. You said I could have a dog if I helped. A brown-and-white one, like when I was a kid."

"You'll get your dog when we get paid."

"Promise?"

"I said so, didn't I?"

The edge of anger told Clive to back off. "Okay." He sweated like a pig despite the cool autumn air. Probably shouldn't have mounded all that salt on his fries during dinner at Colossal Burger. The extra ten pounds he carried around his gut slowed him down, while the creep-show feeling they were being watched made him want to hurry and get the hell out.

Rubbing the lizard tattoo on the back of his left hand, he listened for any unusual sliver of sound. When he was nineteen, a carnival fortune teller told him the lizard was his totem animal and would protect him from harm as long as he honored it. He'd gone out and had the tattoo inked the next day. He wasn't black-cat-superstitious or shit like that but had a healthy respect for evil spirits. Odds were, digging up a body at two a.m. would stir up a few.

At least Hickory Chapel Cemetery was far enough from the roadway that they were unlikely to be spotted behind the church, even with the moon hovering coin-bright overhead. The part of him weirded out by defiling a grave didn't mind the extra light.

Chewing his bottom lip, Clive craned his neck to gaze up at the sky. He was six-three, and the rim of the hole they dug was at least a foot above his head. A few inches deeper and it would be hard to heft himself out, even with Warren giving him a leg up.

He imagined moonshadow slanting from gravestones, spawning patches of black like the maw of open crypts. Somewhere over his shoulder, a night bird started chattering. The sound came from the boarded-up chapel behind them. The place could have been a mausoleum, all dark shadows and stark angles. Who knew what lurked inside, tucked into corners, under broken floorboards? Spiders. Snakes. Rats.

Ghosts.

He tightened his grip on the shovel. "No shit, Warren. I think we've been had. Nobody's buried here."

"Then why would Yancy pay us hard cash to dig this bozo up?" Warren planted his shovel in the earth and rested his forearm against the shaft. "I don't know what you're whining about. I'm doing most of the work. You keep looking around like you're waiting for a serial killer to take your head off."

"Not a killer." Clive lowered his voice. "Monsters. Ain't you heard the rumors about this place? A big black dog. Spook lights." He normally didn't mind dogs—loved them—but the black dog that haunted the cemetery was different. He stilled, tensing when the air carried a shivery whisper of sound to his ears. "Listen! Do you hear that?"

"Hear what?"

Clive's gut turned over, rolling like a tumbleweed. "A bell. Can't you hear it?"

"The only thing I hear is you babbling like an asshat. Get back to work."

"There it is again." Clive peered up at the chapel. "Ain't no bell in that tower, but Kirk said if you hear it ring, you ain't got long for this world."

"And you believed him? Kirk's drunk or high most of the time." Warren nodded toward the shovel. "Keep digging. You want to get out of here, don't you?"

Clive bobbed his head. "I don't wanna get caught, that's for sure." *By the living or the dead.* He strained his ears, but the only sound to pierce the stillness was the wind cavorting among the tombstones. "What do you think the penalty is for digging up a grave?"

"Don't know." Warren stabbed his shovel into the ground. "Don't care."

Clive hunched lower in the grave. If a demonic spirit lingered in the dark waiting to feast on human flesh, hopefully it wouldn't see him. Maybe Warren was right. Maybe he'd imagined that nearly imperceptible dirge, like the solemn toll of a funeral bell in the distance. It was Kirk's fault for filling his head with stupid stories. If he had any sense, he'd listen to Warren and keep clear of their younger brother.

Gritting his teeth, he jabbed his shovel into the soil. His shoulders protested along with his back, but he set to work, matching Warren's pace. They labored in silence, the huffs and grunts of their efforts mingling with the distant sound of traffic. Clive would have sworn hours crawled past, an ungodly stretch of feeling the hair prickle on his neck, his mind crawling with images of maggot-infested coffins and looming death. The old hickory tree overshadowing the grave rattled its branches with a sound like bones clacking together. It was starting to stink in the grave. A sick, cloying stench—half sweet, half rotten—soured his gut.

"Do you smell that?"

Warren never broke his pace. "Keep digging."

Clive wiped sweat from his eyes with a grubby hand and tried to concentrate on something else—a long shower, a cold six-pack. He murmured prayers to his totem animal. The work would have gone faster with Kirk helping, but Warren drew the line at including him. Kirk had screwed up too many times.

Like when he'd dragged Clive along to the pretty red-haired lady's house saying they were going to look at puppies. Clive had thought he might leave with a pup, but there weren't any animals there. Just the woman and her husband, and then Kirk had gone batshit crazy.

Humming under his breath, Clive put his weight into digging. Humming stopped his mind from toggling back to that tiny house on Mill Street. The gruesome spray of blood splattered over walls and floor.

"Looks like a fucking abattoir," Warren had said when he'd hauled their asses out. He'd beaten the shit out of Kirk that night. In an opioid haze, Kirk had blubbered and moaned, threatening to *"cut out your fucking heart."* The next day, he could barely crawl from bed, hobbled by the beating. Warren wanted to write him off permanently, but they were blood. When Kirk was well enough to function, Warren kicked him out with only his clothes and twenty bucks to his name. He told Clive to forget what happened on Mill Street.

He only wished he could. Sometimes he was certain he was going straight to Hell for his part in the butchery. Maybe that's why he feared the black dog and the tolling church bell more than Warren. Too bad regret didn't bring people back from the dead.

"Do you think we got ancestors buried in this place?"

Warren maintained a furious pace with the shovel. "Don't know. Don't care."

Clive blew out a breath. "What the hell *do* you care about?"

"Keep your voice down!" Warren cuffed him.

"That's it!" Clive heaved his spade to the ground. "I'm done. I don't care how much Yancy is paying. There ain't no—" He stopped suddenly, spurred to silence by the look on Warren's face. His brother stared past him, focused on a patch of earth at the head of the pit.

Clive turned slowly, noting where the soil had jiggled away from his fallen shovel. A skeletal finger pointed in his direction. A finger that seemed to condemn him for his part in a heinous crime.

Mill Street.

Warren was oblivious. "Damn." He slumped against the edge of the pit. "I think we just found Gabriel Vane."

Chapter 2

October 10, 1799

Gabriel blew on his hands to warm them as he slid into a pew beside Jasper. If his friend was bothered by the cold, he gave no indication. The chapel was small, newly built, the smell of sawdust as heavy as the twin augers of anger and fear boring through the heart of every man in the gathering. Gabriel counted twenty, but more filed through the rear door. Too many people spoke at once, tossing out opinions, clamoring to be heard.

"Silence!" Standing by the pulpit, Atticus Crowe banged the butt of his musket against the floorboards. "We will get nowhere with everyone bellowing at once."

"And we will get nowhere sitting on our arses." Cyrus Herman bulldogged his way to the front. "I lost half a dozen birds last night, Atticus. We need to do something about the bloody beast and do it quick. If it keeps up this slaughter—"

"It got my young sow night before last," Ira Blake cut him off. "Ripped her up like parchment. My missus darn near had a heart attack when she come on the remains the next morning."

"Slaughtered four of my chickens," someone called from the back.

"Eight of mine," another voice chimed in.

"Would have got my cow if my coon hounds hadn't chased it off," Thaddeus Keel added.

Atticus held up his hands. "We're formulating a plan to hunt the beast."

Gabriel stirred restlessly. If there was a plan, no matter how sketchy, it was time to share the details. The mood was growing uglier, weighted by the slick sweat of fear. Leaning closer to Jasper, he lowered his voice. "Does your father really have a plan?"

His friend rolled his shoulders. "I don't know. Normally, he confers with Vernon Hode."

"Where is Hode?" Gabriel craned his neck to look around the chapel. Together with Atticus, Vernon Hode had assumed a leadership role among the men of the remote village and outlying farms. "I don't see him."

"Enoch said he's in mourning." Jasper's older brother, Enoch, was a frequent visitor to the Hode house, usually calling on Vernon's middle daughter, Abigail. "They say Hode got word his mother died in the Old Country. He's sworn off all visitors."

Gabriel grimaced. "But surely he understands the importance of this meeting?"

"Enoch sent word through his hired hand, but the man turned Enoch away at the gate. Vernon says he can't break from religious obligation and will see no one for a period of weeks."

"That puts the full weight of the beast on your father's shoulders." Gabriel frowned. He looked to where Enoch stood behind Crowe, several steps to the right. As oldest son, he was there to keep order if the meeting got out of hand. Tempers ran high, but if anyone could instill sense in the group, it was Atticus.

In the small chapel it was easy to imagine him in the role of a fire-and-brimstone preacher, delivering judgment on anyone who questioned his authority. He didn't stand behind the pulpit—that was reserved for Jasper's Sunday sermons about serving the Lord. Gabriel's friend was young to be a pastor—nineteen, to Gabriel's eighteen years—but he'd agreed to shepherd their flock until an ordained man of God could be found. The chapel had been built in the hopes of attracting just such a minster to the village. The ground to the rear had yet to see a single grave cut into the sod.

"What happens when this beast tires of our pigs and chickens?" The crack of Thaddeus Keel's voice drew Gabriel back to the present. "When it decides to feast on our children and our women?"

"Don't be absurd." Musket butt-end to the floor, Atticus wrapped his hand around the stock, his brows furrowed in a thunderous line. "Have you not heard a single thing I've said? We must hunt the creature. Track it during daylight hours when it will surely be holed up in a den."

"And leave our womenfolk unprotected?" Cyrus shook his head. "I will not entertain such nonsense." A chorus of voices rose in agreement, men talking over each other, striving to be heard. Gabriel felt their fear, understood their anger.

The creature had come from nowhere, a plague for the last two weeks. What began as sporadic attacks progressed to almost nightly occurrences. Farms were raided, livestock slaughtered. Villagers and farmers alike sequestered inside once the sun set, fearful of what the darkness would bring. Sometimes the foul beast didn't bother to eat its kill, plundering as if for pleasure. Other times, it left little more than bones to mark butchered prey.

A few people had spied the creature—Cyrus, along with Farley, the tanner. Both claimed it was far too large to be a natural wolf but said it ran on all fours and was lupine in shape. In the mind of many villagers, it had taken on a supernatural aura. Some whispered of demons and monsters, fiends that haunted the Old Country. Others talked in hushed tones of werewolves. Men slept with muskets beside their beds, and women hunched over prayer books and Bibles.

Gabriel thought of Dinah. He'd been courting Jasper's sister since spring and had every intention of asking Atticus for her hand. Were it not for the untimely appearance of the beast, he might have done so already. He understood Cyrus's protest, the fear of the other men. If anything happened to Dinah because she was left unprotected, he would not have the strength to continue. Yet, someone needed to see the demon-creature cornered and killed.

"It will only take a few," he whispered.

"What?" Jasper frowned at him.

Determination rooted in Gabriel. For Dinah and their future, he would do what was needed. Gripping the pew in front of him, he shot to his feet. "It will only take a few." He pitched his voice, shouting over the others. "It isn't necessary for all to go, only a handful. Let stealth be in our favor."

One by one, those nearest turned to look at him, their arguments fading.

Atticus extended his hands, palms down, motioning for quiet. "You have something to say, Gabriel?" The strength of his voice overpowered any lingering protests, the room succumbing to silence.

Gabriel tightened his hands on the pew. His opinion did not carry the weight of his elders, but in this, he could do what they could not. If he was successful, the victory would surely play in his favor when he asked Atticus for Dinah's hand.

"Cyrus makes a valid point about leaving our womenfolk unprotected."

"And what affair is that of yours?" Atticus's scowl etched a crevasse into his face. "You have no wife to concern you."

"Should I be so fortunate in the future, I would want others to protect her and my family, as I am ready to protect theirs. What good is it to send groups of men traipsing into the woods? So many will only alert the creature to the hunt while stripping our village and farms of protection."

"Hear! Hear!" someone shouted from the back.

Atticus stood straighter, his frown deepening. "You have another suggestion?"

"A small hunting party." Gabriel drew a breath. He had not seen the creature himself but had witnessed the bloody destruction it wrought. It would be no easy task to flush out the beast and bring it down, but for Dinah and the safety of his village, he must try. "I will go. I ask only for one or two others to join me."

Stunned silence fell over the room. For a period of five seconds no one spoke; then Jasper stood beside him. "I will go with my friend."

"I will go, too."

Gabriel turned his head. Hiram Blum stood two rows behind, across the aisle. A gruff man with a large frame and a squared-off face, he'd appeared in the village a week ago, taking odd jobs for room and board. Little was known about him, but it was rumored he'd once served under Washington. A good ally to have in a fight.

Gabriel nodded. "I am honored to have you both at my side." He clapped Jasper on the shoulder then turned to face Atticus. "We will need provisions and enough ammunition to last several nights. The creature must be close, to frequent as often as it does. If we are unable to deliver a carcass by the Sabbath next, we will return for fresh supplies." He stood taller, proud when Atticus nodded agreement. Respect gleamed in the older man's eyes, admiration previously lacking.

"How say you?" Atticus called to the assembly.

"Aye!" The group answered as one.

Within moments, Gabriel and Jasper were surrounded. Men pummeled their backs, shook their hands, wished them Godspeed and a dozen other regards. Elation displaced anger, sweeping the vinegar of fear from the chapel. Through the throng, Gabriel watched Hiram Blum slip from the crowd. The big man hesitated near the door, then cast a glance over his shoulder. A second later, he eased outside.

But not before Gabriel had caught the feral yellow glint of his eyes.

* * * *

Present Day

Elliott hooked his backpack higher and stepped outside. He'd delayed as long as possible at school, texting his mom to say he was going to stay late and join the science club. He'd probably have gotten around to joining anyway, but after today, he needed a quick out to save his butt. Accidentally sending Rodney Townsend sprawling in the cafeteria had skyrocketed the move to the top of his list.

Rodney and his friends made it clear they planned to kick his "sorry ass" after school, so Elliott had done the only thing a coward could—he'd wasted an hour in the science lab watching the clock inch closer to 4:00, praying his tormentors had taken the bus home. Mr. Knoll had been glad to welcome him to the group, but Elliott barely heard a word the teacher said, his mind on the incident in the cafeteria. If only he'd been looking where he was going instead of burying his nose in his cell phone, he would have seen Rodney carrying his lunch tray. The other boy had been talking over his shoulder to Finn Carrigan but, of course, the fault was Elliott's when they collided. No way could Rodney—badass and mouthy—be in the wrong.

Rodney blundered backward into Finn, who'd dominoed into Troy Weaver. All three had gone down, but only Rodney had been carrying food. Only Rodney ended up wearing a plateful of macaroni and cheese, a corn dog slathered with mustard, and gobs of chocolate pudding. It might have been comical if Elliott wasn't the one who caused the mess.

He'd gaped with his mouth hanging open, cell still locked on *Simon's Cat* while the cafeteria roared with laughter. By the time the three boys had scrambled to their feet, Rodney snarling in his face, Mr. Fielding and Ms. Trevor arrived to pull them apart. Elliott had tried to apologize, but the humiliation couldn't be undone. In math class, Rodney had lobbed spitwads at the back of his head when Mrs. Martinez wasn't looking. Between classes, Finn tripped him in the hallway, sending his glasses flying. Troy kicked them to Rodney, who did his best psychotic goalie impression with a spectacular block and rebound. Only Mr. Lafferty's timely intervention as he stepped from his classroom to see what the ruckus was saved the glasses from being crushed. But even the mocking laughter of everyone who'd witnessed the spectacle hadn't been enough to satisfy Rodney.

"We're going to kick your sorry ass, Camden," he'd told Elliott before the start of next period. Lafferty saddling him with a detention for the following week hadn't helped.

Elliott lived in fear the remainder of the day, going out of his way to avoid his tormentors. When three o'clock rolled around, he hightailed it to Mr. Knoll's classroom but spent the time fighting the urge to throw up. At least it was Friday. He didn't have to face school tomorrow. If he could make it home, he'd be okay. Rodney and the others might forget everything by Monday.

Yeah. Right.

He'd worry about Monday when Monday came. Fake the stomach flu or something.

Elliott licked his lips. His palms were sweaty, and his mouth was dry. Outside, a couple parents had arrived to pick up students who'd stayed for afterschool activities. Elliott hustled past and up the sidewalk to the road. No sign of Rodney, Finn, or Troy anywhere. When he reached the crosswalk, he considered himself in the clear. He lived close enough to walk home, but the other three would have needed to catch a bus. The thought of skirting Hickory Chapel Cemetery without a group of other kids walking in the same direction made him nervous, but the trade-off was worth not getting his butt kicked.

He was halfway to the chapel when he heard snickering. A glance over his shoulder blew open his worst fear—Rodney, Finn, and Troy casually following behind. The single glimpse was all it took to propel him into a panicked run. The quick pounding of feet and a vicious, "You're dead, Camden!" convinced him to beat the pavement as hard as he could. The chapel whizzed by in a blur. Then he did the unthinkable—they wouldn't chase him into the cemetery.

Gulping for breath, he veered from the sidewalk, backpack bouncing as he clambered up an embankment of overgrown grass. The browned husks of foxtails and nettles snagged his jeans, chickweed crunching under his sneakers like stale peanut shells. The bank was steep, the old chapel set on a hill overlooking the south end of town. Elliott was almost to the top when he risked a glance over his shoulder.

All three scrambled up the hillside, Rodney in the lead. If they caught him, there'd be no one to help, no one to see them gang up on him. At least on the sidewalk, a car might have stopped. Someone might have chased the three off if he yelled. He'd been an idiot, stupidly setting himself up for a beating.

Elliott dashed for the cemetery, certain they wouldn't risk the monsters. Panting, he raced through the graves, haphazardly zigzagging between headstones. A weird twilight hung over the place, too many trees to let the pale autumn sun warm the ground. His breath rasped in his ears, tangled with the threats of the other boys. They'd followed him into the graveyard, gaining with every step.

"We're gonna make you sorry you were born, shithead."

"Should have stayed at your old school, douchebag."

"You're dead meat."

Elliott neared the back of the cemetery, realized there was nowhere to go. He darted to the right, casting a hasty glance over his shoulder. It took only a second for his foot to strike air and the world to upend in freefall.

He plummeted into a pit, his backpack battering against him with the full weight of science and algebra textbooks. His teeth clacked together, triggering a jolt of pain up his jaw. His glasses were flung from his face as his hands and knees struck earth. Frantic, he groped through the dirt, one knee digging deeper into the soil.

"Holy shit." Rodney Townsend's voice came from somewhere high overhead.

Elliott's fingers curled over the glasses. His head swam with the gritty musk of loam and weeds. Slowly, he came to his feet.

Rodney, Finn, and Troy were on their hands and knees, staring down at him from above.

"You dipshit," Rodney said. "You fell in an open grave."

Elliott choked on panic, realizing the other boy was right. There was no casket, just the empty hole in the ground, perfectly suited for a coffin.

"Freaky." Troy grinned.

Elliott looked for a handhold, but there was nothing to support his weight. He'd once heard modern cemeteries held vaults to contain coffins, but this was a just a dirt cavity, dug in a time when bodies were buried in pine boxes. Did that mean there were bones under the soil?

New terror strangled him. "Help me out."

Rodney laughed. "Don't think so."

"Hey." Finn jutted his chin toward the pit. "Why's an open grave back here? They stopped burying people in Hickory Chapel Cemetery long ago."

Rodney shrugged. "Who cares? Let douche-boy hang out here for the night, and the monsters can take care of him."

"You can't do that." Elliott feared he'd piss himself. In a little over an hour it would be dark. "Quit screwing around. Help me up. I'm sorry about lunch."

"You should have thought about that before," Troy said.

"We can't leave him here," Finn countered.

"Why not?" Rodney stood, dusting his hands free of dirt.

"Get serious. It's gonna get cold once the sun goes down. People are gonna be looking for him."

"Quit being a wuss, Carrigan. You're starting to sound like your uncle."

"Yeah. Cop talk." Troy snorted. "'Fraid he's gonna toss your butt in jail? Like mother, like son." He snickered.

"Shut it, Troy."

Elliott's gaze ping-ponged between them. He didn't know what they were talking about, just knew he wanted out. He dug his hand in his pocket and fished out his cell phone. The glass was cracked, probably shattered when he fell. His stomach sank when he pushed the power button and nothing happened.

Cold sweat broke out on the back of his neck. "My phone's broke."

"Bad luck," Rodney said.

"You can't leave me here all night."

"You won't last the night. Once the sun sets, you're monster chow."

"Yeah. Try not to wiggle when you get chomped on." Troy flipped him the finger. The two boys walked away, trailing laughter. Only Finn Carrigan remained, staring down with a look of uncertainty.

"Please." Elliott wet his lips, his voice passing from his throat in a tremulous whisper. "I'm afraid. The monsters…"

"Hey, Carrigan." Rodney's call drifted from farther away. "You coming or what?"

Without a word, Finn swiveled and darted after his friends.

Fighting tears, Elliott closed his eyes. Someone would miss him. Someone would come.

He tried the phone again, but it was shot. Shrugging the backpack from his shoulders, he stared up at the top of the pit. He stood five feet, and it was at least another two feet above. Weird that the tomb was so deep, but maybe graves were dug deeper in the old days because of foraging animals. Thinking took the edge off his fear. If he jumped high enough…

A few attempts and he knew it was impossible.

"Help!" Elliott tilted his head back and yelled as loudly as he could. "Someone—anyone—help me!" His throat grew raw after several minutes of hollering. Falling silent, he strained to hear. The scuttle of wind across dry grass twined with a faint hum of distant traffic and the rattle and clack of tree branches. No answering voice. No footsteps rushing to his aid.

Dejected, Elliott sank into a corner of the pit and hugged his knees to his chest. If he stayed still and didn't move, maybe the monsters wouldn't know he was there.

Maybe, maybe, maybe.

A glimmer of green on the other side of the grave snagged his attention. His breath caught.

An eye?

Slowly, he crawled forward, inching cautiously on hands and knees. Instinct told him to stay low, appear nonthreatening. If it was a monster, it was a small one. Elliott was almost on top of the thing when he realized it was a piece of glass partially buried in the dirt.

He dug it free, then wiped it clean on his sweatshirt.

Not glass. A crystal or a gem.

He held it up to the light.

It looked like an emerald.

Chapter 3

October 10, 1799

"Your father and the others are gathering provisions as we speak." Gabriel sat next to Dinah in a ladder-back chair drawn close to the hearth. A roaring fire filled the gathering room with warmth, and a slice of late-day sunlight yawned over the rug-covered floor. On the dining table, an oval basket held an assortment of plump red apples and fat chestnuts. Someday he would have a house like this with its strong timber construction, double chimneys, and a gambrel roof. He already had plans to expand on the two-room cabin he'd built with money inherited from his parents. The only one to survive the voyage across the Atlantic, Gabriel had found himself orphaned at fifteen, alone in a new country. A newly *formed* country.

"Jasper will be going with me," he added, though Dinah had probably already heard the news. Word spread fast in the village.

"I expected he would." Her fingers stilled on the shirt she was darning. The steady back-and-forth creak of her rocker echoed beneath the sibilant hiss of the fire.

"Hiram Blum is coming, too."

"A capable man, they say." She wouldn't look at him, her gaze trained on the chaotic dance of flames in the hearth.

"Dinah." Leaning forward, he clasped her hand. "It is best this way. We will rid the village of the beast."

Drawing a breath, she searched his face. "Why does it have to be you? And why Jasper? I do not doubt your ability, Gabriel, or that of my brother, but there are older men, more skilled in the woods."

"All with wives or loved ones."

"And what am I? I had hoped there was a promise between us." Her lashes dipped, pale as her hair. His own hair was darker blond, ash to her alabaster. She was a vision, blessed with both grace and beauty where he only had hard work to recommend him.

He could still recall the first time he saw her, the sun setting flame to the white-gold curls framing her face. He'd asked where to find the tanner, then stammered his gratitude when she'd pointed him in the right direction. Two days later, he'd introduced himself to her father as a new landowner on the outskirts of the village. He'd bought his own livestock and dutifully tended his humble acreage. Yes, he'd been young to establish himself, but he'd learned farming techniques as a child. He'd been sixteen when he'd settled in the area, waiting a full year before seeking to court Dinah. He was not a wealthy man, but nor was he poor.

He rubbed her hand, her skin chapped from scrubbing laundry and kneading dough. Someday he hoped to hire servants, so she might live in a small manner of luxury.

"Allow me this task with your blessing, Dinah. If I am successful, your father will look upon me with new regard. He will not refuse when I ask for your hand."

"He will not refuse now."

He wanted to believe her but suspected Atticus entertained the thought of someone flush in land and money for his youngest daughter. Fern was already wed, the wife of Oren Inghram, leaving only Dinah, Enoch, and Jasper at home. Who would cook and clean for Atticus when Dinah was married? His wife had passed, the victim of a wagon accident five summers before Atticus arrived in the village.

No, as favorable as the village elder could be at times, Atticus sought a man of means for his daughter. A homesteader capable of supporting him in his dotage and lending hired hands to aid with the chores of his household.

"I will not take the chance." Gabriel's future with Dinah was too important to risk with a rash proposal. "If I slay the beast, others will look to me as a hero. Your father will not be able to refuse my request for your hand."

"You are already a hero to me."

He smiled, then kissed her lightly. "I pray you understand why I must do this."

Setting her sewing aside, she nodded. "Wait a moment."

He rose with her when she stood, their fingers trailing apart. The sweep of her long skirt whispered across the floorboards as she left the room.

Several moments passed before she returned with a small wooden box clasped in her hands.

"This is precious to me, Gabriel. Old and powerful."

His gaze dropped to the container. The top had been etched with the carving of two interlocking circles, a heart laid over the center. "What is it?"

Dinah opened the box, turning it so he could see inside. A crude green gem, the size of a quarter dollar, rested in a scrap of white linen.

He looked from the stone to her face. "I don't understand."

"It is a protection stone. An emerald imbued with the power to cleave one soul to another. In the wrong hands, it can also destroy."

Gabriel fidgeted, the explanation sounding much like witchcraft.

"I know what you're thinking." Dinah closed the lid, tucking the box close to her chest. "But there is no evil in this thing, only in the hearts of those who would possess it."

"Are you..." He wet his lips, fearful to ask. "Do you practice—"

"Witchery?" She shook her head. "But there are traditions I cherish from my heritage. This stone was given to me by my great-grandmother on her deathbed. She chose me to guard it, requesting only that I reserve it for a man with a pure heart. I believe you are that person, Gabriel." Carefully, she withdrew the stone from the box, then placed it in his palm. "This is my pledge to you—a pledge to bind us together. One that will keep you safe for as long as I live. It will protect you and bring you back to me. Until we are wed, I make you the stone's guardian."

The weight of the gem was warm against Gabriel's skin. He did not believe in protection spells or wards, but for their future, he would do as she asked. "I will bring it back to you." He slipped the emerald into his breeches. "And before a fortnight has passed, I will seek your hand in marriage."

* * * *

Present Day

Jillian pulled into the parking spot behind her brownstone, already focused on unloading groceries and taking Blizzard for a walk. The husky would be pacing, alerted by the sound of her Accord off the terrace. Silencing the engine on the blue sedan, she flicked a glance in the rearview mirror as an unmarked car with flashing lights sped past. Before she could process the image, Tessa Camden popped up beside her driver's door.

"Jillian." Tessa pressed one hand against her lips as if restraining herself from pounding on the window. The other clutched a cell phone with a poppy-colored case. A ponytail secured her curly hair, but multiple strands had worked loose around her face, giving her an unkempt look. The frowzy wisps heightened the uptight edge in her eyes. "Have you seen Elliott?"

Jillian stepped from the car and was immediately blindsided by Tessa's panic. She faltered backward against the door. "N-no. Not since last night. Is something wrong?"

Of course, something was wrong. The woman practically pulsated anxiety.

Wave after wave of desperation crashed over Jillian, the blast so strong she fought to breathe. She needed her safety buffer. Needed Blizzard to anchor her in reality and keep her from being swept into the maelstrom of Tessa's turbulent emotions. Tightening her fingers on the door handle, she struggled to ground herself and sucked down air.

Tessa was immune to her distress. "He stayed after school to join the science club." Her gaze darted left, then swung right. Across the street and back again. Anywhere that might divulge a much-needed glimpse of her missing son. "He should have been home by now. He should have been home long ago." Biting her lip, she stared at her cell as if the answer lay there. "I tried calling and texting, but he doesn't respond. Nothing."

"Did you try calling the school?"

"They're gone for the day. I told Elliott he could stay afterward, but he was supposed to be home before I got home from work. Normally, he'd go to his grandmother's until I got home, but she's working at her antique shop today. It was just a half hour he'd be alone. I thought...he's so responsible for his age. What could go wrong?"

"His grandmother?" Jillian was still putting the pieces together. "You mean Imelda?"

Tessa bobbed her head. "I tried to reach my cousin, Dante, but his phone goes straight to voice mail. I thought he could help search, but he must be painting. He shuts his phone off when he's working."

Jillian tried to keep up with the conversation, but the funnel had been opened to Tessa's emotions. The other woman's steadily mounting terror bludgeoned her.

If Elliott were her child, her son...

Her stomach contracted, twisted in a merciless grip. This was every parent's worst nightmare. A thing that stole breath and shriveled the heart.

Tessa was on the verge of hyperventilating. "I called the police and gave them Elliott's description...all the details. They're sending someone over to talk to me, but I thought maybe… I hoped you—" Her voice broke, tears welling in her eyes.

Jillian gripped her hand. "It's going to be all right." The platitude fell from her tongue, hollow words that made her eyes prick with moisture. It *had* to be all right. "What can I do to help?" She wrapped her arm around Tessa's shoulders, trying to block the other woman's grief. She needed to be strong, a foundation of support. However raw her empathic nature, she couldn't let Tessa face the trauma alone.

"I was going to drive to the school. Follow the roads he would have walked." Tessa wiped tears from her face with shaking hands. "But I'm afraid to leave the house in case Elliott comes home, and the police are on their way. If I could only reach Dante."

"Do you want me to go?"

Tessa gaped at her through wet lashes. "To get Dante?"

"No, I—" Jillian fumbled for words. "I meant the school."

"I need Dante. He'll know what to do."

"Okay." She couldn't turn away from the desperation in Tessa's voice, the heart-wrenching mixture of hope and misery in her eyes.

Blizzard would be pacing. There were perishable groceries in her car. "Do you have an address?"

Relief flooded from Tessa, gratitude so strong it nearly knocked Jillian off her feet. "I can text it to you." They'd exchanged phone numbers for emergency purposes shortly after Tessa moved in—the single concession Jillian allowed herself. If not for Madison, she never would have offered up her number when Tessa suggested it, but the memory of her sister covered with her husband's blood had taught her some compromises were necessary.

Tessa's thumbs flew over the screen of her phone, tears trickling down her cheeks. Jillian heard an answering ping in her purse when the message was received. Before she could extract her phone to examine the text, Tessa's ringtone kicked in, blaring "I Will Survive" by Gloria Gaynor.

"Oh!" Without glancing at the caller ID, Tessa hit connect, then quickly pressed the phone to her ear. "Elliott? Elliott?" Silence reigned as she listened to the caller. Within seconds, her expression changed from one of expectant urgency to staggering relief. "Oh, dear God, thank you. Thank you!"

Sagging against Jillian's car, she lowered the phone.

"Was that Elliott?" Jillian asked.

"No. The police. They found him. He's safe." Whatever else she tried to say couldn't be understood for the gut-wrenching force of her sobs.

Jillian wrapped her arms around her and hugged her close.

* * * *

Blizzard never had a proper walk, but she managed to hustle him outside so he could relieve himself.

Jillian dropped her groceries on the counter, dumped the perishable items in the refrigerator, then loaded Blizzard in her car and pointed the Accord toward the east end of town. The drive would make up for his missed walk, and having the husky close would help settle her nerves. The headache still pounded at the back of her skull, but her pupils had returned to normal, negating the need for the tinted glasses around her neck.

She'd left Tessa to wait for Elliott, grateful to undertake the short drive to Dante DeLuca's home. Far better she wasn't there when the police arrived. Even after three years, her memories were too strong—the sight of a squad car, the staticky crackle of a radio, the ghastly swath of emergency lights across the lawn.

The blood.

"I'm sorry to have to tell you, Ms. Cley." The female officer had a small mole to the right of her mouth reminiscent of a beauty mark from Hollywood's gilded age. Her blue eyes were direct, weirdly translucent in the half-light of dawn, but sympathetic. "Your brother-in-law is dead."

Jillian's heart plummeted. She'd suspected as much. "What about my sister? What about Madison?"

"Mrs. Hewitt is alive but unresponsive. She's being transported to Hode's Hill General Hospital."

Jillian looked past her to where medics loaded a gurney into a waiting ambulance. "I need to be with her." She lurched forward, but the officer restrained her, gripping her arm.

"Let the medics do their work. If I take you to the hospital, will you have a way home?"

Jillian stared at the woman, unable to comprehend the question. A second passed, then another. She gulped. Nodded. "Thank you." Fighting nausea, she clutched her stomach. "There was so much blood."

"It wasn't from your sister." The officer steered her toward a patrol car. "It belonged to Boyd. I think you already know whoever did this wanted him to suffer."

Jillian tightened her hands on the steering wheel, swallowing bile as fresh nausea washed through her. Sweat soaked into the heavy braid resting against the back of her neck. Now wasn't the time to dwell on the past, but the memories were aggressive, without restraint. Confined to the rear seat, Blizzard whined and paced.

"It's okay." She tossed the dog a glance in the mirror. "I'm going to be okay, boy. We're going to be okay." She owed Officer Sherre Lorquet a debt of gratitude for suggesting a therapy dog. The woman must have seen something in Jillian's face the morning of Boyd's murder to know she'd never recover on her own. If only Madison's healing were so simple.

Breathing easier, Jillian made a turn onto Grant Street. Friday traffic was heavy, but she managed the congestion without too much difficulty. As if sensing her heartbeat and pulse had returned to normal rhythm, Blizzard lay down, crossing one paw over the other. Jillian reached back to scratch behind his ears.

"We need to help Tessa and Elliott. You like Elliott, don't you?"

Blizzard's tail thumped against the seat.

She made another turn onto Highmore, then a right onto Crescent. "Shouldn't be much farther." Normally, she had little reason to venture into the east end of town, an area comprised of sprawling homes on four- and five-acre lots. Tessa said her cousin usually favored a small apartment near Pin Oaks Senior Center, but lately had been staying at a larger property he'd inherited from his father.

Last summer, Dante DeLuca had been the subject of several soundbites, an activist who'd made it his mission to stop Hode Development from tearing down Pin Oaks to make room for luxury condos. After a slew of bad press, it came to light the plan had been to construct a new and improved building in another area of town. A disgruntled subcontractor had leaked premature information in an attempt to give Hode Development a black eye. After the hoopla died down, Dante faded from the spotlight.

"Looks like this is the one." Jillian stopped at the end of a cul-de-sac, staring up at an oversized two-story with a cement driveway and integral three-car garage. An oversized pole barn, crowned by a red cupola with brass weathervane, stood to the rear. Ornamental shrubs and bright orange mums lined the driveway, overshadowed here and there by chestnuts and oaks that had yet to shed their leaves.

With the hour sweeping toward six, darkness had begun to feather the edges of the sky. Several lights glimmered behind Palladian windows, warm yellow against the sleek silver of twilight.

Jillian stepped from the car and turned to Blizzard, already engaged in thrusting his nose outside. "Stay here. I'll only be a minute." Closing the door, she studied the imposing asymmetrical lines of the house. Varying roof pitches plus a brick-and-stone façade marked the home as contemporary New American, but a corner turret with towering windows made her think of forgotten eras. There was something both welcoming and brooding about the house; the latter heightened by the swift fall of twilight.

She hurried up the walkway, then up several brick steps to a recessed entrance. Double doors accented with leaded glass and scrolled ironwork were backlit by amber from within. Jillian jabbed the doorbell, then counted off seconds while she waited for someone to answer. She had to press the bell twice more before Dante finally appeared on the threshold.

Given the artist's brush and paint-dotted rag in his hands, she'd probably interrupted his work.

"I don't know you." His reaction was odd. True, but odd. Although close in age, Jillian had spent her childhood and teen years—times when they might have crossed paths—in a private school.

"I'm Jillian Cley."

"What do you want, Jillian Cley?" Surprisingly, the question was curious rather than rude. "Now that I think about it, you look familiar. Maybe I do know you."

"I don't think so." She shifted from foot to foot, finding it impossible to read him. Even when someone didn't subconsciously broadcast their feelings, Jillian was usually able to radar in on a sliver of emotion without trying. "I live next door to your cousin, Tessa."

"Ah." The flash of a smile. "The lady the monsters will get."

"I—" Flummoxed, she searched for something to say.

"Sorry." He held up a hand. "A joke. Elliott and I—"

"Elliott is why I'm here." Weird joke aside, she wanted to deliver her message and return home where she could retreat into the safety of a world without hysterical neighbors and missing children. "Tessa has been trying to reach you, but your phone is going straight to voice mail."

"I'm working." His brows drew down, black over hazel eyes. "Is something wrong?"

Quickly, Jillian told him what happened.

"Shit!" Dante dug his cell from his pocket and began punching numbers. "I'll get there as soon as I can." Retreating into the foyer, door yawning behind him, he pressed the phone to his ear. "Contessa?"

Jillian was forgotten as he began firing questions at his cousin, wanting to know if the police had arrived, if Elliott was home. Apologizing for not being available when she needed him. His restless movements broadcast agitation, but it was as if an invisible shield separated him from Jillian.

She sprinted down the steps and raced for her car.

Dante DeLuca was a total blank.

* * * *

Detective David Gregg killed the flashing lights on his Mustang's grille before driving up the rutted lane to Hickory Chapel. Two squad cars and a slick top were parked in front of the dilapidated church. Finn sat hunched in the back of the nearest cruiser, nervous and morose even from a distance.

He'd deal with his nephew later.

"Thanks for calling me." David greeted Officer Del Desmond when he stepped from the car. He flicked a glance to the patrol vehicle with Finn. "What did he say?"

"Not much." Desmond was clean-shaven, twenty-six to David's forty-four years, but the rookie officer could have easily passed for a college freshman in the right light. Probably why he'd been given the job of talking to Finn. "He and some other kids were screwing around in the cemetery, and Elliott Camden fell into the grave."

Nice and pat. Reeking of garbage.

"Screwing around, huh?" David stuffed his hands into the pockets of his overcoat. "Is the Camden kid okay?"

"Yeah. Mostly scratches and bruises. Scared more than anything. If I'd tumbled that far, I would have broken a leg, but kids are resilient. Anders was going to suggest the mother have him checked over by a doctor to be on the safe side—in case he hit his head or something."

"Makes sense." Anders must have been tasked with taking the boy home. "What about the Camden kid's story? Did it match Finn's?"

"Close enough. He stayed after school to join the science club, then met up with Finn and some other kids while walking home. They decided to check out the cemetery, and he fell into the grave because he wasn't looking where he was going."

"Anyone say who these other kids were?"

Desmond shook his head.

"Finn say why it took him so long to call for help?"

The young cop shrugged. "Afraid he'd be in trouble."

"Yeah." David tried to keep the sour edge from his voice. "That's about the size of it." He hadn't spent twenty years as a cop without knowing when someone was lying through their back end. Finn could double-dance around the truth, but sooner or later he'd trip over his own bullshit.

David indicated the unmarked Taurus beside the patrol car. "Where's Lorquet?"

"At the site. Head to the back. Thorton is around, too." Desmond glanced from David to the patrol car. "You going to talk to your nephew?"

"Not now. Stay with him, huh?"

"Sure thing."

Hands in pockets, David trudged through the rubble of a broken walkway. Time had done a number on the chapel, battering and weathering the building until all that remained was a husk. Jagged holes gaped in the roof where shingles were missing, and most of the windows had been boarded up. Once white, the clapboard siding was dingy gray where the color hadn't flaked off entirely. The whole thing had a depressed aura, exaggerated by the dense slate of twilight.

As a rookie cop, he'd chased teens from the site more than once, especially on Halloween. Kids wanted to test the legends. Brag they'd survived the night in a graveyard haunted by church grims and corpse candles.

Over a decade ago, Spencer Wright had been killed when struck by a car. David still recalled his name, haunted by his death. He'd been one of the first officers on the scene, only two weeks on the job. Of Spencer's two friends with him that night, Alex Price had babbled about tolling church bells, but Dante DeLuca hadn't said a word. The kid simply shut down, refusing to confirm or deny what had happened.

There'd been other trouble after that, but thankfully, no deaths. Kids still trekked there like clockwork every Halloween. Was Finn buying into the folktales?

Lately his nephew had been hanging around with Rodney Townsend and Troy Weaver. Weaver wasn't too bad, but the Townsend kid had "smart aleck" and "troublemaker" written all over him. He'd never heard Finn mention Elliott Camden, but Finn could be stubbornly close-mouthed when he wanted. A trait learned from his prick of a father.

Don't go there.

David blew out a breath and made his way into the cemetery. Chemical weathering, acid rain, and erosion had all taken a toll on the grave markers. Many of the stones were leaning, a few broken, all surrounded by clumps of weeds and overgrown grass. He spied Thorton canvasing the perimeter and acknowledged the officer with a short wave.

Leaves crunched under his shoes as he made his way to the rear of the cemetery. Sherre Lorquet was in the farthest corner, squatting by an open grave. A decrepit-looking hickory tree hunched over her shoulder, bowed over the tomb like a sentry in mourning. Sherre stood when she saw him, dusting her hands on her pants. The area had yet to be roped off; mounds of fresh dirt scattered in humps behind the church. Fallen hickory nuts littered the ground.

"What do you think?" She indicated the narrow ditch. "Halloween trick?"

"Could be, but we're weeks from Hell Night." He looked for a grave marker. "Do we know the identity of the remains?"

Sherre consulted a small notebook. "Gabriel Vane. The headstone is over here." She walked around the edge of the pit. Unlike the tall limestone and granite markers denoting other graves, Vane's headstone was recessed into the ground. David could barely read the lettering, but someone had tended the plot, ensuring the slab was free of mold and weeds. Drawing a small flashlight from his pocket, he flicked on the beam, then dumped light on the stone.

Gabriel Vane

B. 1781

D. October 21, 1799

"That's a hell of an old grave."

"Could be the first in the cemetery." Sherre hooked sleek black hair behind her ear. "The original chapel on this site was built when Hode's Hill was a village. Why would anyone want the remains of a body that's over two centuries old?" She tilted her head to stare up at him.

David had watched her come up through the ranks, subject to crap most male cops never had to deal with. Making detective last winter had showed the naysayers what she was made of. Just over medium height with straight black hair and blue eyes, her ancestry was a mixed bag of French Creole, Scots Irish, and African American. They'd passed time on a stakeout once talking family trees and DNA.

He cast a glance around at the neglected graves. "Could be a prank, or a meth-head hoping to score off the sale of old bones. Could even be ritualist."

"Satanic?" Sherre clicked a pen against her teeth. "Not this grave."

David raised a brow. "Why?"

"Did you look at the depth?" She inclined her head to indicate the hole. "Eight feet or better. Not sure why a body would be buried so deep, but there are more recent graves, some as late as the early twentieth century. No need for the perp to dig so far."

"Would our grave robbers know that?"

"You used plural."

"Had to be more than one. Too much work for a single person. And if someone is selling bones to a museum or hoping to fetch black market price, the older the better." He squatted, noting where the dirt and grass had been raked over by slender tines. "Looks like they covered their tracks. What about tire prints?"

"Thorton's on it."

David nodded, standing and dusting his hands. "Shitty day. Did you hear about Coleman?"

Most everyone who worked at the precinct was on friendly terms with their janitor. Coleman often stopped to shoot the breeze in the squad room, sometimes showing up with donuts or muffins from the local bakery. The guy had been working for the city long before David started, and had to be seventy if he was a day.

Sherre's brow knitted. "What happened?"

"He was changing a fluorescent tube when the whole light came loose, mount and all. The thing dropped like a guillotine and sliced off his ear."

"My God."

"Ambulance took him to the hospital, but I guess his heart couldn't stand the shock. I heard he died in transit."

Sherre blanched. "That's horrible! Poor Coleman." She'd been close to him like everyone else. "His wife is going to be devastated."

"Yeah." David dropped his voice. It sucked when bad things happened to good people. "There's a collection going around at the precinct. The place was a mess this morning when it happened." He forced the thought aside. Cops didn't dwell on death, especially when they had no control over it. "You notice anything unusual about Vane's grave?"

Sherre refocused just as quickly. She frowned, the movement drawing attention to the beauty mark at the corner of her mouth. The tiny mole looked damn good on her coppery skin. Too bad the department had a rule about fraternizing.

"You mean other than the fact it's got a recessed headstone and is currently nothing more than an eight-foot ditch?"

"Yeah. What you said—and it's isolated."

Her brows furrowed. "Huh?"

"Take a look." David indicated where they stood in conjunction with the other tombstones. Gabriel Vane's grave was segregated behind the church tower, the singular burial plot removed from the others.

"Shit." Sherre's eyes grew wide. "It's like he was ostracized."

Chapter 4

October 10, 1799

Gabriel poured a dram of Madeira into his cup, then topped off Jasper's. The sun had set hours ago, the robust hearth fire and lantern light inside his cabin holding the heavy night at bay. Every now and then an arrow of wind pierced the chinks in the log walls, a reminder of the autumn chill outdoors.

"You're quiet." Gabriel studied his friend across the table. He didn't doubt Jasper was fit for the task at hand, but worried over the conviction of his heart. "Perhaps you are better served in the village than on the hunt."

"I will not hear of it." Jasper drained his wine. "You are a true friend, Gabriel. I would not have you hunt this beast alone."

"Hiram Blum intends to accompany me."

"As will I. The provisions have already been set. We leave from my father's house in the morning." Jasper pushed the cup away, waving aside the offer of more when Gabriel raised the bottle of Madeira. "I need a clear head for the morrow. As do you, if we are to outwit this creature."

"I've heard it whispered Blum is an excellent tracker."

"Let there be truth in that." Jasper rubbed the ginger scruff of beard on his chin.

Of the men in the village, Gabriel considered Jasper the most diplomatic. Certainly, the most devout. The small chapel tucked in a grove of hickory trees had only heard one sermon thus far. A sad occurrence to think it would stand empty so soon after the last nail had been struck.

"There is no one to preach in your absence." Gabriel drained his glass and stretched, setting off a rickety creak in his chair. His cabin did not have the grand scale or fine furnishings of Atticus Crowe's home, but was serviceable. He was too embarrassed to ask if Dinah would find the rough-hewn furniture beneath her station, so kept his thoughts on the chapel. He'd helped build the church. Driven nails and set boards, along with most every man in the village.

"My father has agreed to stand in and read a passage from scripture." Jasper stared down at his cup. For a moment, the crackle and hiss of flames was the only sound in the cabin. A shadow passed over his face, drawing his lips into a grimace. "You and the others think I am the best choice to stand behind the pulpit until we find an ordained man of God, but I am not sure. There is a great deal of weight in shepherding a flock."

A vexing thought niggled at Gabriel's mind. "Is that why you chose to accompany me on the hunt? To avoid your responsibility here?"

"Of course not." Jasper's tone soured, a tincture of anger darkening his eyes. "I have already told you that as your friend, I will not allow you to face this danger alone. Or even with Hiram Blum." He added the admonition when Gabriel moved to object. "But I cannot help feel a momentary relief to know I will be absent from the chapel."

"That makes no sense." Gabriel wandered to the hearth. He retrieved the poker from its resting place then prodded the logs. "I know you, my friend. Left to your own devices, you would spend hours ruminating on God's word. Your face radiated joy when you shared last Sunday's sermon."

"But I have no joy in tending graves."

The flames danced higher. Clumps of ash tumbled from the wood, steeping the air with the odor of char and burning hickory. Gabriel propped the poker against the stone and dusted his hands. "There are no graves. We have Heaven to thank our village has yet to suffer a death."

"But someone will die eventually. Someone must." Planting his palms on the table, Jasper stood. He strode to the rear of the cabin, restless movements betraying his agitation.

Gabriel studied the clenched line of his jaw, the taut edge of his features. "Death will come to all of us in time."

"You don't understand." Jasper rubbed the back of his neck, his shoulders hunched with unseen weight. "Do you know what my father would have me do?"

Gabriel shook his head.

"There is an old belief that the soul of the first body set in a graveyard remains tethered to the grounds for eternity. It is the responsibility of that doomed soul to protect those laid to rest in the days and years that follow."

"Protect them from what?"

"Night demons. Wights and phantoms. Predators from the Netherworld."

"Jasper, surely you do not believe—"

"No, but my father does. As do most of the people of this village. You joined us after we had already established a community, but the people who reside here—even among the outlying farms—hail from similar regions in the Old Country. Places of standing stones and funerary paths. Hollows and fells. Their beliefs have been ingrained through tradition and folklore." He lowered his voice. "However enlightened they imagine themselves to be."

"But if that is truly their belief..." God forbid Dinah shared her father's archaic superstitions. "...how could they condemn one of their own to such a horrible fate?"

"There is another way." Jasper returned to the table. Sinking into his chair, he glanced up at Gabriel. "A sacrifice may be substituted. Normally, a dog is killed and buried in a plot isolated from the other graves. When churches were made of stone, the animal was often sealed alive inside a wall to die of thirst and starvation."

Gabriel grunted with disgust. "That's a barbaric practice."

"I did not say I condone the custom. Only that it is a communal belief of those who dwell here. Now that the chapel is complete, they await a sacrifice. My father made a point of reminding me after last Sunday's service. Since I have assumed the mantle of clergy, he expects me to carry out the deed."

Gabriel's stomach churned. How had he lived among the villagers for two years and never heard so much as a whisper about the vile ritual?

Because there was no chapel or ground allotted for burial until recently.

He joined Jasper at the table. "Your father is only one elder of this village. Does Vernon Hode share the same belief?" Hode carried as much respect as Atticus among the villagers and farmers, if not more. Rumor said Hode came from icy lands farther north than any other. Likely, his beliefs were different. If anyone could stop the butcher and sacrifice of an innocent animal, it was Hode.

"I don't know." Jasper shrugged. "He hasn't been visible for days."

"In mourning." Gabriel remembered the rumor. "Reason enough to delay such a critical ritual."

Jasper looked surprised. "What?"

"Think about it. If this sacrifice is truly for the people of the village—or should I say, their souls when laid to rest—Vernon Hode should be present. No doubt your father and others will be there."

Jasper nodded, appearing to listen intently.

"Then you have every reason to delay the deed, especially if you are the one forced to carry it through. As the one to offer the sacrifice, is it not your right to set a time of your choosing?" Gabriel poured another cup of Madeira, then did the same for his friend.

This time Jasper did not refuse. He licked his lips. "We will be gone hunting the beast. When we return, Hode will have passed his period of mourning and should be focused enough to attend."

"He will surely be attentive enough to listen to reason." Leaning back in his chair, Gabriel sipped his wine. "More so, you will be a hero when we bag the beast. What better creature to set in the ground to protect against night demons?"

"Hang it, you're right." Smacking his hand against the table, Jasper lurched to his feet. "It is a fell beast that terrorizes us, and a fell beast that will fare best against the denizens of the Netherworld. No phantom or wight will stand a chance against such a creature. Why didn't I think of that? Gabriel, you are a genius!" He downed his wine in a single gulp.

Gabriel laughed. "How charitable of you to recognize my brilliance."

"A subject we will debate again when I hold the upper hand. For now, I freely concede to the better man." Sweeping an imaginary hat from his head, Jasper mimed a bow. He dropped into his chair with a grin. "Enough of my difficulties. Let us speak of something other than fell beasts and problems."

"Such as?"

"My sister."

Caught off guard by the abrupt change of topic, Gabriel tensed. "What of her?" Jasper was aware of his feelings for Dinah, but they rarely spoke of her in that regard.

"Nothing so troublesome as you think. Dinah told me she gave you a gem that once belonged to our great-grandmother. I wondered if you understood the significance."

Gabriel hedged, thinking of the emerald tucked in the pocket of his breeches. Dinah had entrusted him to keep it safe, and he took that vow seriously.

"Is this another tradition from your folklore?"

"Scoff if you will." Jasper helped himself to more Madeira, the pledge of a clear-headed morrow apparently forgotten. "The women among my ancestors have always commanded such stones. There are few left in the world. My great-grandmother claimed to have one of the last."

"Why only women?"

"The power the gem possesses is believed too tempting for a man to resist. A path to certain ruin."

Dinah would not have given him anything dark in nature. He shifted, disturbed that more and more the emerald reeked of witchery.

"But I have the gem. A man."

"Aye." Jasper acknowledged by draining the last of his wine. "Bestowed upon you by a woman as her pledge of protection and love—an entirely different circumstance. My ancestors considered it a great honor to receive such a blessing. Dinah might have imparted her pledge of protection to me, but she chose you instead."

"Jasper." Gabriel swallowed. "I hope you do not resent your sister for—"

"Nothing could be further from the truth." Jasper cut him off with a wide grin. "Her choice speaks volumes. She knows you will bear my safety in mind as I bear yours, but her pledge goes to the man who holds her heart. I expect you will do the honorable thing and approach my father for her hand."

Gabriel relaxed. Of course, his friend would know. "When we return. With the beast." He raised his cup, then drained it dry. "You are not the only one who needs that creature to change his future. Pray for both our sakes the monster dies swiftly."

* * * *

Present Day

David tossed the keys to the Mustang on the table inside the door, then shrugged out of his overcoat. Hands in the pockets of his hoodie, Finn brushed past and made a beeline for the hallway.

"Not so fast."

"What?" Heaving an exaggerated exhale, Finn turned, his mouth screwed into the frown of the century.

Great. Overall, the kid wasn't bad, but lately his attitude had been working on David's nerves. Probably the influence of Rodney Townsend.

"So now you're speaking."

Finn shrugged.

He hadn't said a word on the drive from the cemetery, though David hadn't talked much either, busy stewing over Finn's latest exploits. He didn't doubt the story Finn fed Desmond was a load of hogwash. Already this week the kid had missed curfew twice and neglected three homework assignments. David had gotten a call from the principal requesting a parent/teacher conference. Too bad he wasn't actually a parent. He needed to come up with a better way of controlling Finn's routine. His own was often unstable, the scattershot hours of a detective sergeant.

He pointed to the couch. "Sit."

Without a word, Finn dragged his feet across the carpet, then slumped into the cushions, arms folded over his chest.

David didn't say anything for a time, letting Finn fidget on the sofa while he flipped on the gas fireplace, then set the stereo system for something low and soothing. Another day, he might have pumped it full of classic rock, but the scream of electric guitars and bass drums wouldn't help his headache.

He wandered to the bathroom, located the economy-sized bottle of Excedrin, then tumbled a few into his palm. After swallowing them with a mouthful of water, he braced his hands on the vanity and stared into the mirror. Originally, when he'd leased the two-bedroom apartment off River Road, he'd planned to use the spare bedroom as an office. He'd had a sleek, contemporary desk, bookcase, and filing cabinet set up for three months before his sister ended up in prison—again—and he'd had to dump everything in storage to make room for Finn's bedroom set. He couldn't really blame the kid for having an attitude, given his parents.

David washed his hands then walked back into the living room, toweling them dry. Finn hadn't moved, still wedged into the sofa, gaze turned out the sliding doors to the balcony. If he slouched any farther, he'd fold into the cushions.

"So." David dropped into the chair across from him. "Let's talk about what happened this afternoon."

Finn's gaze slewed from the balcony, settling on David's face. He had his father's piercing blue eyes, his mother's curly black hair. When he wasn't sulking, his features could be open, even congenial. Right now, he looked like someone who'd swallowed a frog.

"Is this interrogation time?"

Little shit. The kid could play cool when he wanted.

David breathed deeply and counted to five. Ten gave too much leeway, and Finn knew exactly why he was in trouble.

"How do you know Elliott Camden?"

"School."

Brilliant. Who didn't love a one-word answer?

"Try again. He doesn't fit your circle of friends."

Finn shrugged. "He's a new kid. You can check the records."

A little too confident. This wasn't the avenue to take.

"What were you doing in the cemetery? You should have caught the bus home."

Finn took sudden interest in a thread on his jeans. He picked the edge. "We stayed after...a few other kids and me."

"What other kids?"

"Just some guys. You don't know them." *Pick. Pick.*

"How were you going to get home?"

Shrug. "One of the kids has an older brother. He was gonna come get us."

David wondered how long it had taken him to stitch the story together. Whatever had happened in the cemetery—he was sure it involved Rodney and Troy and equally certain the Camden kid was not a friend, probably the target—he was grateful Finn had done the right thing. He could have bailed like the others but had stayed and called for help. He'd put his neck on the chopping block, but it was clear he had no intention of ratting out his friends.

How did parents deal with crap like this on a regular basis?

David rubbed his eyes. "Since when do you decide to stay after school and not tell me? We've been through this. It's important that—"

"Yeah, I know. I need to stay out of trouble." Finn mimicked the lecture with venom. "Otherwise they might not let me go home when Mom's done doing time for her latest screw-up. Did you ever think maybe I don't want to go back? That maybe I'm sick of her promises to stay clean?"

He couldn't fault Finn the acid, not with Mandy as a mother. David's younger sister wasn't cut out for kids, a reality Finn had grown wise to years ago. The first time she'd fallen off the opioid wagon, Finn's father had stepped up to the plate, despite being equally ill-equipped to handle parenthood.

At least the prick had tried. Not so anymore.

A struggling paper products salesman, Reece Carrigan had fallen into the lap of luxury fourteen months ago when he'd hooked up with a greeting card heiress at a convention. Since then he'd been off the grid in Seattle, living with his soon-to-be bride. A woman who'd made it plain her affection didn't extend to the adolescent son from a previous marriage. *"I don't care where he goes, but not here, thank you very much."*

Never a stand-up guy to begin with, Reece's involvement with Finn had dwindled to an occasional phone call and a monthly support check, the latter of which Mandy used for pills. This time her fumble came with a two-year prison term, a sentence David prayed would be shortened over time for good behavior. If he hadn't agreed to become Finn's guardian, his nephew would have ended up in foster care. After four months, there were still gaping holes and hurdles in their relationship, with him undertaking the responsibility of meeting halfway.

"Look, I know you got a raw deal."

Finn snorted. "I don't need another reminder about people being only human"—air quotes—"or how parents aren't perfect and can make mistakes."

"Fine." Compassion wasn't going to work. The kid had a stick up his butt and had made up his mind to be bullheaded. "This isn't about your mother, anyway. It's about you and what you did. Or failed to do. You should have called me."

Finn drew back, the surprise on his face indicating he'd expected the prison card to get him off the hook. At the very least, lighten the fallout.

"Okay, I should have called." His gaze shifted sideways, the sign of someone thinking rapid-fire. "But we decided kind of quick. This afternoon. I…I thought I'd be back before you got home and didn't want to bug you. You're always on cases"—playing for truth, but using it as a lie—"and I…I was thinking of joining the science club."—faltering, trying to find a foothold—"You know how I like reading about aliens and stuff."

David made a noncommittal sound and tossed the towel aside. His nephew watched him as if trying to gauge whether his story had been bought.

Fat chance.

Reclining in his chair, David hooked his ankle over his knee. It was getting on in the evening, a reminder he'd have to start dinner soon. Something quick but healthy. He did a mental inventory of the refrigerator and came up with chicken he could throw in the oven. Maybe roast a few vegetables, toss with noodles or rice. As a bachelor, he usually nuked a pre-packaged slab or dumped something processed in a pot. Everything had changed since he'd taken custody of Finn.

Time to meddle. "So, you joined the science club?"

Finn shook his head. "It was lame. I decided not to."

"Too bad."

"How come?"

"Because you're going to join now."

Finn lurched forward on the couch. "Huh?"

"I think it will be good for you." *Keep you away from Rodney and Troy.* David tried not to smile. "I'll call on Monday and sign you up."

"But—"

David stood. "I also think you need someone to look after you on nights I work late."

"You don't mean—" Clearly horrified, Finn shot to his feet. *"A babysitter?"*

The smile fought to emerge, but he tamped it down. "If that's what you want to call it." He headed for the kitchen. "I'm going to start dinner. If I were you, I'd break out the books. I know it's Friday night, but you have three homework assignments to catch up on."

* * * *

Muttering under his breath, Eli Yancy paced in the basement of his life-coaching building. The business was still new, and he hadn't gotten much past outfitting the upstairs with an office and waiting room. A stainless-steel sink, exam table, utility cabinets, and a glaring retractable light reminiscent of an operating theater completed the lower level—much as they had when he'd worked for Leland Hode. Yancy had barely left the place since last night.

Tired, functioning on a short fuse, he shot a glance at the bones on the exam table. Vane's skeleton had been intact, remarkably well preserved. A death investigator or curator would have done flips for remains in such pristine condition, but Yancy had no appreciation for historic value, regardless how out of the ordinary. His wheelhouse spun on profit.

The passage of several months had done nothing to lessen his opportunistic nature. Leland Hode had once labeled him a greedy bastard, but Hode hadn't minded doling out a sizable salary to keep his hideously deformed son hidden from the world. After Ford Hode's death, Yancy and Leland had parted ways, the facility at Wickham shut down. Ford's body was never found, no one the wiser he'd been the blue-skinned "drifter" who'd committed suicide by leaping from the remains of the Old Orchard Truss Bridge.

With Leland's life in a shamble, he'd been eager to divest of Wickham, selling it for pennies on the dollar when Yancy approached him. It had been easy to obtain life-coaching credentials, an occupation he viewed as being on the trendy side of profit. Having Jillian Cley design a website was step one in building his contact base. He'd already netted a few clients by word of mouth. Probably could have lined up more if he hadn't gotten sidetracked by a cache of old notes written by his great-grandfather.

What Yancy really wanted—the prize he craved—was the single item *not* on the table with the collection of bones.

"It had to be there." He'd read his great-grandfather's notes over and again until he could almost recite them by rote. Heath Yancy had been the historian of the family, someone who *did* care about ancestry trees and moldy eras. When he'd died at the outstanding age of one hundred two, his binder of deeds, birth, death and marriage certificates, handwritten notes, and photos had passed to Yancy. If it hadn't been for Heath's written remarks about the binding stone, Yancy might have trashed the whole collection.

Gripping the short end of the table, he glared at Warren Porter. "You didn't look hard enough."

Porter shook his head. "I told you—there was nothing else in the grave. It's like the guy wasn't even buried in a coffin. No wood fragments, nails—nothing."

"I don't give a shit about nails and fragments. I told you to look for an uncut emerald."

"You told us to bring you his bones, and we did." Warren extended his hand, palm up. "I want paid."

It's what he got for working with lowlifes. Cursing silently, Yancy crossed to a black metal desk in the corner. Last night, he'd stashed an envelope in the center drawer before Warren and Clive arrived with Vane's bones. They'd expected payment on delivery, but he'd told Warren to come back this evening, wanting to ascertain the idiot brothers hadn't tried to stiff him with some derelict's skeleton.

Most of all he wanted the damn emerald.

"Twenty-five hundred as agreed." He offered the envelope but yanked it away before Porter could grasp it. "Five hundred more if you go back."

"What?" Porter's face darkened.

Yancy tossed him the envelope. "Vane's bones don't mean anything. It's the emerald I want. The emerald you failed to deliver. It has to be in the grave."

Warren pawed through the cash, making certain he hadn't been shorted. "Cops are crawling all over the place. They've got it roped off."

"Give it a day or two for the hoopla to die down. You have to go back before they fill in the hole."

"You're crazy. I'm not getting caught."

Yancy sighed. Porter was broad-shouldered and square, built like a fireplug. In a fit of temper, he'd inflict massive damage, but he was also easily manipulated by money. The trick was to nail down the right amount. "One thousand."

Porter rubbed his jaw, mulling it over. "What if we don't find the stone?"

"Then you get jack shit."

Porter's ruddy complexion flamed red. "Hell, it could be anywhere. If it was buried with Vane, it might have dropped when we hauled out his bones."

"Exactly. And the first place it would fall is back into the grave." Imbecile! Did he have to spell out everything? Lack of sleep was making him brusque. He needed to crash soon. "Are you in or not?"

"Yeah. Okay." Porter heaved a breath. "Clive, too." He shoved the envelope in the back pocket of his jeans. "I don't get why you're so sure it was buried with him."

"It wasn't." Yancy focused on the bones arranged on the table. Vane hadn't been tall, no more than five-nine. He'd keep the remains a while longer, then find a way to dump them when things cooled down. His great-grandfather would have denounced his actions as sacrilege, spending most of his life tracing the Yancy family tree back to Fern Crowe Inghram, the oldest daughter of Atticus—an elder of the village that eventually became Hode's Hill.

Soured by thoughts of the past, Yancy ground his teeth. Atticus Crowe's name should have been on the town charter, not Vernon Hode's. Maybe he couldn't change history, but he could do what his ancestor couldn't—claim the emerald as his own.

"I don't get it." Porter still hadn't left, hovering by the door, one hand wrapped around the knob. "If the stone wasn't buried with Vane, why are you so sure it's in his grave?"

"Because, you oaf, he swallowed it."

* * * *

Saturday morning, Jillian filled a bowl with oatmeal and berries, grabbed a cup of French roast coffee, then carried her breakfast to the kitchen table. The previous owner of the brownstone had enlarged the area by removing a built-in nook, adding a huge center island with cooktop and installing French doors where a set of double windows had been.

The doors opened onto a deck, equal in size with the terrace below. As the last home in a row of six, she had a partial view of the adjacent field and an unobstructed view of Hickory Chapel jutting from a hillside in the distance. It was one of the reasons she'd bought the property. Even when she didn't visit the cemetery, his resting place was in sight. It was important he know he wasn't forgotten.

Blizzard nosed her leg, a thank-you for his morning walk, then strayed into the kitchen to sniff around his food bowl. His toenails clicked on the hardwood floor.

Jillian sipped her coffee and opened the newspaper. Despite not craving social interaction, she liked to keep up with town events. Anything of note was more detailed online, but the paper was great for local color—something in abundance now that Halloween was so close.

She scanned announcements while she ate, pausing to read a few in detail. The annual Halloween Parade was scheduled for the thirtieth, beginning on the northern end of River Road. Closing subsequent streets meant traffic would be blocked from her end of town. If the weather was decent, she might take in the sights of the river from her front stoop, the parade no more than a penny whistle trill in the distance.

A flip of the page drew her attention to a splashy advertisement several columns wide. In honor of Halloween, Hode's Hill was holding its first Masquerade Pub Crawl, a mashup of all things spooky and Carnivale. Several taverns and grilles were participating, clustered together in a strip locals commonly called Pub Place.

Part of her wanted to attend, get out more. But too many people would be bunched together, swirling in costumes, wearing—

Masks.

Not really themselves. Pretending. Make believe.

She spread her fingers over the ad.

Could she shut out others for a single night if she did the same? If she hid behind a mask and imagined herself a different person?

Startled by the thought, she pulled her hand away. Immediately, her gaze fell to the headline below the ad.

Halloween Hoax or Deliberate Desecration—One Editor's Opinion

A photo of Hickory Chapel was tucked in the bottom corner. Shot from the cemetery, the picture showed the weathered, boarded-up church from the left side, a strip of police tape cordoning off a plot to the rear.

Jillian's heart beat faster. Pulse pounding, she flew through the article.

Anyone who has lived in Hode's Hill for any length of time knows to avoid Hickory Chapel and the old cemetery it overshadows. For centuries, there have been rumors of tolling church bells and restless ghosts. The hauntings are said to increase in the weeks leading up to Halloween. Every year, local teenagers dare each other to stay overnight, several usually bold enough to take the challenge.

Shenanigans. Halloween fun.

Not so anymore.

A person or persons unknown has violated the grave belonging to Gabriel Vane and removed his remains. According to his tombstone, Vane died in 1799. Police estimate the depth of his tomb at eight feet or greater, requiring the grave robbers to expend remarkable effort to complete their task.

Why this grave? Why Gabriel Vane?

Circumstance was brought to light when children playing in the cemetery happened upon the open grave. A twelve-year-old boy fell into the pit but was not harmed. Police arrived to discover a scene straight out of a Victorian novel when bodysnatching and the sale of bones were common practice.

Hickory Chapel has no place on the Register of Historic Places. The graves entrusted to its care have long been forgotten. Neglected. Efforts to create awareness for funding by the Historical Society have been stymied at every turn, resulting in abandonment. This lack of interest, apart from oft-told ghost tales, could be why grave robbers targeted the site.

Halloween hoax or deliberate desecration?

Either way, a sad affair for a town which should have a stronger appreciation of its past.

Jillian's breath fluttered between her lips. It took several seconds before she realized she'd bunched the corner of the paper into a ball, her hand fisted around the newsprint. Blizzard sat beside her, prodding her leg with his paw.

No, no, no!

It wasn't possible. Not his grave. Not his.

She thrust from the chair and paced off a tight circle. What did she do now? There'd been nothing to prepare for this.

Blizzard back-danced two steps and barked.

Her gaze shifted to the husky. The dog whined when their eyes met. "He's gone, Blizzard. Gone." The word stuck to her tongue. What would her parents have done? Her grandparents or great-grandparents? Her mother's voice rang in her ears:

A man dies two times but must never die three. It's up to you and Madison to see Gabriel Vane never suffers the Third Death.

Breakfast forgotten, she bolted for the foyer. Blizzard loped on her heels, toenails clacking loudly. Jillian threw open the closet, grabbed her pea coat, then snatched Blizzard's leash. Her emotions were in turmoil, spikes of near-tangible upheaval that made the husky restless. He fidgeted as she clamped the leash to his collar.

"It's okay, it's okay." She was barely conscious of repeating the mantra, whispered efforts to calm them both. "We're going to the cemetery." She needed to see Gabriel's grave for herself. Once there, she'd have a better idea of what to do. There had to be a clue, however vague, of who was at fault for the theft.

Maybe Sherre would have more information.

Jillian had kept in touch with the law enforcement officer following Boyd's murder. The trail had grown cold, but the motive had been clear from the start—he'd crossed the wrong people. If Madison's mind hadn't shattered, she could have ID'd the killers.

Jillian groaned.

"Madison." Would her sister even understand the significance of what had happened?

In her mind, Gabriel Vane had already suffered the Third Death.

* * * *

There were far darker places that catered to ghosts than cemeteries.

Dante parked in front of the redbrick building and silenced the ignition of his 4Runner. He studied the plaque riveted to the right of the entrance door, a glossy black rectangle with white lettering.

ELI YANCY, CERTIFIED LIFE COACH

Finally, a name attached to a building designated only as "Wickham" after the road on which it squatted. Dante's father had died within that square of red brick over a decade ago, the accident that caused his death as shrouded in mystery today as it had been then.

Fifteen was too young to lose a parent, especially when that parent remained an enigma. Salvador DeLuca had never talked about his work except to say it involved medical science. After his death, Wickham remained as it had before—a facility without markings of any kind, a place of questionable practices.

Growing up, Dante had kept his distance. It wasn't only his father's death that made him shy away, but an underlying disease that seemed to seep from the knots and fissures in the ground. Like Salvador, he was able to pick up on preternatural vibrations, a gift not without a downside. Fingering the medallion under his shirt, he realized his father must have faced his share of monsters too. Why else a medal of the Archangel Michael, commander of God's armies? Michael was a protector, defender against darkness and demons.

Stepping from the vehicle, Dante pocketed his keys. He closed the door and glanced around the parking lot. This early on a Saturday morning, the place was deserted. Not that he'd noticed many cars since Eli Yancy hung his shingle. Wickham was situated far enough from town to raise eyebrows for a practice of any kind. Maybe the guy liked the isolation and thought his clients would, too.

Stuffing his hands in his jacket, Dante forked from the sidewalk in favor of the grass. He walked around the back of the building, conscious of the wind whistling through tree branches. Gnarled oaks and towering sycamores clustered several hundred yards to the rear, mammoth pines dotted like sentries around the sides. Sometime, long ago, the area had probably been densely wooded.

He couldn't say why he was here, or why the damn spot drew him even as it repulsed him. Something told him his father wasn't the only one who'd suffered.

Tilting his head, he stared up at the stark structure. There was nothing appealing about it, a series of small windows recessed under the eaves like shuttered eyes, barely enough to provide light. The interior would have to be bleak, swathed in the harsh glow of fluorescent tubes. Even with the morning sun casting leaf shadows on the ground, the place reeked of something defiled.

It's how he'd painted it.

A vision from memory, storm clouds gathered behind it. He hadn't brought the canvas with him, but one look was all it took to know he'd captured its essence.

If only he understood what that essence was.

No good will ever come from this place.

The thought was his, but the words belonged to someone else.

Dante turned and looked at the cluster of trees.

Long ago, someone had nearly died here.

Chapter 5

October 11, 1799

"Tracks?" Gabriel asked as Hiram Blum dismounted and squatted to examine something in the weeds. The sun hovered behind a plateau of clouds to their right, indication of their northeasterly path. The beast had struck overnight, raiding Cyrus Herman's chicken coop, slaughtering half a dozen birds. Most of the remains were left uneaten, convincing Cyrus *"the damn animal butchers for pleasure."*

The beast's end couldn't come soon enough for him or the other farmers. In the village, men had taken to barricading their doors, fearful the foul creature would develop a yen for human flesh.

"Coyote scat. Too smooth and shiny for our wolf." Hiram dropped a chunk of offal, then dusted his hands. "We keep going." Standing, he pointed in the distance. "This way."

Gabriel nudged his sorrel ahead as Hiram mounted. Behind him, Jasper brought up the rear, leading a pack mule loaded with provisions. Though it had been Gabriel's idea to hunt the wolf, he was content to let Blum lead. Hiram seemed to think like the creature, choosing the direction it would go, the wooded habitat it should favor, even the boundaries of territory it would roam.

"Our beast could cover over a hundred miles in a day," he'd said when they'd met at the church an hour before dawn. Unwelcome news for so small a hunting party. He'd assuaged their fears by adding, "Could, but won't. This creature knows where to fill its belly. Life is good here. It will not roam far."

Gabriel breathed easier. Atticus and several other men gathered to see them off, Dinah the only woman among them. She'd squeezed Gabriel's hand and wished him a safe journey, daring nothing more in mixed company. Before departing, Jasper offered a prayer, beseeching God to grant them victory on their quest. Several hours had passed with the gray haze of dawn yielding to the sallow light of late morning. Here and there they picked up tracks among knots of Indian hemp and ryegrass, thorny weeds or clumps of bittercress. A short while ago, they'd discovered prints paralleling a creek bed, a sight that left Hiram tight-lipped and grim. It wasn't until Gabriel had gotten a good look at the muddy impressions that he understood the older man's reaction. No common wolf had paws of such size or claws half the length of sickles. He'd seen similar tracks ringed around the carcasses of dead chickens and pigs, but the reality struck deeper this time. The beast they pursued was no mere predator, but a monster of abnormal proportions. The thought stayed with him long after they'd left the tracks behind, abandoning the stream for denser woods.

The weight of Gabriel's long rifle rested against his back, secured by a shoulder strap. It comforted him to know the weapon's range was accurate over two hundred yards. He wasn't a marksman but was proficient enough to have won several shooting titles at holiday fairs. From an early age, he'd handled a gun, a necessity of living on a farm where livestock made easy prey for wild animals. When he'd purchased his own acreage, he'd replaced his father's musket with the slender long-barreled rifle, a weapon designed to hit what he aimed at.

Let the beast come.

The sooner he killed it, the sooner he could seek Dinah's hand in marriage.

Jasper rode up beside him, trailing the pack mule. "We should stop soon. Water the horses and allow them to rest. I fear the sun will not favor us this day."

"Aye." The cloud cover had grown heavier, the air cooler. "If we break now, we can push through 'til nightfall." Darkness, in unison with the beast, was not something he wanted to contemplate. "Hiram." Gabriel pitched his voice to carry. "Let us find a place to make a brief camp."

The big man acknowledged with a wave. Ten minutes later they stopped in a small clearing where ground water formed a narrow stream. The horses drank their fill while Gabriel, Jasper, and Hiram shared salted fish and cups of hard cider. They made no fire and spoke little, each wrapped in private thoughts. Gabriel's drifted to Dinah and the emerald she'd given him. Idly, he fingered the gem, tucked in the pocket of his overcoat. Would her gift truly keep him safe? If the beast was as sizable as they feared, he and the others needed added protection.

"You carry a fine weapon." Hiram swallowed the last of his cider, then flung the clinging residue from his cup with a flick of his wrist. He indicated Gabriel's rifle, propped against the trunk of a hefty ash. "May I?"

"Aye." Gabriel was proud of the weapon. It had cost him a pretty penny, but the Pennsylvania long rifle was as beautiful as it was deadly, constructed with a maple stock and a brass patch box. "I bought it from a gunsmith in Lancaster after I came to America." He'd known even then he'd need a serviceable weapon if he planned to take up farming. "The bore is rifled, not smooth like a Brown Bess. I've heard it said you can bark a squirrel from a tree at three hundred yards." Heat rose to his face with the exaggeration, leaving him feeling a bit like a schoolboy trying to impress an elder.

"Ever do it?" Hiram ran a thick-fingered hand down the stock, then held the weapon up to spot through the sights.

"No." He felt foolish admitting the truth.

"Ever kill a man?"

"No." Gabriel flung a glance to Jasper, noting his friend looked as startled as he by the question.

Hiram returned the gun to its resting place. "I carried a Bess under Washington."

"Did you…did you ever…" Gabriel couldn't form the question. A man didn't fight in that war without taking the life of his enemy.

"The general had a regiment of frontiersmen with long guns he used as marksmen. The rest of us fired volleys with smoothbores then moved in with bayonets."

Gabriel grimaced. Close quarters killing. He'd noticed Hiram's current weapon of choice was a musket-style gun with a tubular magazine. He'd never seen anything like it but heard someone in the village say it was an Austrian military rifle called a *windbusche*, or "wind rifle." He couldn't summon the nerve to ask how it worked.

"I…I had heard you'd fought under Washington," he stammered instead.

"Did you now?" Hiram strode to his horse. He packed away his tin drinking cup, then tightened the straps on his bedroll and saddlebags. "Rumors follow a man, but not all are true." He looked over his shoulder. "You remember that, boys. It's time to get a move on, don't you think?"

"S-sure." Somehow, Gabriel felt as if he'd just surrendered leadership of their group, not that it mattered. This excursion wasn't about ego or proving himself to a former soldier. He was a farmer, nothing more. All he craved was a simple life with Dinah. If Hiram Blum could help bring that about, he'd willingly follow the man into the damn creature's den. "Lead the way, Hiram."

* * * *

Present Day

Jillian attached a leash to Blizzard's collar then stepped aside as he jumped from the back of the Accord. Even trained in the role of therapy dog, some things remained instinctual to her beloved husky, too ingrained by breeding to overcome. One of the first things her handler had told her was "never let your dog off leash when you're outside."

"We don't have to worry about that, do we, boy?" Jillian scratched behind his ears. She'd made the mistake only once, spending three hours combing the riverbanks and city streets to track him down. Blizzard had eventually shown up not far from home, a muddy mess, his fur riddled with briars, tail wagging and tongue lolling from his mouth. He'd had his fun, but any running after that incident was done on a leash with her jogging at his side.

"I wish Madison could run with us." Her gaze tracked to Rest Haven, the private care facility at the front of the parking lot. She'd been doing what she could to ensure her sister maintained her private room. Boyd's life insurance had only gone so far, and even with Madison's disability subsidy, the funds were starting to dwindle. The mere thought of moving her sister—once so vibrant and active—to a state-funded institution made her sick in the stomach. "Something will work out. Something has to."

Either Madison would recover, or Jillian would need a windfall.

Or a miracle.

She bit her lip. "Come on. We might as well tell her the news." She started walking, Blizzard falling in beside her. At the entrance to the three-story building, she punched out a security code, waiting for the lock on the door to flash green before she continued into the lobby. Rosella, the daytime receptionist, greeted her and asked her to sign in.

"How's my sister today?" Jillian scratched her name in the log book.

Rosella's eyelids lowered. "Quiet." She'd come around the desk to greet Blizzard, but now returned to her seat. "Abbie is her day nurse. She had her down earlier for breakfast, but I don't know that she ate much."

"Okay. Thanks." Quiet was better than the alternative—days when Madison relived Boyd's murder and wouldn't stop screaming. Food, regardless of how she felt, had become a mechanical function Madison performed during more agreeable moments. Jillian doubted she would understand the significance of Gabriel Vane's grave being robbed but felt obligated to tell her. There was a time Madison had visited his burial site on a regular basis.

When the elevator doors closed behind her and Blizzard, Jillian took several deep breaths, preparing herself to block the bombardment of stray feelings waiting on the floors above. It was harder here. Maintaining her detachment in a facility devoted to the care of those who couldn't function in society due to mental or emotional disabilities was almost impossible, but after three years, she'd learned to seal herself in a cocoon. The first time she'd visited Madison, she'd left in tears, on the verge of a nervous breakdown from the mental barrage. Still a wreck after months, she'd crossed paths with Sherre Lorquet, who'd suggested a therapy dog.

Blizzard pressed against Jillian's leg, an extension of the shield she'd built. Stepping from the elevator was like stepping into a slow-motion world. The nurses at the station desk were familiar with her and merely nodded, continuing their work as she passed. A few patients shuffled down the hallway, some escorted by aides, others on their own. Madison's room was at the end, facing front. Jillian passed several doors, a few open, others closed tight, thoughts and feelings seeping from them all.

Once in Madison's room, she breathed easier. The sight of her sister sitting in a chair by the window brought the hint of a smile to her lips.

"Look, Blizzard. Madison probably saw us pull into the parking lot." She crossed the small room—fitted with a bed and dresser near the door, a small seating area and table by the window—until she eased in front of her sister. Madison didn't raise her eyes or turn from her study of the dozen-plus cars tucked into orderly rows outside.

Blizzard whined softly and lay down nearby. Jillian dropped the leash, set her purse on the table, then eased into the opposite chair. Madison's expression was blank, her once shoulder-length coppery hair cropped close for convenience. Her face had grown thin, her body frail after three years of living in a world only she could see. Jillian picked up her hand, rubbing her thumb over the bony knobs of her sister's knuckles. Madison's arms resembled sticks sheathed in whey-colored flesh. Two years older, she might have been half a dozen or more based on her haggard appearance.

"Madison. It's Jillian. Blizzard's here, too. Can you look at me?" She opened her mind. Wanted to feel something. Anything. But like Dante

DeLuca, Madison was closed to her. Her sister's mind had shattered on the day Boyd died. Witnessing a murder was enough to push anyone over the edge, but an empath? What must it have been like to sink into the black abyss of Boyd's terror, the mind-blowing edge of his pain? To *feel* his death as if it were her own?

Leaning forward, she gripped Madison's hand tightly. "I just left Hickory Chapel and the old cemetery where Gabriel Vane is buried. You remember Gabriel?" *One of us has to. One of us has to keep him alive in our memory.*

The images returned in rapid succession—an open grave surrounded by yellow caution tape, the marker she'd lovingly tended over time with the barely legible scrawl of his name, the boarded-up chapel hunched at her back like a silent guardian.

"Gabriel's gone, Madison. Someone dug up his grave and stole his remains." She squeezed slightly, pressing on Madison's fingers. Slowly, her sister swiveled her head, her gaze resting on Jillian.

Madison's eyes were blue-green, once a vivid teal when caught in the right light. Today, they appeared washed-out, faded like old denim. Her mouth tightened, accentuating fine white lines at the corners. She wouldn't speak. She never did. The only sound to issue from her throat was the high-pitched wail of her screams.

Jillian wet her lips. "Do you remember Mom and Dad telling us we had to keep Gabriel in our memory? It was our responsibility to see he was never forgotten, a duty our family has carried for generations." Remembering Gabriel and the importance of their obligation might piece together some fragmented part of Madison's mind. It wasn't as if Jillian had never tried before, but Gabriel's remains had never been missing. Thinking about the potential damage sent a flutter of anxiety through her stomach.

"Madison, I know you can hear me. I know you're in there somewhere." Gripping both of Madison's hands, she squeezed harder. If only touch could reach where she couldn't. "Gabriel's life was taken against his will. You still have a life, if you'd only crawl out of the dark place you've created for yourself."

Her sister's stare was blank, as it always was.

Overcome by despair, Jillian looked out the window. At the cars in the lot below, the white cement sidewalk stretching to either side, flanked by boxwood hedges slowly browning with the rust of autumn. Anywhere but into the empty shell of the person sitting across from her.

Three years. How much longer could she do this? Time after time of sitting and pleading with someone who'd allowed themselves to be stripped of all they were.

As if sensing her thoughts, Blizzard whined and shuffled to a sitting position. He nosed Madison's leg, but Jillian's sister gave no indication she knew the dog was there. His tail thumped weakly against the carpet. The low-pile nap was the same bleached almond as the walls. Peaceful, serene.

Drab.

The lack of color helped reinforce the impression there was no life in the room.

Jillian refocused on her sister. "Mom told us that a man dies three times. Once when he dies. Once when he's buried. And once when there is no one left to remember him. When that happens, he suffers the Third and Final Death. Remember how Mom used to take us to Hickory Chapel Cemetery when we were little? We helped her tend Gabriel's grave. Then when she and Daddy died in a car accident, it was up to me and you to look after Gabriel. We used to take turns before"—the words stuck in her throat—"before Boyd was killed."

In the first weeks after her brother-in-law's murder, Jillian had feared mentioning his name to Madison, but soon realized doing so had no effect. Somewhere under all the horror she'd suffered, Madison must have known Boyd signed his death warrant the day he started dealing drugs.

The corner of Madison's mouth tipped up in a feeble smile.

"Maddy?" Jillian's heart lurched. Who was she smiling about—Boyd? Gabriel? Some dusty memory of their mother or father? Giddy elation boomeranged from Jillian's head to her feet. "Maddy, you're smiling. You—"

The meager hint of amusement vanished in half a pulsebeat. Madison stared blankly, the emptiness of her gaze carving a black chasm through Jillian's heart.

"No. Oh, no." She buried her face in her hands, but after three years, had no tears left.

* * * *

Jillian couldn't remember the last time she'd cried over her sister. In the beginning, she'd spent days huddled in bed, sobbing uncontrollably. It didn't help that Boyd's killers had never been caught. The murder scene indicated two, possibly three men. Boyd was bad news from day one, but he hadn't deserved to be butchered like a pig. In forcing Madison to watch, his killers had murdered her, too. Maybe that's why they'd left her, broken and howling by the mutilated remains of her husband. Slitting her throat would have ended her misery, but they must have known her mind was blown. Why else would they leave her alive, giving her the chance to ID them? If only she could talk.

"I hate this drive." Jillian gritted her teeth, fingers white-knuckling on the steering wheel. Every time she made the forty-minute trek to Palmer Point and Rest Haven, her mind blundered into the past. Madison's shaky suggestion of a smile had reawakened memories of Mill Street and her joy when she and Boyd had bought their small house. For someone who barely held a job, Jillian should have questioned where the money came from. Boyd flitted from random paycheck to random paycheck while Madison had just started a new career in real estate, nowhere near established or lucrative enough to afford a mortgage.

"Damn you, Boyd. Why'd you have to set your sights on my sister?"

Blizzard paced in the cramped back seat. The dog could read her moods like a book.

She sent him a glance in the rearview mirror. "I'm okay, just ticked. Lie down. In another twenty minutes, we'll be home."

She passed Eli Yancy's office on the left, a black SUV she didn't think belonged to Yancy in the lot. Maybe she'd fiddle with his website when she got home. She was behind schedule as it was, and a few hours on the computer might prod her from her bleak mood.

Ruminating on the thought, she jerked to awareness when her car engine died.

"What the—" The steering wheel locked in her suddenly sweaty grip and pressing the brake had no effect. Panic shot through her. She fought the wheel, struggling to guide the Accord off the side of the road. When the vehicle finally rolled to a stop, she blew out a breath and turned to make certain Blizzard was okay. Unharmed, the husky nosed her shoulder.

"Sorry, boy." She patted his head. "I don't know what happened." Fortunately, she hadn't been going fast, and there was no traffic this far north on Wickham Road. Placing the gearshift in park, she switched the ignition to the off position, then tried to restart the engine. A half dozen warning lights flashed to life on her dash, but the motor refused to turn over. No sound, not even a click.

"Great." Probably a dead battery. At least she hoped it wasn't anything more involved. "Looks like we need to call Triple A." That meant sitting and waiting for a jump. Not fun, but manageable given her already disastrous morning. A grave robbery, the ghost smile on Madison's face, and now a car that decided to go belly-up.

"They say things come in threes. It can't get any worse." Jillian pressed the power button on her cell. Then pressed it again when nothing happened.

Like a lead weight, her heart plummeted to her gut. "I take that back." She pounded her fist against the steering wheel. "I'm such an idiot. I forgot to charge my phone!"

* * * *

Dante had only driven half a mile when he spied the blue Accord off the side of the road. The hood was up, and a woman with a long, blond braid over her shoulder stared forlornly at the guts of the vehicle. The rear passenger window was cranked down far enough to allow a Siberian husky to thrust his head through the opening. The dog looked far happier than the woman who glanced up when Dante parked his 4Runner behind her car.

"Hey." He jogged toward her, still a few feet away when he recognized her. "Jillian Cley, right?"

She nodded.

"I didn't get a chance to thank you last night for telling me about Elliott."

"Is he okay?"

"Yeah. A few scrapes and bruises. You know kids." His gaze skewed to the side, taking in the open hood and exposed engine. "I'd asked if you're having car troubles, but that's obvious. What's the problem?"

"I don't know. It just died on me. I was going to call Triple A, but my cell's dead, too."

"Sounds like a bad day."

"You don't know the half of it. Any chance you can give me a jump?"

"Sure. I've got cables. Let me pull around in front of you." Dante jogged for his truck. He pointed to the husky, who'd paced to the opposite side of the vehicle, thrusting his head through the window to watch. "Who's your friend?"

"Blizzard."

"Great name." He wondered if Elliott had befriended the dog. The kid was going to need something to get his mind off the fall he'd taken in the cemetery. It was true he'd come through the ordeal with a few scrapes and a broken cell phone, but it's what he hadn't said that bothered Dante. A kid didn't play in a place he was frightened of, and only two nights ago, Elliott had been terrified by the thought of monsters lurking in Hickory Chapel Cemetery.

Dante had a feeling he knew exactly who the real "monsters" were. He'd had more than a few in his past.

Several minutes later, he had his SUV in place, the alligator clamps connected. Jillian's vehicle started on the third try.

"I don't know how to thank you," she said when they'd both exited their vehicles to stand by the cables. "If you hadn't come along, who knows how long I might have been stuck here."

"We'll let it charge for a while. It could be the battery, but it might be the alternator, too. I'll follow you home in case you have more problems."

She seemed surprised. "You don't have to do that."

"It's okay. I want to check on Elliott and Tessa, anyway. I'm supposed to have lunch with them."

"Oh." It was odd how uneasy she appeared, her gaze darting away, then back to his face. "All right. Thank you." She fingered a beaded eyeglass chain around her neck, drawing his attention to the small bits of amber and gold glass. As an artist, he appreciated the way the colored beads complemented the tortoiseshell glasses they secured. Tinted green, the lenses weren't opaque enough for sunglasses, but solid enough to provide protection.

"Light sensitivity?" he guessed, motioning to the glasses.

She blanched. "N-No. I mean, yes. I mean..."

Laughing, he held up his hands. "It's okay. I wear contacts, but some days I fall back on glasses. I've got an outdated pair that makes me look like a cross between a long-haired Clark Kent and a lab rat. At least that's what my grandmother says."

She relaxed noticeably. "Sometimes the light bothers me."

Dante saw no reason for her to lie, but the furtive glance she cast to the side made him think she wasn't being truthful. Weird how some people felt the need to cover up a vision impairment.

"I think we're good to head back now." Leaning over the Accord's open hood, he unhooked the alligator clamps. "Give me a minute to get my 4Runner turned around so I can follow you."

He thought she was going to protest again, but she nodded.

"I wish I could do something to repay you."

"You can."

Her eyes widened in shock.

No surprise there. It might be rude to collect on a favor, but he'd spent most of last summer in the spotlight proving exactly how bad-mannered he could be.

"My cousin needs a friend. You can join us for lunch."

* * * *

Elliott rubbed his thumb over the rough-cut green gem. For some reason it made him feel safe. Downstairs, Jillian and his mom were chatting over coffee. He'd been surprised when Dante showed up and said he'd invited Jillian to lunch. She'd seemed ill at ease, like how he felt when everyone was buddied up with a friend in the school cafeteria.

But his mom hadn't been flustered at all, and soon she and Jillian were talking about dumb stuff like yoga and some masquerade thing for adults. He'd gotten the impression it had to do with Halloween but tuned it out since he was too old for trick-or-treating.

If he wasn't secretly freaked out by the thought of going to school on Monday, he might have eaten more of his turkey/Swiss melt and tomato soup. He downed half, then said he was tired and disappeared upstairs to his bedroom where he could wallow in doom.

What if Rodney, Troy, and Finn thought he'd ratted them out? He'd seen Finn by one of the police cars when the cops hauled him from the grave. Finn looked miserable, sick and worried, like he knew he was in trouble. If that was the case, Elliott was dead meat.

Dropping onto the bottom bunk of his bed, he rubbed the stone harder. He slept in the top bunk but used the bottom for thinking and playing video games. Sometimes, he even sprawled there to do his homework. The bunk beds had been a parting gift from his father around the time of his parents' divorce. *"Think of all the fun sleepovers you'll have with your new friends in Hode's Hill."* Problem was, he didn't have any friends, and the bunk beds, no matter how cool, had been a bribe. At least at night, he could lie in the top bunk and gaze at the glow-in-the-dark stars his mom had affixed to the ceiling.

Elliott caressed the gem. He'd seen his grandma buff her thumb over a rose-colored piece of quartz when she got worked up about something. She called it a worry stone. His gem didn't have an indention like hers, the sides rough and uneven, but it took the edge off the churning in his gut. If only it could work magic. Make the other boys leave him alone. Maybe even help him find a friend.

"Hey, Elliott?" Dante's voice echoed through the door in unison with a knock. "You in there?"

"Um...yeah." Elliott tucked the stone into his jeans. "Come on in."

Dante stepped inside. Parting with a low whistle, he hooked a thumb at the full-wall space mural adjacent to the bunk bed. "When did you add that?"

"Last week." Elliott loved the colorful array of planets, meteorites, and stars. At night, when the room was dark, the planets glowed, just like the stars on the ceiling. "Grandma hired someone to do it as a surprise for me." He'd been fixated on the night sky ever since second grade when his class had taken a field trip to a planetarium. Sometimes, when he couldn't sleep, he'd drag his telescope to the window and angle it up at the heavens. He'd never tell his mom, but maybe Dante.

"Grandma said you used to watch the stars when you were a kid."

"She did?" Dante blinked as if surprised. "I guess so. That was a long time ago." He closed the door with a soft click. "I'm surprised she remembered. Your grandmother and I don't talk much."

"How come? She's your aunt."

"It's complicated." He hunched down and eased onto the bunk beside Elliott. "Ancient history and far too boring to talk about. Besides—that's not why I came up here. You took a bad tumble yesterday. I bet you're stiff today, huh?"

"I'm okay." No sense admitting the truth when it was his own dumb fault. Elliott dropped his gaze, focusing on his thumbs. His fingernails were ragged, rimmed with grime two baths hadn't been able to wash away. The stain came from trying to claw his way out of the grave. Acting like a coward.

The memory sent a pang through his gut. He didn't want to talk about the cemetery any more than he wanted to think about Monday.

"Weird place for you to be playing." Dante's tone was casual.

"I wasn't playing." He wished the emerald was still in his hand. With a little effort he could imagine the hard ridges pressed against his fingers. "I-I was taking a shortcut."

"Through the cemetery?" Dante frowned. "I thought you were afraid of the monsters."

Elliott shook his head, the ping of his heart gaining speed.

The cemetery was a bad place, not because he'd fallen, but because everyone said so. What if there'd been a monster in the grave with him, something he couldn't see? What if it followed him home and he didn't know it? What if it was in the room right now…invisible, squatting in the corner?

He lurched to his feet, his gaze sweeping the room.

"Elliott, what's wrong?"

"Nothing. I don't want to talk about the cemetery." He dug his hand into his pocket—

"What about the other boys you were with?"

—wrapped his fingers around the stone. "They're just some kids I know from school." His gut flopped. *Stop asking me questions. Please stop asking me questions.*

"You're not in any kind of trouble with those other boys, are you?"

"No." He shook his head vehemently, but even then guessed Dante saw through the denial. He might be able to trick his mom, but Dante was different. He lowered his gaze, too embarrassed to talk about how Rodney, Troy, and Finn had bullied him.

"Okay." Dante seemed to sense his mood. "But if anything ever happens—if you are in any kind of trouble—you know you can talk to me, right? And your mom. You should talk to your mom."

Nodding, Elliott pushed his glasses higher onto his nose. "Thanks."

Standing, Dante clapped his shoulder. "Don't be frightened of the cemetery either. The people who are buried there started this town, and we should be grateful to them. If it weren't for their perseverance, Hode's Hill wouldn't exist. You had a scare, but you're safe now."

Safe.

After Dante left, Elliott rolled the word around in his head. There were different degrees of safety. More than likely a monster hadn't followed him home, wasn't squatting in the corner waiting to suck his brains out when he fell asleep. But he'd keep the stone close, just in case. It had protected him in the grave. Maybe it could protect him from anything—or anyone.

Like Rodney, Troy, and Finn.

Chapter 6

October 11, 1799

Gabriel tossed another stick on the fire, then bowed over his plate. The temperature had plummeted once the sun set, the air rimmed with cold where it slithered beneath his heavy frock coat. The root stew they'd thrown together in a cast iron pot, along with a cup of hard cider, helped warm his stomach. He sopped up the last of his meal with a chunk of bread, then set his plate aside, hunching deeper into his coat.

Overhead, stars pirouetted in the gap between pillars of hemlocks and ash. A steady breeze carried the scent of pine and toadstools from deeper in the forest and made the flames of the campfire cavort as though possessed. He fed another stick to the blaze, coaxing it higher.

"You fear the darkness." Hiram's observation contained no malice. Reclining with his back to the trunk of a tree, he sat with his legs stretched in front, crossed at the ankles. "The wind tends the fire well without your help, Gabriel Vane." He drew on a clay pipe, exhaled a stream of smoke, then pointed the end at Gabriel. "Even were that not so, there is no need to fear the night."

"It is not the night that concerns me." Gabriel glanced over his shoulder, peering into the heavy blackness, but it was impossible to see beyond the ring of light.

"Nor I." Jasper pulled his musket closer. "We've entered the wolf's preferred hunting hours. How can you remain so relaxed, Hiram?"

The older man gave a short grunt. "I've crossed trails with this beast before."

"Before?" Gabriel exchanged a swift look with Jasper. "You never mentioned that. Don't you think Atticus and others in the village would have found the information valuable?"

"To what end? Would it make them take up weapons and join the hunt? No." Hiram drew on his pipe. "It is best the speculation remains with me. Were I to share what I know, there would be far too much dissecting. Men arguing the best approach, none with the gumption to follow through on strategy. Rest assured our predator will seek that which is familiar to fill its gullet—chickens and pigs. Stray dogs and sheep. It has no desire to cross paths with us."

"How can you be so certain?" Gabriel wanted to believe him, but doubt wormed under his skin. "Is it because you encountered the beast before?"

"Aye."

Another look exchanged with Jasper.

His friend shifted, tucking into a cross-legged position. "We are not just any members of the village, but your companions on this hunt. We deserve to know."

"Aye, you do. I thought to broach it eventually." Hiram sat forward, firelight picking up a gleam of yellow in his eyes. He was quiet for a time, puffing on the pipe as if seeking the right words. "This beast is known in the deep woods from which I hail. Our legends speak of a fell creature that crawled from caverns buried well below the soil. In those days, there were many of the monsters, and the woodsmen were hard pressed to stave them off. It is said one man—stronger and braver than the rest—cornered and slaughtered the alpha beast, but his victory was not without cost. Gravely wounded, he suffered with fever and delirium for the passage of four sunsets. When he awoke on the fourth night, his eyes gleamed the same yellow as the beast. He was able to think like the creature, track the others to their dens. He became the first Hunter among my people, and from his bloodline others followed. Eventually, over time, all the creatures were slaughtered with the exception of one."

Gabriel's mouth had gone dry. He was barely conscious of the crackle of the fire or the hiss of wind through the trees. "If we're tracking that beast, how did it end here, in this land?" He struggled to fit the pieces together.

Hiram's expression darkened. "Through folly and greed."

"I don't understand."

"But you suspect more than you're saying."

"Aye." Gabriel glanced to the side where Hiram's odd weapon, his "wind rifle," lay within easy reach. "You are a Hunter of that same bloodline, aren't you?"

"How did you know?"

"Your skill in tracking this beast, thinking as it does. I've seen your eyes change color, too."

"I thought I imagined that," Jasper inserted.

"And then there is your weapon," Gabriel continued. "I do not understand how it functions, but I suspect it is deadly."

Hiram nodded. "The balls fire on compressed air. Silent in an ambush. I don't have the range of your long rifle, but a *windbusche* is lethal to one hundred fifty yards. And unlike your rifle, or a Brown Bess, it repeats—thirty to forty shots at killing range."

Jasper's draw dropped. "How is such a thing possible?"

Hiram rolled his shoulders. "I did not invent the gun, merely saw the advantage in becoming proficient with it."

"None of that explains how the creature came to this land." Gabriel was every bit as impressed as Jasper by Hiram's rifle, but the wolf weighed heavier on his mind. Already they'd wasted a day tracking the creature without results.

"I was not the only Hunter in my family." Hiram knocked the dregs of tobacco from his pipe. Darkness painted half of his face with shadow, the other sculpted by the frenzied leap of firelight. "My greatest mistake—and greatest failure—was in thinking I had slaughtered the Endling."

Jasper frowned. "An Endling?"

"The last of a species." Hiram's mouth twisted in a grimace. "I thought there was no longer a need for my skills as a Hunter, so I came here to fight for your Colonies. The war was almost over by the time I arrived, my stint with General Washington amounting to little more than a few months. That is why I say you shouldn't believe everything you hear." He tugged on his bottom lip as if sorting his thoughts. "After that, I drifted from place to place, picking up work wherever I found it. Two years ago, unbeknownst to me, my younger brother, Solomon, cornered the true Endling. He should have killed it, but word had reached him your new country was a land of immense opportunity. Blinded by greed, he crated the beast and boarded a ship, the monster in tow. I'm told he believed someone would pay an extravagant sum for the right to display the creature. His ship was not far from the harbor when the wolf managed to break free. Penned for so long a journey, it was maddened with bloodlust. Solomon and several others were killed. The Endling escaped, flung into the sea by the pitch of the boat and likely drowned—or so the crew thought. Nearly a year passed before I picked up the tale in a tavern, learning of my brother's death secondhand."

Gabriel grimaced, imagining the shock of such a ghastly moment. But rather than remorse, Hiram's eyes burned with anger.

Swearing softly, he stood. "The fool would still be alive had he not let greed overcome him." Pacing a short distance from the fire, he dragged a hand over the back of his neck. "Soon after, tales began to circulate of a fell beast raiding villages and farms. I heard snippets here and there, enough to convince me the Endling was responsible. I tracked the creature for months before arriving in your village."

"If it moved on before, why does it linger now?" Jasper challenged.

Hiram rolled his shoulders. "Perhaps because the pickings are plentiful. It hunts, not merely to eat, but for the thrill of butchering weaker things. This is why it does not willingly choose men as prey. The creature knows nothing of children, but I fear the time will come when it discovers how vulnerable the innocent can be."

Gabriel blanched. "Let it come." He shoved to his feet, no longer concerned by the darkness or the pounding of his heart. It was not fear that fed his pulse, but rage that such a monster should exist. "If it fears our firelight, we should tamp it out. Draw it closer."

"Your anger is warranted, Gabriel, but the beast has gone elsewhere. It will not trouble with us when unguarded prey awaits in the village."

"If you can think like this creature, then why can't you find it?"

"I *will* find it." Hiram stabbed a thick finger in his direction. "And when I do, you will stand clear. I will have vengeance for Solomon. More importantly, I will fulfill the destiny of my bloodline and eradicate this monster from the Earth."

* * * *

Present Day

Jillian spent most of Sunday and a good part of Monday working on Eli Yancy's website. During off moments, she scoured the newspaper and checked her local TV affiliate app for reports of unexplained mishaps. Fortunately, there was nothing of note, leading her to hope the folktales tied to Gabriel Vane's burial plot were only that—legends passed through her family for generations, fables without merit.

On Monday morning, she took her car to the dealer for a new battery, then phoned Eli and suggested a meeting to go over her work to date. He seemed distracted, almost as if he'd forgotten the project, but agreed to see her later in the week.

Jillian kept herself busy throughout the day. By the time mid-afternoon rolled around, she finished her site design and shut down her computer. Calling for Blizzard, she grabbed his leash, then headed outside. The day was pleasant, barely a cloud in the sky, the sun a bright butterscotch ball overhead. Rather than follow their usual trail along the river, Jillian led the dog across the field where Elliott liked to stargaze and headed toward Hickory Chapel Cemetery.

Gabriel's resting place may have been violated, but she'd make certain he wasn't forgotten. She only prayed that with his physical remains no longer entombed, his protection would hold firm for those buried in the cemetery and their descendants.

The steady whirr of a motor reached her as she trudged up the hill leading to the chapel. Blizzard loped ahead, pausing now and again to snuffle among the weeds before trotting forward. A white Ford F-350 was parked at the top of the hill, a flatbed trailer hitched to the back. There was rarely anyone in the cemetery when Jillian visited, and certainly no one that would be doing anything of a mechanical nature as the drone of the motor seemed to indicate.

"Come on, Blizzard." Breaking into a jog, she rounded the corner of the church, heading for Gabriel's burial plot. She'd only run a short distance before tugging sharply on the husky's leash and coming to a dead stop.

A bald man she didn't recognize used an open tractor with a front-end bucket to dump dirt into Gabriel's grave. Judging by the mounds of soil clumped under the old hickory tree, the man hadn't been there long. The city had probably hired him to fill in the hole, considering it a liability.

"No—you can't." She jerked forward, attempting to flag down the worker. The chances of Gabriel's remains being returned to his proper resting place were almost nil if the hole was filled in. If his bones did resurface, he'd likely be buried elsewhere, something she couldn't allow.

"Sir!" She waved her arm, but he worked with his back to her, hard earmuffs wrapped around his head to deaden the rumble of the tractor. She watched as he jerked the machine forward, maneuvering the wide bucket to scoop up another heaping mound of earth. Sensing her anxiety, Blizzard started barking.

Between the husky's loud yap and the drone of machinery, Jillian barely heard the soft, distant toll of a bell. A second later, an ear-splitting *crack* shattered the air. The abruptness of the noise drove her back a step, her gaze sweeping to the ancient hickory.

The gargantuan tree split down the center, the left side folding like a matchstick under the massive load of branches. The top hung suspended for a quicksilver flicker, then plummeted with the speed of a guillotine, crashing onto the bald man.

"No! No, no!" A scream tore from her throat as she raced to help.

The tractor's engine cut out, and in the heavy weight of sudden silence, Jillian was confronted by a tangle of broken branches and bloodied flesh. A single look told her the poor man had not survived, his neck twisted at a grisly angle, eyes open and staring as if he couldn't perceive what had gone wrong.

Fighting tears, she dug her cell phone from her pocket. Her fingers trembled as she punched out three numbers she'd hoped to never use.

The dispatcher answered on the second ring. "Nine-one-one. What is your emergency?"

"Please come quick. There's been a terrible accident."

* * * *

Monday was not as bad as Elliott feared. Finn gave him a wide berth, and while Rodney and Troy took potshots with snide remarks, their need for revenge seemed to have run its course. Either that or the wishstone in his pocket—as he'd come to think of the gem—was helping. It had protected him from the monsters when he was trapped in the cemetery, and he was convinced it had something to do with Rodney and Troy leaving him alone.

Once or twice he tried to wish things into happening, without luck. He willed Mrs. Martinez to give them less math homework, but it seemed she piled on double. Later, he tried willing himself a place to sit at lunch, where he wouldn't have to be alone and could hang out with some other kids, but no one invited him to their table and he was too shy to ask. He considered it a bonus when he made it through the day without getting bullied by his usual tormentors.

Feeling upbeat, he headed outside, past the buses and down the sidewalk to the crossing guard. He was still a few yards away when something slammed into his back and sent him sprawling into the grass.

"Watch where you're walking, doofus." Rodney Townsend faced away from him but glanced over his shoulder, a football in his hand as if he'd only just caught it.

Elliott picked himself up, backpack sliding from his shoulder, glasses askew. A couple kids on the sidewalk stopped to snicker. Others hung out open bus windows, laughing. Kids weren't supposed to roughhouse on the sidewalk, toss balls or Frisbees, or even run, but there was no sense telling Rodney. Any more than pointing out Rodney had been the one to plow into him.

Elliott dusted loose grass from his knees and straightened his jacket. He kept his head down, not wanting to draw attention. Now that Rodney had shamed him, maybe he'd leave him alone. He stepped onto the sidewalk, but Rodney moved to block his path.

"Going somewhere?"

Troy sidled up behind his friend.

Elliott swallowed hard and glanced around, looking for a bus driver or anyone who might help. A couple of kids clustered up ahead, blocking the view to the crossing guard—or the guard's view to Elliott. Cold sweat broke out on the back of his neck, and he dug his hand into his pocket, wrapping his fingers around the wishstone. Rodney and Troy wouldn't gang up on him here. Not so close to school. They couldn't.

He tried to sidestep, and Rodney moved with him, cutting him off.

"Get out of the way," someone snapped.

Elliott pivoted, shocked to find Finn Carrigan glaring at Rodney. He blinked, surprised the order hadn't been directed at him. Now that he thought about it, he wasn't the only one Finn had given a wide berth today.

Rodney shrugged. "Just messing with him." He seemed to deflate a notch. At least his voice dropped, no longer broadcast to everyone nearby. He tossed the football lightly, catching it before it could drop. "Your bus is at the other end of the line."

"I know where my bus is." Finn shouldered forward, bumping into Rodney to move him aside. The other boy grunted but gave way.

Troy snickered. "I think someone's pissed." He grabbed the football from Rodney. "Come on. Let's go catch the bus. Camden's not worth it, and Finn's in one of his moods."

Elliott was grateful when they trotted back the way they'd come. He looked ahead to where Finn had joined the group waiting for the crossing guard and ran to catch up. He made it just as traffic stopped and hustled to cross the street. Once on the other side, kids split left and right, Finn following the path Elliott normally took home. After a few blocks, he was the only one left walking in the same direction. Elliott lagged several paces behind. He was pretty sure Finn lived on the opposite side of town. When the other boy came to a side street and had to wait for the crossing guard to halt traffic, Elliott joined him on the curb.

"Um...thanks for helping me back there with Rodney and Troy."

Finn stared ahead, watching as the guard moved into a break between cars. "They're jerks."

"I thought they were your friends." Elliott fingered his glasses, bumping them higher on his nose.

"Things change."

The guard motioned them forward, and they stepped into the street together. Elliott could just make out the top of Hickory Chapel looming above a knobby hill in the distance. The sight resurrected memories of his fall into the grave.

"I saw you in the cemetery when they hauled me out." He remembered the police cars and the ambulance, Finn waiting grim-faced by the side of a squad car. He didn't know how the cops had found him, only that he'd been crazy-grateful when an officer climbed down into the hole and hefted him up.

He wet his lips. "Did you...did you get in trouble?"

"What do you think?" Coming to an abrupt halt, Finn shot him an exasperated glance. "Look—we were stupid chasing you into the cemetery. It was a dumb thing to do, and Rodney and Troy were asses for wanting to leave you there. My uncle's a cop. Things would have been a lot worse for me if I hadn't called for help."

Surprise slammed into Elliott. "You...you were the one who called?" He never would have guessed. "Thanks. I thought I was done for when I fell into that hole."

Looking mildly uncomfortable, Finn shrugged. He started walking again, and Elliott fell in beside him. The discomfort he'd felt earlier dialed down a notch.

Finn threw him a sideways glance. "You didn't rat us out."

Elliott shook his head. "How did you know?"

"My uncle. One of the other cops told him your story about how we were screwing around up there together. He thinks we're all friends."

Elliott surprised himself by snorting.

Finn laughed. "It is kinda funny when you think about it. Rodney and Troy—"

"You, too. I'm the new kid nobody likes."

"You're not so bad." Eying him, Finn swiped a mop of black curls from his brow. He was several inches taller, making Elliott feel toadish by comparison. It wasn't that he was heavy, just that Finn seemed to exude wiry energy and confidence. Elliott wished he could be so sure of himself. Maybe if he had thick wavy hair and vivid blue eyes like Finn. There were several girls in Elliott's class who drew hearts in their notebooks, then scrawled Finn's name inside with an arrow. He'd never be that lucky.

"You had a chance to land us in some serious shit and didn't take it." Adjusting his backpack, Finn glanced up the hillside as they drew abreast of Hickory Chapel. "Rodney and Troy are ticked because I called for help, but their crap is getting old."

"Is that why you didn't take the bus home?" Elliott was terrified to look toward the cemetery, the memory of being trapped in an open grave too fresh in his mind. From the corner of his eye, he spied a pickup truck with a flatbed trailer parked near the old church. The steady drone of an engine whined in the background.

Finn shook his head. "My uncle wants me to hang with one of the moms in our apartment building while he finishes his shift. But she's got two preschoolers who are hellions, and I don't need a damn *babysitter.*" The final word was spat with venom.

Elliott was going to ask about Finn's parents when he remembered scuttlebutt from school. Finn's dad wasn't around—pretty much like Elliott's—and his mom was in jail. Drugs or something. That had to suck.

Elliott sometimes stayed with his grandmother after school until his mom got home, but she was family and he didn't mind. Having a babysitter would be mortifying.

He decided to change the subject. "How come you're walking this way?"

"'Cause I figure I'm already in trouble. What's a little more?" Stopping, Finn looked up the hill toward the cemetery. "I'll call my uncle to come get me when his shift is done. Either that or take the bus home."

Elliott stared, unable to imagine braving public transportation alone. He'd never have the guts, and his mom would throw a fit. He finally turned to gaze up at the cemetery.

"How come you stopped?"

Finn nodded toward the chapel. "I was thinking about that open grave. Someone had to dig it up."

"So?"

"It was a lot of work. Why go to all that trouble?"

Elliott hadn't thought about it. Why did anyone dig up a grave? To find what was hidden inside. He fingered the uncut emerald in his pocket. "Maybe they just wanted the bones of whoever was buried there."

"Or were looking for something—like buried treasure." A quick grin flashed over his lips. "I'm gonna check it out." He started for the hillside, then glanced over his shoulder. "Wanna come?"

Elliott gaped, trying to process the idea Finn had invited him to tag along. He fought for something to say, but before he could speak, a loud boom ripped through the air. The shockwave boomeranged from his head to his feet, chased by the unmistakable sound of something heavy crashing to the ground. A woman's high-pitched scream raised the hair on the back of his neck.

"Holy shit!" Finn bolted for the cemetery.

Swallowing his fear, Elliott raced after him.

* * * *

Finn was sure he was in deep shit. Not only did he skip riding the bus home, but he ended up in Hickory Chapel Cemetery amid uncontained chaos. The woman Elliott called Jillian had blocked their path to the heap of broken branches behind the chapel. He'd understood someone was buried under that tangled mass and the results weren't good, but it wasn't until his uncle arrived with several other cops, a firetruck, and an ambulance, that he realized the seriousness.

Jillian made a call to Elliott's mother while the firemen worked with saws, cutting away branches to reach the man imprisoned underneath. Long moments passed, his uncle in the thick of things, coordinating between cops and paramedics. Finn heard shouts about a lack of vital signs, saw the deathly pallor of an arm jutting between yellowed leaves. The air reeked of fresh-cut wood and trampled hickory nuts. Someone made a call to the coroner, and he fought the urge to be sick.

His uncle pulled him aside, hugging him tightly and shielding his view as the body was removed. He expected to be sent home, but everyone was involved with something—cleaning up debris, talking to the ambulance attendants, roping off the area where the accident occurred, or keeping crowds away.

"Elliott!" A woman with curly dark hair ran up the hillside, a frantic expression on her face. A second later she engulfed Elliott, then bent, babbling questions close to his face. Finn overheard snatches. Was he hurt? Why was he in the cemetery again? What happened?

Random people began to throng at the base of the hill, watching from a distance, onlookers attracted by flashing lights and sirens. A man with his hair in a ponytail exited a big 4Runner a block down, then raced past the group, ignoring the orders of a uniformed cop to stay back. He beat a path to Elliott and the curly-haired woman.

Finn's attention shifted to a guy in a brown bomber jacket. He hadn't noticed him before, but somehow he'd managed to get past the cops, hovering on the opposite side of the fallen tree. Squat and broad-shouldered, he blended into the background. There was something in the way he watched the activity around the grave that raised flags in Finn's head.

"Hey." Noticing Elliott had wormed free, he caught his elbow and steered him from the adults. "See that guy over there?" He pointed to the man in the bomber jacket. "He shouldn't be here."

"How do you know?"

"Everyone else has a job to do. All he does is watch what's going on like he's calculating something."

Elliott looked confused. He was probably still reeling from the idea that someone had died. Finn tried not to think about it. Dwelling on the guy in the brown jacket helped mute the ugliness of what had taken place. Later tonight, when he was alone, he'd mull the whole thing over. Better not to have an audience if he ended up hurling.

"I think he could be the guy who dug up the grave." He was grasping at straws, but connecting imaginary dots gave him something to do. A part of him had always liked the idea of trying to think like a cop.

"He couldn't have done it himself," Elliott said.

Finn reconsidered the strange man. Good point. He was beefy and fit, but it would take a single guy too long to unearth all that dirt. He shrugged. "If he didn't do it alone, I bet he helped."

"Do you think he had anything to do with the tree?" Elliott looked green as he eyed the fat nest of branches.

Before Finn could answer, the man ducked behind the blind side of the chapel. "Hey, he's leaving!" Seconds later, he rematerialized, tramping down the hill in the direction of the school. As far as Finn could tell, there were no cars around. "He must have walked here. Probably heard the sirens and hiked over."

"That doesn't mean he was the one who dug up the grave. He could have been curious about what happened." Elliott looked pleased with himself for having arrived at a simple solution.

Maybe Finn *was* reading too much into things. "Yeah. I guess so."

"Finn!"

He was distracted when his uncle called and waved him over.

"Shit. Now I'm in trouble." Sooner or later he knew he'd have to own up to why he'd disobeyed David's orders to stay with Mrs. Foltz after school. Shooting Elliott a resigned glance, he hoofed over to his uncle.

David dropped a hand onto his shoulder. "I'm going to be tied up for a while. I've got no clue what you were doing here in the first place, but we'll talk about that later. I'm going to have one of the uniformed officers drive you home. You can stay with Mrs. Foltz until my shift is over."

Finn's heart sank. "Uncle David, her kids are terrors."

"Um…" Elliott sidled close. "I'm sure my mom wouldn't mind if Finn came home with us and stayed for dinner. Uh…we've got some math homework we could work on together."

Finn tried to keep shock from his face. Had Elliott just saved his butt?

His uncle gave Elliott a swift, appraising glance. "You're the boy who fell into the grave the other day. Elliott Camden."

Elliott nodded.

Finn found his voice. "I told you we were friends."

"You did." Something about his uncle's expression indicated he wasn't convinced. "Let's check with your mom, Elliott, then we'll figure out what Finn's going to do."

Elliott pointed to the group of adults talking quietly among themselves. "That's her. The lady in the red jacket with the black hair."

As his uncle moved away in the direction Elliott indicated, Finn stepped to the other boy's side. "I owe you."

Color rose on Elliott's cheeks. "You saved me from Rodney and Troy. Just returning the favor."

"Maybe." Finn eyed him openly. "Did you really mean that about staying for dinner?"

"Sure." Elliott stuffed his hands in his pockets. "My mom makes great spaghetti and meatballs."

* * * *

When Detective David Gregg introduced himself to Tessa, Jillian led Blizzard away. She'd been trying to find a way to speak with Sherre Lorquet ever since she arrived. To all appearances, the coroner had finished with his grim task, the body loaded into the ambulance for transport. The fire crew was still working in the background, trying to clean up the debris pile. Someone had righted the tractor and rolled it off to the side.

The sight of it sitting empty punched a hole in her stomach. Her natural empathy kicked in, leading her down a trail of the man's life. Did he have a wife? Children? Was his wife anxiously checking her watch, frantically sending texts, wondering why he was late in coming home? Had someone notified her of his demise? Was she sobbing even now, children huddled close, unable to comprehend how she'd face another hour, another day without the man she loved?

Stop. Just stop.

Jillian pictured the family Labrador pacing in the background, keyed up by the woman's sobbing. A small child clutching her ragdoll, tears brimming on the surface of her eyes. "Mommy, what's wrong? Where's Daddy?"

With a soft woof, Blizzard pressed against Jillian's legs.

The sound drew her back to the moment. Made her grope for the tinted glasses looped around her neck. One hand tangled in Blizzard's soft fur as she slipped the lenses over her dilated pupils.

"Thanks, boy. I'm okay now." She fought to slow her breathing.

Several paces away, Sherre stood with her head bowed, speaking into her mic. Jillian waited until she was through before moving to her side.

"Sherre." Somewhere in the past they'd moved past "officer" and then "Detective Lorquet" to friendship. "Do you have a moment?"

"Jillian, now's not a good time."

"But the tree—"

"The fire company thinks the ground must have been hollowed out by a small sinkhole. The base of the tree shifted. As old as it was, the weight set off a chain reaction and cracked the trunk up the center." Sherre pressed her lips together. "A freak accident."

Jillian gnawed her lip. She had no proof to contradict otherwise. How could she ever hope to explain the removal of Gabriel Vane's protection was at fault for the tragedy?

"Um…I wanted to ask you about the bones that were stolen the other day. Do you have any leads?"

Sherre blinked as if she hadn't heard correctly. "That's not my focus right now."

"I realize that, but it's important." Tightening her fingers on Blizzard's leash, she plowed ahead. "It's connected."

"What is?"

"What happened here today…" She knew she sounded like an idiot. "The bones."

Sherre wedged her hands on her hips and stepped closer. "What happened here was an accident. Tragic, but accidental. It has nothing to do with—"

"You won't believe me if I tell you the truth." Jillian knew she pushed the envelope but could already feel the malevolent touch of something sinister in her gut. "I told you the truth about Madison, and you believed me. You *know* why I need Blizzard as a therapy dog."

Sherre glanced away before swinging her gaze back. "Are you going to tell me this has something to do with empaths?"

"No, but if you believed me then…" She halted, flustered. "Sherre, I heard a bell toll before the tree fell. It was a death knell."

"You're talking about the folklore associated with this place." Sherre shook her head. "No one takes those legends seriously."

"I do."

"Detective Lorquet." One of the firemen hailed her from a spot near the decimated tree. "Can I see you a minute?"

It gave the detective the out she needed. "I've got to go."

Jillian gripped her arm before she moved away. "This is just the first accident. The first of many." She watched as Sherre jogged toward the fireman, the sour miasma of fear ballooning in her stomach.

"Hey. You okay?"

Lost in her thoughts, she gave a startled jerk when Dante DeLuca touched her arm. "Dante—" She forced a shaky smile to cover her confusion. "I didn't realize you were here." She glanced around, looking for Tessa. "Is—"

"Over there." As if anticipating her question, Dante pointed to his cousin. "She's talking to one of the detectives." He offered his hand to Blizzard, who snuffled around his fingers before being rewarded with a scratch behind the ears. "Thanks for calling about Elliott."

"How did you know?"

"I was on the phone with Tessa when your call came through. She told me what happened as soon as she was done talking to you. I thought I'd better drive down to make sure she and Elliott were okay."

"It's wonderful how you look out for them." Even if she couldn't read his emotions, it was easy to see his concern was genuine. "I tried to keep Elliott and Finn—the other boy—away from the site of the accident. I think they know the poor man didn't survive, but…" She closed her eyes briefly. "It was such a freak thing. Sherre said a sinkhole under the tree caused the trunk to crack."

"Sherre?"

"The detective I was talking to." She nodded in Sherre's direction, noting the detective was still busy conferring with several firemen. It wouldn't be long before they hustled nonessential personnel out of the area, her and Blizzard included.

"I overheard you tell her this was the first of many accidents." Dante surveyed her levelly.

"I—"

"It's a good thing you were here when the accident happened," Dante continued as if he hadn't expected a response. "Although it's an odd place to visit." His smile was quick and effortless. "Why *were* you here?"

She wet her lips. "I took Blizzard for a walk."

"In a cemetery?"

"I'm not sure what you're asking. Or implying." Damn, she wished she could read him, but it was as if he had a shield in place, an impenetrable barrier that kept him isolated from others.

"Nothing upsetting." A second passed before he heaved a sigh and tilted his face skyward as if steeling himself for something. When he met her eyes, his gaze was nonjudgmental. "Look. I don't want you to take this the wrong way, but I'd like to talk to you. Not now, but at some point later when things settle down."

Curious, she angled her head. "About what?"

"The bell you heard. The death knell."

She sucked down a breath.

Dante compressed his mouth in a tight line. "I've heard it, too."

Chapter 7

If Gabriel had any doubts of Hiram's ability to think like the Endling, his skepticism vanished the next day. When Jasper questioned why they hadn't continued the hunt at night, Hiram explained the farms the beast favored were too scattered with too much ground to cover.

"Now with a full belly and its thirst for carnage slaked, our wolf will be sluggish. Slow to scent danger. We need to venture deeper into the forest, away from the greensward." He nodded to the east where white birches grew tall and straight, thick as wheat. "The Endling will seek rest in a place that does not leave it vulnerable. A hollow or cave, something that allows it to sleep protected."

They set out early when the sun was barely above the horizon. Within an hour, Hiram had picked up a path of "dullings."

"See how the grass and weeds are shiny with dew?" He indicated the clear droplets clinging to the tips of grass and weeds. "Plants hold onto that moisture, but if something passes and wipes it clear, a dull spot is left behind."

It took several seconds for Gabriel to sort the patches of dry foliage from those glittering with dew. In time, he discerned a pattern. "Whatever passed here must be large."

"Aye." Hiram drew rein, then dismounted for the third time that hour. Squatting, he examined the leaf depressions in the ground. "Whatever beast passed, it was in no hurry. Walking without fear, moving slowly." Pressing his hands flat, he got down on all fours and lowered his head, bottom eye pressed to the soil. He hovered briefly, gave a soft grunt, then pushed to his feet. "We're following the right path, lads. I'd be willing to wager these compressions were made by the Endling, though I can discern no solid print."

"Then we move on," Gabriel said.

Over the next two hours, Hiram pointed out more signs of passage— broken twigs, an occasional tuft of hair snagged by brambles, diagonal walk patterns that revealed part of a heel lobe or inner toe. The trees grew thicker, the paths swaddled in moss-slick stones and soil detritus. Occasionally, they came upon a shelf of rock or ground cavity where water collected. By the time the sun was almost directly overhead, the tracks became more frequent, clear depressions with elongated claws and heel pads.

Hiram drew to a halt and surveyed the terrain. "There will be rock caves here. Look for a cavity or fissure, any kind of hole that might conceal a creature while it sleeps."

Jasper spotted the burrow first. Twenty minutes into their search, he indicted a small hollow cut into a hillside. The crevice looked pitch black from the outside, barely wide enough for two men to pass through together. Judging by the height of the opening, they would need to stoop to enter the den, an advantage to the slumbering beast within.

Almost immediately the horses grew jittery, sidestepping and refusing to go forward. Hiram motioned everyone to dismount, then led them back several hundred yards to a safer distance. Even then the horses shuffled hoof to hoof, Jasper's bay giving a nervous whinny.

He rubbed his hand over the horse's muzzle. "They're spooked."

"I can't fault them." Gabriel tethered his mount, then slipped his rifle from his shoulder to check the flint and frizzen. Beside him, Hiram drew his wind rifle.

"You're the experienced hunter." Gabriel deferred to Hiram with a nod. "But I would think logic dictates one of us flush the beast from its den, the other two primed to fire when it flees."

"You think wisely, Gabriel Vane."

Jasper wet his lips. "It will be dangerous confronting the creature in its lair, a task no one should have to assume. Let us draw straws."

Gabriel shook his head. From the moment he'd seen the cavern, he'd mentally worked a plan. In order to win Dinah's hand, he needed to prove himself to Atticus. "There's no need. I will go."

Hiram frowned. "Why is that?" The wind scattered dark hair about his face.

"It is only logical. I am the smallest and quickest. The beast's den does not appear large, far too restricted for a man of your size, Hiram."

"And I?" Jasper challenged. "I am only a few inches taller than you."

"But we both know I am the swifter runner, should it come to that." Gabriel laid a hand on his friend's shoulder. "And you have a spiritual flock to tend in the village until such time God sends another to take your place. I will be fine, Jasper."

Hiram was still scowling. "You do not know this creature as I do."

"No, but it is a beast with heart, lungs, and blood as any other four-footed animal, and like any other animal, it will surely die." He slipped his hand into the pocket of his frock coat, fingering the gemstone Dinah had given him. She had vowed the emerald would protect him. It was time he put that promise to the test.

"Come, gentlemen. Let the predator become prey." Swinging the barrel of his rifle up against his shoulder, Gabriel headed for the Endling's den.

* * * *

Present Day

It took a solid day for the accidents to gain momentum. Jillian scanned the news app on her phone, finding several tragedies, most nothing more than a footnote. Two construction workers died when a defective crane boom fell at a jobsite. A drunk driver lost control of his car and plowed through a convenience store window, killing himself and the teenage clerk inside. A woman died in a freak accident when the outside deck she was standing on inexplicably collapsed. A window cleaner suffered fatal injuries when the scaffolding he was on plummeted six stories to the sidewalk below.

She set the phone aside and rubbed her forehead, propping her elbows on the breakfast table. She had agreed to meet Dante later that evening, and there were still several hours until her appointment with Eli Yancy. In the interim, she could try to appeal to Sherre again, convince her how important it was to return Gabriel's bones to his resting place. She needed to visit Madison, too. Make sure her sister was all right. Like many people in Hode's Hill, Jillian and Madison were at risk for tragedy. Their connection to Gabriel Vane could either play in their favor or factor against them. It took less than twenty minutes to change clothes, pull her long hair into a ponytail, and get Blizzard situated in the back of the car.

In the parking lot of the care facility, she spied a familiar gray Taurus. Sherre Lorquet was leaving the building as Jillian approached the entrance. The timing couldn't have been better. It warmed her to know Sherre still visited Madison regularly, especially given the drive to the facility.

"Two visitors in one day." Jillian drew Blizzard to a halt as Sherre bent to fuss over the dog. "Madison should be pleased."

"Do you think she knows?" Sherre gave Blizzard a last scratch beneath his muzzle, then straightened, hooking her hair behind her ear.

"I have to believe she does. Somewhere inside. I don't suppose it does any good to ask if she was different today?"

A pained expression crossed Sherre's face. "It wasn't a good visit. They had to give her a sedative."

Jillian sighed. "She must be reliving the past again. Boyd's death is stuck in her head like a skipping record. She won't break free and move past it."

"Sit down for a minute?" Sherre indicated a wooden bench just off the sidewalk.

Blizzard took a few moments to nose through the grass after the two women were seated. Lacing his leash between her hands, Jillian stared across the parking lot to the stream of traffic on Barrington Avenue. The steady drone bordered on melodic, white noise that blended into the background. The breeze carried the scent of yellow and orange chrysanthemums, arranged in stone planters by the entrance.

Jillian looked at Sherre. "Are you going on duty?"

"In another hour. I've been running errands and wanted to see Madison."

"I don't suppose you have any new leads on Boyd's killers?" The case had gone cold long ago, but Jillian couldn't stop herself from asking.

Sherre shook her head. "Something might still turn."

The answer was the same each time Jillian asked. At least there was someone in the Hode's Hill PD who hadn't written off the case as closed.

"You've done more than I could hope for, Sherre." The detective was one of the few people she trusted implicitly. "You visit Madison. You helped me get Blizzard, and you haven't given up. That's all I can ask."

"I wish it were more." Stuffing her hands in the pockets of her military-style denim jacket, Sherre slumped against the bench and extended her legs. A jogger passed farther down the sidewalk, headed to the street. "It's been hard to accept the whole empath thing you and your sister have going on." She slanted a sideways glance at Jillian. "Monday, when you were in the cemetery, you were wearing those glasses." She nodded to the tinted lenses looped around Jillian's neck. "Was it because—"

"My pupils were dilated." Sherre had seen her like that before, the black of her eyes nearly obliterating the green on the morning Boyd was murdered. When she'd run across the street to her sister's home, babbling hysterically, pupils blown open, Sherre had first suspected she was high on something. The cemetery had brought a quieter kind of remorse. "The man on the tractor—"

"His name was Henry Teale."

That made it worse. "I don't think I can hear more." She looped her fingers over Blizzard's collar, scratching the dog in an effort to anchor herself. She didn't want to know if Henry had a wife. If he'd left parents, brothers, and sisters behind. If he coached his son's little league games or read his daughter stories before tucking her into bed each night.

The sudden sting of light made her flinch.

"Shit. That's unreal." Sherre watched her with a stunned expression.

Jillian slipped the glasses over her eyes, conscious her pupils had expanded.

"Were you thinking about him?" Sherre pressed.

"Just like Monday afternoon in the cemetery." Jillian bowed her head, grateful when Blizzard pressed against her. "It's what an empath does—putting themselves in someone else's shoes. Living their pain as if it were her own."

"Like your sister did with Boyd."

"That was different." She raised her head, thankful the tinted lenses hid the moisture in her eyes. "She watched him die. There was no way to close her heart and stop the horror. That's what I can't get past—that she's forever caught in that moment of terror, living it over and over. Maybe it would have been more merciful if she'd died, too."

"Get that shit out of your head." Heat kindled in Sherre's eyes. "Boyd was bad news. He'd been on HHPD radar for over a year. Madison was too naïve to realize he was up to his neck with the wrong people. He crossed the line and paid for it. Your sister was an innocent victim."

Jillian looked back to the street. The late morning sun was dazzling, spiking through the trees on Barrington, splattering leaf-shaped patterns over the dingy asphalt. A pair of bicyclists, male and female, turned the corner and headed northbound at a leisurely pace. Seconds later, a red Camaro whizzed by in a splashy blur of candy-apple gloss and chrome.

She heaved a sigh. "I suspected Boyd was involved in something illegal. He could barely hold a job but always had money to burn. I think Madison liked the idea that he played on the edge. She was always attracted to the wrong kind of guy." Admitting the truth soured her stomach.

Before she could shake off the gloom, the angry blare of a car horn intruded. Tires whined over asphalt, kicking up the blistering burn of heated rubber. The stench lodged in her throat, thick as syrup, and the street exploded in a kaleidoscope of candied red and sun-bright metal. Mangled wheels and spokes soared airborne. A second later, the female bicyclist struck the windshield of the Camaro and slid to a broken heap on the hood.

Bolting to her feet, she raced for the scene of the accident, Sherre already three steps ahead.

* * * *

Eli Yancy paced in his office at Wickham, the one he'd dressed with a glass-topped desk, two side chairs, potted plant, and a coffee bar. He'd been trying to reach Warren Porter for two days, but the good-for-nothing lout wasn't answering calls. Yancy had been careful not to leave anything incriminating on the messages, just demands that Porter contact him as soon as possible. With one hand stuffed in the pocket of his pants, the other holding his cell pressed to his ear, he strode past the window for the fourth time, listening to Porter's phone cycle through several rings.

"Yeah?" Finally, the man answered.

Yancy blew out a breath. "Where the hell have you been? Didn't you get my messages?"

"Got 'em."

"Then why didn't you call?" A pause as he imagined Porter beetling his brow, trying to come up with a plausible lie. "Never mind." He didn't have time for the Neanderthal's shortcomings. "Did you go back to the cemetery?"

Porter guffawed into the phone. "You're shitting me? Are you trying to tell me you didn't see what happened there on Monday?"

"I saw." Yancy waved a hand in the air. The damn knuckle-dragger was going to use the hoopla as an excuse. "There was an accident. So?"

"A guy freaking died. On top of that, he had the grave half filled in with dirt before he bit the Big One. No way can I clear that out."

"Get your brother and dig it like you did before."

"Not happening. Between cops and reporters, the place is too hot. There's a busted tree sitting on top of a sinkhole, and if you think I'm going anywhere near that shit, you're out of your freaking mind. Besides—if the emerald fell into the grave when Clive and I hauled out Vane, the kid who took a spill could have found it."

Yancy opened his mouth. Closed it with a distinctive clack of teeth. In three quick strides, he was at his desk where he'd left the *Hode's Hill Daily Echo* lying folded open. An editorial about the grave robbery blasted him like a snide accusation. What an idiot he'd been!

"Damn it, you're right." How had Porter managed to get one up on him? "Any idea who the kid was?"

Porter huffed a grunt of air. "Not my problem."

"Make it your problem. Find out who he is and if he has the stone."

"Forget it. You can keep your money. I don't screw with kids."

A dial tone droned in Yancy's ear. Swearing, he punched the disconnect button.

Of course, the kid found the emerald.

Yancy's research had been meticulous. Dinah Crowe's binding stone was never recovered despite a thorough search of Vane's house and possessions by Atticus Crowe. It only made sense Vane had swallowed the emerald at some point before his death. Yancy still remembered the elation he'd felt when arriving at such a clever deduction. Too bad all that brilliance hadn't stopped him from overlooking the obvious.

How the hell was he going to find out who the kid was? Names of juveniles were protected by both cops and the press.

From the window he spied a blue Accord pull into the parking lot. Just what he needed. Another appointment about his website. The emerald was all that mattered now. Once he had the stone, the whole business could go belly-up for all he cared. Used correctly, the gem would open doors to prestige and money.

He'd have to deal with Porter later. Decide what he was going to do with the bones in the basement. How he was going to get the blasted emerald.

Straightening his shirt in an effort to look professional, he ground his teeth and headed for the door.

* * * *

Jillian drew a deep breath, grabbed her laptop and purse, and stepped from the car. After the events of the morning, she should have canceled the appointment, but she wanted to finish the website and put the job behind her. Yancy had paid half up front, the other half due on delivery. The money would go into an account for Madison's care, funds that continued to dwindle with every passing month.

It wasn't simply that she needed the money, but there was something about the project that didn't sit right. Every time she talked to Yancy he'd forgotten what they'd discussed before. He'd been so particular in the beginning, micromanaging details and requesting daily updates. Now, he agreed with most anything she asked, quickly cutting her short as if her questions were a nuisance.

She'd yet to see any cars at Wickham—the local name too ingrained for her to think of the building by any other name—and wondered how he was going to make a profit. He'd told her he already had several clients he provided life-coaching services for, probably online or by phone. Each time she passed on the drive to Rest Haven, the lot was empty. The only vehicle she'd ever spied at Wickham had been Dante's 4Runner. Could he be one of Yancy's clients?

Stilling a tremor in her hand, she opened the rear car door. "Come on, Blizzard." She picked up the husky's leash. "We can do this."

She closed her mind to the image of the woman lying broken on the hood of the red Camaro, her boyfriend bent over her sobbing, the driver of the car white with shock. She'd left Sherre on the scene when the ambulance arrived, her empathic nature on overload as she alternately placed herself in the shoes of the boyfriend and the young driver, both of whom were going to be emotionally scarred for life. At least the woman had been breathing when the EMTs put her in the ambulance. She'd call Sherre for an update later, needing to know the woman survived.

With Blizzard at her side, she walked down the short sidewalk to the front door. The slant of the roof cast shadows at the entrance. Patches of cool blue and slate nestled in the corners. She tried the door but found it locked. A second later, Yancy appeared on the other side of the glass.

"Sorry. I'm not open for business today." He motioned her inside. "Just doing some private work in my office." His grin was too quick to be genuine. "I'm behind on a few things, so hopefully this won't take long." Blunt and short as always.

"It shouldn't." Jillian had never met him at Wickham and did a quick scan of the surroundings. The room on the left was outfitted as a waiting area with two upholstered armchairs, a small sofa, and a glass coffee table. An abstract painting with random splashes of apricot, orchid, and sienna hung above the sofa, and an artificial tree stood in the corner. Light was provided by two floor lamps with a cluster of upturned shades as if the poles sprouted lilies. The whole area was spotless, somehow sterile-looking despite what appeared as an effort to be trendy.

"I see you have your dog with you." A flicker of distaste passed over Yancy's face, masked by an artificial smile. "This way." He gestured to an open door on her right, then followed behind when she stepped into his office, the room every bit as sparse as the waiting area. His glass-top desk held a folded newspaper, scratch pad, computer screen, and little else. Sliding into a chair, Jillian dropped Blizzard's leash, then settled her laptop case on her knees. Without being instructed, Blizzard sat obediently at her side. Yancy took the seat across from her, behind his desk.

"Can I offer you some coffee?"

"No, thank you." She had a feeling the offer had been made from protocol rather than any true desire to be courteous. Coffee would have only soured her stomach anyway after the events of the morning. Even thinking of the acid brew made her queasy.

She unzipped her laptop case. "We can look at your site on my laptop. Or if you prefer your screen, I can give you the backside URL. The site hasn't been published, but I'm hoping we can work through the final tweaks today."

"Yes, I'd like that." Yancy moved the newspaper aside, motioning her to set her laptop on the desk. His fingers were long and spidery, a match for his tall, wispy frame. With thinning blond hair, close-set blue eyes, and a pale complexion, he'd always reminded Jillian of a mortician.

As she booted up her laptop, she caught a sideways glimpse of the article Yancy had been reading. The paper was folded open to the editorial about the violation of Gabriel's grave. The accompanying photo showed the old hickory tree—taken before its destruction—and the caution tape roped around Gabriel's burial site.

"Oh." The gasp slipped from her lips involuntarily.

Noticing her eying the paper, Yancy tapped the page. "Dreadful thing, that."

"Yes." Jillian fought to pull herself together. Mentally, she wasn't sufficiently prepared for the meeting with Yancy, the distraction of the newspaper article making her think of the recent string of accidents. She feared even the latest involving the bicyclist was connected. The collision might have happened outside of Hode's Hill, but it wouldn't surprise her to learn the woman's ancestors were buried in Hickory Chapel Cemetery.

Ducking her head, she quickly tapped several keys on her laptop. "At least Elliott was okay."

"Elliott?"

"The boy who fell into the grave." Jillian opened a browser window and loaded Yancy's website.

He drew back, steepling his hands under his chin. "You know him?"

"He lives next door to me."

"Is that so?"

As the website loaded, Jillian swiveled the laptop so Yancy could see the final design. She'd put a lot of thought into the psychology of color for his gender-neutral target audience, using a palette appealing to both men and women.

"I've used cobalt and sage as the primary colors to capture your message, with a touch of sandstone for contrast." She pointed toward the screen as she relayed her reasoning. "The pages are predominantly white, but the variations on blue and green are trigger colors that work well in advertising. Blue relays the trust and reliability of your confidential services, while green speaks to the potential for growth and abundance clients can achieve under your tutelage." It sickened her to realize she didn't believe a word of what she was saying. She'd never hire Yancy as a life coach. The man creeped her out, yet here she was trying to paint him as highly reputable.

It didn't matter. He wasn't listening.

"Yes. Yes." He waved a hand at the screen. "That all looks satisfactory."

"But I haven't even started to show you the site."

"I'm sure it's fine." He withdrew a pen and checkbook from his jacket pocket. "Let's settle up. Unfortunately, I've forgotten the amount on the final bill."

Jillian told him the figure. "Do you want me to make the site live?"

"That's fine."

Once again, it felt as if he wanted to finish quickly, the website an annoying distraction rather than the primary tool of a man who hoped to find the bulk of his clients online.

"I'd feel better if you reviewed it first."

He tore off the check and handed to her. "If you insist. I'll look it over in the next few days and call you by the end of the week."

"All right." She keyed the browser closed. It was his money. If he wanted to part with it so easily, that was fine with her. She slipped the check into her purse, then closed her laptop.

"Tell me, Jillian." Yancy had folded his hands on the edge of the table, a tight smile on his thread-thin lips. "That must have been quite a fall Elliott took. I imagine it shook him up a good deal."

She nodded absently, only half listening as she packed the laptop in its case. "I'm going to need you to sign off on the website. I'll email the final paperwork by the end of the week after you've had a chance to study the site in detail."

"That would be fine. The boy didn't say anything, did he?"

Startled, she raised her head. "Excuse me?"

Yancy's smile faltered before holding steady at a higher wattage. "I was just thinking what a frightening experience it must have been, alone in that hole. I understand the thieves removed the bones, but a grave that old..." He let his voice trail away. "There was likely debris in the pit. Elliott might have fallen over something or picked something up—an old coffin nail. A piece of wood or a stone..."

Her stomach twisted. She pushed the ugly thoughts away by raising a hand. "I don't want to think about it. All that matters is that Elliott is fine." Hiking the laptop strap onto her shoulder, she stood.

"His parents must have been so worried."

"His mother was beside herself."

Yancy nodded somberly. Sagely. "Well. As you said—it all worked out in the end." The sham smile returned as he held the office door for her.

She exhaled in relief when she finally stepped outside into the parking lot. A few more days, then she could officially write Eli Yancy off her client list. The hour couldn't come soon enough.

"Come on, Blizzard." Quickening her step, Jillian hustled to her car.

* * * *

And just like that, he was back in the chase.

Heaving a relieved sigh, Yancy dropped into his desk chair and tilted his head to gaze up at the ceiling.

"Thank you." He had no idea who he was talking to but didn't care. Whether by virtue of some higher cosmic force or archaic powers-that-be, he'd just been handed a treasure trove of information.

Jillian had no idea she'd just sang like the proverbial canary. He hadn't been able to wheedle a last name for Elliott, but hunting one up wouldn't be hard to do. Best of all, when he'd mentioned parents, Jillian confirmed the boy's mother had been "beside herself." No reference to a father, which meant the guy was out of the picture, or at least not in residence. That left a woman and a child in the house by themselves.

What to do?

He picked up his pen, absently clicking the end as he worked through the dilemma. A simple confrontation should take care of matters, but he couldn't be seen accosting a child. Someone needed to put a scare into the kid. Rough him up and find out if he had the emerald.

Porter was out. He'd already made it clear he wanted nothing to do with the situation. Not everyone was up to being hard-assed with a kid. Even career criminals got willy-nilly about shit like that.

He considered Clive only briefly, writing him off as too much of a simpleton. The oaf stumbled through life thanks to the tolerance of his older brother.

But there was a third Porter. One he'd only heard about and never met. Clive had wanted to include him on the grave robbery, but Warren squashed the idea the moment it was mentioned. From what Yancy gathered, Kirk Porter was a wild card—young, crazy, and dangerous. Just the kind of person he needed.

A man willing to cross any line if the money was right.

Chapter 8

October 12, 1799

Gabriel crept with all the stealth he could muster, muffling his footsteps as he inched toward the cave where the Endling slumbered. A trickle of sweat wormed down the back of his neck; his palms gummed with perspiration where they gripped the stock of his long rifle. The gun would be unwieldy in the cramped interior, but it was his only weapon, and he had no intention of entering the den unarmed.

Behind him, Hiram and Jasper took up positions in the trees, waiting for him to flush the beast from its lair. If all went according to plan, the result would be a slaughter, the wolf caught in a deadly crossfire between Hiram's wind rifle and Jasper's musket. In less than an hour they'd tie the vile carcass to their pack mule and head home.

Gabriel wiped sweat from his upper lip. He hadn't expected to be so nervous. The closer he drew to the cave, the ranker the air became. The stench of masticated animal skin and feces assaulted him. His gut rolled over and crawled into his throat. Drinking unsteady gulps of air, he breathed through his mouth. He forced himself to think of Dinah. Of the gem tucked into his pocket. For the woman he loved, he'd face more than a predator in its lair, however horrific the beast.

A horde of fat blow flies swarmed near the entrance of the cave. He swatted the cloud away and ducked inside, fighting to still the ragged hitch of his breath. The air was cooler in the cave, but clammy with the sticky touch of residual moisture. His boot sank into the soggy ground with an audible squish. He sensed ribbons of water dribbling over the craggy walls, but the pall of darkness was too opaque to see far. Something moved in the gloaming with the click-clack of claws against rock. The hair prickled on the back of his neck, propelling his heartbeat higher.

What feeble light existed was blotted by the silhouette of the beast. An abomination of sinew and ragged fur, it reeked of death. Of disease and spoiled meat left to rot in the sun. Gagging, Gabriel jerked his rifle into position.

The confines of the cave hampered the length of the gun and made it difficult to maneuver. Before he could get off a shot, the monster slammed into him. His head and shoulders struck rock, teeth clacking together with a jolt that traveled the length of his jaw. He tried to twist free, but the beast pinned him to the ground, fetid breath hot against his face. The creature's eyes were the pale mustard yellow of phlegm, its fangs long and curved.

Gabriel's finger convulsed on the trigger. In the enclosed space, the blast of the rifle was deafening.

The Endling jerked and bellowed, flung backward. Claws raked across his chest, peeling skin like shavings whittled from a stick. A roar of pain and rage, twice as thunderous as the gunshot, exploded in the cave. Gabriel scrambled to his feet, one hand clutching the rough, wet stone behind him. He fumbled to load another shot, but the creature bounded past, racing for the exit.

Within seconds, the twin discharge of weapons split the air. The fire of Hiram's wind rifle followed in rapid succession. One hand pressed to his torn shoulder, Gabriel limped outside.

The beast lay on its side, its fur a macabre patchwork of blood in the raw sunlight. Despite the gaping holes drilled through its torso, it fought to raise its head. He approached slowly, Jasper one step behind. A toxic mix of fear and hatred burned in the Endling's eyes. Gabriel expected to feel loathing, triumph for their victory. Instead, he was overcome by relief that he could put the grim hunt behind him. He fingered the emerald in his pocket.

Hiram lowered the barrel of his gun to the monster's head. "It's over."

Gabriel turned away when the rifle blast splattered bone fragments and blood across his boots.

* * * *

Present Day

Evening had settled by the time Dante pulled onto the side alley by Tessa's brownstone and exited his 4Runner, sketchbook tucked under his arm. Traffic lumbered past on River Road, the glow of headlights cutting a swath through the gathering soot of night. Quickening his pace, he rounded the corner by a tall streetlamp, the fixture like all those lining River Road reminiscent of a bygone era.

Maya Sinclair's brownstone occupied the end of the row, a home he'd visited over the summer at the request of a friend. It was the last time he'd conducted a séance, reaching out to the ghost of a nineteenth-century medium who'd lingered in Maya's house. Unfortunately, the apparition who'd answered his summons was not Lucinda Glass, but a destructive phantom of a darker nature. He hadn't tampered with a spirit circle since. Should probably have his head examined for considering it now.

But he couldn't erase the memory of what he'd overheard Jillian tell the female detective in the cemetery: *I heard a bell toll before the tree fell. It was a death knell.*

He could still recall the eerie peal on the night Spencer Wright died. Was it possible Jillian had seen the same unspeakable things he'd watched slip from the Aether? Creatures he'd later drawn in the sketchbook tucked under his arm?

Most of his friends had started to shy away from him around that time. The kids at school thought he drew monsters because of what happened to his father, but he'd sketched them because he couldn't get the hideous things out of his head. His grandmother had forced him to see a counselor after several teachers voiced their concern about the macabre things he doodled on homework assignments. He'd sucked it up for a few weeks and suffered through the sessions to pacify her, but never told anyone about the monsters he'd seen. Not even Alex Price. Alex would have spilled his guts if he'd caught so much as a glimpse of the ghouls at Hickory Chapel. Instead he drifted away like everyone else, shell-shocked by Spencer's death.

An accident.

Just like the death of the man on the tractor had been accidental, both fatalities following the toll of an invisible bell. Jillian might label him crazy—think he should have his head examined—or she might be the one person in Hode's Hill who would understand what he had to say.

Dante jogged to the last brownstone on the corner, then sprinted up the steps. Jillian expected him, but that knowledge didn't downplay a sudden case of nerves. It wasn't every day he exposed his abilities to others. *I can communicate with the spirit world. My monsters are real.*

Pressing his thumb on the doorbell, he counted off seconds until Jillian appeared.

"Hi." She offered a tentative smile. Blizzard crowded into the doorway beside her. "Come in." She gripped the husky's collar and urged him back, allowing Dante to enter.

"Thanks for agreeing to chat with me." Blizzard's tail thumped against his leg, and he bent to greet the dog.

"I made coffee." Her gaze dropped briefly to the sketchbook. "Come into the kitchen."

He followed her down the hallway, noting the soft palette of colors that flowed from room to room. Pastels and neutral shades, nothing jarring or loud. Everything from wall tones to the bleached hardwood floors was designed to soothe. The curtains on the French doors were light and airy, the pale white of cumulous clouds, crowned by a string of fairy lights.

Jillian motioned him to the table in the dining area, then headed to the kitchen. "I've got soda if you prefer." Unlike Tessa's home, which was cordoned off in sections, the entire area was open, creating one large sprawling room.

"Coffee's good. Black is fine." Dante slid his sketchbook onto the table then crossed to the French doors. Given Jillian's townhouse was the last in a row of six, the view from her main floor was mostly unimpeded. Twilight silvered the landscape with a veil as soft as the muted colors indoors. "You've got a great view. I didn't realize you could see Hickory Chapel from here. A lot of people get freaked out by the sight of that old church."

"Because of the legends?" Jillian carried two mugs to the table. She set one beside his sketchbook then took a sip from hers. "I'm not frightened by them."

"What about the bell?"

Her eyes narrowed. "I think you should tell me why you wanted to talk to me."

"Fair enough. Let's sit down." He noticed Blizzard never moved far from her side. When she sat, the dog sat beside her, his expressive eyes watching intently.

"It's okay, boy." She smoothed the husky's fur. "Lie down." Her gaze returned to Dante. "The other day you told me you'd heard a bell, too."

"When I was fifteen." Briefly, he told her about the Halloween night he, Spencer, and Alex spent in the cemetery, omitting the part about the monsters and the black dog.

A vein of horror touched her eyes. "I'm so sorry about your friend."

"It was a long time ago. We were young and stupid. Never should have been screwing around up there to begin with. The whole thing was a freak accident. If Spencer hadn't been so scared by that damn bell, he never would have blundered into the street. The thing is…" He hesitated, uncertain how receptive she'd be to the supernatural. "After it happened, I poked around in the history of Hode's Hill. Did you know there's a legend that says hearing a church bell at Hickory Chapel is a sign you, or someone close to you, will die soon?"

Her mouth tightened. She fingered the tinted glasses looped around her neck. "I've heard that."

"Has it occurred to you that both Spencer and the man on the tractor died after hearing the bell toll?"

"His name was Henry Teale." Lowering her head, she averted her gaze. "He was wearing a hard headset like construction workers use. I doubt he ever heard the ringing."

"Even so, it signaled his death. As unexpected as Spencer's."

She continued to look away, her shoulders growing rigid, muscles tightening as if she sought to shut down. Something was happening he couldn't explain, as if the woman across from him battled an unseen force. He detected nothing of a supernatural nature, but that didn't necessarily mean anything. He wasn't always able to navigate the layers of the Netherworld. If a spirit was present, it moved through the Aether beyond his reach.

"Jillian, what's wrong?"

Her face crumpled. Frantically, she groped for her glasses.

"Jillian, look at me." He stretched across the table and stayed her hand.

Heaving a sigh, she raised her head. Her gaze swiveled to catch his, the green of her eyes swallowed by the full black moons of her pupils.

Stunned, he pulled away. "My God, you're an empath."

* * * *

Unable to mask her shock, Jillian drew back. She no longer thought about hiding behind her glasses even though the overhead light stung her eyes. Her mind had been caught up in a whirlwind of thoughts surrounding Henry Teale—his wife, children, family. People she didn't know but whose pain she continued to channel as if it were her own. Once started on that path, her empathic nature kicked into overdrive, threatening to shatter her heart.

And then Dante had said the unthinkable. *"My God, you're an empath."*

She stared, open-mouthed. "How did you know?"

Bonelessly, he slumped in his chair. "Your pupils are a dead giveaway."

She didn't buy it. "No one else would put two and two together like that." A shockwave pulsed against her temples, spurred by realization.

"Most of what I feel comes from empathy, but there's a small part that goes beyond that. A semi-psychic ability that allows me to key in on the emotions of others." There was no sense denying the truth when he saw so plainly. "Normally, I have to enforce a mental wall to keep those feelings out. They can be overwhelming. But from the moment I met you…" She leaned forward, bracing her forearms on the table. The pieces were beginning to fall into place. "I haven't been able to read you at all. You have your own shields in place."

Dante's gaze was direct. "You're perceptive."

Something didn't add up. "You're not an empath." It was becoming easier to think, thoughts of Henry growing scattershot, less distinct. "But you've managed to erect your own buffers. It isn't emotions you want to keep out." Her heartbeat quickened, her breath catching in her throat. "You can sense the spirit world."

"Well done." His smile was tight. "Before coming to see you, I'd hoped you'd be open to that possibility. Your empathic nature should make it easier for you to believe what I have to say."

She wasn't certain she wanted to hear. "Which is?"

"Do you believe in ghosts?"

Hiding behind her coffee cup, she took a slow sip and studied him across the brim. "What if I said yes?"

"If that's the case, I think you might be receptive to my suspicions about Hickory Chapel Cemetery. I'm convinced something horrible must have happened there a long time ago. Something unspeakable."

She shifted uneasily. "Such as?"

"I'm not sure, but I think it's tied to what's going on now—the tree, the accident…"

"There have been other accidents." She told him about the reports from her news app and the incident she'd witnessed on Barrington Avenue.

His brows drew together. "You think they're related?"

"I know they are."

"How?"

She shook her head. "You first."

"Fair enough." He was silent for a moment, seemingly collecting his thoughts. He fingered the edge of the sketchbook. "My father died when I was fifteen. His death triggered something in me. Not long after, I started to sense the spirit world."

"You think he passed a gift to you?" She'd heard of such things happening but had never encountered anyone with an inherited power. When it came down to it, she'd never encountered anyone with a spiritual gift at all.

"Maybe. A few others in my family had the same gift. I think I was always connected to the Aether, but as a kid I wrote off most of my experiences as déjà vu or the result of an overactive imagination. The first true encounter I had was the night Spencer died."

"The bell."

"It was more than that. I saw things. A large black dog—"

"The guardian of the church."

"You know about that?"

Her mouth had gone dry. In all the years she'd tended Gabriel's grave, she'd never seen him manifest. Many of her ancestors believed he would assume the guardian form of a dog if and when he did, keeping with ancient tradition. "A church grim." She wet her lips, tightening her hands around her coffee mug. On the floor, Blizzard shifted as if sensing a change in her mood. "According to folklore, the grim is a guardian spirit. Its job is to protect the souls of those in the graveyard from devils, witches, and thieves. Night creatures or anyone who would try to profane hallowed ground. When someone is slated to die, the grim tolls the church bell."

Dante studied her across the table. She didn't have to be a mind reader to know he was thinking of Spencer and Henry Teale.

"There's more." It was suddenly hot in the room, as if the walls closed in. She tried to stay focused, forcing herself to breath evenly. Blizzard pushed to a sitting position and nudged her leg. She dropped her hand onto his back, taking comfort in his presence. "A dog was often buried alive beneath the cornerstone of the church. When it died, its spirit took the form of a grim."

"Do you think that's what happened at Hickory Chapel Cemetery?" Dante's expression hovered between interest and revulsion. "That somewhere prior to the founding of Hode's Hill, our ancestors rounded up a dog and sealed the poor thing in a tomb?"

"No." She said the word so softly, it barely carried. Eyes downcast, she studied her coffee, the brown liquid the same murky hue as a freshly turned grave. "Someone else was meant to be the guardian spirit of Hickory Chapel. You asked me before why I was in the cemetery." Her gaze flashed to his face. "I was there to visit a grave. The first one ever set in that place. It belongs to Gabriel Vane."

Dante's brow crinkled. "Isn't that the guy they dug up? Someone stole his bones?"

"Yes." She couldn't keep the disgust from her voice. "But no one understands the importance. Death draws darkness—monsters and creatures of the Aether. It's always been the way of cemeteries, but there has always been a protector to chain those monstrosities in place. With Gabriel gone, they're no longer restrained and are free to roam the city. They'll seek out descendants of those buried at Hickory Chapel. I bet every one of the people who suffered an accident recently has an ancestor buried in the cemetery." She slumped in her chair when he made no reply. "You think I'm insane, don't you?"

"No. But I want to know how you know all this."

She drew a deep breath. Out of options and in need of an ally, she told him of the three deaths.

"Why is it your job to ensure Vane is never forgotten?"

"Because my family is connected to his. One of my ancestors, Atticus Crowe, was a village elder before the founding of Hode's Hill. The story is that a horrible plague swept through the community. Many people died, but Gabriel was the first. Atticus oversaw his burial in the cemetery. A number of men gathered and formed a power circle, praying over him, asking that his spirit become the guardian of those who were buried afterward. Atticus lost two of his four children to the plague. I'm descended through his oldest son, Enoch."

Dante tapped his fingers lightly against the sketchbook. "It's your job to ensure he's never forgotten in order that there's always a protector?"

"More or less. I have a sister, too." She rarely spoke of Madison to others. Whatever walls Dante had held in place were gone. No longer guarded, he'd allowed her to see the side of him he secreted from the world. That trust spurred her to do the same. The only other person who understood her empathic nature was Sherre, and even she had been skeptical at the start. Still was at times. Dante was not only receptive to her abilities but had sensed them. His gift was every bit as burdensome as her own, making him the ideal person to confide in.

"Madison is in a private care facility in Palmer Point. I was coming back from visiting her the day my car battery died near Wickham."

He nodded as if recalling the incident. "Is she ill?"

"Not physically. She was born with the same empathic abilities I have. Three years ago, she witnessed her husband's murder. The shock shattered her mind."

His face contorted. "My God."

Jillian dug the fingers of one hand into Blizzard's fur, kneading rhythmically to ground herself. "The man she married got involved with the wrong people. Drugs, maybe more—we don't know everything Boyd was mixed up in. He lived a double life, but most of it didn't come out until after his death."

"What happened to him?"

"They had a small house across from me on Mill Street. I was renting at the time." She steeled herself to continue. "It was fun having them as neighbors at first, but then people started showing up at all hours of the day and night to see Boyd. I tried to tell Madison something was going on, but she didn't believe me. One morning, a few hours before dawn, I heard sirens. By the time I got across the street, cops were pouring into the driveway. I didn't even think—I just blundered into the house. Madison was on the floor cradling Boyd's head in her lap. He'd been stabbed repeatedly." The sight washed over her even as she fought to dial back the pain and emotion the memory resurrected. "There was so much blood."

Dante reached across the table and gripped her hand. "I'm sorry I asked."

She shook her head. "Madison's never been the same since. She hasn't said a word in three years. Sherre Lorquet, the detective I spoke with at the cemetery, was an officer on the case. She's the one who suggested I adopt a therapy dog to help me through the trauma." She turned a wistful smile on Blizzard. "I only wish the solution would have been as easy for Madison."

"What do the doctors say?"

"That she has to come out of it on her own. I keep hoping, but nothing ever changes. The worst part is they never caught the person or persons responsible."

Grimacing, Dante shoved his coffee aside. "I'm sorry, Jillian. There are too many monsters in the real world. If anyone can reach your sister, I would think it would be you."

"I used to think so too, but after three years, I'm not certain. She lives in a different world, trapped in her head. In the past."

"If you think it would help, I'll visit her."

She tilted her head, surprised he would make the offer. "How would that help?"

"I don't know that it would, but sometimes when people are trapped in limbo, they're more open to the spiritual world. Part of my gift is picking up impressions of events that happened in the past. Do you know Maya Sinclair?"

"Of course. She lives on the opposite corner." Jillian had become friendly with Maya after the librarian moved into the end unit brownstone last year. "We grab lunch together now and then, and sometimes she joins me when I'm walking Blizzard." How did you say you were causal friends without sounding like a snob?

Dante seemed to read between the lines. "A few months ago, I helped Maya rid her home of a ghost that had become trapped in the Aether, unable to move forward in her spiritual journey. I picked up impressions of events that happened in Maya's house. I'm not saying I'll be able to pick anything up from Madison, but I'm willing to give it a try if you think it might help."

She'd experimented with everything else when medical doctors and psychologists failed. Spiritual counselors, homeopathic remedies, a Reiki master. At one point she'd even hired a hypnotist to regress Madison to a point before Boyd's death. Nothing worked.

"Thank you for offering." A hesitant smile touched her lips. "It couldn't hurt."

"What about Friday?"

"Okay."

He nodded. "We'll work out the details. Right now, I need you to look at something. Remember when you said cemeteries attract monsters from the Aether?" He shoved the sketchbook across the table. "Look inside. I drew those when I was fifteen."

Uncertain what she would find, Jillian opened the cover. The image on the first page made her stifle a gasp. The atrocity spawned a string of gooseflesh on her arms. Steeling herself, she turned the page. Dante was silent as she flipped through the sketches, each one more horrific than the last.

He'd drawn things of nightmare. Creatures that dangled from trees or wrapped around tombstones. Monstrosities with double heads, bloated flesh, protruding fangs, tattered wings. Unspeakable horrors that slithered over the ground, loped on all fours, or oozed from burrows. Beasts with disjointed limbs, gummy tentacles, and scythe-like horns. By the time she reached the end, she felt defiled, touched by something unholy. Breathing deeply, she flipped the cover shut.

Dante's gaze was steady. "Did you notice the similarity in each sketch?"

Her mouth was too dry to speak. She shook her head.

"Look again."

Her reluctance must have shown.

"It's important, Jillian."

She rubbed her temple, glanced down at Blizzard, who watched her intently. Finally, she propped her elbow on the table, cupped her forehead in her palm, and opened the cover. She'd paged through three sketches before she realized what he wanted her to see. Stunned, she sat up and flipped through the previous drawings to be certain. Suspicions confirmed, she rifled to the end of the book. A single element appeared in every sketch.

"The monsters—creatures—whatever they are. They're all chained to something."

"Or were."

Her stomach rolled over. "It's as I feared. They've been released on Hode's Hill to seek out the descendants of the people buried in the cemetery."

"What about the accident you saw on Barrington Avenue?"

She shook her head. "I don't know. Maybe their reach extends past Hode's Hill, or maybe that really was just an unfortunate accident. A coincidence given the timing." She pushed from her chair and started to pace. "This is horrible. All those years I believed a tradition passed down through my family, but you've proved it's real. Somehow, I have to convince Sherre to focus on finding Gabriel's remains. As long as he isn't in his resting place, he can't fulfill the duty of guardian. Who knows what kind of havoc these things can create." Whirling, she spun to face him. "You're connected to the supernatural. You've even seen these things, which is more than I have. Isn't there a way to stop them?"

"I don't have an answer to that." He'd turned sideways in his chair to face her, one arm looped over the back. "Up until a few minutes ago, I didn't even know why those things were in the cemetery." He stood, then joined her near the French doors. Blizzard hovered close by, keyed to her mood. "I came here because I overheard you mention the bell. I thought you might have seen the same things I did the night Spencer died. Now that I know you didn't, I have to chalk the experience up to my affinity with the spirit world."

Jillian gazed up at him, frightened by the thoughts ping-ponging in her head. It was one matter to know the removal of Gabriel's bones would result in accidents for innocent people, another to realize the horrific creatures behind those mishaps. Such abominations would stop at nothing short of—

Death.

The thought drilled through her with the power of lightning.

"I have to call Sherre." She darted for the kitchen, where she snatched her cell phone from the counter. Frantically, she punched out a series of numbers.

"What are you doing?" Dante followed as far as the large center island.

"Every one of those people I told you about—they all died."

"Yeah?"

She pressed the phone to her ear, listening as it cycled through a series of rings. "I don't know what happened to the woman on Barrington Avenue. If she—"

"Lorquet." Sherre's no-nonsense greeting echoed in her ear.

"Sherre, it's Jillian." She held up a hand to stall Dante as she spoke into the phone. "I just wanted to check and see how the cyclist was after the accident today. Did you hear anything?"

"Just a short while ago." Sherre released a breath, her tone casual now that she recognized her caller. "I was going to phone you later. The woman's going to be all right. She has a broken arm, multiple bruises, and a concussion, but nothing life threatening."

"Thank God." Wired only moments before, Jillian deflated with relief. "What about the driver?"

"Uninjured. Shaken up as hell, but that's understandable. We're still working out the details. The boyfriend's a witness, and there was a bystander who saw the whole thing, so we'll get it sorted. I'm just thankful no one was seriously hurt."

"Me, too." Jillian considered pressing about Gabriel but sensed now wasn't the time. "Thanks, Sherre." She needed to focus on Dante. After she hung up, she turned to face him. He squatted beside Blizzard, roughing the husky's fur as if recognizing the dog was keyed to her moods.

"The woman I saw hurt in Palmer Point is going to be okay. She was injured, but nothing too serious." As she rounded the island, Dante stood.

"You still haven't explained—"

"Maybe she isn't part of what's happening, or maybe she was just lucky." Jillian gave Blizzard a few pats so he'd know she was okay, then crossed to the pantry where she kept his treats. "The whole accident could have been a coincidence."

"Let's hope so."

"I still think the only way of preventing more accidents from happening is to find Gabriel's bones and return them to his grave."

Blizzard crossed the kitchen and sat attentively as she fished a biscuit from a bag of dog treats. "I can appeal to Sherre again, but maybe there's another way of finding out what happened." Blizzard took his treat gently, then carted it off a few paces to chew with his head lowered.

Jillian refocused on Dante. "If you really can communicate with the dead, could you reach Gabriel?"

"Maybe." Dante rubbed the back of his neck. He blew out a breath then paced to the glass doors, where he stood staring into the night. Twilight had already faded, replaced by the slant of licorice shadows and a faint glimmer of starlight. Farther away, an occasional car passed, the red gleam of taillights swallowed by distance. "I've been thinking of trying to communicate with a spirit—any spirit—connected to Hickory Chapel, but severing the veil between the living and the dead isn't without danger."

She stepped to his side. "But you said you helped Maya."

"I did." His mouth tightened as he stared down on her. "The séance I held wasn't without risk. Sometimes, when you try to summon a particular spirit, something else might answer. There are no safeguards."

Her heartbeat quickened. She understood what he was trying to tell her. Anyone or anything could answer that call.

Including the monsters of Hickory Chapel Cemetery.

Chapter 9

It took two days' journey to return to the village, the beast draped over the pack mule, secured with rope. Gabriel felt sorry for the animal burdened with the Endling, the reek of the carcass enough to make him gag. Even with the beast dead, no longer a threat, the horses remained jittery. When they stopped for a brief rest near noon of the second day, he found a stream and washed the welts on his chest. The shock of cold water sent deep shudders through his body, spasms that not even several swigs of hard cider could mute. Jasper applied an herbal salve and makeshift bandage, but the pain was getting harder to ignore.

Hiram studied him as he mounted his horse. "I nary suffered a scratch or bite from the beasts I hunted, and can't speak to the consequences, but you are clearly flush with fever. The sooner we return to the village, the better."

Jasper eyed him with concern. "Can you ride?"

"Of course I can." Gathering his reins, Gabriel hunched deeper into his coat. He didn't know if he was hot or cold, only that with each minute that passed, his misery intensified. By the time they neared the village, his head throbbed and his hair hung lank with sweat. The sun drooped low on the horizon, casting exaggerated shadows across farms and fields. Cyrus Herman spied them just shy of town and raced ahead to sound the alarm.

It didn't take long for people to pour into the streets, all crowding close, all eager for a glimpse of the Endling. Within moments, they were surrounded. Gabriel could barely breathe. Any excitement he'd felt for their triumph had vanished. Hiram cut the beast free, and it struck the ground with a thud. Putrid fluid oozed from its mouth, anus, and ears, but no one seemed to mind the sickly stench, too intoxicated by the victory of its death. Men thumped Gabriel on the back as he slid from his horse. Pumped his hand, immune to the effort it took him to stay on his feet. Barely conscious of the accolades, he fought through the crowd. The only person he wanted to see was Dinah.

He spied her a few feet from the throng, waiting as she'd promised she would be. Her eyes lit with joy, the exultation on her face so pure, that for a single blissful moment he forgot his pain.

"Gabriel!" She threw herself into his arms, hugging him close. "Praise the Heavens! I have been so worried for you, my love. I have already told Father should you seek my hand, he must accept your proposal. Now that you are safely returned to me, surely we can marry."

"Marry...yes." He tried to embrace her, but his arms slid free, too heavy to hold upright. Fire blazed through him. Pasted his clothes to his skin with perspiration.

"Gabriel." Dinah clutched his face between her palms, her voice turning shrill. "Heavens, what is wrong? Why did I not notice before?"

He tried to speak, but no sound came from his throat. The noise of the crowd grew muddy, far away. Gravity opened the ground beneath him, and the street upended to crack against his face. With a grunt, he rolled onto his back. Dinah bent over him, her lovely features contorted in a mask of fear. His gaze dropped to her lips. He watched as her mouth moved, but her words were swept away by the reedy drone in his ears.

His eyes rolled into his head, and a heavy veil of darkness swallowed him whole.

* * * *

Present Day

Each time Jillian opened the paper, scrolled through her news app, or turned on the TV, she hoped to hear Gabriel's remains had been found. But as the days passed without an update, she feared the case had been forgotten. In an effort to make Sherre understand the importance, she phoned the detective and asked to meet her for lunch. They picked a place for Thursday, and after some small talk, Jillian spilled her tale. After chatting with Dante—after stringing all the moldy pieces of folklore together—she knew she couldn't hold back.

Sherre listened silently, her mouth set in a frown as Jillian told her about the plague that swept through Hode's Hill when it was no more than a village. Of Gabriel's death and how Atticus Crowe and others had formed a power circle over him, anointing him through prayer as the guardian of Hickory Chapel.

Jillian talked until her mouth was dry. Until the turkey/avocado melt she'd ordered had grown cold, her iced tea warm. When she was through, Sherre wiped her mouth with a napkin then slid it under her plate.

"You do realize I'm a detective?"

Caught off guard by the question, Jillian drew back. "Of course, I do."

"Then think about what that means." Though Sherre's voice was pitched low, it carried the crack of a whip. "Detect. Clues. Logic." Each word was clipped, bitten off with frustration. "Jillian, I bought into you being an empath. I bought into your philosophy of why Madison is a shell, empty of all except some ungodly memory of her husband being butchered."

Jillian flinched.

"But you can't expect me to believe in hobgoblins and monsters. Accidents and death—because without some ghostly guardian, the denizens of Hell have been unleashed on Hode's Hill." Shaking her head, she fished a few bills from her jacket, then dropped them on the table. "Lunch is on me. I have to go." She stood, ready to leave.

"Wait!" Panicked, Jillian gripped her wrist. "I know it sounds crazy, but before you met me, you never would have believed in an empath either."

Sherre's scowl dug deeper. "That's beside the point."

"Then prove me wrong. Look into the deaths I told you about. I bet every single one of the people who died has an ancestor buried in Hickory Chapel Cemetery. Henry Teale, too."

A look of discomfort crossed Sherre's face. She pulled her hand free and slid it into her pocket.

Immediately, Jillian keyed in on what she didn't say. "There's something you're not telling me."

Sherre glanced away briefly, the quick shift of her eyes, confirmation. "Henry Teale. The city hired him to fill in Vane's grave."

"I figured that."

"I heard he took the job because he has an ancestor buried in the cemetery."

Jillian sank against the back of her chair. "Now do you believe me?"

"I've got to go." Sherre turned away. "No promises."

* * * *

Camped out at her desk, Sherre shot a glance to the wall clock. Eleven fifteen at night. She should have left the precinct over two hours ago but had gotten sidetracked trying to chase down information on Jillian's victims. She should have her head examined for even considering a hocus-pocus explanation but couldn't ignore the nagging voice insisting Henry Teale had ancestors buried at Hickory Chapel. Normally, that wouldn't have been enough to justify digging deeper, but the precinct janitor, Coleman, also had relatives buried there. A member of the Historical Society, he'd routinely lamented the poor condition of the graves to anyone who'd listen. Coleman had died the same day she and David Gregg investigated the theft of Vane's bones. Could the janitor have been the first victim of Jillian's curse?

Propping her elbow on the edge of her desk, Sherre rubbed her forehead. The coffee in the cup at her side had turned to sludge hours ago.

"Late night?" David shrugged from his jacket and dropped it over the back of his desk chair. "I thought your shift ended at nine?"

"It did." She lobbed a glance over her computer screen, watching as he sorted through a stack of mail. Engrossed in research, she hadn't heard him enter. "I got caught up chasing phantoms."

He tossed the envelopes on his desk. "Mill Street?"

"No. I put that to rest for now." She tamped down a wince. Mill Street was never truly at rest, but others immediately thought whenever she hunted information on her own dime, it had to be related to Boyd Hewitt's murder. Fingerprints with no match in any database and bloody footprints with a common shoe size and tread. They should have been able to nail down something from the forensic evidence, but Mill Street remained a tragic blank. The only person who knew what happened in that home— the sole person who'd witnessed the atrocity and who could identify the killers—was locked inside her head and couldn't talk.

Sherre stood. Time to cut and run. "I've had all the fun I can stand. At least you've got a quiet night."

David tossed a glance around the empty squad room. "Where's Desmond? I thought I was babysitting."

"Don't be so hard on the rookie. He's down in records." She plucked her jacket from the back of her chair. "I think the kid's got a crush on the blond girl. The one who likes to go zip-lining."

"Carrie."

"That's it." She snapped her fingers. "Hey, speaking of kids, how's Finn these days?" David often groused how hard it was raising a nearly teen boy, not to mention one who kept smart-assed company. Juggling the chaotic work schedule of a detective with an adolescent couldn't be an easy task.

David shrugged. "Improving. He ditched Rodney and Troy. Finally made a decent friend."

"Oh, yeah?" She pulled on the jacket and flipped up her collar.

"Elliot Camden."

Sherre furrowed her brow. "Isn't he the kid—"

"Who fell into the grave. Yeah. He and Finn have been buddy-buddy since coming across Henry Teale at Hickory Chapel."

Sherre grimaced. "That's an ugly bonding experience. I'm glad something positive came of it."

"Me, too. Elliott's in the school science club, so Finn stopped complaining about me signing him up for it. When I work late, Elliott's mom has been letting Finn hang at her place. He's sleeping over tomorrow night since it's Friday."

"That worked out well."

"Couldn't ask for better." David crossed to the coffee pot. "It's good for Finn to have a positive female role model in his life. He seems to like Tessa Camden and doesn't think he's being subjected to babysitting." He mimed air quotes on the last word, then turned to examine the half-full carafe of Colombian on the burner.

The mere thought of caffeine soured Sherre's stomach. "I'm glad it's working out. I'll see you tomorrow." She turned to leave but drew up short when Del Desmond plodded into the room. The rookie looked shell-shocked, his skin the color of old cabbage.

"Hey, Desmond." Concerned, Sherre took a step forward. "You don't look so good. Are you sick?"

He shook his head, dropping into a vacant chair. "I just found out about Carrie."

"Carrie?" David crossed to Sherre's side.

Desmond's face was slack, his eyes wide. "The news just came through. She was off yesterday. Went zip-lining with some friends. There was an accident..."

Sherre's gut plummeted.

"The line snapped." Desmond dropped his head into his hand. "My God, we were going to grab dinner tomorrow, and now she's dead." He blinked up at them, the misery in his gaze a plea to change the dreadful reality. "Now she's dead."

* * * *

Clive rolled over in bed. He'd been dreaming about Mill Street again. The pretty red-haired woman had managed to twist from his grip, her screams so shrill he'd thought his eardrums would split. She'd flung herself on Kirk, but Clive's brother was high on drugs, possessed of inhuman strength. He batted her away like a bothersome fly, hefted the dripping red knife above his head, then plunged it into Boyd Hewitt's mutilated body.

Again. And again.

So much blood. On the floor, the walls. Kirk was drenched in it.

"Stop! Please, stop!" Clive remembered how he'd sobbed unabashedly, begging his brother to stop the butchery. Kirk had laughed, pushed away from Hewitt, and turned on the woman. If Warren hadn't tracked them down, burst through the back door at that moment—

Make it stop. Make it go away.

Sitting upright, Clive rocked on the bed. All he'd wanted was a puppy. Kirk had promised there were pups at that house, the only reason he'd tagged along. Squeezing his eyes shut, he rubbed the lizard tattoo on his hand. His palms were sticky-wet, and sweat gummed the backs of his thighs to the bedsheets. Maybe if he got up and moved around he could push the memories away.

He plodded to the bathroom in the dark, threw the light switch, then blinked at his reflection in the mirror above the sink. He looked like shit, his pupils contracting to pinpricks. He needed a shower, a shave, and something to take the shakes away. He settled for splashing cold water on his face, pulling on a pair of jeans, then plodding downstairs for a beer. He found Warren sitting at the kitchen table in the dark, his hand wrapped around a can of Bud.

"What are you doing up?" Clive opened the refrigerator and fished for a brew. The light stung his eyes and splashed a yellow rectangle over the cracked linoleum floor. Pressing the cold aluminum can to his face, he slumped against the counter.

Warren still hadn't answered. Clive wondered if he was thinking about the bell they'd heard in the cemetery. The memory scared the shit out of him. He rubbed the lizard tattoo to hold evil spirits at bay, then popped the tab on the beer. "Hey, Warren, how come you ain't answered?" He guzzled beer.

Warren grunted, a resigned sound tangled with disgust. Clive knew he didn't like to be bothered when he was in one of his moods. "Thinking about Yancy."

"And all that money we got?" Clive pulled out a chair and sat at the table. When he thought about the money, the memory of the bell wasn't so bad. "You ever wonder how come Yancy has so much to throw around?"

"Not really."

"You think he's rich?"

Warren snorted contempt. "I think someone paid him a windfall to keep his mouth shut about something. That life-coaching business is a front."

"I guess so." Clive tended to agree with most things his older brother said. Warren was smart. He knew things that made Clive's head spin, like how to program a TV remote and how to use his cell phone to pay at Starbucks. If Warren said the life-coaching gig was a front, then it was a front. It was funny to think Yancy might have been bought off by someone, just like he'd bought them.

Clive poked a finger into his ear, scratching inside the canal. He dug out a hunk of wax, rolled his thumb over the crust, then wiped it on his jeans. "You know what I'm gonna do? I'm gonna get me a dog with my share of the money." Warren had yet to do anything to help him find a pup, and Warren had promised. "A brown one with a white patch on its back like Bodine. Remember Bodine?"

Mentioning the stray mutt that had showed up in their backyard when they were kids might spur Warren into action. Back then, it had taken Clive three days to convince his dad to let him keep it. Kirk said the dog smelled bad, so when Clive wasn't home, he plugged Bodine full of BBs, then dumped his body in a field behind the house. Clive had balled his eyes out when he'd found the pup still feebly clinging to life. Dad said there was nothing to be done for the animal. He'd used his pistol to put Bodine out of his misery. Afterward, he'd used his belt on Kirk. It had taken three weeks for the welts to heal.

Warren pitched him a tired glance. In the dark, his eyes looked like two cavernous holes. "You got more money than a dog's gonna cost."

"Don't care." Clive took another swig of beer so he wouldn't have to look at the empty sockets where Warren's eyes should be. "Alls I want is a brown dog with a white patch and enough money to buy dog food. Maybe a few toys for it to play with. You promised."

"Yeah, I know. We'll look next week, okay?"

"Where?"

"The pound. Bodine was a stray. They got plenty of them there."

Clive felt a spark of hope. "You sure this time?"

"I said so, didn't I?"

Clive had never known his brother to back out on a promise. Satisfied, he grinned. "You can have the rest of what Yancy gave us."

"Funny thing about that." Warren drummed his fingers on the table top. Cheap plastic, it was nothing more than a folding square they'd bought at the local flea market, but it made a decent place to have a bowl of Froot Loops or a cheeseburger and fries. "Yancy ponied up a lot of paper, but he didn't want the bones. He wanted the emerald, remember?"

"Yeah. He said it was some kind of family heirloom." Clive spun his beer can between his palms, studying the small condensation rings it left on the table. Stupid shit. You couldn't get loyalty from a bauble. "I guess it meant a lot to him to part with all that dough."

"That's what I'm thinking, too." Warren tilted his head back and drained his beer. "I think the bastard lied about it being an heirloom. I bet it's worth a fortune."

Clive stared blankly, uncertain where he was headed.

"Remember that kid who fell in the grave? I think he could have found it."

"Makes sense." Clive's gut tightened. He rubbed a thumb over his lizard tattoo. Too bad his totem animal wasn't a dog.

Warren was silent several seconds. Shoving the empty can aside, he leaned forward, planting a muscular forearm on the table. "Probably wouldn't take much to find out who the kid is. Where he lives."

"Huh-uh." Backpedaling in his chair, Clive shook his head, thoughts of Bodine and stray dogs swiftly forgotten. "Don't even think about it." He'd let Kirk drag him into the house on Mill Street under the ruse of getting a pup and was still suffering nightmares because of what happened. "I don't mess with kids, women, or pets."

"Okay. Forget I said anything." Warren held up a hand, his voice dropping to a pacifying tone. "I don't want to mess with a kid, either. It just bugs me, you know? Thinking we missed out on something big. If I knew what Yancy was up to—after I told him to take a hike, he called back trying to weasel out how he could sniff up Kirk."

Clive was sure he blanched. Yancy had called him, too. Probably after striking out with Warren. "What'd you tell him?"

"To take a hike. The less I have to do with Kirk, the better. That crazy-assed bastard will do anything. Yancy must have heard of his rep."

Fear bubbled up from Clive's gut. He hadn't thought twice about telling Yancy how to reach Kirk but hadn't stopped to consider why Yancy wanted the information. Dumb, dumb, dumb! Like Warren was always telling him—he didn't have a filter. He spoke without thinking, acted without thinking, took everything at face value.

Shit. All he'd wanted from the whole messed-up deal with Yancy was a dog like Bodine, and now he might have set bad karma in motion. Best not to tell Warren.

Squirming on his chair, he rubbed his lizard tattoo. "I gotta bad feeling about things."

"Like what?"

Clive rolled his shoulders. "Don't know. Just bad. Didn't you hear that bell in the cemetery?"

Warren smirked. "Not that shit again."

"Don't mock it." Clive pushed away from the table and paced the length of the narrow kitchen. Cold sweat rolled from his hair onto his neck and dribbled down his back. "What if it was meant for one of us? Maybe one of us is gonna die. Maybe it's 'cuz of Mill Street."

"Now I've had it." Warren shoved back his chair and stood. "Mill Street was three years ago. I told you to forget it. Pretend it never happened." He lobbed his beer can at an overflowing bin in the corner. "I'm going to bed."

"I can't forget it!" Clive crowded close, peering down into Warren's face. He might be younger, but he towered four and a half inches over his brother. "All you did was come in at the end and haul us out. You didn't stand there and watch Kirk butcher Boyd Hewitt in front of his wife. I heard she ended up a vegetable in some kind of asylum."

"Her loss." Warren stiff-armed him out of the way.

Worry built in Clive's head. He felt like a pressure cooker, ready to explode. "You ain't listening to me."

"Tell you what." Warren paused in the doorway leading to the hall. "I'll make a deal with you. I'll forget about that kid, and you forget about Mill Street. That way we'll both stay out of trouble." Before Clive could answer, he stalked from the room, swallowed by darkness.

In the sudden stillness, Clive listened to the blood-thump of his heart—

And the distant toll of an imaginary bell.

* * * *

The bad thing about living in a huge house was trying to find something, especially when that "something" was packed away in a dusty attic. Friday morning, Dante carried a mug of coffee up to the attic and studied the mess of oddities tucked under the rafters. Jillian was picking him up at noon to take him to the care facility where her sister lived, but he had several hours to kill in the meantime. Talking to Jillian about ancestors and family had gotten him thinking about his own, particularly his grandmother.

Sonia DeLuca had practically raised him, once living in the big house along with him and his father. Dante had never known his mother, a beautiful but frail woman who'd died of a rare bone disease a few months after he was born. Once or twice he'd thought about trying to contact her spirit but always ditched the idea in the end. He'd never tried to communicate with his father, either. The dead deserved their rest, the crossing of realms exacting a harder toll on them than the person doing the summoning. He just wished he'd known his mother. Wished he understood the truth behind the accident that took his father's life. The details of Salvador's death had always been murky, but given the settlement his employer paid, there had to be negligence involved. At fifteen, Dante hadn't been savvy enough to push for information. If his grandmother did, she'd never relayed the specifics.

Five years ago, Sonia moved to Pin Oaks Senior Center and gave Dante's aunt, Imelda, the bulk of her possessions to sell. Imelda owned an antique store that specialized in vintage items, but some keepsakes didn't translate well. Sonia had been a hoarder with a special fondness for old photos, letters, newspapers, and documents. Dante never understood the reasoning behind half of what his grandmother tucked away but knew she'd spent years researching the history of Hode's Hill. He could always visit and chat with her to learn what he needed but preferred not to involve her in supernatural theories about guardians, monsters, and church grims.

As a kid, he'd often seen her bent over a large book, jotting notes, adding diagrams and tiny boxes with names. Looking back now, Dante was sure she'd been constructing a genealogy of the founding families of Hode's Hill. Sonia had lost interest in the project after Dante's father died. He'd rarely seen her with the book after that, but odds were it had to be stored in one of the trunks or cartons she hadn't wanted to part with.

Blowing out a breath, he surveyed the hodgepodge of items strewn over the floorboards.

Even so close to Halloween, it was stuffy in the attic, the air musty with a combined reek of rough-hewn wood, crumbling newspapers, and mothballs. Wherever he looked, some forgotten memory was wedged beneath the rafters—trunks, cartons, boxes. A tall bureau that had once belonged to his father, a pitcher and bowl set made of milk-glass his grandmother had cherished, stacks of folding chairs used for lawn parties, old toys and board games—some he recognized—a broken patio fountain, curtain rods, discarded tools. Sorting through the mess could take hours.

122 *Mae Clair*

One of these days he was going to have to clean out the clutter and think seriously about selling the house. It was too freaking big for one person.

Grabbing a folding chair, he flipped down the seat, then pulled over the closest box. Several photo albums were wedged inside, and he spent a few minutes paging through faded memories before moving on to the next carton. He rummaged through stacks of magazines and newspapers, medical science articles his father had saved, old receipts and tax documents that should have been shredded years ago. Standing, he wedged a hand in the small of his back and stretched. He'd barely made a dent in the mess, but it felt like hours had passed. A glance at his watch told him the assumption wasn't far off the mark. Jillian would be arriving in another forty-five minutes.

It had grown brighter in the attic, late morning light streaming through a trio of half windows set high under the eaves. Dust motes did a lazy dance in the broken beams and added to the thick coating on top of the bureau. He could have written his name in the powder, sketched an image. His lips quirked at the thought of outlining a monster in the dust. Out of curiosity he yanked open the top drawer.

The book he remembered his grandmother holding lay inside.

"Shit." The book was the only item in the drawer, a thin volume longer than it was tall. The shape and size reminded him of a hotel guest register or an accounting ledger, but the pages were unlined when he flipped through them. His grandmother's spidery handwriting detailed names and dates, arrows drawn between neat container boxes to indicate relationships and parentage. He shuffled back to the first page and eyed the title: *A rough genealogy detailing the founding families of Hode's Hill.*

Bingo.

Grinning, Dante shoved the drawer shut. It stuck halfway, the old wood swollen by the stuffiness of the attic, refusing to budge. He set the book aside and tried to force it closed. It moved a few inches, screeching under the pressure, then held fast as if something blocked it from inside. Dante yanked the drawer from its slot and bent to peer in the opening. Even with sunlight angling through the windows it was too dark to see much of anything in the deep cavity. He felt along the sides and back of the hole but came up empty. Shrugging, he hefted the drawer to align with the slot.

"What the—" The angle exposed a small book taped to the underside.

Dante pulled it free. The initials S.D. were stamped in gold leaf in the bottom right corner. S.D. for Salvador DeLuca. His father had often had personal items monogrammed.

Swallowing hard, he opened the book and examined the first page.

I feel it when I least expect it, lingering like a disease. The color blue has haunted me since I was a child, a whisper of my life to come. Now, it hovers near, wrapped in the guise of the monster I treat. From the start I fear this has been my destiny, a madness light will not breach. How else can I justify my role of Dr. Frankenstein to L's monster? I have no doubt Blue will turn on me one day, driven by the experiments I subject him to. Blue may well be L's son, but he has become my personal demon, one who grows to abnormal size and strength. If I die, it will surely not be an accident, but by Blue's hand. It will be because I allowed myself to be corrupted by this wretched place. I fear it is blighted and has been for centuries.

No good will ever come of Wickham.

Chapter 10

October 18, 1799

Gabriel blinked, consciousness returning slowly as he struggled from a deep slumber. His surroundings were vaguely familiar, the bedroom outfitted with a tall standing wardrobe, rocker, and washstand with pitcher and bowl. He rested in a four-poster bed, far finer than the small cot he slept on at home. Curtains were drawn over the windows to blot the light, but from the hint of red beyond the heavy fabric, he guessed the time near sunset. A fire burned in a hearth in the corner.

Bits of memory floated through his mind—Dinah tending him as he labored with fever, Jasper pacing in the distance. He remembered his friend coaxing liquid through his lips, Dinah pressing a cold cloth to his forehead. He'd twisted with nightmares of the Endling. Ugly dreams in which the beast had mauled his throat instead of his shoulder. Remembering the wound, he fingered the fresh bandage wrapped over his chest. The area was tender, but the ragged starburst of pain had faded.

The sound of footsteps drew his attention to the door. Dinah appeared on the threshold carrying a wooden tray laden with a soup bowl.

"Thank heavens you're awake." Quickly, she deposited the tray on a small table by the bed. When she gripped his hands, her touch was papery and warm. "It has been four days, Gabriel." She eased onto the edge of the mattress, her face drawn by lines he'd never noticed before. Deep shadows bruised the flesh beneath her eyes, and a thin sheen of perspiration clung to her cheeks.

"I feared you would never awaken." Worry colored her voice. "Father had you brought to Enoch's room when you passed out. We have been tending you while Enoch and others from the village look after your farm. Everyone is so grateful for what you, Jasper, and Hiram did in killing that dreadful beast. Hiram told Father how you went into its lair and confronted the creature alone. He called it an Endling."

Gabriel's head was spinning. Four days had passed? He was in the bedroom of Dinah's oldest brother? He barely remembered riding into town—the crowd pressing around him, men slapping his back in boisterous greeting, the stench of the Endling clotted thick in his nostrils.

"Dinah." He lifted his hand to her cheek. "You look flush."

"'Tis nothing." She lowered her eyes. "A mild fever."

"From tending me?" His stomach roiled. He'd assumed his illness had been caused by infection in the wound, not any malady he could pass to others.

"Surely not. It is the autumn chill, nothing more." She swiped a stray tendril of hair from her face with the back of her hand. "I brought you hot broth, hoping you'd be able to stomach a little food." She indicted the bowl.

He should be hungry after four days, but the paleness of Dinah's skin had unsettled his stomach. "Perhaps water instead."

"I'll fetch you some." She crossed to the pitcher and bowl, then poured a glass. Her normal grace was absent, weariness seeming to hang on her delicate frame. Four days of tending to his health had taken a toll.

He swallowed half the water when she passed him the glass, the splash of cool liquid blissful against his parched throat. He reached for her hand as she resettled on the mattress. "The emerald brought me back to you, as you said it would. I have kept it safe all this time."

The hint of a smile touched her lips. "I told you it had bonded us together. It could do naught but bring you back as I commanded."

"You commanded?"

"That is the magic of the stone. To protect—or destroy, should it be used for ill. As long as I live, the gem will answer to no one but me."

He set the glass aside and rubbed his temple. What she said smacked of witchcraft, but he had no understanding of the Old Powers. All he knew was that the emerald had returned him safely to the village. To her arms. He longed to hold her close but feared the impropriety of the bedroom setting.

"I would ask your father for your hand."

She averted her gaze. He had thought to see joy on her face, but she looked stricken.

"Dinah, what is it?"

"Now is not a good time, Gabriel." She wet her lips as though fumbling for words. "Jasper...for the last day, I have tended him as well as you. He has taken ill with a high fever."

"How can that be?" Gabriel's gut plummeted. "I remember him at my bedside. Something is surely wrong." He moved to fling the sheets away, then realized he was clothed only in a nightshirt. "Dinah, see to your brother." He gripped her hand, willing his urgency onto her. "I must get dressed and investigate how this happened. Jasper did not suffer the slash of the Endling. My wound likely became infected on the journey home, but that is no cause for him to be ill as well."

Once she left, he located his clothes on a rocker and dressed quickly. He flung open the curtains, then paused at the mirror to secure his hair in a loose pigtail. The light of the setting sun caught his eyes and reflected off the surface.

Yellow, like Hiram's. Yellow, like the Endling.

He stilled, recalling what Hiram had said about the first Hunter among his family. The man who'd been savaged by the alpha wolf.

"He suffered with fever and delirium for the passage of four sunsets. When he awoke on the fourth night, his eyes gleamed the same yellow as the beast."

Whirling, he plunged his hands into his hair and stalked across the room. Such depravity could not exist! Had the foul beast tainted his blood the same as the alpha had tainted the original Hunter? He paced back to the mirror, then angled his head, studying his reflection. The faint flare of yellow was unmistakable.

"Hiram." He said the name aloud. "I must see Hiram."

Gabriel dashed from the room. Before he looked for Hiram, he would check on Jasper. No wonder Dinah was exhausted, tending to them both. After he spoke with Hiram, he would return and take up Jasper's care. Dinah needed to rest and recoup her strength.

He found her in the doorway of Jasper's room, wilted against the frame as if she lacked the strength to stand on her own. All color had fled her face. Her cheeks gleamed wetly with tears, and her eyes were unfocused, staring straight ahead.

"Dinah. Dearest." He took both of her hands in his. "What is wrong? Please speak to me."

Her gaze shifted, aligning with his. Her mouth moved, and a single tear fell on her lips, gone white with shock. "It's Jasper. He's dead, Gabriel. Jasper is dead."

* * * *

Present Day

When Jillian arrived at his house, Dante had her park her Accord in his driveway. Blizzard was more than happy to bound into the back of his 4Runner. Because the husky was so friendly, it was sometimes difficult remembering he was a trained therapy dog.

Jillian explained how Blizzard was schooled to sense her moods plus act as a buffer between herself and others. People naturally tended to focus on Blizzard, shutting down any stray emotions that might otherwise brim over into her head.

"I guess he's used to this trip, huh?" Dante tossed a glance to his passenger as he drove toward Palmer Point. For the time being, he put the piece his father had penned about Wickham and someone named "Blue" out of his head. He'd promised Jillian he'd do everything he could to help her sister. It was important to stay focused on Madison and her needs. "Does your sister ever respond to Blizzard when you visit?" Sometimes people, especially those who'd been crippled emotionally, felt safer interacting with animals.

Jillian shook her head. "Rarely. I've tried placing her hand on his fur. Sometimes she moves her fingers, but most times she sits there unmoving. She doesn't react to much of anything." She adjusted her seatbelt, shifting to face him. "Thank you for driving. I didn't expect that."

"No problem." The forty-minute trek wasn't exceptionally long, but the roominess of his vehicle made the time pass more comfortably. "Blizzard seems to like the extra space in the back." He shot a glance to the rearview mirror, noting the husky lying comfortably on the rear seat.

Jillian smiled. Since their discussion last night, she was more relaxed with him, as if she'd found a kindred spirit. He knew what it meant to be burdened with an unusual gift. Not everyone accepted the uncommon and the strange. His own gift was the sole reason he and Tessa's mother didn't speak.

Jillian smoothed back her hair. She'd left it loose today, a cascade of blond that tumbled to her waist. She wore a black pea coat over faded jeans and a white blouse. Her tinted glasses were looped around her neck within easy reach. He guessed she was rarely without them, a shield to hide behind when needed.

The drive was scenic, mostly two-lane back roads. They passed Wickham then continued east, the sun blazing yolk-yellow in a turquoise sky. Pastures, meadows, and fields dotted the countryside, offset by a hodgepodge of scattered rural homes. Farther along, they passed a pumpkin patch, the fat orange gourds a reminder Halloween was less than a week away.

Dante made a right turn when Jillian prompted, the road every bit as winding as the one they left behind. "Did Tessa say anything to you about the masquerade event that's going on next Saturday night?"

"You mean the Halloween pub crawl?" She bobbed her head. "I saw it advertised in the newspaper. She told me she was thinking of going."

"She's going, and she's dragging me with her." The things he wouldn't do for his cousin. Even with the years they'd spent living apart, she was still like a sister. "Why don't you go with us?"

She flinched slightly, the recoil barely perceptible. One hand curved around the chain holding her glasses. "I don't know...all those people. I don't do well in crowds."

"I don't, either. We can hang out together, and if you get uncomfortable, we'll leave."

Jillian cast him a questioning look. "What about Tessa?"

"She'll be fine. Maya is going, too. Her boyfriend's out of town on business."

"Collin Hode?"

"You know him?" Most everyone in Hode's Hill knew *of* the Hodes, but whether they knew the family personally was another matter. Dante had been a thorn in Collin's side last summer as he waged a public campaign against Collin and his father, Leland, to preserve Pin Oaks Senior Center. Weird the difference a few months could make. Now he and Collin were friends.

"Maya introduced me to Collin shortly after they started going out together." Jillian shifted her purse from her lap to the floor as if attempting to get more comfortable. "Do you remember all that stuff last June after the Fiend Fest? Leland Hode was attacked, and there were rumors about a blue monster running around town."

Dante palmed the wheel through a bend in the road. The Fiend Fest was an annual event Hode's Hill threw every June to commemorate an old urban legend about a nineteenth-century creature who'd terrorized the town. It was good fun, but last year the event had taken a bizarre turn.

"The guy who jumped off the Old Orchard Truss Bridge..." He tried to remember how the pieces fit together. "The drifter they think attacked Leland. Wasn't his skin blue?"

"That's what I heard." Jillian shifted her gaze out the window as a bank barn and silo rolled past. "The reports said he had a rare skin disease. It's a shame they never found his body."

"Yeah."

Blue.

Dante jostled the thought aside. He'd examine it later when he could put the drifter in better context with the notes his father had penned. "You didn't answer my original question."

Jillian lobbed him a surprised glance. She wasn't getting off the hook that easy.

"Do you want to go to the Masquerade Pub Crawl with me and Tessa?"

She hedged. "I don't have a costume."

"There's still time to get one if you want, but I think a lot of people are just showing up in masks."

"What are you going to do?"

"I haven't decided."

She bit her lip. "Can I think about it?"

"Sure." The artistic side of him liked the idea of a masquerade, but he understood her hesitancy. Shutting down her empathic nature was only one hurdle. Jillian possessed a semi-psychic gift that worked in conjunction with her empathy. Flipping that switch off would be harder to do.

They talked companionably for the rest of the drive. He told her about his artwork and gallery, and she talked about her web design business, including a recent client who'd set up a life-coaching practice at Wickham. He'd seen the sign for Eli Yancy and had thought the location odd, but he'd been biased toward the spot ever since his father had died there.

No good will ever come from this place.

The voice he'd heard at Wickham flitted through his head, reciting the exact words his father had written. He shuttled the oddity aside, locking it in the same chamber where he kept "Blue" and his father's reference to someone he'd labeled "L."

When they arrived in Palmer Point, Jillian directed him to Rest Haven. The lot was mostly empty, so he parked near the entrance. Once inside, they signed in at the front desk then took the elevator to the third floor.

Dante's first impression of Madison was one of damage. He didn't have to touch her to know she was broken inside. They found her sitting in a chair by the window, a spot Jillian said she favored. She looked tiny and frail, shrunken in on herself, as if she would crumble under the slightest pressure.

"Madison, this is Dante DeLuca. He's a friend of mine." Jillian's introduction brought no response. Pressing her lips together, she pitched him a resigned glance.

"May I?" Dante indicated the chair in front of Madison. With a nod, Jillian perched on the foot of Madison's bed, keeping Blizzard at her side.

Dante eased into the chair, his eyes never leaving the frail woman across from him. He could see hints of Jillian in the curve of her cheek, the blue-green spruce of her eyes. At one time she would have been stunning, but her face had grown too thin, her cheeks sunken and slack. Her red hair was cut short, cropped close to her head, her arms skinny like matchsticks. He picked up one limp hand and gazed into her eyes.

It was like looking into a cloud. Milky and opaque, as if she kept a cloak held tightly about her. "Jillian." He kept his gaze on Madison's, staring into those empty, vacuous eyes. "Have you ever tried to use your empathic abilities on Madison? To feel what she's feeling?"

"There's nothing inside her to reach." Jillian sounded tired. She shifted on the bed, crossing one leg over the other. "Other times all she does is scream. When she's like that, her mind is too chaotic. It's like being plunged into a maelstrom."

"She's caught in the past when that happens." He didn't want to reawaken her trauma, but there had to be a way to reach her. To peel back the cocoon she'd sealed herself in.

It was easier with places, where he could pick up vibrations of spirits. Graze the memories that still lingered. When impressions were strong enough, they became folk memories, imprinted on a place for anyone perceptive enough to read them. Murder left a taint unlike any other. Given the savageness of Boyd's death and the short length of time that had passed, the folk memory of his killing would still be strong.

"What happened to the house on Mill Street?" The question was for Jillian, but he kept his gaze on Madison. Staring into her eyes was like looking into a well with no bottom. Is that what she saw inside her head? An infinite blackness from which there was no escape?

He felt himself sinking deeper. Jillian's voice came from far away.

"I hold power of attorney for Madison and sold it. The money has gone for her care, but it wasn't much. After the murder, no one wanted to touch the house."

"A stigmatized property." He'd heard of such things happening. He sensed Jillian nodding.

"An investor bought it. Now it's a rental."

"Mill Street." This time his words were solely for Madison. She cocked her head. Something flitted through her gaze as if a lock had tumbled open in an unseen place. He felt himself sliding into a prism where thoughts and images fragmented like pieces of a kaleidoscope.

A broken lamp...an overturned chair...a man's body sprawled on the floor...clothing drenched in blood...a black lizard...a butcher knife dripping red...

Madison moaned low in her throat.

He tightened his grip on her hand, felt sweat bead at the back of his neck.

Blood pooled on the floor, oozing from the man's body...a black lizard... the knife sweeping downward...blood spraying onto the walls...a bloody hand gripping the knife...

If only he could see the killer's face. But the impressions were disjointed, shattered like panes of cracked glass. Pain rooted in his temples, splintered behind his eyes.

...a black lizard...

Madison's voice climbed in a sudden, keening wail.

Releasing his grip, Dante jerked backward.

"No! No, no, no!" Clutching her head, Madison bobbed forward in her chair. "Make it stop! Please make it stop!" She rocked in place. Back and forth, back and forth.

"Madison!" Jillian bolted from the bed and hit the nurse call button. In the next instant, she was crouched at her sister's side, one arm looped over her back. "Shh, shh, it's okay, Maddy. You're safe. Nothing can hurt you." Tears streamed down her face. "Can you look at me? Please, Maddy?"

Dante grabbed Blizzard's collar and pulled the husky out of the way. His head felt like it was going to roll from his shoulders, the throbbing in his temples intense enough to reduce his eyes to slits. A fist slammed into his gut, and he fought the urge to puke. Somewhere in the back of his head, he was aware of Jillian babbling through her tears. Of Madison's ceaseless rocking, her face wet and shiny.

When a nurse sauntered into the room, probably expecting no more than a routine request for aid, all chaos broke loose.

"She talked!" Jillian was still hunched over Madison, her eyes wild with a mix of desperation and excitement. "Get a doctor! Get someone! Hurry up, damn it. My sister talked!"

* * * *

Jillian wanted to spend the night, but Dante insisted she go home. He stayed with her at Rest Haven until almost midnight. After the few brief words she'd said, Madison fell back into stony silence. Doctors were summoned, and soon medical personnel began trooping in and out of

Madison's room. Dante waited outside with Blizzard while specialists, nurses, and aides arrived in various groups, some pushing medical equipment, others conferring in hushed whispers. Jillian stayed glued to her sister's side through the long hours of exams and a barrage of medical tests. At one point, there was talk of moving Madison to the hospital for more conclusive tests, but the idea was eventually vetoed for fear it would cause her to relapse.

Doctors agreed she'd had a breakthrough and more were likely to follow. In the same breath, Jillian was cautioned her sister's next words might come in days, weeks, or even months. All signs indicated she *would* speak again, but patience was the key.

Dante took Blizzard outside at various times to walk the husky and let him do his business. He ate in the cafeteria, then brought food up for Jillian when she refused to budge from her sister's bedside. Madison had fallen into what appeared to be an exhausted sleep, something he was sure he'd triggered. He'd reawakened the horror of her husband's murder but had also found a way to blunder through her shell where no one else had. A little more time and he might have seen the killer's face.

"I'm going to get a hotel in Palmer Point so I can be close in the event of another breakthrough," Jillian said somewhere after ten thirty.

"I don't think that's a good idea." It took some wheedling, but Dante eventually convinced her it would be better to go home. He reminded her the doctors said it could be weeks or even months until Madison spoke again. "The worst thing you can do is build up false hope. Stay positive and let time run its natural course."

"Maybe you're right." He guessed it was the three years she had invested in waiting that made her concede. She fell asleep on the drive home, curled in the seat of his 4Runner.

By the time they pulled into his driveway, he could feel his own muscles yielding to exhaustion. The day had been draining, more mentally than physically, just as taxing. Trying to banish a lingering ache, he massaged his temple.

Jillian stirred. She came awake rubbing her eyes. "What time is it?"

"Close to one."

Her shoulders slumped. "I need to get home."

"In the morning. You're not driving anywhere this late at night, especially as tired as you are. I live in a behemoth." He jutted his chin to indicate the sprawling home visible through the windshield. "It's got plenty of spare bedrooms. You can take your pick."

She sighed. "Dante—"

"No arguments." He was out of the vehicle and around the side before she could finish the protest. Opening the door, he extended his free hand to help her down. "As a plus, I'll make breakfast in the morning. How's that?"

The shadow of a smile touched her lips. "We didn't even talk about what happened when you connected with Madison."

"Tomorrow." *Blood. A black lizard.* "I'm too tired. Let's call it a night."

She slid from the 4Runner, then opened the back door to gather Blizzard's leash. The husky bounded to the ground, shuffled his nose through the grass, and stretched.

"I really owe you for everything you did today." Jillian lifted her face to gaze up at him.

"No, you don't." She seemed as frail as her sister. Maybe it was the fact her exhaustion showed so plainly. With her blond hair unbound, disheveled around her face, she looked like a wraith, something the wind might blow away. "But I think you need a break from all the stress you've been under." Hooking an arm around her shoulders, he led her from the driveway toward the house. "Next Friday you can set everyone and everything aside—Madison, Vane, Hickory Chapel Cemetery—and enjoy yourself for a night."

"Ah." A sliver of amusement crept into her voice. "The Masquerade Pub Crawl."

"It would be a nice way to say thank you." He drew away to insert his key into the lock. "I'm just saying." The grin he flashed was calculating. "If you wanted to."

"You're not bashful about pulling strings."

"So I'm told." He opened the door and waved her inside. "And I'll take that as a yes."

* * * *

Dante was true to his word. Jillian awoke the next morning to the scents of freshly brewed coffee and bacon. She'd slept soundly, despite being in unfamiliar surroundings. The bedroom was spacious with a color scheme of toasted almond and rose. She'd used nothing but soothing tones in her own home, a conscious effort to create a relaxing environment, and welcomed the airiness of the color palette. After slipping into the adjoining bath, she freshened up, then pulled her long hair into a ponytail. Blizzard was nowhere to be seen.

She dressed quickly, noting she'd slept until almost ten. Sitting on the edge of the bed, she scrolled through her cell phone for messages, hoping there would be word from Rest Haven.

Nothing.

Discouragement fluttered awake in her stomach, but she hammered it down. Dante was right. She needed to stay positive and not lose sight by getting her hopes up too soon. Flipping to her text messages, she found a brief notice from Yancy. The website met with his approval, and she should publish it. At least that was one project she could put behind her.

Gathering her purse and coat from a bedside chair, she slipped her phone in the bag then wandered into the hallway. Dante hadn't lied when he said the house was a behemoth. It took a moment to get her bearings and conjure an image of the hallway from last night.

The house appeared to have front and back staircases. She descended the one to the front, feeling like a movie star making a grand entrance as she followed the sweeping curve to the bottom. From the foyer she trailed the smell of coffee, bypassing a two-story great room, elaborate formal dining room, and a study overflowing with books.

Dante stood in the kitchen, adjusting the flame beneath a pan of bacon. A short distance away, Blizzard lay beside a massive center island with dark walnut millwork and a granite top. The remaining cabinetry was white, fusing English country and French bistro for an upscale look that was both trendy and classic. The deeply coffered ceiling and rough-cut stone accents made her feel like she'd stepped into an English manor.

"Good morning." Her tidy brownstone suddenly felt like a shoebox.

"Morning." Dante flashed a grin, then motioned to the counter. "I made coffee, but I can do tea or espresso if you'd rather."

"Coffee's fine." Blizzard wandered over, and she bent to rough the husky behind the ears. "How'd you sleep, boy, huh?" His tail swayed back and forth. "Poor guy is probably hungry, especially smelling all this good food."

"I'll take that as testament to my cooking skills." Dante cracked an egg over a skillet. "Hope you like scrambled." He looked different this morning, his dark hair unbound. Because he usually wore it in a ponytail, she hadn't realized how long or curly it was.

"Scrambled sounds wonderful." She couldn't remember the last time she'd had a full breakfast. "I should take Blizzard for a walk."

"I already did that. He ate, too."

Jillian located a cup beside the pot and filled it with coffee. "I'm afraid to ask what you gave him."

He laughed. "Don't worry. I have a friend who drops by now and then to talk art. When he does, he usually brings his dog, so I stock some food. Blizzard got the usual canned variety."

"All this hospitality." She slid onto a stool at the center island, then relaxed against the chair's high back, coffee mug cradled in her hand. "What can I do to help?"

He pushed the eggs around the skillet with a spatula. "Would you like toast?"

"No."

"Then just sit there and relax." Within a few minutes he had their breakfast plated up—scrambled eggs with bacon and fresh fruit. They ate in the adjoining breakfast room, an open area with floor-to-ceiling windows on three sides and sun tunnels overhead. The view was picturesque, overlooking a stone patio and the gentle slope of the rear yard. A stand of trees guarded the perimeter, their colorful leaves creating a backdrop of cinnamon, poppy, and gold.

Jillian took the last bite of fruit from her plate, then set her fork aside. "Thank you for breakfast. It was delicious."

Dante offered a quirky smile. "Passable. Especially after a late night."

The observation gave her the opening she needed. "You never did tell me what happened when you connected with Madison." It was still unthinkable that after three years of silence—except for screams—her sister had finally spoken. Maybe Maddy's phantom smile last week had been the beginning of a greater breakthrough.

"I figured you'd get around to asking sooner or later." Dante puffed out his cheeks, then exhaled. He fiddled with his fork, prodding a piece of cantaloupe as if mulling over what to say. "I did pick up impressions from Madison, but they were disjointed. Random flashes. Bits and pieces of things here and there."

Jillian tensed. "Did you see faces?" If he'd gotten into Madison's head, seen what she had, there was a chance he could identify Boyd's killers.

"No faces. Mostly—" He grimaced. "Blood."

She rubbed her forehead. "What else?"

"The knife. A black lizard."

She angled her gaze to catch his. "A lizard?"

"A *black* lizard." He stressed the clarification, then shrugged. "I don't think it was an actual lizard, more like a symbol. I don't know why it's important, but it means something to Madison."

"It might mean something to Sherre, too." Her mind engaged in mental cartwheels, Jillian shoved to her feet. "It might be a gang symbol, or it could have something to do with the drugs." She started to pace. "Maybe one of the killers was wearing a T-shirt with a lizard. It could be anything."

"It could." Dante pushed his plate away. "You always say killers. Are you sure there was more than one?"

"Yes." She flexed her hands. "Someone restrained Madison while the killer attacked Boyd. There were bruises on her arms, and the police recovered two sets of fingerprints."

"What about the neighbors? No one saw anything? Heard anything?"

"The next-door neighbor heard Madison screaming. He's the one who called the police. He thinks he saw three people running from the backyard but couldn't give any kind of identification. It was still dark, and all he saw were shapes moving around. He's an elderly man and his eyesight is poor."

"I'm sorry there hasn't been closure."

"It's more than that. I want the killers caught, but mostly I just want my sister whole." Gripping the back of her chair, she regarded him across the table. "I'm worried about her, Dante. She's already frail. What if something happens to her because of what's going on with the cemetery and Gabriel's remains? Even a minor accident could be fatal for Madison."

"That's not likely to happen when she's in a care facility. And speaking of Vane, I have something I want to show you." He shoved back his chair and stood. "I'll be right back."

While he disappeared down the hallway, Jillian cleared the table. By the time he returned, she had their plates in a sink full of soapy water.

"I found this in the attic." He plopped a ledger-sized book on the center island.

Drying her hands on a towel, Jillian stepped closer. "What is it?"

"Something my grandmother used to fiddle with." He opened the cover and paged through several sheets. "A genealogy of the early families of Hode's Hill. You mentioned Atticus Crowe before."

She nodded. She knew her own family lineage but not that of others.

"Look." Dante pointed to a genealogy chart.

Fascinated, she slid onto a stool, angling the book for a better look. Atticus was there, including her own line that flowed through his oldest son, Enoch.

"This is amazing." She traced her finger down the page, picking up names she'd heard bandied around by members of her family—Margret and Herman Woods, Eliza and Marcus Billings, Melissa and Bryan Farner. Even her own grandparents and parents where there—Jane and Nathan Bricker, Amelia and Wade Cley. At the very bottom, she saw her name and Madison's.

"I don't believe it." Shock washed through her as she lifted her gaze to Dante. "Your grandmother traced my entire family line back to Atticus and his wife, Myrna Felty. When you look at this chart, you'll understand how the line flows through both the men and women in the family."

"I get that, but I thought you said Atticus had four children."

"He did." She pointed to a few scribbled notations off to the side. "Your grandmother jotted it here. Dinah and Jasper both died in 1799."

"There's a fourth one." Dante bent over the book, tracing a different line with his finger. "It looks like the oldest daughter, Fern, married someone named Oren Inghram." Shifting the book closer, he began paging though the contents. "Why does it fall on your line and not on Fern's?"

"I don't know." She'd never stopped to consider Fern. "Maybe because the responsibility has to flow from the eldest son in the ancestry."

"Here's Fern's family tree." He studied it for a moment, a frown growing as he scanned the names. "This is interesting."

"What is?"

"Take a look at the last entry in the hierarchy." He pointed. "Seems to me you mentioned that name only yesterday."

Her gaze dropped to the spot he indicated, and her breath escaped in a rush. His grandmother had scrawled a single name in flowing script at the bottom of the page.

Eli Yancy.

Chapter 11

Life had turned upside down, become unrecognizable. Clinging to the shadows, Gabriel darted between homes, Dinah's emerald clutched tightly in his fingers. In a matter of three days, the world as he'd known it had tumbled into oblivion.

Dinah had died in his arms.

Within thirty-six hours of Jasper's death, she succumbed to the same ailment that had claimed her brother. A sickness that swept through the village, striking one victim after another without discernment for age or status. Little Gail Hodgers passed in the same hour as her grandfather. Phillip Edwards was found the next morning, along with his wife, Beatrice, and all four of their children. William Todder, his mother, and a spinster aunt all perished within minutes of each other. It didn't take long for the word "plague" to circulate or for rumors of the supernatural to fester.

No malady could be so swift, so savage. The sickness had sprung from nowhere.

People began to look at Gabriel, remembering his injury and how ill he'd become after suffering an attack from the Endling. Atticus Crowe fell into despair when Jasper passed. When Dinah ailed, he put two and two together, starting to whisper that both of his children had tended to Gabriel. He pointed out the odd yellow cast of Gabriel's eyes. When it became apparent that Dinah would not recover, something inside him snapped. His daughter was the first to realize it.

"My father has convinced the men of the village you are possessed by a demon. He has lost all sanity to grief." Her voice was no more than a thready whisper when Gabriel cradled her in his arms. "Do not let him have the emerald. I fear how he might use its power. In the wrong hands, the stone can inflict horrible destruction. He will try to use it to vanquish the plague, but the power will corrupt him. If there is any hope for those who remain, you must keep it safe. I will not see the morrow, but as I love you, we shall surely meet again in a better place."

He'd crushed her to his chest when she'd taken her last breath. Was still cradling her, tears dampening her hair, when Atticus burst into the room.

"Do not touch her, filthy scum!" The older man shoved him from Dinah. "You have done this! Brought this unholy sickness to our village. There is no hope for any who remain until your life is forfeit, demon!"

Gabriel backed further into the room. Crowe was no longer a man he recognized, his face twisted with rage, eyes fired by fanatical righteousness. Something had transformed him—hatred, mania, grief—whatever the fuse, he'd crossed the line of sanity.

Throat dry, Gabriel shook his head. "You don't know what you're saying."

Other villagers crowded into the small space. He looked over their angry faces, noted Dinah's brother, Enoch, blocking the doorway. Had they not once laughed together, shared brandy, and raced horses across summer fields?

Atticus thrust a finger in his direction. "Look at his eyes. Do they not gleam yellow like a devil's? Did I not say he is at fault for this heinous plague?"

"Aye," Cyrus Herman agreed. "He is possessed of evil. It must be him that brought the illness upon us."

"No." How could they misjudge him after he'd risked his life to safeguard them? "My eyes gleam because of the Endling. Ask Hiram."

"Hiram is dead." Atticus spat the words in judgment. "Taken by the same fell fever that claimed Jasper and now Dinah." He did not move to touch his daughter.

"Swift action must be taken to bring an end to this vile sickness." Cyrus stepped closer, his posture signaling aggression.

"Aye." Farley, the tanner, muscled in beside him.

Recognizing the time for talk had passed, Gabriel plowed into Atticus. He never slowed even as Dinah's father reeled backward, staggering into Cyrus and Farley. Gabriel bludgeoned shoulder-first against Enoch. Hands grappled him, but he blundered free, managing to thrust past Enoch as Jasper's brother buckled at the waist. In the main room, he vaulted the sofa. Was halfway to the door when he snatched an oil lantern and shattered it on a straw rug. Flame and oil spread quickly, the men on his heels forced to bat down the fire before it could spread.

Darkness enveloped him outside, the touch of the night barely noticeable as he ducked between houses.

Jasper. Dinah. Hiram. All dead.

A cold fist twisted his gut. He fought the urge to retch and shoved the grim truth from his mind. Panting, he slipped into deeper shadows. There was no one left to help or offer a voice of reason. Atticus had turned friends and neighbors against him.

Vernon Hode.

The face of the village elder flashed through his mind. Hode had as much clout, if not more, than Atticus, and he hadn't bought into the hysteria that claimed the rest of the small populace. If Gabriel could reach him, there was a chance he might restore order.

Behind him came the sound of angry footfalls and cursing. Men he'd once called friends, spreading out to hunt him like a beast.

He risked a glance around the corner of the building that shielded him. Atticus Crowe stood in the middle of the street, a tall, thin shadow with a face like the grave.

"You must pay for these deaths, Gabriel Vane. For the innocent lives taken by this unholy sickness. Run, but I will find you. This I vow—your body will be the first in the ground, made protector of the souls you have claimed. Do you hear me, Gabriel?" He thrust a fist to the sky. "As God is my witness, you will not live to see the dawn."

* * * *

Present Day

Kirk Porter was nothing like his brothers. If Yancy hadn't been so desperate, he would have written the guy off the moment they crossed paths. Physically, Kirk wasn't imposing, a thin, wiry twenty-something who barely stood five-nine. But what he lacked in height and girth he more than made up in intensity. There was something about his eyes—obsidian black and needle-like—that cut Yancy to the quick. Plain and simple, Kirk Porter gave him the creeps.

But the man had no qualms about roughing up a kid. He was game for just about anything.

"I need you to get rid of these bones." Yancy motioned to Vane's scattered remains, laid out like a museum exhibit on his exam table. Warren Porter had brushed him off when he'd tried to get contact information on Kirk, but Clive had been more gullible offering up what he needed. Afterward, Yancy had a brief discussion with Kirk by cell phone. The youngest Porter brother agreed to meet him in the basement office at Wickham.

Kirk made a slow circuit around the table, his movements light-footed as a panther. "I said I'd rough up the kid. Dumping bones is extra." With a slow curl of his lip, he prodded a femur. "This the guy that got dug up from the cemetery?"

"What if it is?" Yancy stiffened his spine. It had been easy to maneuver Warren, far simpler to manipulate Clive. Kirk felt like an eel, too slippery to read.

"No biggie." Propping a shoulder against the wall, he fished a cigarette from the pocket of his jeans, then lit up with a cheap disposable lighter. The fingers of his right hand were yellow, stained with nicotine, the nails long like a woman's and filed to a point. "You got a boat?" He flicked a thumbnail against his teeth, exhaling a long stream of smoke.

Yancy fought the urge to cough. "What's that have to do with anything?"

"The river can be a dumping ground if you weight things right."

He hadn't considered that. It was off season for fishing, but there were probably a few places left where he could get a jon boat. "I can rent one."

"Too messy. You'll make a paper trail." Kirk took another drag off his cigarette, then flicked it to the floor and crushed the butt under his sneaker. Pig. "I know a guy. I'll take care of it, but the rental costs you extra."

"Deal." He was past caring how much. "Get rid of the bones and get me the emerald. Do it all by the weekend, and I'll double your payment."

"Shit, man." Kirk flashed cracked, uneven teeth. "I would have done that anyway, but I know a good thing when I come across it." He wiped his palm on his jeans and held out his hand. "Shake and you got a contract."

Yancy figured the handshake was as worthless as Kirk's word.

He shook anyway. He had a feeling people didn't say no to Kirk.

* * * *

Saturday night Dante carried a beer and his father's notebook into his studio. The canvas he'd worked on sporadically since summer remained unfinished. Anyone else looking at the easel would call the painting complete, but something was missing. An element he couldn't put his finger on. Maybe it was because he loathed the subject—Wickham—yet something about the place spoke to him. Wouldn't let him rest.

He took a swig of beer then set the bottle aside. Dropping into a chair, he paged open the notebook he'd found in the attic. As a kid, he used to tell his friends his father worked for the government, and his job was top secret. In reality, he had no idea what his father did or even who employed him. After his death, everything was handled through an attorney representing the shadow company Salvador worked for. Dante had been too young to pursue the matter, and his grandmother never followed through, satisfied by the establishment of a trust fund that would see Dante never wanted for anything.

When he was old enough to ask specific questions about his father's death, his grandmother brushed them off, saying she didn't know the details of the accident. Even now he believed her—his grandmother had always been honest with him—but part of him suspected she didn't want to know the truth of what Salvador had done at Wickham.

If he were honest, his father had been different the last few years leading up to his death. Secretive, withdrawn. Dante recalled waking in the middle of the night once and wandering downstairs to find his father sitting at the kitchen table in the dark with a half-empty bottle of whiskey. From his slumped posture and hitch of his shoulders, it was obvious he was crying.

The sight left Dante so shaken he'd returned to his bedroom and lain awake the entire night. He'd never said a word of what he'd seen to anyone. Never acted any differently toward his father.

His gaze dropped to the notebook where Salvador had penned words about madness, Wickham, and Blue. The only entry the book contained. Dante's father had been as cognizant of the spirit world as he was, if not more so. Had something at Wickham corrupted him? Turned him into a man who took on the "role of Dr. Frankenstein to L's monster?"

He skimmed snippets of the passage:

...it hovers near, wrapped in the guise of the monster I treat.
...a madness light will not breach.
...Blue may well be L's son, but he has become my personal demon.
...Blue will turn on me one day, driven by the experiments I subject him to.
...grows to abnormal size and strength.
...If I die, it will surely not be an accident, but by Blue's hand.
...I allowed myself to be corrupted by this wretched place.

Dante rubbed his forehead. No wonder his grandmother hadn't wanted to know the truth, that the wrongful death payout had been so large. Gut instinct told him his father had been killed by the person he'd dubbed Blue. Someone of abnormal size.

Like the blue-skinned drifter who'd jumped from the Old Orchard Truss Bridge last June. One and the same?

Dante's stomach roiled, the beer he'd drank turning to acid. The drifter had never been identified, his body carried away by the Chinkwe River.

Had his father truly become so corrupted by the taint of Wickham that he performed experiments on another living being? He ran his fingers under the chain of his Saint Michael's medal, the ugly glare of understanding like a spotlight. His father had never been employed by a company, but by a single person—the unnamed "L." Someone powerful enough and rich enough to pay Salvador a hefty salary then dole out a settlement when he died and keep the whole fiasco under wraps.

The only man Dante knew with that kind of clout was Leland Hode, Collin's father.

Dante lifted his gaze to the painting of Wickham and suddenly understood what was missing—flames to burn the wretched place to the ground.

* * * *

Dante woke Sunday morning with a pounding headache. He had a vague memory of calling Collin three times then hanging up before the calls went through. He'd lost track of the beers he'd downed, but thought he'd crawled into bed sometime after two in the morning. If his father was a monster who'd conducted medical experiments on another human being, what good would it do to drag up that depravity?

His father was gone. Wickham was a stigma of the past and Blue was dead, the victim of a suicide. Maybe Collin already knew what had gone on in that vile brick building. A falling out had happened between Collin and Leland last June. Maybe by keeping the truth from Dante, Collin had been protecting Salvador's memory. Who the hell wanted to learn their father was Dr. Frankenstein?

Dante stripped off his clothes and trudged into the bathroom. He stood in the shower with the water turned to cold until he drove the ache from his head and the dust from his thoughts. Learning the truth would not change the past. He'd tell no one of what he'd discovered, at least not as it related to his father or the Hode family.

Decision made, he finished showering and dressing. His first order of business was to return to Wickham. The impression he'd felt the day he'd helped Jillian with her car had been faint, barely perceptible. More energy was needed to awaken the folk memory, probably more than he had. He'd talk to Jillian and see if she was willing to help. If there was a way to channel her empathy, it might mean the difference between reading the past and coming up blank.

He made coffee for breakfast along with a piece of dry toast, enough to buffer the acid left over from his beer binge. He waited until after ten to phone Jillian.

She answered on the fourth ring. "Good morning."

"Morning. Any news on Madison?"

"Nothing." Her disappointment was palpable. "I just got off the phone with her doctor. The staff at Rest Haven are monitoring her closely, but there's been no change."

"I'm sorry. You have to give it time." He imagined her reaching down to pet Blizzard. The dog was probably glued to her side, given the sorrow in her voice.

"I know, but it's hard. Thanks for calling and asking. I appreciate what you did. In three years, Madison hasn't responded to anyone. You're the first person who got a reaction out of her."

"I'll try again if you want." He dumped the dregs of his coffee down the drain.

She was silent a moment. "Let's give it a week and see what happens. I have a feeling something has to break."

"If anyone is in tune with feelings, it's you."

She laughed. "Thanks. What do you have planned for today?"

"Actually, that's why I called. Since you did the website for Yancy, you probably know his business hours. Is he usually there on Sundays?"

"No. And after learning he's descended from Atticus Crowe, I can't stop being creeped out that he's a distant relative."

He imagined her shuddering. "Do you think he knows about Gabriel?"

"I don't know. The last time I was in his office, he had a newspaper on his desk with an article about the grave robbery." He sensed a frown in her voice. "Now that I think about it, he kept asking about Elliott."

Dante felt a stab of alarm. "Elliott?"

"Not by name. When I saw the article, I made a reference to being relieved Elliott wasn't hurt. After that he kept asking questions."

"What kind of questions?"

"Stupid stuff. He wanted to know if Elliott found anything in the grave…a coffin nail or a stone. Who thinks of those kinds of things?"

"*Why* would he think of those kinds of things?" Dante rubbed his temple. He'd function a lot better without the edge of a hangover clouding his mind. "I'm going to take a drive to Wickham. Would you mind coming along?"

He sensed when she hedged. "Sure, I guess. But what's at Wickham?"

He left the kitchen and headed down the hallway for the front door. "Remember when I told you about folk memories, and how I can read the impressions of events that happened in the past if they're strong enough? I think something vile happened at Wickham, and I want to find out what. I might need your help to do that."

"How?"

"I'll explain when I get there. Can I pick you up?"

"Now? Okay. See you when you get here."

Dante stopped in the foyer to grab a coat. He was still shrugging into the garment when the doorbell rang. Surprised, he opened the door to find Tessa and Elliott standing on the front porch.

"Contessa. What are you doing here?"

"Wow." Her smile was quick, her tone laced with humor. "I don't normally rate a full name greeting. Why do I get the idea you're not pleased to see us?"

"No. It's just—I was on my way out."

"Oh. Bad timing." She dropped her hands to Elliott's shoulders. "We missed you in church and thought we'd drop by to see if you wanted to grab breakfast."

"Sorry." He felt stupid. Didn't know if he should invite them in or step outside. At least she hadn't badgered him about why he'd missed Mass. "Maybe another time?"

"Sure. We're still on for Halloween night, right?"

The masquerade. "Yeah. I talked Jillian into going, too."

"Great."

Dante glanced down at Elliott. "Sorry I'm going to miss breakfast." No sense mentioning his stomach wouldn't have been able to handle it anyway.

"That's okay." Elliott fiddled with a stone, tossing it lightly in his hand. "I told Mom to call first, but she didn't listen. She figured if you weren't in church, you must be painting and would have your phone off."

"Late night." Dante rifled a hand through his hair. He hadn't bothered tying it back. "I overslept."

"Well, we won't keep you from wherever you're headed." Tessa nudged Elliott from the doorway. He back-stepped, lost his balance, and dropped the stone.

Dante stooped to pick it up. Strange rock. It looked a little like an emerald, but of a rougher cut. "Hey what's this?"

Elliott held out his hand. "My wishstone."

"Your what?"

"Like Grandma has a worry stone, only mine's for wishes."

Dante grinned and dropped it into his palm. "Does it work?"

"I wished for a friend, and now Finn and I hang out together."

Dante pitched Tessa a questioning glance.

"Finn Carrigan. He was the boy at the cemetery with Elliott when... when the tree fell."

When that poor man died. The unspoken words dangled between them.

"Well, hang onto it." Dante clapped Elliott on the shoulder. "It's unusual-looking."

"Come on, Elliott. We've held Dante up long enough." With a parting wave, Tessa headed for her car.

Elliott lingered, looking like he wanted to say more. Dante crouched lower. "Is there something else you wanted to tell me?"

The boy nodded, leaning close. "It protects me from monsters, too." His voice had dropped to a whisper. Monsters were their own special secret. He stared up at Dante, eyes wide behind the lenses of his glasses. "Do you know why?"

"I couldn't guess."

"Because I found it in the cemetery. It was in the grave I fell into."

Chapter 12

October 21, 1799

The passage of the night took a toll on Gabriel. Whether from cradling Dinah on her deathbed, or the natural process of the sickness, by the time he slipped from the village, he was flush with the same fever that had claimed so many others. He knew his farm would be the first place his pursuers searched, so he ran in the opposite direction, toward a knoll dense with trees. The autumn foliage would help conceal him, and the leaf-strewn ground would make him harder to track. If he could make it through the wooded terrain, Vernon Hode's homestead lay on the opposite side.

Hode had not been seen since before Gabriel, Jasper, and Hiram left to track the Endling. Gabriel had always looked to him as a man of formidable strength and reason. If anyone could return sanity to the village, it was Hode.

Stopping to catch his breath, he bent over, hands on knees, and drank ragged gulps of the cold air. He dug Dinah's emerald from his frock coat. If the illness took the same course with him as it did others, he would be dead in less than three days. Whatever magic his beloved had woven into the stone could no longer protect him. That power had been severed with Dinah's death.

A steady, distant baying drew him upright.

Dogs.

Atticus must have realized he'd try to reach Vernon Hode.

Caught in a nightmare, Gabriel closed his eyes. It wasn't possible to be hunted this way. To be tracked like an animal as they had tracked and cornered the Endling. The roles of predator and prey kept shifting, but it didn't matter. He fisted his hand around the emerald. Whatever happened to him, he'd made a promise to Dinah.

"Your father will not have the stone."

Atticus's threat needled into his head. *"This I vow—your body will be the first in the ground, made protector of the souls you have claimed."*

Cold sweat broke out on his forehead and tracked to his jaw. A guardian soul for the chapel cemetery. Atticus had expected Jasper to sacrifice a dog, but Jasper was gone.

And, this night, Atticus had named his own sacrifice.

Propelling himself forward, Gabriel prayed for the strength to reach Vernon Hode.

* * * *

Present Day

Jillian was thankful to find the lot at Wickham deserted. Yancy didn't advertise Sunday hours, but that didn't mean he might not be there working.

Dante parked his 4Runner in a spot at the far end, away from the building. On the drive over, he'd told her about Elliott's "wishstone" and how he'd found it in Gabriel's grave. Her stomach had been in knots ever since.

He killed the ignition. "You haven't said anything for a while."

"I know." She worried her bottom lip between her teeth. "I told Yancy that Elliott lived next door to me. Suddenly, I have this horrible feeling." Twisting, she shifted to face him. "Why would he ask if Elliott found something in the grave unless he expected something to be there?"

"You think he's the one who took Gabriel's bones?"

"I don't think he could do it himself, but that doesn't mean he isn't involved. He seems to have money to burn. He could have hired someone."

Dante draped an arm over the steering wheel. "Maybe you should share your thoughts with your detective friend. What's her name? Sherre?"

"No." Bad idea. "She already thinks I'm a nutcase for believing the grave robbery is the reason behind all the accidental deaths. I'm just worried about Elliott."

"He'll be okay." He opened his car door, then hesitated. "What about you? You don't have Blizzard for a buffer."

He'd asked her to leave the husky at home, something she rarely did. Dante had said he needed all her empathy and psychic energy open to him while he tried to focus on the folk memory he believed lingered at Wickham.

She'd never liked the place. Was that why? Because the part of her that was tuned to emotions had zoned in on something that occurred here ages ago?

She fingered her glasses. "I'll be okay. Just tell me what you need me to do."

"Come on." He led her around the back of the building where oaks and sycamores clustered several hundred yards to the rear from the lot. Ducking beneath the branches, he wove his way deeper into the pocket of trees.

Surprised, Jillian tugged the collar of her pea coat closer to her throat and followed on his heels. He'd taken about thirty paces when he stopped suddenly and stood motionless. Sunlight mottled the ground in piebald patches and filtered through branches that had shed most of their leaves. The air was redolent with the odor of loam and fungi.

"Dante?"

Ignoring her, he pressed one long-fingered hand to the trunk of a towering birch. The breeze scattered the black hair from his face. His eyes were narrowed, focused on something she couldn't see.

A memory?

He trailed his hand down the bark, stepped around the tree, then squatted to examine the ground. Seconds passed in silence. Finally, he stood and faced her.

In that quicksilver moment, when their eyes met, she felt what he did. The impressions he latched onto blindsided her.

A young man in Colonial garb, his clothing torn and muddy...several men ringed in a circle...torches...dogs...another man, tall and thin, his face contorted with hate.

The bristling force of the man's hostility made her stagger backward. For a second, she thought he was Yancy, but his coloring was all wrong. Dark instead of fair. Yet the features were the same. High brow, sharp cheekbones.

Atticus Crowe.

The name mushroomed in her head. Atticus was a man she'd always thought worthy of respect. Seeing him now, he harbored nothing but hate.

Fear and desperation slammed into her, sharp as lightning, but the emotion was not from Atticus. She choked and nearly stumbled.

The young man!

Crowe hefted a knife.

No! It couldn't be!

But she knew, even as the tears fell from her eyes.

The young man being restrained by the others was Gabriel Vane.

* * * *

Dante shoved her iced tea closer. "Drink. You'll feel better."

Jillian twined her hands around the glass but didn't raise it to her lips. "I'll be all right. I just need a moment." Far more than a moment. It had been over a half hour since they'd left Wickham. Dante took them to a downtown hole-in-the-wall eatery named The Knot. Located on Fourth Street among a strip of other cafes and bars, it fell within the district locals called Pub Place—the area designated for Saturday night's Masquerade Pub Crawl.

On a Saturday night, The Knot would be pulsing with music, wall-to-wall with a crowd who favored mingling and craft beers. On a Sunday afternoon, it was a quiet haven for friends to chat over flavored teas and vegetarian dishes. She'd ordered a shaved cauliflower salad to Dante's asparagus and goat cheese sandwich, but her appetite was lacking. The experience at Wickham had left her eyes dilated far longer than usual.

She took a sip of the tea, then removed her eyeglasses. The subdued lighting of The Knot slowly eased the edge from her nerves. The place was long and narrow like an alley, with faux-brick walls, a hardwood floor, and mounted lanterns that resembled teardrops.

"Sorry." She poked at her salad. "It's one thing absorbing emotions, but to actually see something that happened…" She met his gaze, appreciating his gift in a whole new light. "Do…do you think Gabriel died there?"

"I don't know. You told me he died of a plague." He took a bite of his sandwich. She was used to guys who favored burgers and fries, not asparagus and goat cheese.

"I always thought he did. That was the belief in my family, but the memory you tapped into makes it seem like he was killed by Atticus."

"If that's the case, how did Gabriel end up as the guardian of Hickory Chapel Cemetery? Atticus doesn't seem like a praying man to me."

"No." She recalled the prayer circle she'd believed in. How the men of the village had gathered around Gabriel's grave and beseeched God to make his spirit the protector of those buried after him. A stray thought surfaced—chilling and unthinkable. Centuries ago, villagers had buried a dog alive to ensure protection for their departed. If Gabriel hadn't died at Wickham…

She shoved the idea aside. No one, not even Atticus, could be that heinous. And yet, the cemetery had attracted creatures far more monstrous than the normal cessation of life should draw. And Gabriel's grave was so deep, segregated from the rest.

So very, very deep.

"At least now I understand why Wickham carries a malevolent taint." Dante's voice intruded on her thoughts.

She flicked him a surprised glance. "You've felt that, too?"

"Always." He slumped back against his chair, his expression sobering. "I told you my father died when I was fifteen. What I didn't tell you was that he died in an accident while employed at Wickham."

Her lips parted. "I had no idea."

"You mean you've never heard I'm a bohemian who lives off a settlement from the accident?" He snorted sour amusement. "I thought that was common gossip."

"Dante, I never—"

He waved her protest aside. "Ignore me. Every now and then I get bitter." Gaze lowered, he rested his wrist on the edge of the table and idly turned a glass of water in his hand. "The truth is I no longer think what happened at Wickham was accidental, but I think my father brought his death on himself. I'm positive the place corrupted him." Sitting forward, he shoved the glass away. "At least, that's what I have to believe if I want to remember him in a good light."

Jillian was tempted to prod further, but Dante looked around for their waitress.

"Ready?"

She nodded. Her stomach was still too unsettled to eat more.

Dante flagged the server over and asked for the check. Once she left, promising to return, he dug for his wallet. "Are you willing to take this thing one step further?"

Confused, Jillian cocked her head. "What do you mean?"

"Do you want to find out the truth about what happened to Gabriel?"

Of course she did. "How?"

His grin was sharp, more barbed than cordial. "Ask him."

She grew very still. "You're talking about a séance."

"It's what I do. And with Halloween around the corner, it's the perfect time."

"Okay." She took a deep breath. "Count me in."

* * * *

Late Monday morning, Jillian drove to Rest Haven, staying for several hours with Madison. Her sister seemed to have more color to her face and a higher level of alertness in her eyes but remained silent throughout the visit. Jillian chatted about trivial matters—the weather, colorful Halloween decorations she'd noticed on the drive over, Blizzard's newest chew toy—then read aloud from *The Great Gatsby*, one of Madison's favorite novels, just so her sister would hear her voice. Finally, she told Madison about the séance.

"I'm nervous, but I think it's something I have to do." Jillian sat in her usual spot, a chair drawn close to the window, Madison across from her. A few feet away, Blizzard lay with his head on his paws, content at the foot of the bed. But for the occasional footsteps of someone passing in the hallway, the room was quiet. Jillian turned her gaze out the window where clouds hung heavy with rain.

"Nervous is too tame a word. I'm scared, Maddy. We've tended Gabriel's grave for so long, but to summon his spirit seems wrong." The dismal gray sky matched her mood. She struggled not to let her bleakness show. "I trust Dante. In the short time I've known him, we've become close. I know he'd never do anything to put me at risk."

He'd told her for the séance to be successful, there should be at least four sitters in the summoning circle, but that six would be better, and each person should have a personal connection to her. He'd agreed to ask Tessa, and she said she'd ask Maya. Her neighbor was not only a friend but had hosted a séance last June. Unfortunately, Maya was going to be out of town on Friday, the night Dante had chosen to hold the séance—Halloween Eve.

Shifting, she crossed her legs and relaxed against the back of her chair. "I'm going to have to ask Sherre." The detective was already invested to a degree, even if she didn't buy into what Jillian had told her about the rash of odd deaths in Hode's Hill.

Madison lowered her gaze and plucked at a stray thread on her slacks. Her fingers were thin, her nails bare and clipped short. There'd been a time when she'd paid for biweekly gel manicures, but the days of having French-tipped nails or berry-red polish were a thing of the past. Selfishly, Jillian wanted that person back. The sister who dropped by unannounced, forgot to return the shoes she'd borrowed, and who phoned at all hours of the day and night just to chat.

Despite her natural empathy, Madison had never sealed herself in a cocoon the way Jillian had. Maybe because Madison didn't have the additional burden of fringe psychic abilities, or maybe she'd just been better at managing empathy. Whatever the knack, Jillian had admired her ability to detach. That habit had allowed her to experience more of life—right up until the moment Boyd died and the skill failed.

Suppressing a surge of melancholy, Jillian stood and paced a short distance away. Alerted by her mood, Blizzard raised his head.

"It's okay, boy. I'm just going to make a phone call." Locating her purse on a table by the door, she fished inside for her cell. With her back to Madison, she pushed the button to dial Sherre's number.

"Lorquet." She'd caught the detective at work.

"Hi, Sherre. It's Jillian."

A moment of silence. "If you're calling about Gabriel Vane, or anything connected to him, now isn't a good time."

Jillian read between the lines. "I'm not calling about the deaths." She wanted to ask if Sherre had followed through and investigated but understood the message—*don't ask.* "I'm with Madison."

"How is she?"

"Since she spoke last?" Jillian had phoned Sherre on Saturday to give her the news. "Still no change, but I'm hopeful. Her color is better today, and she seems more alert, even if she isn't talking."

"That's good. I know her doctors said it could take time. If you're looking for leads on her case, now that she's improving, I don't have anything new."

"It's not that."

"If she does recover, you realize she'll be able to ID Boyd's killers."

Jillian chose not to dwell on Sherre's use of *if* instead of *when.* She hadn't thought about what Madison's ability to speak would do for the detective's cold case. "She'll need time to adjust. I want Boyd's killers found as much as you do, but right now my focus is on getting her whole."

"She's on the right path. You've waited this long."

"I know." A rustling traveled through the line as if Sherre rearranged papers on her desk. "Are you working Friday night?"

"Saturday. They've got me on for the Masquerade Pub Crawl."

With everything else going on, Jillian had forgotten she'd promised to go with Dante and Tessa. If she couldn't scare up a costume, she'd at least have to find a mask. "That's good, because I have a strange request."

The shuffling stopped. "Strange? From you?" Sherre laughed. "Nah."

At least the detective maintained a sense of humor. "Stranger than usual. I'm hosting a séance Friday night and was hoping you'd attend."

Dead silence.

"Sherre?"

"Séance, as in ghosts? Spirits of dead people? That kind of thing?"

"Yes."

A pffing noise. "I didn't realize you were into Halloween."

"It's not about Halloween."

"Then why are you holding a séance?"

"To contact Gabriel."

Sherre muttered something she didn't catch.

"Sherre, it's important. If I'm right about Gabriel and the reason people are dying, Madison and I are targets, too. I can take care of myself, but Madison doesn't have the same luxury."

"She's not going to get hurt in a care facility."

"Anything can happen."

Several seconds of silence. "Why ask me?"

"Because Dante said the people who attend should be connected to me, and you're invested whether you want to admit it or not. You have been from the moment you responded to the call on Mill Street."

"Maybe." Sherre didn't deny the connection or its inception. "Are we talking about Dante DeLuca?"

"Yes. He's conducting the séance."

"The same Dante DeLuca who was a royal pain in the ass about Pin Oaks?" There was no disguising the incredulity in Sherre's voice.

"You're forgetting he's also the one who got my sister to talk when no one else could. Will you come?"

"It sounds like amateur hocus-pocus to me. I hope DeLuca isn't charging you."

"He's a friend who's trying to help. I'm asking another friend to do the same."

"That's not fair."

Jillian forced herself to stay silent. Sometimes the only way to accomplish a goal was through a low blow.

Sherre exhaled. "I'll think about it."

"Sherre—"

"It's the best I can do. I'll call you later." The line clicked in her ear.

Swearing under her breath, Jillian switched off her phone. She turned back to the window. Madison was no longer in her chair but sitting cross-legged on the floor beside Blizzard.

"Pretty dog." Her sister smiled broadly and stroked the husky's fur.

Chapter 13

October 21, 1799

They were coming.

Men with dogs and guns. Men he'd once called friends and neighbors.

Gabriel stumbled as he zigzagged between the trees. He hadn't put as much distance between him and his pursuers as he'd hoped. The fever was spiking, slowing him down, dripping sweat into his eyes with each step. At this pace, he'd never outrun them, and he'd surely never reach Vernon Hode.

He shook his head.

What the hell was wrong with him?

His death might be a foregone conclusion, but that didn't mean he had to yield to violence. Let the fever take him as it had others. He'd be damned if he'd allow himself to be a sacrifice.

He stopped to draw a breath and glanced down at the emerald in his hand. Filtered moonlight splattered the ground around him and defined the rough edges of the stone. Atticus would claim it if he was caught, and if he tossed it, he risked the chance of someone stumbling over it—whether minutes, days, months, or even years from now. For Dinah's trust, he must ensure that never happened.

His lips were dry, his mouth parched, but the gem wasn't that large. If he forced it, he might be able to work it past his throat.

Behind him, the chorus of baying grew louder. Closer. The wind carried the faint sound of men calling to one another. He didn't have the luxury of debate. Whatever happened to him, he would ensure his promise to Dinah remained unbroken.

Closing his eyes, Gabriel tossed the emerald to the back of his throat. He swallowed with effort, forcing the stone deeper into his gullet. Soft tissue tore, shredded by the gem's jagged edges, and his gag reflex kicked in. He fought the urge to retch, bending double, sweat popping like beads of dew on his forehead. A taste like hot metal flooded his mouth. He spat blood and stumbled forward, attempting to vault an overturned tree. In the darkness, he misjudged the step, and his ankle twisted. The pungent tang of decayed leaves clogged his head as he sprawled to his knees.

Get up!

He forced himself to move, slipped on the leaf-strewn ground, and hobbled to his feet. The air reverberated with the clamor of his death sentence—footfalls and baying so close he was certain he wouldn't live to see the dawn.

* * * *

Present Day

A rollercoaster.

There was no better word to describe the peaks and valleys of Jillian's emotions. Discovering her sister petting Blizzard had catapulted her into the stratosphere. The endearment "pretty dog" had never sounded so sweet, Madison's smile equivalent to a sunburst at the zenith of a pitch-black night. No further words had followed, but the flattery she'd offered Blizzard convinced Madison's doctors she continued to separate from the darkness that imprisoned her.

Jillian had celebrated by going to dinner with Dante, Tessa, and Elliott. Tuesday found Madison uncommunicative again, content to sit by the window and stare into space. Blizzard might not have existed for all the attention—or lack of attention—she bestowed. Elation spun into a mundane waiting game, the plodding hours made bearable by renewed splinters of hope. Jillian reminded herself to be patient. Every step, no matter how minor or infrequent, was improvement.

Tuesday evening, she'd just finished drying dinner dishes and was talking to Dante on her cell when another call came through.

"It's Rest Haven." Anticipation made her voice catch. "I've got to take this."

"I'll hold." Dante sounded every bit as anxious as she did. "If it's news about Madison, I'd like to know."

"Back in a flash." Heart pounding, Jillian switched to the other call. "Hello?"

"Jillian Cley?"

"Yes?"

"This is Nurse Hollinger from Rest Haven."

She was familiar with the woman. Had spoken with her multiple times. "Has there been a change with Madison?" She held her breath, poised for the news her sister was speaking. Digging her nails into her palm, she counted the seconds until Hollinger's somber voice sounded in her ear.

"I'm sorry to be the bearer of bad news, Ms. Cley, but your sister was the victim of an unfortunate accident that caused her heart to stop beating. Please come as soon as you can."

* * * *

Jillian was shell-shocked. She had no other words to describe the heavy fog through which she moved. She'd flown out the door even as she relayed the news to Dante. He'd insisted she drive to his house rather than straight to Rest Haven. Because the stop was on the way, and because she feared her emotional stability, she'd conceded. Within seconds of arriving, Dante hustled Blizzard into the back of his 4Runner, her into the passenger seat.

She fought back tears.

"Her heart stopped beating. Please come as soon as you can."

After all she and Madison had done through the years to keep Gabriel's memory alive, her sister had fallen victim to the monsters of Hickory Chapel Cemetery. It was so unfair, especially when Madison had been on the verge of a breakthrough.

Dante reached over the center console to squeeze her hand. "It's going to be okay."

She wiped away a tear. "Her heart stopped beating."

"But they were able to revive her." He reminded her of Nurse Hollinger's parting words. Madison had been enjoying a quiet dinner in the dining room when a new resident suddenly became violent and threw a chair across the room. Jillian's sister was struck full force in the chest, the blunt trauma sparking a condition Nurse Hollinger called "commotio cordis." The electrical system in Madison's heart short-circuited from the shock of impact. For a full minute, fifty-six seconds, she'd been clinically dead, the victim of a freak accident. Two aides, working in tandem, were able to restart her heart through CPR. She'd eventually been taken by ambulance to Palmer Point Hospital, listed as unconscious but stable.

"It's just not fair." Blizzard poked his head from the back seat, nosing beneath her arm to offer comfort. Jillian hugged him close. "Everything was going so well. Madison made more progress in the last few days than she has in years." Her tears soaked into Blizzard's fur.

Dante rubbed her shoulder. "She survived Mill Street and she survived this. Your sister is going to be okay."

Biting her lip, Jillian nodded. She wiped tears from her face. "I thought she'd be safe in Rest Haven."

"I did, too."

A sedan passed in the opposing lane, the white glare of headlights sweeping through the car. Jillian studied Dante. "Then you think the accident was because of the curse?"

"I do." He kept his attention on the road, hands locked on the steering wheel. "The sooner we have the séance, the better. I have most everything together I need. Did you talk to Maya?"

"She's going to be out of town."

His mouth tightened. "Then we move ahead anyway. It doesn't matter how many sitters we have. At this point, it's more important to channel what energy we have into contacting Gabriel."

"I asked Sherre to come." Concentrating on the séance helped shift her focus from Madison. Her stomach was in knots, but there was nothing she could do for her sister until she arrived at the hospital. "She said she'd think about it."

"That's not good enough."

"No, it's not." Resolution settled like a rock in her stomach. "Once we reach the hospital and I've had a chance to see Madison, I'll call her."

* * * *

Sherre carried a glass of white wine and a dinner plate into the living room, then collapsed on the couch. From habit, she switched on the TV then flicked through the channels. Part of her wanted something to keep her mind occupied, the other part couldn't stand the noise. Her head pounded, making the grilled cheese sandwich she'd toasted on a griddle less than appetizing. Setting the plate on the coffee table, she rubbed her eyes and folded back against the sofa cushions.

It was nearly ten o'clock at night, and the day had been grueling. Not because of an excess of calls, but because her mind kept tripping over potholes every time she thought of Carrie, the records clerk; Coleman, the janitor; or Henry Teale. Not to mention the host of other people who'd met untimely ends. Jillian had filled her head with stories of phantom church bells and curses. Reluctant to buy into old wives' tales, she'd dug through historical records and death certificates only to discover the people who'd died each had ancestors in Hickory Chapel Cemetery.

But was that enough to motivate her to attend a séance? The blare of a siren rose in the distance, the wail faint and far away. It was a city sound, one she'd heard countless times. Any other night she might have switched on her scanner, ready to bolt out the door if needed. But the shrill noise carried an ominous edge, one that made her want to stay sealed within the walls of her apartment.

"Shit. Get a grip." It was just a siren, far from supernatural.

Far from the eerie toll of a church bell.

The jangle of her phone startled her. Thankful for the intrusion, she dug the cell from her pocket, noting the caller before answering.

"Jillian. Is everything all right?"

"No." Jillian's voice was strained, tremulous with emotion. She drew a shaky breath. "There was an accident tonight."

Sherre's belly clenched. "Madison?"

"Someone threw a chair. It hit her in the chest and short-circuited her heart."

"What the hell?" In an instant, she was on her feet, gut ballooning into her throat. "She...she can't be—"

"They were able to revive her."

"Thank God. You mean she was—"

"Dead." Jillian's voice was monotone. In the next second, she hitched in a breath as if fighting tears. "I can't lose her, Sherre. I can't."

"I know." If there was anyone who grieved every bit as much as Madison, it was Jillian. After three years of watching the sisters suffer, Sherre no longer had the stomach to deny even the most ludicrous request. "What do you want me to do?"

"Say you'll come to the séance Friday night. Nine o'clock."

"I'll be there." She hung up the phone. Moving mechanically, she carried her wine and grilled cheese into the kitchen, dumped the wine down the sink and the sandwich in the trash. The pounding in her head was like a sledgehammer. She barely made it to the bathroom before she threw up.

* * * *

Jillian spent the night in the hospital, curled up in a chair by her sister's bedside. As a therapy animal, Blizzard was greenlighted to stay, but Jillian asked Dante to take the dog home with him. He left close to eleven, promising to return the next morning. Throughout the night, various hospital staff filtered in and out of the room, checking periodically on Madison and recording her vital signs. Jillian's sister slept soundly, and somewhere after one in the morning, Jillian eventually fell into an exhausted sleep.

She woke to a beam of sunlight slanting across her face and pronounced stiffness in her neck. Groggily, she rubbed her eyes.

"Hi." The voice was familiar, one she'd barely heard in three years.

Jillian froze, her gaze flashing to the bed. Madison relaxed against the pillows, sheets drawn to her chest, an uncertain smile on her lips. For the first time in thirty-six months, her eyes were unclouded, intelligence visible in every line of her face. Her smile inched higher. "I've missed you."

Sobbing, Jillian collapsed at the bedside.

* * * *

The day was consumed by a battery of exams and questions. Consulting doctors, specialists, and nurses. Prodding, blood samples, machines. Madison was out of her room for most of it, wheeled to this or that department, for this or that test. Jillian ate lunch in the cafeteria with Dante then asked if he would take Blizzard for one more night.

"I need to speak to Madison. Alone. Without doctors and nurses hanging on her every word. Without—"

"I get it." He held up his hand. "I need to put things together for the séance, anyway. You're still going through with it, right?"

"Of course." Madison had survived "death," but others might not be so lucky. Thus far, no one had been. Keeping Gabriel's memory alive might have made the difference for Madison, but Jillian still had a responsibility to the residents of Hode's Hill with ancestors in Hickory Chapel Cemetery. "The doctors seem to think Madison will be here for two more days. As long as she continues to do okay, they're talking about moving her to a rehab center to help rebuild her strength."

"Sounds logical." Dante swirled sugar into his coffee.

Jillian nodded. "Rest Haven made sure she got up and walked each day, but she's lost a lot of weight plus strength and mobility." She plucked a corner from the chicken salad sandwich on her plate and nibbled the bread. Soup would have been better given her stomach had been twisted into a fat knot from the moment she'd awakened.

At thirteen minutes after two on a Thursday afternoon, the cafeteria wasn't crowded. Three nurses shared salads at a table by the entrance. Nearby, an older couple talked over bowls of fruit cocktail. A young mother pushed a stroller with a sleeping baby through the food line, sliding a red tray one-handed along the serving counter. A few people sat hunched over cell phones or laptops, and occasionally an overhead page requested someone report to lab or X-ray. A typical hospital cafeteria, it looked the part, right down to the sound-absorbing ceiling tiles, potted ferns, and ergonomic chairs.

Gaze downcast, Jillian took another bite of her chicken salad. Blizzard lay beside her chair, keenly watching the activity around him.

"I thought you'd be happier about your sister." Dante shoved his plate aside, only crumbs remaining from his sandwich.

"I am happy." Overjoyed. Ecstatic. But there was a downside to that giddy euphoria, too. "With all the tests Madison has been going through, I've had time to think about what it means—three years of her life gone. She's going to need more than physical help to readjust."

"I'm sure her doctors will tell you what kind of counseling she'll need." The corner of his mouth pulled into a frown as he studied her. "It's all good, Jillian."

"I know." He probably thought she was an idiot. Or doomsayer. Likely both. For three years, she'd looked forward to the day Madison recovered, and now her gut was in turmoil. "I'm just scared. I came so close to losing her." Fear was the true culprit of the emotion plaguing her. "I'll feel better once Gabriel's remains are back in his grave."

"Forget about Gabriel until Friday night. He's my problem." He cracked a smile. "Leave the ghost, the grim, and the monsters to me."

The knot in her stomach unraveled. "Thanks for taking such good care of me."

He laid his hand over hers where it rested on the table. "It's my pleasure."

* * * *

Jillian drew her chair closer to her sister's bed. The barrage of tests finally over, both she and Madison could breathe easier. The revolving door of doctors, nurses, technicians, and aides had sputtered to an infrequent appearance. Dante had left with Blizzard, promising to return and pick her up after visiting hours. For three years Jillian had used the husky as a shield, but now that Madison was talking again, she didn't feel the need to rely on Blizzard as a buffer between herself and others.

Madison reached for her hand and held fast. "I feel like you're always sitting by a window talking to me."

"Then you remember my visits?" Surprise made Jillian tighten her grip.

A hint of sadness crossed Madison's face. Her color had improved, but her cheeks were hollow, much too thin. "I remember more than you think."

Jillian swallowed hard, unable to ignore the elephant in the room. A delicate Goliath, the thought had vulture-circled since morning. "Boyd?"

Madison released her hand. In the span of a pulsebeat the soft blue-green of her eyes darkened to winter pine. Looking away, she curled the sheet beneath her fingers. "I know he's dead."

Jillian barely breathed. She held herself rigidly in place, terrified the slightest movement would prevent Madison from talking.

"We fought." Her sister gazed across the room as if the memory played out on the distant wall. "I knew he was dealing, but I thought it was penny-ante stuff. He told me it was just weed. A few downers. I didn't know how serious it was until the night he was killed." Her attention returned to Jillian. "He was scared. Really scared. He'd crossed someone he shouldn't have. Shortchanged them or gave them bad junk. I don't even know." She pressed her fingers to her temples and rolled the fragile skin in circles. "All I remember is hearing a noise. Like someone trying to get in the house. And then—" She dropped her hands to her lap where they lay like broken things. "Nothing."

Jillian's mouth was dry. "Nothing?"

Madison squeezed her eyes shut. "I wish it was more. In some part of my head, I know I've relived that night over and over again for the last three years. But now it's…" She turned a hollow-eyed gaze on Jillian. "Gone."

"It's all right." Jillian squeezed her hand, fear chasing a tumbleweed through her belly. Now that Madison was no longer in a catatonic state, would she become a target for Boyd's killers? Sherre would know the odds and what steps should be taken to keep Madison safe. As long as there was no press on her recovery, she could stay under the radar. Jillian had wanted her sister whole. Hadn't wanted to badger her about the identity of the men who'd murdered Boyd, but her survival could well depend on her ability to ID them.

She leaned forward in her chair. "Whatever happened that night is in the past. The important thing is for you to concentrate on getting well."

"They never caught them, did they?" Madison's gaze was direct. "The men who killed Boyd?"

"No." Jillian hated admitting the truth. A sticky wave of heat crept up the back of her neck. Had her sister realized she was a potential target?

Madison dropped her head against the pillows and stared up at the ceiling. "I told him I was going to leave him."

"I didn't know." If only she'd left sooner.

"The only thing that sticks in my head about that night is a lizard. A black lizard. But I don't know what it means."

Dante had seen a black lizard.

Frustration drew Madison's brow into a crinkled line, balled her hands into fists. Sudden tears made her eyes gleam with green lacquer. "I hate that I can't remember."

It didn't matter—the lizard—any of it.

"You spent three years remembering." Jillian gripped her arm. "You were trapped in a nightmare. Whatever Boyd's faults, he wouldn't want you living that over again. Maybe that's why you *can't* remember." Standing, she began to fuss with the sheets, adjusting them over Madison's waist, smoothing them at the foot of the bed—all signals to end the conversation.

"Do I even have a house anymore?" Madison's voice was thin.

Jillian ceased her restless movements. A prickly lump lodged in her throat. She hadn't wanted to go down this path so soon. "I had to sell it. The money has been going for your care at Rest Haven."

Madison looked away, her mouth a papery line. "I couldn't live there anyway."

"I moved, too." Jillian sat close beside her on the mattress. "I bought a brownstone on River Road. It has plenty of room. When it's time, you'll move in with me."

"And be a burden all over again."

"Stop it." The harshness of her tone surprised her. Sighing, she folded her hands together and pressed them briefly to her lips to compose herself. "Maddy." When she spoke, her tone was soft, but her shoulders stiffened with the sharpness of her mood. "I've waited three years to talk to you again. I know the road ahead is going to be challenging, but I'm not going to let you face it alone. Please don't ever think you are a burden."

Closing her eyes on a rush of tears, Madison folded against her. Jillian held her tightly, her cheek pressed to the short strands of her sister's hair.

"I'm just so exhausted." Madison's voice was broken.

"You've had a long day." Jillian stroked her back, a single harrowing thought popping to the surface.

And you died.

* * * *

Dante fiddled with the kitchen radio until he found a clear station. "Thriller" by Michael Jackson blared from the speakers. Satisfied, he adjusted the volume then grabbed a soda from Tessa's refrigerator. At the table, Elliott scooped the innards of a fat pumpkin into a garbage bowl.

It was Thursday night, Jillian was with Madison at the hospital, and Tessa was picking up a costume for Saturday's masquerade. As a favor, he'd agreed to undertake pumpkin-carving duty with Elliott. Not that he minded. The kid might be too serious at times, but he was family, and Dante enjoyed spending time with him.

He took a swig of his soda as Elliott dug a handful of seeds and stringy fibers from the pumpkin.

"Are you going to make triangle eyes?" Elliott asked.

"I can make them however you want." The rot-like smell of pulp wafted from the table where Elliott knelt on a chair. "I sketched some designs for you to look through." Dante tapped a paper tablet on the counter. "We can make it goofy, scary, or weird. You decide."

"Not scary." Elliott scissored his fingers above the bowl, flecking off chunks of orange flesh. "Thriller" ended, segueing into a commercial.

"Get your ghoul on this Saturday night with Hode Hill's first Halloween Masquerade Pub Crawl. Starting at seven, quaff spirits and enjoy devilish meals at your favorite Fourth Street eateries, each decked out for spook-tacular fun. Live music, blood-curdling costumes, and, of course, the best in local brews. Put on your mask, or come as you are, but make no bones about it—you're sure to have a fang-tastic time."

"Mom said you're taking her and Jillian to that masquerade thing." Elliott seemed to have picked up on the commercial. The ad transitioned to one for a car dealer who assured his unbeatable prices weren't just "witchful thinking."

"Yeah, we're going to the masquerade." Dante set his bottle aside. "I heard you're having your friend over and your grandmother is going to stay with you until your mom gets home." He and Imelda might not be on speaking terms, but he admired her for the attention she lavished on her daughter and grandson.

Elliott bobbed his head. "Finn's spending the weekend. He's coming over after school tomorrow night."

"Sounds like Finn is becoming a good friend." Having Elliott adjust to his new school had been one of Tessa's biggest concerns. She'd confided he'd kept mostly to himself before the move, withdrawn over his parents' divorce and too shy to make friends. Whether he knew it or not, Finn Carrigan had taken a load off her shoulders.

"We like a lot of the same things. Space stuff and UFOs." The bulk of the pumpkin's innards were clumped into a sticky marshmallow in the bowl. Elliott picked up a spoon, then began to scrape the remaining strings from the fleshy insides. "Finn's dad doesn't come around either. He lives with his uncle."

No wonder the two boys had bonded. "What's his uncle do?"

"He's a detective. His name's David Gregg."

Small world. David Gregg had been one of the cops who'd responded to Hickory Chapel Cemetery the night Spencer was killed. "What about Finn's mom?" Having a father out of the picture was one thing, but it was odd for both parents to be AWOL.

Elliott scrunched his mouth to the side as if working through how to reply. "She's in jail." He nudged his glasses higher with the back of his wrist. "Finn doesn't like to talk about her. He said she's a drug addict and cares more about getting high than she does about him."

Dante felt like someone had punched him in the gut. The soda he'd ingested turned sour. No kid deserved an MIA father, but the thought of a mother who favored pills over her own child was reprehensible. "It's a good thing Finn has his uncle."

"Yeah." Elliott set the spoon on the table, then reached for a paper towel to wipe his fingers. "His uncle works weird shifts, but Mom's been letting Finn hang with me when he does. Like this Friday and Saturday night."

Halloween Eve and Halloween. Cops would be on high alert for vandalism and pranks that got out of hand. Hopefully, no one would be stupid enough to camp out in Hickory Chapel Cemetery, like he, Spencer, and Alex Price had done.

"Mom said we can have pizza Friday night. We're gonna stay up late and watch scary movies since you guys are gonna be next door at Jillian's for game night."

Dante was the one who'd contrived the excuse for Tessa. She didn't want to tell her son she was participating in a séance, so Dante had suggested a board game night for adults. In some respects, it wasn't far from the truth. In the late 1800s, séances had become a form of entertainment with people forming "home circles" to communicate with the dead, often gathering around Ouija boards, or trying to produce spirit-rappings.

"Scary movies, huh?" That part surprised him. "Aren't you worried about monsters?"

Elliott crossed to the sink, then turned on the water to wash his hands. "Not the movie kind. They're not real."

"But others are?"

Elliott rolled one shoulder into a shrug. "Finn told me he and the kids he used to hang out with made that stuff up about the cemetery to scare me. He said the folktales about the place aren't really true."

Dante knew otherwise but didn't want Elliott thinking differently. "Maybe you don't need your wishstone anymore."

"Maybe." Elliott switched off the water, then dried his hands on a clean paper towel. "I'm ready to carve the pumpkin. Can we look at your drawings?"

"Sure." Dante grabbed the tablet from the counter and passed it to him. He threw his empty soda bottle into a recycle bin. "Any chance I could borrow your wishstone for a few nights?" He'd been trying to find a way to work around to the subject from the moment he'd arrived. Gut instinct told him the gem had belonged to Gabriel and having something of Vane's during the séance created a better chance of reaching his spirit.

"Sure. I guess so." Elliott tilted his head to stare up at him. "How come you want to borrow it?"

He hated lying but knew he'd only frighten the kid if he told Elliott the truth. "I want to make a few wishes. You said it helped you."

"Uh-huh." Elliott sucked on his bottom lip, his gaze dropping briefly as if giving the matter serious thought. He dug the stone from the pocket of his jeans and stared down at the rough shape in his hands. "A lot of the monsters…they were really the kids at school. They laughed at me, and no one wanted to be my friend."

"I'm sorry, Elliott." Kids could be freaking cruel.

"I guess I don't need this anymore." Elliott extended his hand, offering the stone. "Finn isn't my only friend; he's my best friend. A lot of the other kids talk to me now, and we have fun together." He dropped the stone in Dante's palm. "It brought me luck, but I think I'm supposed to pass it on so someone else can benefit." Elliott studied him with a deliberative manner. "When you're done with it, you have to give it to someone else, okay?"

"Okay." With an inner sigh of relief, Dante fisted his hand around the stone. He knew exactly who he'd give it to—Gabriel Vane, the emerald's original owner.

Chapter 14

October 21, 1799

Gabriel groaned and rolled onto his side. The night air smelled of dog and sweat, the rancid perspiration of men trapped by fear. He forced his hands under him, his palms clotted with blood and dark soil. They'd stripped him of his coat, the biting cold making him shiver. A single blossom of heat pulsed below his heart where his tunic was plastered to his chest by something sticky and wet.

Grunting with effort, he tried to rise. Someone planted a foot against his hip and shoved, thrusting him face-first to the ground. He became conscious of boots ringed around him, the hot breath of a dog as it strained at the end of a rope, the steeple of a bell tower looming overhead.

Hickory Chapel!

Nausea bubbled up from his gut. He was no longer in the woods, far removed from any chance of reaching Vernon Hode. He wasn't afraid to die, but not like this. The sound of multiple spades sinking into the earth made his head spin. *Merciful God in Heaven, not like this.*

Gabriel ran his tongue over his lips. Tried to find his voice in the pitted, torn tissue of his throat. The emerald had shredded his gullet like a straight-edge. "At-Atticus."

His voice was a ragged thread, easily overshadowed by the grunt of labored breathing and the splatter of loose soil, flung against the ground. How many hours had they been working at the task? How many had he lain unconscious? He recalled a grave already half-dug in the rear of the church, internment for the first of the plague victims. No bodies would be buried there now, the spot segregated for him alone.

Struggling to stay alert, he rolled onto his back. The bell tower pinwheeled above him, backlit by icy stars on a stygian sky. Torches flickered beyond the ring of men and dogs, the frenzied jump of flames casting monstrous shadows on the flat chapel walls. Pain made him drift briefly, faces bobbing in and out of his consciousness—Dinah, Jasper, his parents.

He longed for death. Prayed for it. Was pulled back from the edge when someone grabbed his ankles and dragged him closer to his grave. Pebbles, leaves, and crushed hickory nuts prickled his back. The ragged tear below his heart pumped hot blood over cold flesh. Wildly, he looked about for Enoch but couldn't spy him among the ring of somber faces. He hadn't been in the woods either, which left Atticus as his savior.

"You can't do this." His voice was a coarse thread, pockmarked by the hard hitch of his breath. "It's sacrilege. Atticus, you…you defy Jasper's church."

"Do not tell me what I defy!" With a roar of anger, Atticus kicked him in the ribs.

Gabriel grunted and folded in half.

"For the love of God, don't do this."

"You will not speak of our Lord, foul demon." Atticus's tone was ruthless, nearly unrecognizable. "Cyrus. Everett. Put Vane in the grave. I will throw the first shovelful of dirt."

Gabriel's head flopped back when they lifted him, one man grabbing his ankles, the other his arms. The rough handling tore the flesh around his wound and ripped a scream from his throat. Through the poison of terror, he thought he heard someone tramping away.

The open pit gaped below him—seconds only before he was thrown, his body tossed like worthless garbage. He managed to twist mid-air, angling to take the bulk of the impact on his arm, hip, and thigh. Breath rattled between his teeth and pain exploded the length of his side. A ring of somber faces stared down from above, the features of men he'd once called friends contorted by hatred and fear in the torchlight.

Monsters. God save their murderous souls, but they looked like monsters.

Atticus hefted a shovelful of dirt.

"At least kill me first." Gabriel pushed against his dirt prison. The sky reeled as he staggered half upright.

"Your passing will be swifter if you lie down and accept your fate." Atticus shoveled more dirt into the grave. The other men joined him, working in silence, unwilling to meet Gabriel's eyes.

Loose soil rained down on him, the spades singing a death dirge. The prison was narrow, the dirt coarse. Clods of mud and stone pelted his head and back, driving him to his knees. The barrage was violent and swift. As if by exerting themselves, the men could finish quickly and forget their shameful deed.

Blood dribbled into Gabriel's eyes. He clawed at the sides of the pit in an effort to escape the brutal pummeling. A chunk of stone struck his temple and sent him sprawling. Sheer terror spiked into his head. It couldn't end like this, suffocated by cold soil. Buried alive.

Get above the dirt. Find a way out.

He tried to scrabble upright but toppled to his side. Soil rained down in a deluge, each blow siphoning breath from his lungs. Mounds of earth piled higher—covering his face, pinning his legs and hips. His heart labored, thumping terror into his skull. Weakly, he tried to writhe free, but there was little strength left in muscles cramped by pain and ravaged by fever. Pinpricks of light exploded behind his eyes. Somewhere up above, one of his killers pulled the cord in the church tower.

The last sound Gabriel heard was the mournful toll of a bell.

* * * *

Present Day

Clive walked to the pound to look at the dogs. He could have taken his car, but it was only a few miles by foot and he needed to think. Warren had told him he could bring a pup home next week. They had plans to check out the pub crawl tomorrow night, and Warren said it wouldn't be good to leave a dog at home.

He thought about getting a pup anyway and skipping the crawl but figured a few days wouldn't hurt. Besides, it would be cool to wear a mask. Warren said the bash was going to be a cross between a Halloween party and a Carnivale celebration with food and entertainment. Lots of people would be there.

Pausing at a cross street, Clive waited for a green minivan to pass before he walked to the other side. On the main road, a bus chugged by, spewing a puff of exhaust. A panel on the side advertised the masquerade, showing a woman in a sequined blue mask with elaborate plumes of feathers. It made him wonder if the devil mask he usually wore for the annual Fiend Fest was going to cut it.

With a mental shrug, he stuffed his hands in the pockets of his hoodie. Too late to worry about it now. As long as he could get burgers and beer, he'd be happy.

He picked up his pace, passing a few people walking in the opposite direction. Mostly business types on lunch break from a nearby corporate center, a few with cell phones glued to their ears.

He could never sit behind a desk. Not just because he wasn't smart enough—the boredom would get to him. He'd taken the day off from his job driving a delivery truck for Hode Development so he could spend a few hours at the pound. As he got closer, his feet dragged. What if he couldn't find a dog that looked like Bodine? What if he did and Kirk just shot it up like that poor stray when they were kids?

Clive's stomach flip-flopped. Spying a bench beneath an oak tree, he sat down and stared moodily at the passing traffic. On the opposite side of the street, a guy walked a golden retriever. The dog trotted on its leash with its head high, tongue lolling happily from its mouth. Damn it, he wanted a pup that would do that, too. Why did Kirk have to ruin everything?

Because the bastard's bad news.

He should have never given his brother's phone number to Yancy. Thinking about the goof made his stomach clench tighter.

Eventually, he'd have to work up the nerve to tell Warren what he'd done. Warren would call him a dumb ass, then tell him to forget it when Clive's feelings got hurt. Warren groused at him a lot, but he looked after him, too. Kirk just looked after Kirk.

Clive dug his cell from his pocket. The cool air made him sniffle. He dragged a sleeve under his nose and hooked his ankles beneath the bench. The sun was bright—it looked like a glob of butterscotch candy—but autumn was starting to take hold. Maybe he'd stop somewhere for a hot apple cider and piece of pumpkin pie after he finished at the pound. In the meantime, he had to do something about Kirk. He kept thinking about the kid Warren had mentioned, the one who'd fallen into the grave they'd dug up.

Switching to his texts, he found Kirk's contact information and thumbed out a message: *did Yancy call u*

It took a few minutes for Kirk's reply to ping back. Clive used the time to watch the guy with the golden, noting how the dog offered a friendly nose to anyone who stopped. When he was done, he'd hike across the street and say hello.

After a while, an emoji thumbs-up flashed on his screen.

Clive keyed in a new text: *what did he want*

Not important

was it about a stone

Why

about a kid

Several seconds passed. Finally, Kirk's reply came through.

Don't worry about it

An ill feeling washed over Clive. He squirmed on the seat as his thumbs flew over the screen.

don't do nuthin stupid

Like??

mill street

This time the delay was longer. Clive chewed the inside of his cheek, head bowed over his phone. Finally, a ping followed by Kirk's message.

Grabbing lunch. Later

Clive slumped against the bench. He thought of the bell he'd heard the night he and Warren dug up Vane's bones. Something bad was going to happen. He was sure of it.

Worriedly, he rubbed his lizard tattoo. His totem animal would protect him, but what about Warren? What about Kirk?

Kirk had killed Bodine, and he'd killed that man on Mill Street, but he wouldn't really harm a kid.

Sweat broke out on the back of Clive's neck.

Shit.

Maybe the best outcome for everyone would be if something bad really *did* happen to Kirk.

* * * *

Dante arrived at Jillian's brownstone before any of the other sitters on Friday night. He carried several duffle bags inside then declined her offer of wine. Needing something to take the edge from her nerves, she sipped a glass of Riesling as she watched him set up.

"Your table is perfect because it's oval." He covered the surface with a dark navy cloth then brushed a hand over the fabric to smooth away wrinkles. "Ovals are conducive to communication with the spirit world. Rectangles and squares—any kind of rigid lines—create barriers."

"I suppose that makes sense." She hoped her nervousness didn't show. Lately, she felt like a rubber band, stretched in different directions. Madison had been discharged to a rehab center that morning, and Jillian had spent the day getting her sister settled. She'd taken her usual evening walk with

Blizzard, then ate a premade salad she'd picked up from a local deli. Dante had showed up just after seven thirty.

He wore all black tonight—jeans with a chambray shirt, his hair secured in a tight ponytail. The only spot of color to his clothing was the gold medallion looped around his neck. She'd noticed it before but had never asked about its meaning. Given they were about to hold a séance, it seemed an appropriate time.

"Is that a religious medal?" She motioned to the glimmer of gold visible beneath the open collar of his shirt.

"The Archangel Michael." He set a bag on the table and unzipped the top. "It belonged to my father. I'm rarely without it, especially when conducting a séance."

She didn't like the sound of that. "Should I be concerned?"

"There's nothing to be afraid of." He pulled several squat candles from the bag and set them on the table. Blizzard watched from a spot on the floor near the doors to the deck. "I always begin any séance with a prayer. Saint Michael protects against darkness and demons."

"And monsters." She said the words for him.

"Try not to think about the cemetery. Summoning works better if the energy is positive."

"I'll do my best." It was a tall order considering the hypersensitive state of her nerves.

He took his time setting up, placing various items in different corners of the room—a basket with chunks of fresh bread, another with herbs and autumn flowers, several pillar candles of differing heights.

Jillian nibbled on a thumbnail. "I never realized how many things were needed for a séance."

"Not all mediums work the same way."

"So, you're officially a medium?"

"More or less." Dante drew the drapes over the French doors, blotting the ambient light from outside. "The bread, herbs, and flowers are to make the spirit feel welcome. The candles are for us. So we can see."

"Why can't we just leave the lights on?" Blizzard picked up on her jittery nerves and walked closer. She ruffled his fur distractedly.

"Most séances are conducted in the dark. Light is used for protection in the event things go south." Dante unzipped a second bag and set two items on the table. A handheld spotlight and a small tape recorder. He lifted the spotlight. "If there's a problem—if a spirit turns hostile—I'll use this to flood the room. That's a signal for you to switch on every available light you can."

"Now you're scaring me."

"Don't worry." His smile was reassuring. "Everything will be fine."

She dusted her hands against her arms to ward off an inner chill. "What's the tape recorder for?"

"Sometimes spirits interact on a level we can't hear. If that happens, I'll be able to pick up sounds on the audio playback we might otherwise miss."

She breathed a little easier given how calmly he explained everything. He'd conducted séances before and clearly knew what he was doing.

Tessa joined them around eight forty-five, and Sherre showed up a few minutes later. Jillian made introductions, then the group took their seats at the table. Dante went over the same details he'd shared with Jillian. When he was done, he placed a rough-cut green stone, a clear plastic baggie containing dirt, and a small handbell on the table.

Sherre zoned in on the items immediately. "What are those?"

"Something to connect us to Gabriel Vane." He picked up the stone. "I can't say for certain, but I think this belonged to Vane and was probably buried with him."

"How did you end up with it?"

"My son found it." Tessa twisted a silver ring on her hand. Jillian couldn't tell if the action was prompted by nerves or habit. "He was the boy—"

"Who fell into the grave. I remember now." Sherre's gaze swiveled back to Dante. "What about the dirt? Did that come from Vane's grave, too?"

He nodded. "I went to Hickory Chapel Cemetery and collected it earlier tonight. A spirit will naturally home in on soil from their burial place."

Jillian's palms grew sweaty. The conversation was starting to sound like something from a B horror movie, and those always ended badly with the characters picked off one by one. She reached for Blizzard, who sat beside her chair, and rubbed his fur. Even the husky was on alert as if he sensed something unusual taking place. "What about the bell?" It looked like an antique, something a teacher might have used in the days of one-room schoolhouses to call the class to order.

Dante fingered the handle. "Despite what you might have seen in the movies, spirits rarely communicate vocally. It's more likely Vane will pick something to use as a channel. Handbells go back to the earliest days of spiritualism and allow the dead to converse through a series of yes or no answers."

"Like ring the bell if you can hear us. That kind of thing?" For someone who hadn't wanted to attend a séance, Sherre zeroed in on the nuances quickly.

"Exactly. When I give the signal, Jillian will switch off the lights, then we'll join hands. It's possible nothing will happen tonight, but if it does, don't break the circle."

Tessa twisted her ring with greater force. "What could happen?" Definitely nerves. Jillian's own felt like they were going to crawl up through her throat.

"Any number of things." Dante looked at each of them in turn. "The cues might be visual or audible. The temperature could drop, the candles could flicker, or something could move. It's possible you might even see a manifestation."

A ghost.

Jillian reminded herself Vane would not want to hurt them. He couldn't possibly. Not after all she and her family had done to keep his memory alive through the centuries—what she was currently doing in an effort to see his remains returned to his resting place.

She glanced down at Blizzard, noting the watchfulness in his eyes as he gazed up at her. "Will Blizzard be all right?" She could take him upstairs and lock him in her bedroom, but he was a stabilizing presence and she needed that tonight.

"He'll be fine. If anything, he'll sense Vane's presence before we do. Animals are more in tune with the spirit world than humans." Dante opened the baggie and spilled dirt onto the table. He placed the gem beside the small mound, then centered the bell higher above both, creating a triangle. "One final warning before we begin. I'm going to try to reach Gabriel, but there's a chance something else could answer."

Sherre shifted uneasily. "I don't like the sound of that."

"It's always a risk when communicating with the dead. If anything goes wrong, I'll break the circle and flood the room with light." He tapped the spotlight beside his chair. "If that happens, everyone draw back from the table and switch on as many lights as you can."

"Dante." Tessa sent him a worried glance. "I know you've done this before, but—"

"Everything will be okay, Tess." Dante covered her hand with his. "I won't let anything happen to you or anyone else in this room."

She breathed deeply and nodded, seeming to draw confidence from his assurance.

"Jillian." Dante signaled for her to douse the lights.

She stood and flipped the switches, swathing them in blackness but for a few patchy halos of candlelight. An amber corona spread on the table where a single squat pillar provided illumination. Jillian returned to her seat, fighting to banish thoughts of night demons and ghouls.

Keep the energy positive.

It was Halloween Eve. A time for pumpkin carving, glow-in-the-dark spiders, and harmless pranks. Heart pounding, she joined hands with Dante on the left, Sherre on her right. Tessa finished the circle, her eyes liquid black pools in the darkness.

Bowing his head, Dante recited a prayer for protection. Jillian added her own silent plea and imagined Tessa doing the same. Of them all, Sherre seemed unfazed, as if she was merely killing time.

"Spirits, welcome." Dante sat straight, his voice firm. "We come before you to communicate with the ancestor of one who is present. We have formed this circle to reach Gabriel Vane. There are gifts in the room, and our hearts are free of negative energy." He waited a pulsebeat. Two. "Gabriel Vane, can you hear me? If you are with us, give us a sign of your presence."

It took concentrated effort for Jillian to resist holding her breath. Her gaze swept the room, darting into the dark recesses untouched by candlelight. While her nerves were strung taut, she sensed calm, even skepticism from Sherre. Could the detective's cynicism impact the circle? Second dragged into eerie second. Despite the roominess of her home, Jillian felt abruptly claustrophobic.

"Gabriel Vane, are you here?" Dante's voice was measured and cool.

"Nothing's going to happen," Sherre muttered.

He sent her a sharp glance. A warning not to speak.

Sherre rolled her eyes, and Jillian began to fear she'd made a mistake by inviting her.

Just that quickly, a change came over her. An otherworldly presence brushed against her mind, the touch puzzling, yet strangely familiar.

"Gabriel?" Her voice was overly loud in the stillness. Beside her, Blizzard stood with his head and tail lowered. Fur bristled on the back of his neck as a low rumble built in his throat. She wanted to tell him to sit, but her mouth had gone dry. Fear knifed through her as swift and sharp as a honed blade. Before she could catch her breath, the temperature plummeted. Cold air blew through the room and sent the candlelight into a chaotic dance of flickering flame.

Tessa uttered a strangled sound and tried to swivel in her seat. "What's happening?" A note of hysteria crept into her voice.

"Maintain the circle." Dante's order was firm, but his gaze narrowed. "Jillian, what do you see?"

She hadn't taken her eyes from a spot by the glass doors. "A patch of shadow. Utter blackness." Her gaze swiveled between the other three. "Can't you see it?"

"Who is it?" Dante's question supplied her answer.

"I...I don't know." She wanted to believe the phantom was Gabriel, but the presence was remote, merely an impression on the fringe of her mind.

"Ask who it is."

If only it were that easy. "How?"

"In your head. Use your empathic abilities."

Fear had made her close herself off. It was one matter to open herself to the feelings of others, but to do the same with a spirit who had crossed the bridge to Summerland made her blood run cold. Blizzard butted against her leg, his presence infusing her with strength. He'd stood beside her—protector and companion—through the worst moments with Madison. It only made sense he'd do the same now.

Bolstered by the husky's loyalty, Jillian opened her mind. Within seconds she was struck by a hodgepodge of impressions, the images whirling past so quickly it was like watching a movie on fast-forward. Through it all, a single aura feathered her mind. "It's him. Gabriel Vane." She heard his voice as if he spoke inside her head. "He says he was drawn by the stone."

Jillian's gaze dropped to the gem on the table. The cold was growing, slithering up her back along with a creeping sense of terror. There was something else in the room. A malignant force that lurked beyond the fringe of darkness. She imagined it oozing over the floor, black and oily, inching closer.

"He says we must be careful." Gabriel projected urgency into her thoughts. "The stone is powerful. It's meant to bind soulmates together and offer protection, but in the wrong hands, it can also destroy." If only she understood its properties.

Blizzard back-stepped and barked, the sound high-pitched and eerie.

"The gem belonged to Dinah Crowe." The face of a pretty blond-haired woman filled her mind, chased by a torrent of warmth. Gabriel had loved her. Lost her.

Atticus Crowe's daughter.

Jillian closed her heart to his sadness, trying to focus on the stone. *Please, Gabriel, help us.* Cold spots popped like balloons around the table. "He's restless. Angry."

"Because someone violated his grave?" Dante's voice anchored her in the present.

"Yes—No." She felt herself floating, pulled to a distance past. "Not now, but a long time ago. He couldn't escape." Darkness swept over her, the odor of tightly packed earth and stone filling her head. "They—oh, God!" Tears flooded her eyes. "They buried him alive."

Gabriel's breath catches, and for a moment there is only lightness and air. Then the earth closes around him, his senses clogged by leaf-mold and the sour stench of his fear. A keening builds in his ears. Muted at first, it climbs in volume, an unholy clamor unlike any he has ever heard. It resonates with thunder, the violent snake-kiss of lightning.

Death is coming for him.

He fights against the restriction of his mud tomb, but for every fraction he gains, the sludge grows heavier, pushing him deeper into a dank grave. Dirt clogs his mouth, blocks his throat. Starved for air, his lungs balloon against his ribcage.

Contract, expand again.

He breathes in dirt and tries to scream. His mouth is full of mud and the cobweb-like netting of tiny stones. In his mind, his cry rolls above the treetops, over the bell tower, fading into the village he once called home. He is beyond escape, betrayed by men he imagined friends. Their treachery is a knife like no other.

Death sidles closer, oiled and slick with raven feathers.

Gabriel lashes out with every waning trace of strength, but the battle has been decided. His eyes roll into his head. Maddeningly, consciousness remains, in mockery of his terror.

Somewhere far above in a place he cannot touch, fire forks across the sky. Clouds gather—tattered gray vessels speared by pale icicles of moonlight. The sight is dazzling, his fear stifled by awe. There is a strange sense of peace with the fire of Heaven singing him to sleep. Mud and earth strangle the last quiver of breath from his lungs.

He thinks of Dinah. Imagines her arms reaching out to him. He should feel hatred for the men who have brought him to this end, but death takes him quickly, casting him into the silt of the underworld.

His consciousness fades as the chapel bell tolls his passing.

With a gasp for air, Jillian jerked back to the present.

"What did you see?" Sherre stared at her wide-eyed.

"I—" Her voice cracked, her mind still pulsing with Gabriel's thoughts and feelings. Heart pounding, she glanced across the room, but the patch of shadow was gone. Something dark and meaty had slithered into its place.

As her eyes touched the shape, the table jumped and jittered, dancing like someone shook it by the legs.

"What's happening?" Tessa tried to draw back, but Jillian clung to her hand.

The bell upended and rolled onto its side. It swayed back and forth in a small arc, the striker lying dead against the inside curve. Impossibly, the air reverberated with a *brang-clang, brang-clang* as if an invisible hand swung the bell up and down. Gooseflesh broke out on Jillian's arms. A small whimper escaped her throat.

"Dante!" Tessa's cry bordered on panic.

Blizzard snarled—a challenge so feral, Jillian momentarily forgot her fear. She would have grabbed his collar but was afraid of breaking the circle. The table rocked again, and she screamed.

Something crouched in the corner. A mass of sinew and bone. Misshapen and squat, it possessed no true form but appeared scraped from the ilk of nightmares. Red eyes glowed in a skull the cold white of cadaver flesh. Jillian tried to look away but couldn't tear her gaze from the monstrosity. This thing—an abomination of bloated appendages and pasty skin—couldn't possibly be Gabriel Vane.

She whimpered again, and the sound propelled Blizzard into action. With a snarl, he bolted for the corner where the dead thing dragged itself across the floor. Wind spun a cyclone through the room, snuffing the candles in a single, powerful gust.

"Break the circle!" Dante yelled.

"Blizzard!" Jillian raced for the lights. "Stay back, Blizzard!"

Her hand smacked down on the switch at the same moment Dante released a blast of light. The husky gave a strangled yap, followed by a high-pitched whine. The sound catapulted Jillian's heart into her throat. Somewhere behind her, she heard Tessa sobbing.

"Blizzard!" Jillian flew across the room, then dropped to her knees, wrapping her arms around the husky's neck. He pressed into her quaking arms, his agitation nearly tangible.

"Shh, it's okay." She buried her face in his fur.

"What the hell just happened?" Sherre's voice cracked like a whipcord.

Jillian looked from the dog to the detective, who was on her feet, her normally coppery skin blanched the color of egg cream. She didn't seem frightened so much as angry. At the table, Tessa sat sideways in her chair, wiping away tears.

Dante stood behind her, rubbing her shoulder as he studied the room. "My guess is Gabriel Vane just happened."

"But that's not all." Jillian thought of the misshapen thing in the corner. The oily substance she'd imagined oozing over the floor, and the winter blast of cold air. "There was something else here, too." She met Dante's gaze and saw he understood.

"What?" Sherre prompted.

Jillian knotted her fingers in Blizzard's fur. "Monsters." She felt cold to the bone, her voice barely a whisper. "There were monsters here, too."

* * * *

Jillian tugged the quilt closer around her shoulders, but the chill had settled deep. She sat on the sofa in the living room, sipping the cup of hot tea Dante made for her after Sherre and Tessa departed. Tessa had been anxious to return home to check on Elliott and Finn after the unsettling events of the night, and Sherre left—if not a staunch advocate of the curse—at least a firm believer in ghosts. She promised to devote more energy to recovering Gabriel's remains.

"How are you doing?" Dante joined her on the couch.

"Cold." She set her tea on the coffee table and offered a weak smile.

Earlier, he'd packed up his supplies and removed every trace of the tools he'd used during the séance, going so far as to carry the duffle bags out to his 4Runner. Jillian was sure he did it to appease her. All three women had been shaken by what happened during the séance, but only Jillian had seen the malignant creatures crawl from the darkness.

Burrowing deeper beneath the quilt, she tried to block the memory. The séance had left her shaken enough to switch every lamp in the living room to full wattage. She'd done the same with other lights on the first floor and even the second. When she slept tonight—*if* she slept at all—it would be with every lamp in the house blazing like a sun gone nova. The brighter, the better.

Dante seemed to sense her anxiety. "Just cold?"

"And scared." She wasn't afraid to admit the truth. Blizzard pressed against her legs, and she sank her fingers into the husky's fur. "What if one of the things I saw tonight comes back? What if they're still here?"

Dante grasped her hand. "I promise you, nothing is here."

"How can you be so sure?"

"Because I did a cleansing while you were here with Blizzard." His thumb tracked over her knuckles. "I dispelled all negative energy and residual darkness. The things you saw tonight were probably from Hickory Chapel Cemetery. A sampling of the evils Vane is supposed to protect against."

"But I have ancestors buried in the cemetery. And now those things know about me. Where to find me." She'd never felt so vulnerable or afraid. The idea of night creatures bringing chaos to the town and causing deaths had been alarming before, but even when Madison had been struck down, Jillian imagined herself immune.

"Maybe this will protect you." Taking her hand, Dante dropped Dinah's emerald into her palm. He folded her fingers over the edges. "Until we can return this to its rightful place, you should keep it. You're descended from the same line as Dinah."

Jillian's stomach seesawed as she gazed down at the stone. "I can't believe Atticus and the others buried him alive."

"I'm sorry you saw that." Dante looped an arm around her shoulders and drew her closer.

Thankful for the added warmth, she nestled against this side. Emotions she understood, but the spirit world was beyond her grasp. "Did you pick up anything on the tape recorder?"

"Just static."

Jillian sighed. "Then we're no closer to learning where Gabriel's remains are hidden. All we gained is the knowledge the gemstone Elliott found really did belong to him, and—" She stumbled over the words. "The manner of his death."

"It confirms our suspicions about Atticus Crowe and why nothing good comes from Wickham."

She angled her head to look at him. "You said the place corrupted your father."

His mouth tightened. "I have to believe that. It's the only thing that makes sense."

"Then it's probably corrupted Yancy, too. If he really wants the stone, and he knows Elliott has it—or *thinks* he does—he might be willing to do something crazy. The gem belonged to Dinah, and according to your grandmother's notes, Yancy is descended from Fern, Dinah's sister. Yancy must have discovered how powerful the stone is."

Dante worked his jaw as if mulling over the connections. "It all comes back to Crowe."

"What do you mean?"

"Everyone's linked through him. Gabriel was in love with Dinah. Your line is descended through Crowe's oldest son, Enoch, and Yancy is descended through Fern."

"Why is that important?"

"I'm not sure." He drew back, then stood and paced away from her. Stopping before the window, he flicked the drapes aside. For several seconds he considered the darkness, then turned and slid his fingers into the front pockets of his jeans. She could almost see the wheels turning in his head. "Before any of this happened, you thought Atticus Crowe was a good man."

She'd never been so wrong. "I know differently now. He buried Gabriel alive."

"What else did he do?"

"Isn't that tragedy enough?"

He waved her aversion aside. "Crowe was influential. Persuasive enough to make Gabriel's neighbors turn against him. Not just ostracize, but kill him—in one of the most horrific ways possible. To have that kind of sway, he must have been powerful."

"I don't understand what you're getting at."

"If Crowe had that much authority, why doesn't the town carry his name?"

Jillian frowned. Her heartbeat quickened. Through all their reasoning, they'd overlooked one critical element. She suddenly understood what Dante wanted her to see.

"Where was Vernon Hode when Gabriel was killed?"

Chapter 15

Sweat plastered Atticus Crowe's hair to his brow. He smelled of mud and grass and the grime that worked beneath the weathered cracks in his skin. Burial was dirty labor, not for the faint of heart. He tossed his shovel aside, then worked at rolling down his sleeves.

"Do you think he's dead?" Cyrus Herman stared at Vane's grave.

"Of course he's dead." The jittery tone of Cyrus's voice chafed Atticus's nerves. "He's been without air far longer than any man can hold his breath."

"He stopped screaming over ten minutes ago." Thaddeus Keel spat a wad of chewing tobacco onto the soil. Nothing jumpy or indecisive about the coon hound master. "It's done. We should go home." He stomped to the hickory tree where he'd leashed his dogs.

"Agreed." Atticus respected Keel's bluntness. The rest of the group could do with toughening up now that the deed was finished.

"My gut's off." Cyrus held his stomach with one hand and used the other to massage the ropy skin around his neck. In the torchlight, his face looked pasty, mottled with shadow.

"Then go home to your wife and have her make you a tonic. The rest of you tend to your sick." The thought of Dinah and Jasper lifeless in their beds made Atticus grind his teeth. His children would be the first to receive Vane's protection when their bodies were set in the ground. "Two of my children are dead, but yours still live. We did the right thing."

"How can you be so sure?" Ira Blake wiped grungy hands over his tunic. "I've never killed anyone before."

"You think the rest of us have? He was a demon, not a man."

"Doesn't matter." Keel ripped the restraining rope for his dogs from the tree. "It's too late to be second-guessing the deed."

Cyrus staggered and dropped to his knees. Atticus heard retching. A few of the men shuffled their feet. Bowed their heads and mumbled among themselves.

"We must tell no one what we've done," Andrew Whitley said.

Others agreed.

"Fools!" Atticus thrust between them. Their remorse sickened him. "Have you forgotten that Vane brought this wretched malady to our town? That he cursed us and watched our loved ones die? How many have we lost—friends and neighbors who even now wait to be buried in the ground we have sanctified through his sacrifice?"

"But he loved your daughter." Climbing to his feet, Cyrus wiped a shaky hand over his mouth. "Maybe we were wrong. Jasper was his closest friend."

"And he killed them!" Atticus spat the words with all the hatred he could muster.

"Your son, Enoch, wouldn't even follow us into the woods." Everett Donner's accusation was wobbly, his skin sweat-slicked and pale. Visibly unsteady, he glanced among the group. "Wait a minute. Where did Farley go?"

"What did you say?" Ira Blake's voice lurched up an octave. He swiveled his head from side to side, sweeping his gaze between the trees and the chapel. "Farley's gone?"

"He can't have left." Whitley clearly didn't want to believe one of them had deserted.

"I should have done the same!" What little blood remained drained from Cyrus's face. "Farley must have crept off while we were...were..." Bending double, he dry heaved.

"Find your spine, man!" Atticus resisted the urge to strike him. "All of you! I have never seen such a group of cowardly, weak-willed men."

"I take exception to that." Thaddeus Keel eyed him across the circle, his features cut from granite.

"That does not apply to you, Thaddeus. At least one of you recognizes the demon's curse is broken. The sickness will pass, and no more will die. That is all any of you should concern yourselves with."

Cyrus shook his head. "I was blinded by fear. We should have gotten Vernon Hode's opinion before taking action."

Damn the bastard. "Hode is in mourning." Damn Hode, too. "There was no time."

"You should have made time." The crunch of leaves underfoot preceded Vernon Hode's presence in the circle. Torchlight flickered off hair white as snow, brows the black of printer's ink. Hode had two inches on Atticus, but his demeanor made him seem taller still. His gaze raked over each man in turn. Even Thaddeus Keel looked away.

Atticus stiffened. "You have no business here."

"Your son has made it my business."

Atticus's gaze swept past Hode to Enoch, who lingered on the fringe of the circle. Damn the boy for his betrayal. He must have run to Hode like a frightened cur, not man enough to stomach the justice Atticus meted. "You disappoint me, Enoch."

"Where is Gabriel?" Eyes wild, Enoch swiveled his head, looking everywhere but at the mound of dark earth segregated behind the chapel. As if he *couldn't* look there.

"You know where he is." Atticus stabbed a finger at the grave.

Hode stepped forward, his mouth a grim slash. "You killed him."

"We buried him." Keel spoke from his place by the hickory tree. One hand gripping the rope that restrained his three hounds, he held the dogs back. "Someone knifed him in the woods not far from your place. We saw to it he received a proper burial."

"In the dark of night with no clergy or coffin?"

"It was Atticus." Cyrus folded an arm over his middle. He heaved bile onto the ground, then wiped his mouth with his sleeve. "Atticus knifed him, and we let it happen. We believed he was possessed by Satan."

"Shut up, Cyrus." If Hode hadn't been between them, Atticus would have struck the other man down.

"It's no good." Cyrus's words grated like gravel. "What we did was wrong. Farley was right to leave when he did."

"The tanner was here?" Hode directed his question to Cyrus.

"Aye." The other man bobbed his head. "He left before we put Vane in the grave. The boy was still alive when we buried him." Fat tears tracked through the grime on his face. "He screamed for us to stop, but we shoveled dirt onto him until he had no voice left. No air. Until he was quiet."

Groaning, Enoch staggered toward the chapel and dropped to his knees. Lips moving soundlessly, he clasped his hands behind his neck and began rocking back and forth. Back and forth.

Cyrus webbed a hand over his face. "God, forgive me. What have I done?"

"You ask forgiveness now?" Hode's lip curled with derision. "After you willingly bloodied your hands with Gabriel's death? After you defiled the hallowed ground meant for our loved ones when their time has ended? Your boy, Seamus, is only twelve. What if he were older, Cyrus? What if that were *your* son in the grave?" He speared a finger at the dark mound of soil.

"Enough." Atticus had heard all he intended. "You have no right to stand in judgment. You have been locked away in mourning while we were left to deal with the Endling."

"Enoch told me Gabriel killed the beast."

"Aye. Hiram Blum and Jasper had a hand as well. You know that."

"Only because you defied my mandate that no one should set foot on my property until my time of mourning had passed. You arrived with news on the very eve the Endling was killed—badgering your way into my home, puffed up and proud, braying about Jasper's hand in the killing."

"The boy stood his part. Why should I not spread the news?"

"You boasted because you thought it would stand favorably in my eyes. How long have you hoped for a marriage between my Abigail and your Enoch? Do you think I am blind, Atticus? It has been your ambition to join our families over the village, but it is not power I crave. Nor have I ever."

"It only makes sense for us—strong as we are—to oversee the others."

"America left that mode of thinking behind when they broke from their English masters. These men are neighbors, not subjects."

A few shuffled uncertainly. Thaddeus Keel spat in the dirt. "Is that the measure of it, then, Crowe?"

"No." Atticus felt his control slipping. "Abigail and Enoch should be wed because they care for each other."

"You're wrong, Father." Enoch stood and approached on wobbly legs. "I visit the Hode residence because I wish to court their maidservant, Nellie Renault."

The laundress? How could he have been so blind—his son in love with a mere servant? He was sure the color drained from his face. Nellie Renault was the daughter of a French Canadian trader and a seamstress. The family barely had two coins to rub together.

"Now you see the mistakes you have made?" Hode's voice held challenge.

"It does not matter." He would confront Enoch later. No son of his would marry so poorly. "Vane brought the plague upon us." He stared at Hode. "In your mourning, you did not witness the deaths of those who passed from the sickness. The ailment shows no discernment between healthy and weak, young or old. Dinah and Jasper were both struck down."

A flicker of pain crossed Hode's face. "I am sorry for your loss, Atticus."

"I do not want your sympathy. I have saved our village through Vane's death. While you stayed huddled in your house, mourning because of some antiquated religious code, *I* ensured the curse was broken."

"No." Lips thinning in a hard line, Hode shook his head. "I'm afraid you are sadly mistaken."

* * * *

Present Day

Kirk Porter took a final drag from his cigarette then tossed the butt over the side of the jon boat. The water looked black and oil-slick, patchy with globs of gold like the moon had barfed. Fortunately, there was enough cloud cover for the small boat to move undetected through the shadows. He kept the throttle low, the running lights off. It was cold as shit near three in the morning, but the bitter air went with the territory. So did the reek of weed-rot and motor fuel.

According to Yancy, his lazy-ass brothers had been the ones to steal the bones from Hickory Chapel Cemetery. It might have even been them getting paid to dump the moldy things if Warren hadn't balked about roughing up a kid. Before Kirk took the job, Yancy wanted him to ditch the bones.

A test.

Like he was going to back out because it was a kid. Screw that.

Good thing he knew a guy, who knew a guy, who knew a guy. Toss in some meth—a chance for repeat business—along with a C-note, and suddenly he had a boat for the night.

He toed the sack at his feet, wondering how the guy had met his end in the first place. Didn't matter. He'd been chucked in the ground centuries ago.

"Hope you don't mind the change of scenery, dude. You're going in the drink."

He already knew where he'd ditch his cargo. The same spot he'd dumped the knife he used to kill Boyd Hewitt. Who would have thought the waters around the Hode estate would make such a good dumping ground?

Grinning, he popped a beer and raised a toast to Collin Hode. Hode's mother had named their elaborate manor home Amethyst Hall while still married to Leland. That marriage had gone belly-up last summer. Now it was just Hode and his stuck-up bitch mother living in the sprawling mansion. Both would have hit the sack hours ago. Even better, the place squatted in the middle of the Chinkwe River, reachable only by private road from the North Bridge or by water. No one ventured close without an invitation, especially not from the river side. Which was why it was so perfect to get rid of unwanted garbage.

Kirk eyed the sack. "Nothing personal."

The boat puttered past Amethyst Hall, the mansion hidden by trees. Slow going, but he was almost there. A little farther out, he could anchor and heave the bag over the side. The river bottom was pocketed with holes in that spot, cavities deep enough there was no chance of Vane's remains washing up on shore. He'd added extra weight to be on the safe side, but if the bones did eventually surface, so what? Yancy was in the clear.

Biding his time, Kirk glanced across the river where a series of faceless buildings jutted against the sky—the south end of River Road. Pole lamps lined the walking path by the water, but the strip was mostly dark.

The kid lived in one of the brownstones at the far end. He'd already scoped out the location. Half the town was going to be at the masquerade pub thing tomorrow night, which meant there was a good chance the kid could be alone. Either way, it would be Halloween. Between the crawl and the usual Hell Night vandalism, the cops would be scattered thin.

Piece of cake.

Kirk chugged his beer.

＊ ＊ ＊ ＊

Elliott rolled onto his stomach, thrusting an arm beneath his pillow. It was almost three in the morning and he couldn't sleep. Either from the chocolate pumpkins and candied popcorn he and Finn had scarfed while watching *The Sixth Sense,* or from the idea of seeing dead people. He wasn't sure which. The movie gave him the creeps—even though he'd seen it before and knew about the twist ending—but he hadn't told Finn.

When his mom came home that evening, she'd seemed on edge, switching on every light in the house. He hadn't really minded after the movie but asked her if something was wrong. She'd brushed him off, saying she had a headache. Before going to bed, she'd double-checked the locks on the front door, then left the hallway lamp burning. If Finn thought her behavior odd, he never said anything.

Elliott flopped onto his back. From the top bunk, the glow-in-the-dark stars on the ceiling were so close he could almost touch them. On the adjacent wall, the mural his grandmother paid to have installed emitted soft pinpricks of light where the planets of the solar system orbited the sun. Finn declared it far cooler than the drab bisque paint of his uncle's apartment, complaining his room had little character.

Elliott decided Hode's Hill wasn't so bad even if his father had ditched him. School was looking up now that he and Finn were friends and plenty of other kids accepted him. Lacing his hands on his stomach, he stared up at the ceiling. *Star light, star bright.* Sometimes sleep wasn't all it was cracked up to be.

The curtains on the window were open, swept to the side, inviting ambient light onto the floor. Even though the moon was only a quarter full, the thought of stargazing drew him.

Slipping from bed, he grabbed his glasses from the nightstand, then padded barefoot to the window. Traffic was nonexistent on the street below, a stray set of headlights passing in the distance over the South Bridge. The Chinkwe River cut a black ribbon between shores overlooked by a sprawling mass on the horizon.

Amethyst Hall.

He fingered the telescope by the window. Several times, he swiveled the lens between the thickets of trees, trying to catch a glimpse of the mansion. Each time, he gained nothing but an eyeful of branches and leaves.

Looking toward the sky, Elliott angled the telescope up toward the moon.

"Hey, what are you doing?" Finn thrust his blankets aside and pushed from the bottom bunk.

Elliott glanced over his shoulder. "I couldn't sleep, so I thought I'd fiddle with my telescope."

Yawning, Finn knuckled an eye. "Anything good out there?"

"Just the moon. Wanna see?"

"Sure." Finn stepped close, peering through the viewfinder when Elliott directed. He gave a low whistle. "Cool. I might have to ask my uncle for one of these."

"That'd be great. We could stargaze together. Um—unless you think that's dumb."

"No way. It's great having someone who likes the same things I do. Rodney and Troy never wanted to talk about space or UFOs. I just wish I knew more."

"It's easy. I'll show you." Elliott angled the telescope for a better view, then pointed out different craters and terrain markers. It would have been better with a full moon, but Finn didn't seem to mind.

After a while, Finn stepped back. "Do you ever look at other things? Planets and stuff?"

"Sure. When the viewing's good." Elliott thought about mentioning what months made for the best observing but realized there was something that might impress Finn more. "I look at other things, too."

"Yeah? Like what?"

"Amethyst Hall." From the time he'd first heard about the place, he'd wanted to catch a glimpse of the mansion. "I can't really see anything though. There's too many trees."

"Let's try." Finn angled the telescope down from the sky. With his eye glued to the viewfinder, he swept the barrel left, then right. "Hey, check this out."

"What?" Elliott knew he couldn't have spied anything. It was too dark, and Amethyst Hall was buried behind a fence of pines, oaks, and sycamores.

"Holy shit!" Finn's voice lurched up an octave. "There's some guy on the river dumping a sack over the side of his boat."

Elliott crowded close to peer through the viewfinder. "Something's wrong. That boat has no running lights."

"Don't be a moron. There's no running lights because the guy doesn't want anyone to see what he's doing."

Elliott drew back but kept his fingers wrapped around the eyepiece. He stared across the top at Finn, his skin suddenly clammy. "He dumped something." A finger of ice danced up his spine. "Do you think it was…a body?"

Finn took another glance. "The guy's leaving." He plopped to a seat on the floor.

Elliott's skin crawled. "No one goes out on the river in the middle of the night unless they want to get rid of evidence. It had to be a body."

"The sack was too small."

"Not if it was a kid." Elliott thought he might throw up.

"Shit." Finn dropped his head back to stare up at the ceiling. Knees braced apart, he stared at the faux stars overhead. "Maybe I should call my uncle."

"Now?" Elliott sat cross-legged beside him. "My mom will freak. She already seemed out of it when she came home tonight—like she was scared."

"I picked up on that, too." Finn climbed back to his feet to peer through the telescope. He was silent a moment, sweeping the barrel left and right. "The guy's gone. I don't see him anywhere."

"We should forget it." After falling into a grave, Elliott wanted nothing to do with anything creepy. "Halloween's tomorrow. Maybe it was a prank."

Finn stared down at him. "At three in the morning? On the water in a dark boat?"

Elliott realized how crazy it sounded. Standing, he stared out at the river. "So, what do we do?"

"Nothing." Finn made the decision for both of them. "At least not now. Tomorrow I'll tell my uncle. If there's anything weird going on, he'll figure it out."

* * * *

David Gregg arrived unannounced on Tessa Camden's doorstep a little after ten Saturday morning. He rang the bell wondering if Finn had told her he planned to drop by. In retrospect, he probably should have called himself, considering how great she'd been at having his nephew as a frequent houseguest.

He hunched his shoulders against the brisk air as he waited. Windy today, and it was scheduled to get worse. A few of his coworkers were already calculating how the weather would impact the masquerade. David figured partygoers would be more inclined to stay in the various pubs than spill into the street, which could factor into fewer incidents. Mix crowds with alcohol and late-night hours, and there were usually a few mishaps. At the very least, the wind should keep teens from snooping around Hickory Chapel Cemetery.

The door cracked open. "Detective Gregg." Surprise registered on Tessa's face. "Is something wrong?" That answered his question about Finn.

"Everything's good. I just wanted to talk to Finn and Elliott."

"Both of them?" Surprise gave way to concern. Drawing back, Tessa made room for him to enter. "The boys are in the kitchen finishing up breakfast. I made them scrambled eggs."

"I'm sure Finn appreciates that." David stepped past her into the entryway. The house smelled of bacon, coffee, and pan-fried potatoes. Thankfully, he hadn't wakened her or caught her in a bathrobe. Dressed in jeans and a zip-up sweatshirt, she had her dark hair scraped up in a high ponytail. Some people were slow risers on a weekend, but he'd never been one of them.

"I thought maybe Finn would mention he called me."

He'd already been at the precinct two hours when he got Finn's phone call about a lone boater dumping "something" in the river at three in the morning. It was probably nothing, but a lot of crazy stuff went on over Halloween, and the Chinkwe made a convenient place to get rid of unwanted garbage. Two years ago, a plastics manufacturer had been caught trying to unload waste products rather than dispose of them properly.

"No, sorry." Tessa shook her head.

"I won't take up much of your time."

"Is Finn okay?"

"Fine. He's having a great time staying over. I really appreciate it."

"It's no problem at all." Her smile was quick and genuine. "Finn's a good kid, and he and Elliott get along so well." She led him down the hallway. "Can I get you some coffee?"

"No, thanks. I think I've already had a potful. Did the boys tell you what they saw last night?"

She stopped shy of the kitchen, her expression yielding to one of alarm. "Saw?"

Through the open doorway, David spied Finn and Elliott at a dinette table, finishing up breakfast. "It's nothing that—"

She wheeled away from him. "Elliott." Her voice rose in pitch, edged with a note of panic. "Detective Gregg is here. He says you and Finn saw something last night."

Both boys swiveled to face her, deer in the headlights.

"Uncle David." Finn found his voice first. "I didn't have a chance to tell Mrs. Camden you'd be coming over."

"Obviously." David stepped past Tessa into the kitchen, touching her elbow briefly to reassure her. "It's nothing to worry about."

"I'm sorry." Deflating, she shook her head. "I've been on edge lately." She walked past him to the counter, where she retrieved a cup of coffee. "Last night was...upsetting. I was afraid the boys might have seen—"

"All we saw was a boat." Elliott was clearly befuddled. "What did you think we saw, Mom?"

"It doesn't matter." She took a sip of coffee. "But I want to hear about last night."

David used the next few minutes to coax the complete story from Finn and Elliott. Afterward, he asked to see Elliott's telescope. That sent the boys racing upstairs while David and Tessa followed behind. Once in the bedroom, both boys took turns looking through the telescope until they agreed on the location where they'd spied the boat.

"This is it." Elliott stepped back, offering the viewfinder to David.

He bent to peer through the lens. "South of Amethyst Hall." The water was deep there, the river bottom riddled with holes. "Are you sure about the time?"

"I saw the clock on the nightstand when I grabbed my glasses."

"What about the guy?" David looked from Elliott to Finn. "Could you make out anything about his features?"

Both boys shook their heads.

"He was wearing a hoodie," Finn said.

"And he had his face turned to the side." Elliott stood in front of a colorful floor-to-ceiling mural of planets and stars. Between the mural and the starscape on the ceiling, it was no wonder the kid had a telescope.

"But he definitely dumped a sack." Finn seemed to appreciate that David hadn't brushed off their story and was taking the time to question them. Exciting stuff for a twelve-year-old.

"Not a big sack. Kinda like a duffel bag." Elliott spread his arms to indicate the size. "It looked sorta lumpy."

Finn nodded. "He might have had it weighted down, but it was hard to tell."

They were picking up steam, playing off one another as the words tumbled out. David could see excitement building in Finn's eyes, spilling over to Elliott. What had seemed scary at three in the morning was now an adventure—something to speculate about and imagine how they would tell their friends at school on Monday.

"It was too small to be a body." Elliott adjusted his glasses.

"Unless it was a kid." Finn spoke with authority. His vivid imagination didn't go over well with Tessa, who gasped. Apparently, she hadn't considered a corpse.

"Finn, you're scaring Mrs. Camden." David remembered what it was like to be his nephew's age. "Besides, you're both letting your imaginations run wild. It's not unusual for someone to dump garbage, even building materials, in the river." He hoped his words would put Tessa at ease. She hadn't elaborated about what upset her last night, but the cause clearly factored into her jittery nerves today.

Hugging her arms to her chest, she stepped closer to the window. "Then you think it's probably nothing?"

"Most likely. If anything should happen to turn up, I'll let you know."

"Thank you."

"You'll be at the masquerade tonight, right? I seem to remember Elliott's grandmother would be"—he stopped himself from saying *babysitting,* knowing Finn would cringe—"staying with the boys."

Tessa nodded.

"I'll be in and out of a couple different venues keeping an eye on things. If I have any news and we cross paths, I'll let you know. Otherwise, I'll follow up later."

She relaxed visibly. "Thank you, Detective."

"David."

A flush crept up her neck, but she nodded. "Please call me Tessa."

Finn and Elliott exchanged a glance. With a shake of his head, Finn rolled his eyes.

Smartass.

Chapter 16

October 21, 1799

Atticus narrowed his gaze on Vernon Hode. "What do you mean I'm 'sadly mistaken'?" The group of men ringed around them had gone deathly still. Even Keel's coon hounds were subdued, heads lowered as if scenting danger. The wind scattered dried leaves at their feet. "The illness has been vanquished. Vane is dead, and his curse has been broken."

"There was never a curse." Hode's eyes held a combination of pity and disgust.

"You speak from ignorance." Atticus retrieved his frock coat from the ground. Curse Hode for showing up when the deed was done as if he had a right to sit in judgment. "You didn't see Vane's eyes. He was possessed, infected by the Endling." Brusquely, he swiped dirt from the garment.

"He may have had some odd connection to the beast, but he didn't carry a plague." Hode spoke with authority. "He certainly didn't bring *this* plaque to the village."

"How would you know?"

"Because you brought the illness, Atticus."

"Lies!" All night he'd fought a toxic mixture of rage and grief. The poison exploded, splattering the inside of his skull with the ferocity of a cauldron boiling over. "Ignorance I may tolerate, but slander I will not bear. How dare you malign my name!"

Hode didn't flinch. "There is no slander in truth."

A few of the men shuffled uneasily.

"Atticus cannot be to blame." Cyrus worked his jaw back and forth. "He lost two of his children."

"Due to his own foolishness."

"Perhaps you best explain." Thaddeus Keel's pronouncement mirrored the grumbling of the group.

Hode's answering nod was curt. "There was a reason I asked to be left in mourning. My instructions were clear—no one was to set foot on my property until a time of my choosing."

"A matter that bears no weight." Atticus ground his teeth. The long night was waning, and he still had children to prepare for burial.

"That is where you are wrong. I was not grieving but confined to my bed by illness. I posted notice of mourning to keep others away, not wishing to risk someone inadvertently contracting the sickness and spreading it through the village."

"Sickness?" Cyrus looked befuddled. "You can't mean—"

"It is an old malady, one that runs in my family." Hode kicked a loose stone and sent it skittering into the shadows. One of Keel's hounds whined low in its throat. "I have struggled with the disease for decades. It lasts no more than a week—two at most—but it is contagious when it strikes. During that period, I sequester myself and avoid contact with others."

"But why did you not tell us?" Cyrus protested.

"Because my business is my own. I should not have to air my infirmity. Better you should think I grieved than learn the truth and grow fearful of the illness. I have lived among others all my life without allowing the malady to spread. I take precautions, but those precautions were breached."

Andrew Whitley's face had gone pale. "Atticus came to see you. To tell you about the Endling."

"Aye. Disregarding my edict, he forced his way into my home. He saw that I was sick."

"No." A cold slug wormed through Atticus's gut. "You were only resting."

"Recovering. The plague cannot kill me—I have carried it too long, built up a resistance to the ailment—but I can still pass it to others."

"Then *you* are at fault." Blood thrummed against Atticus's temples. He stabbed a finger at Hode.

"Is that how you see it?" A gust of wind scattered hair about Hode's face. "First you accuse Gabriel. Murder him. Then, when you realize your mistake, you wish to foist blame on me. I took measures to keep the malady confined. Had you not ignored my order, innocent lives would not be lost, and Gabriel would still be alive. No one would have died, including your own children. You carried the sickness into the village, Atticus, not I."

Cyrus pawed the back of his neck. "Then Vane was not possessed by a demon? I see no end to this confusion."

Keel spat tobacco juice onto the ground. Muttering rippled through the circle.

"Do not listen to this insanity!" Fear crippled Atticus as he lurched forward. It wasn't possible. Couldn't be possible. "Vane was the spawn of Satan as I professed. If *I* carried the disease into the village, then why am I not sick?"

"For the same reason that none who stand here are sick." Hode shifted his gaze from one man to the next. "Illness claims its victims randomly. Not all who come in contact with an infection succumb to sickness. I should not have to explain basic curative principals to you. Nor should I have to clarify that Gabriel Vane would *not* have risked his life to track and kill the beast vexing our village, only to return and curse you with a plague. For God's sake, use your head! The boy was your neighbor. He hoped to marry your daughter, and Jasper was his closest friend."

Cyrus groaned. Folding in half, he slumped to the ground. "Dear God! Dear God, I have been blind! This is too much." Burying his face in his hands, he choked on tears.

Keel shook his head. "There's nothing to do for it now. Vane is dead, and there's no taking that back."

"Atticus deceived us." In the torchlight, Ira Blake's skin gleamed beet red. "He convinced us Gabriel was possessed by the Devil. He turned us into killers."

"He didn't turn you into anything!" Hode's voice cracked with thunder. "*You* brought this upon yourselves." He looked from Blake to Everett Donner, to Whitley, then Keel, and finally to Cyrus still sobbing on the ground. "It was your own fear and superstitions that brought you to this end. You believed what you wanted to believe so you could offer up a sacrifice for an antiquated practice steeped in wickedness." He shook his head. "You repulse me. Every last one of you. Well, you have your sacrifice. You killed an innocent boy and will have to live with that guilt for eternity. If you have any decency left, you'll make certain he is never forgotten." With a final curse, he wheeled away from the group then stalked into the darkness.

Sniffling, Cyrus wiped dirty fingers under his nose. "He's right. We should get a marker."

"There will be no marker." Hode's sanctimonious speech left a bitter taste in Atticus's mouth. "He can say what he wants, believe what he wants, but I know differently." He cast a scathing glare at Cyrus. "Get up off the ground." A kick to the leg made Herman scramble to his feet. "We have other burials to attend, starting tomorrow. Now that Vane is in the ground, his spirit will protect those who follow."

"I will never believe as you do." Enoch had been quiet so long, Atticus had forgotten he was there.

Slowly, Atticus turned to face his son. Enoch stood toe-to-toe with him, his expression grim. "I have stood by your side from the beginning, Father, but no more. From this day forth, you will share no part of my life. The thing you have done tonight cannot be forgiven, even by blood."

Atticus's mouth twisted. The boy was talking madness. "You are not thinking clearly. You don't know what you're saying."

"I have *never* thought as clearly as I do now. I have been tending Gabriel's farm and plan to purchase the land. I will care for it as he did, in his memory. And I will ask Nellie Renault to be my wife."

Atticus felt a small piece of his life crumble. "Do not be foolish."

"I will also make certain Fern knows of your hand in this foul deed." Enoch ignored the admonishment. "When my sister learns of what you have done, she will want nothing to do with you, either. You will be alone." His son had never spoken so coldly, his eyes hardened to chips of ice, his expression marked by contempt. "To grow old and die in isolation. When the time comes, you will be buried in Gabriel's cemetery. For make no mistake, it is his now. If ever his bones are removed, I pray the protection you sought from him is renounced twofold, and the monsters you fear are released to wreak havoc on you and the descendants of all those who stand here tonight."

"Imbecile!" Atticus wasn't sure if his anger came from hostility or fear. "That includes your own line."

"Yes." Enoch smiled grimly. "You have brought me to that end, Father. When the demons come hunting, I pray you remember who is at fault for unleashing them."

* * * *

Present Day

Jillian slipped inside The Knot with Tessa and Dante. She'd hadn't taken the time to purchase a costume for the masquerade but had found a white eye mask beaded with faux pearls at a boutique shop in Palmer Point. White netting and an ostrich plume were bunched in a showy cluster near her temple. Making do with what she had, she'd paired the mask with a long black skirt, black boots, and a white silk blouse. The ensemble wasn't much of a costume, but given the variety of outfits and near-costumes she saw, she didn't feel out of place.

"Wow, it's loud!" Tessa laughed and leaned close, pitching her voice to be heard above the pulsing beat of music and a rowdy din of voices. After paying at the door, they'd been given orange wristbands to wear, their ticket into the venues participating in the event. Several local music groups were scheduled to appear at various restaurants, and light hors d'oeuvres were included in the cover charge. A few October brews had special pricing, but everything else was at cost.

Maybe The Knot wasn't the best place to start the night. At a little after eight, people were already spilling in the door, jostling elbow to elbow. Dante had dropped them off, then vanished to find a parking place. Costumes ranged from guys in ratty jeans with "Fiend" masks to others decked out in full Halloween regalia. Zombies and witches seemed to be popular—Tessa had chosen the latter for her costume—but others favored steampunk garb or elaborate Venetian Carnivale attire. Everyone wore a mask of some sort, though some of the men had already pushed theirs up on their heads. The mashup of masquerade and Halloween seemed to have attracted double the crowd one event alone would have drawn.

"Hey, I made it!" Dante squeezed in beside them. "I had to park four blocks down, but I found a spot." He smoothed back the crown of his hair, the long strands secured in a ponytail at the base of his neck. "The wind is really picking up. It's crazy out there." Stepping aside to let a guy in a clown outfit past, he straightened his bowtie. "How do I look?"

"Extremely dapper."

Jillian had to agree with Tessa's assessment. Dante wore a tailored burgundy coat with black pants, a white shirt, and a tightly fitted black vest. For accent, he'd added gold gloves and a gold mask with a black top hat and walking stick. He could have passed for a ringmaster on loan from the big top.

"With two gorgeous women on my arms"—he offered them each an elbow—"how could I appear anything but?"

Tessa grinned. "You'd get higher marks if you found us a table and drinks."

"Drinks I can handle. A table's iffy." He led them through the crowd. "Hopefully, Maya's already here."

They found her seated with another woman at the bar. Jillian recognized Ivy McDowell from the library where Maya worked as a reference librarian.

"Hey, you made it!" Maya waved them over. Dressed in a Carnivale gown of dark blue embroidered with lace trim, she wore a matching tricorn hat. An enormous ostrich plume and peacock feathers sprouted from the brim, accented by a cluster of teardrop crystals. Her face mask—complete with gold-rimmed eyes, rouged cheeks, and powder-pink lips—was perched at the top of an acrylic stick. "We tried to save you stools, but the place is packed. I wish Collin could have made it. This is going to be the talk of the town for days."

"I'm already in love with the pumpkin ale." Ivy sipped a dark draft from a tall pilsner glass, then slid from her stool. "Why don't one of you sit down? We've been here for a while, and I need to use the ladies' room."

Jillian motioned for Tessa to take the seat. She was too jittery with nerves, trying to downplay the scintillating energy of the crowd. Every table was taken, servers scurrying between the aisles with platters of food and drinks hefted high overhead. Most wore cadaver makeup with a thick noose knotted loosely about their necks. Macabre, but the place *was* called The Knot and Halloween sometimes pushed the envelope of taste.

Dante touched her arm. "What can I get you to drink?"

"Chardonnay, thanks. I'm not much for beer."

"Tessa?" Dante glanced at his cousin.

"I'll try the pumpkin ale."

Behind them, a new group of partygoers spilled into the pub. "Damn! I don't think we're in Kansas anymore, Toto." A man dressed as a vampire shook out his cape. "That wind is freaky."

His companions laughed, and several others turned to look out the windows. It was too dark to see anything beyond the glass, but Jillian imagined she heard blustery gusts above the whine of electric guitars. Whatever the weather outside, it didn't mute the high energy level in the bar.

A few minutes later, Ivy returned from the ladies' room. "I'm going to grab a plate of hors d'oeuvres. Any requests?"

"Food." Dante passed Jillian her wine.

"I guess that means you get potluck."

Maya laughed. "I'll come with you and grab a plate, too. I'm sure he'll eat whatever we come back with."

Jillian watched the two weave through the crowd.

Dante motioned for her to take the vacant bar stool. "Hungry?"

"A little." She hadn't eaten since breakfast but needed her nerves to settle first. Without her tinted lenses, surrounded by the boisterous crowd, she felt vulnerable. At least the mask concealed her to a degree.

He leaned closer, lowering his voice. "Sometime I'd like to take you out. Just the two of us."

It was clearly her night for being discombobulated. "We've been out before." Her heartbeat quickened as she gazed up at him. "Several times."

"To talk about curses, Gabriel Vane, or ghosts. It would be nice not to have to share you with a dead guy." He slipped off his mask. "How about it? I know you've got a lot on your plate with Madison, but if you get an evening free next week, I'd like to take you to a nice restaurant. Maybe Italian."

She couldn't remember the last time she'd been on a date. Sometime pre–Mill Street. Feeling a flush on her cheeks, Jillian lowered her head. "Italian sounds good." She was thankful her mask would hide most of her color. "I'll leave Blizzard at home."

"Deal breaker." His voice was deadpan.

Jillian glanced up sharply. "What?"

"Kidding." Grinning, he extended his hand. "Would you like to dance?"

Before she could answer, Tessa took her glass. "I'll hold your drink for you." She must have overhead part of their conversation. Jillian hoped not all of it.

Dante kept her on the floor for two dances before they joined the others at the bar. By that time, Maya and Ivy had returned with hors d'oeuvres, and they all spent a few minutes munching and talking. Ivy got chatty with the guy seated beside her—a square-jawed type with steampunk goggles and a military-style black coat. After a while, she left with him, saying they were going to check out some of the other places on the crawl. Dante took Tessa for a spin on the dance floor, then Maya. Jillian danced with Tessa and found herself relaxing. By the time the next song kicked in, the entire group stayed on the floor.

"I think I need a real meal." Tessa pressed a hand to her forehead when the final notes of "Play That Funky Music" drew to a close. "What if we try Sharks? I heard they've got their club sandwiches on special."

"Sounds like a plan." Dante steered the three women from the dance floor. "We just need to brave the wind."

Outside, chill gusts blew partygoers up and down the sidewalks, but most people seemed to take the weather in stride, loitering under overhangs where music and lights spilled onto the street. The whole area was brightened by neon bar signs, streetlamps, and the headlights of passing cars.

At Sharks, they managed to snag a table as another group was leaving and stayed until almost eleven. Maya made her goodbye a short time later, and Jillian began to think of doing the same. She could always call a cab. As designated driver, Dante had switched to soda a while ago, but she could tell he was enjoying the band Sharks had booked and probably wasn't ready to leave. She should have grabbed a ride with Maya.

"We can't call it a night yet." Tessa seemed to sense where her thoughts were headed. "I haven't had a fun night out since..." She frowned as if giving the matter serious thought. "My divorce. How pathetic is that?"

"Pathetic." They'd all removed their masks some time ago. In the hazy light of the pub, Dante's hazel eyes were walnut brown. "As your only cousin, it's my sworn duty to correct the oversight."

"Oh, yeah? How?"

"Let's check out April's next door. They've got great craft beer."

"I thought you were drinking soda?"

"I am, but you aren't." Grinning, he cast a glance at Jillian. "How about it?"

Not wanting to be the one to put a kibosh on the fun, she smiled agreement. At April's, they crowded into a corner of the bar, each ordering a seasonal draft. The ale tasted of pine and citrus, but it was lighter than some of the others Jillian had sampled that night. After a while, Tessa left to use the restroom, and Dante fell into a discussion with the guy beside him about eighteenth-century painters.

Maybe it was because the man was wearing a black bodysuit with a glow-in-the-dark skeleton on the front and back, but Jillian suddenly felt uneasy. The time inched close to midnight, and she was beginning to drag. She'd enjoyed the evening but had reached her limit and wanted to go home and crawl into bed.

Her thoughts spun to Gabriel—a cold grave, his brutal death. If the monsters of Hickory Chapel Cemetery had been free to wreak havoc before, how much more likely were they to cause mayhem on Halloween, a night when the boundary between the living and the dead grew thin?

Shivering, she glanced about the bar. There hadn't been a death in days. Maybe the curse had a limit and had run its course.

Her attention was snagged by two men at a table by the door. Both were big, the first with a buzz cut and hooked nose, the second with wavy brown hair and an angular jaw. The younger of the two had a Fiend mask at his elbow, both sans costumes in jeans and sweatshirts. From the slouched posture of the first man and his attachment to a long-necked bottle, he was on his way to a roaringly good drunk.

The second man looked moody, chin propped in hand as he studied the crowd. When their gazes locked, he swiftly averted his eyes, withdrawing like a turtle into a shell.

Tessa returned from the ladies' room. "What did I miss?"

Jillian fought against a yawn. "Me. On the verge of turning into a pumpkin."

"I think I'm right there with you." Tessa retrieved her mask from the bar. "It's going to be late Mass tomorrow for me and Elliott." She batted Dante on the shoulder. "Hey, driver, are you ready to call it a night?"

"I could be persuaded." He offered a shrug to the guy he'd been talking with. "Nice chatting with you, but I've got two impatient ladies ready to leave."

"Be thankful, dude. I don't even have one."

Dante grinned. He shook the guy's hand, then stood. "Okay, ladies, I'm ready if you are."

Jillian gathered her purse and slid off the bar stool. As she turned back to the door, she realized the man with the Fiend mask had left, the table where he'd sat now vacant. In the crowded room, that flagrant spot of emptiness was glaringly noticeable—like a tomb no one would touch.

Jillian looked away from the sight and hurried toward the door.

* * * *

The beers Clive had quaffed didn't settle well in his stomach. Warren had downed a mix of drinks all night—everything from ale and Jack to rum and vodka—but his brother had an iron gut. Always had. Clive had fun in the beginning of the night, but the later it got the bleaker his mood grew. He kept thinking about the man with the golden retriever yesterday. He'd wanted to pet the dog, but by the time he'd finished texting Kirk, the guy had left. Clive headed to the pound like he'd planned, but there were no pooches that resembled Bodine. All the dogs had looked at him with sad eyes, and he'd left alone, feeling depressed.

Like now.

Something bad was going to happen. The pretty lady at the bar had been an omen.

She'd reminded him of the woman on Mill Street—blond hair instead of red, but with features that looked the same. His stomach had rolled over when he saw her, memories of what Kirk had done pummeling him like blows from a hammer. He'd had to fight the urge to hurl, grateful when Warren said it was time to leave.

The cold air helped chase away the sweats. He pawed a hand over his face.

"How far away did you park?" Warren hunched his shoulders against the wind and fished in the pocket of his bomber jacket.

"Up across the street." Clive started walking, but Warren hung back, cupping his hands to light a cigarette. The harsh smell wafted to Clive as his brother exhaled, churning the acid in his gut. Balling up his Fiend mask, he stuffed it in his coat, saddened that fun had given way to folly. The wind hurtled leaves against his feet. Chased bits of litter between parked cars and set utility wires into a mad dance overhead.

He just wanted to go home. Crawl into bed. Forget the woman at the bar. *Shit!*

There she was again—walking on the opposite side of the street beside a guy in a burgundy jacket and a woman dressed as a witch. His steps lagged as he studied her.

What if she *was* the woman from Mill Street? Hewitt's wife had ended up in a mental ward, but what if she'd recovered? Dyed her hair? He wet his lips as a white sedan sped past, cruising through a yellow light. He waited for the traffic signal to cycle to red.

Already several steps ahead, Warren glanced over his shoulder. "Get your ass in gear. It's freaking cold. I want to get to the car." He exhaled smoke through his nostrils. There were a few people around—pockets of partygoers still in costume.

"We should wait for the walk signal." *Wait until she's a few blocks away.*

Warren swayed slightly. "Screw the signal. Do you see any cars?" He jiggled a hand at the empty street.

Clive shook his head but stayed rooted to the sidewalk.

"The hell with you." With a drunken backhand wave, Warren blundered into the crosswalk. "I'll see you at the car."

He'd only taken three steps when a loud *boom* jerked him to a halt. Pivoting, he cast his gaze skyward. A utility cable plunged from its mooring, ripped free by the wind. Sparks spurted from the end, a shower of blue-white death lighting up the night.

Warren stumbled. Dove to the side, but was too inebriated to avoid the spitting, writhing snake. The wire lashed about his waist, ripping a scream from his throat. His arms and legs locked in place as the sickening stench of burning clothes and flesh filled the air.

"Nooo!" Heart pounding, Clive raced toward his brother.

The cable skittered free, eel-slick, sin-black. Warren crumpled in a contorted heap, hunched over like a turtle. His eyes gaped wide and sightless, spittle pooling from his mouth onto the ground. All around him, the street plunged into darkness, pole lamps and pub lights extinguished in the wink of an eye.

"No, shit no!" Clive dropped beside him, deep sobs wrenched from his gut. A car screeched to a halt a few feet away, the white glare of headlights blinding him. He felt like a sideshow display in that garish circle, his brother's bent form exhibited for all to see.

"It's my fault, all my fault. The bell was meant for me." Pulling Warren against his chest, Clive rocked the broken form, fat tears splattering on his brother's singed clothing. The smell of char would have choked him if horror hadn't wedged a lump in his throat. All around him people poured from pubs, their shouts like blackbird chatter. Some screamed, others cried. More than one yelled for an ambulance.

"All right, get back. Stay back. Police." A man's authoritative voice sliced into his misery. He heard the crackle of a radio, the clump of footsteps on asphalt. A siren wailed in the distance.

"My fault, my fault." The ring of zombies and masked partygoers retreated. A man squatted beside him. "You need to let me see."

"He's dead." Clive sucked his bottom lip. Looked up into weathered features, hair silvered with frost at the temples.

"I'm Detective David Gregg." The man placed a hand on his shoulder. Clive wiped snot from his nose. "My brother's dead."

"Let me be the judge of that." Gregg glanced aside. "Thorton. Anders. Get this crowd back and get more light up here."

Someone pulled Clive away. He managed two steps before slumping to the curb. Gregg bent over Warren's inert form, checking his pulse, pressing an ear to his chest. He looked up at a woman in a leather jacket and shook his head. She closed her eyes briefly then nodded. Turning away, she spoke into a handheld microphone. Two police cars rolled in from the opposite direction, the strobe of red-and-white lights making his head spin.

He pressed his hands to his temples. "It was meant for me."

"Think you can tell me what happened here?"

He glanced up to find the woman in the leather jacket gazing down on him. She had dusky skin and a tiny mole like a beauty mark at the corner of her upper lip. He focused on the mole. "I heard the bell, not him."

"What bell?"

"In Hickory Chapel Cemetery." He rubbed his lizard tattoo. Why had it failed him? "I'm the one who should have died."

"My name is Detective Lorquet. I want to help you."

"Too late." He swabbed away tears.

"Sherre?" The soft sound of a woman's voice intruded. "Can I help?"

Clive glanced up, and there *she* was—standing like an avenging angel behind the detective—her white blouse spectral in the corona of emergency lights, long hair a waterfall of silver flame.

"Jillian, you shouldn't be here."

Clive scrambled to his feet. "It's because of Mill Street."

"*What?*" The woman's face drained of color. Her gaze dropped to his hand. "A lizard tattoo. A black lizard." She looked like she might throw up. "You were there."

He tried to shake his head, but his neck tendons froze in place. Up close, he realized she wasn't Hewitt's wife, but looked similar enough to be family. The insight made him suppress a whimper. "You're her sister. Like Warren was my brother."

The woman shrieked. The sound cut him, banshee-swift and lethal. In the next second, she was in his face, pummeling him with her fists, spitting curses.

"Jillian!" A man in a ponytail snagged her waist and hauled her back.

"That's enough!" Detective Lorquet stepped between them. "Stop it now, Jillian. Stop." Her voice was ice and steel.

Chest heaving, tears glittering in her eyes, the blond-haired woman glared at Clive. "If you heard the bell, you're dead. You know that, don't you? You *deserve* death for what you did."

Her hatred stung like acid. "It wasn't me." He wrung his hands, wishing he could talk to Warren. Hot tears streamed from his eyes. "Kirk was crazy that night. He told me we were going to look at a puppy. I wanted a pup, but when we got there…" He choked, remembering the smell of Boyd's blood, the woman's hysterical screams. "I held her back because I didn't want her to get hurt. That's all I did. I swear, *I swear!*" Folding in half, he bowed his face in his hands. Sobs bulleted from his gut like shockwaves.

"Kirk who?" Lorquet squatted in front of him.

"My…my brother, Kirk Porter." The memories came back, scurrying rodent-swift through his skull. He clutched his head and rocked. "Make it stop, make it stop. I want Warren."

The woman named Jillian made a sound of disgust. "I can't believe after all this time…" She turned away, burying her face against the man with the ponytail. He wrapped his arms around her, holding her close.

Clive burrowed into a tight ball, wishing he had someone to hold. He thought of Bodine, the soft press of fur against his cheek. Somewhere in the background, he heard David Gregg talking to Lorquet. The words were jumbled like pieces of a puzzle…something about an APB…about Kirk.

He was still sniffling when a uniformed officer hauled him to his feet. Lorquet read him his rights as the clean-cut cop slapped cuffs on his wrists.

His heart triple-timed against his breastbone. "I want Warren."

"Put him in a car." Lorquet's expression was stony.

The uniformed cop led him away, throngs on the sidewalk parting to let them pass. "I want Warren." Why wouldn't they listen to him? He craned his neck, twisting to gaze over his shoulder, but the crowds had closed behind him. "Why can't I see Warren?"

The cop wrenched him to a halt at the rear of a police cruiser and reached for the door. His stomach catapulted into his throat. Bending double, he heaved beer and chunks of food onto the ground.

"Gah!" the cop backpedaled in disgust.

Clive inhaled snot. "I wanna die. I don't want to be alone."

"Neither did I." The blond-haired woman stared at him across the roof of the car, the perfect lines of her face cold marble in the moonlight.

He wobbled upright. Hunched a shoulder against his cheek to sop up tears. Something in her eyes flayed him to the core. "I just wanted a dog." Why didn't anyone understand? "That's why I helped Warren dig up the grave at Hickory Chapel. We gave the bones to Eli Yancy for money so I could have a dog like Bodine. That's all I ever wanted."

"You're lying."

"No. It's the truth. I'd never hurt anyone intentionally." They had to believe him. His whole world was falling apart. Warren was gone, and Kirk— "Ask my brother. Ask Kirk. Yancy called him because Warren and I wouldn't take money to rough up a kid." He was babbling and knew it, but didn't care. "Something about a green stone, like an emerald. Kirk does shit like that, not me." He might have said more if the cop hadn't recovered and yanked open the door. A hand clamped on his head, forcing him down into the rear seat. Locked inside, he drew his knees to his chest and listened to the labored hitch of his breath.

"Stupid shit." Warren's reprimand echoed in his head. *"You screwed up again."*

"I did. I'm sorry."

"Doesn't matter. You heard the bell."

He nodded, tears soaking into the collar of his coat. "Will you wait for me?"

"Don't I always?" A slight chuckle. *"Hurry up. I got you a dog."*

Clive grinned through his waterworks and sucked back a glob of snot. "Does he look like Bodine?"

"Hell, he is Bodine. Get your lazy ass in gear. We're waiting."

Clive tipped his head back, smiling up at the roof of the car. The cop spied him through the window and bent down to peer inside.

"Hey. What are you grinning at?"

"Warren and Bodine." He welcomed the soft peal of a bell only he could hear—still smiling when his heart exploded.

* * * *

Kirk slipped inside the back door of the brownstone. The lock was easy to pick, the property mostly dark at twenty after twelve on Halloween night. He'd waited until the woman had fallen asleep watching TV in the living room, the two boys upstairs. The woman woke briefly when he clasped a hand over her mouth, her eyes popping at the sight of a leering devil staring down at her. The Fiend mask was perfect for Halloween, even better to conceal his features. He knocked her unconscious before she could scream.

Piece of cake.

Adrenaline ripped through his veins as he flexed the surgical gloves tight around his fingers and wrists. He'd been stupid when he'd killed Hewitt—left prints all over the place, but he'd been stoked on drugs. Tonight, his head was clear. Tonight was about fun.

Kirk crept toward the steps.

Oh, boys...

He'd thought to find the Camden kid alone, but the little shit had a friend staying over. Didn't matter. He could scare the bejesus out of two as easily as one, make the little suckers piss themselves. He'd never roughed up a kid before, but there was always a first time.

At the top of the stairs, he spied a blue-gray sliver of light beneath a door to the left like a TV was playing. A soft murmur of voices made him prick his ears, but he couldn't distinguish words. No matter. He slipped a butterfly knife from his back pocket and flicked it open. Sucking air through the holes in the Fiend mask, he crept down the hall until he was close enough to press his ear against the door.

Laughter. Something about a gym teacher with a face like a camel.

Kirk closed his hand around the doorknob. Adrenaline spiked to his brain. He kicked the door wide and burst into the room, flashing the knife in a showy arc. The boys were seated on the floor in front of a TV. Both scrambled to their feet when they saw him. Their screams bounced against his ears, but it was a woman's high-pitched shriek that froze him in his tracks.

* * * *

Jillian dug through her purse for her keys.

"Do you want me to stay?" Dante closed his hands over hers, stilling her twitchy fingers as he stared down into her eyes. "I'm not sure you should be alone tonight. I can sleep on the couch."

A sliver of warmth pierced the ice encasing her heart. "I'll be all right. It's just...a lot to absorb." Tessa had already moved away, climbing the steps to the rear door of her brownstone. Jillian wanted to do the same. Wanted to forget the ugly events of the last half hour and crash into bed. Tomorrow, when she could think clearly, she'd dredge up Clive Porter's face and the black lizard tattoo on his hand. He hadn't seemed like a killer, and that confused her. If anything, he'd seemed as lost as she felt. She'd almost pitied him.

Then just like that he was gone—his heart giving way in the rear of the patrol car.

Because he'd heard the bell at Hickory Chapel Cemetery.

It was too much to process. Tomorrow, she'd think about Clive. About Madison and Mill Street and the search for Kirk Porter. At least Sherre had alerted the police in Palmer Point and placed a call to the rehab center where Madison was in recovery. If Jillian hadn't been so exhausted, she might have driven there tonight. Sherre had promised to question Eli Yancy, too.

A triangle of light severed the darkness as Tessa opened the rear door and slipped inside. Jillian smiled at Dante. "Thanks for your concern. I'll be okay. I—" The words were choked from her throat as a flood of emotion engulfed her—fear, shock, a torrent of anxiety. "Tessa!"

She bolted for the brownstone as Tessa's screams pierced the night.

* * * *

"Damn." Kirk slipped inside the bedroom door. The two boys had backed up against the far wall. "Don't move. Don't make a sound."

The one with the glasses bobbed his head, all wide eyes and white skin.

"Bullshit." The dark-haired one was the problem. "He's got a knife, not a gun." He ripped a lamp from the dresser. Kirk was halfway across the room when the kid hurled it at his head.

"Run!" The boy was thoroughbred fast, bolting past while Kirk grasped at air. He flung the lamp aside with a wild sweep of his arm. The other kid scrambled after the first, thrown to his knees when his foot snagged the edge of a bunk bed.

"Elliott!" A woman's scream rebounded up the steps, followed by the rapid thud of footfalls. He grabbed the smaller kid and dragged him backward toward the window. Yancy had said the Camden brat wore glasses.

"Where's the stone? The emerald?"

The kid made a strangled sound, eyes boggling behind his glasses. His skin turned the color of wet flour, and he looked like he might pass out. Kirk shook him hard.

"I'm not going to ask you again, shithead." He cast a glance out the window. The drop down was too far. "Give me the stone and I won't hurt you." He pressed the blade against the boy's neck, felt his body stiffen like someone had wrenched his spine straight. The other boy grappled a cell phone off the dresser, frantically keyed in a security code.

"Drop it or I'll slit his throat."

His fingers froze on the phone. Eyes wide, he licked his lips. "Okay. Whatever you say." Raising his hands in surrender, he dropped the cell like it was contaminated. Behind him, a woman in a witch's costume rushed through the door.

"Elliott!" She would have lurched forward, but a guy with a ponytail grabbed her, holding her back. The two regarded him across the room.

Tightening his hand on his knife, Kirk smiled behind his Fiend mask. "Well...I sure as hell hope one of you has my stone."

* * * *

Jillian took one look at Imelda, half-conscious on the living room sofa, and dashed from the room. If Tessa or Dante viewed her swift departure as cowardice, neither had a chance to voice an objection. She was out the front door and racing for her brownstone, the wind cold against her face. On the stoop, she fumbled for her keys, the deluge of emotion she'd felt in Tessa's home pulsing through her veins. The boys were terrified, their fear tangled up with something dark and sinister.

Someone dark and sinister. Kirk Porter had taken money to "rough up a kid." What were the odds he'd show tonight after his brother had branded him Boyd's killer?

Blizzard nosed up against her the moment she stumbled inside. Racing past him, she flew up the steps to her bedroom. A flood of yellow blinded her as she flipped on the light switch. Frantic, she yanked open the top drawer of her dresser then rummaged inside until she found the emerald. The gem was exactly where she'd left it, tucked beneath a red silk scarf. Keyed to her hysteria, Blizzard barked and danced restlessly.

She had no time to calm him. No time to do anything but punch out Sherre's number one-handed on her cell as she raced down the steps clutching the stone.

"Lorquet."

"Something horrible is happening." Jillian's voice was urgent and shrill. "I'm at home."

"Jillian?"

"Please send help. My neighbor's house—Tessa Camden. Hurry!" She dashed outside. Blizzard's frantic barking was muffled by the closed door.

Imelda wobbled up from the sofa as Jillian dashed inside Tessa's living room.

"There was someone here." Sobbing, Tessa's mother pressed a shaky hand to her head. Fear puddled at her feet and spread outward to engulf Jillian. The quagmire of fright was nothing compared to the bombardment of raw emotion tumbling down the steps from the second floor. The combination of terror and dark insanity struck Jillian like a fist to the gut.

He's up there.

Her brother-in-law's killer. The man responsible for Madison's psychosis.

"You're safe now." Jillian guided Imelda toward the front door. "My house is unlocked. I've already called the police. Stay there."

"The boys—Tessa—"

"Please go." Jillian bolted up the stairs. When she reached the hallway, it was like hitting a visceral wall of emotion. Tessa's terror blasted through her like lightning. She sucked down a breath and clamped her mind shut, a steel trap to repel feeling. Anything less and she could end up like Madison.

Tessa and Dante stood in front of the door to Elliott's room, blocking her view of the interior. Spying her over his shoulder, Dante gave a short shake of his head.

Stay away.

"I'm not going to ask again," a gruff male voice said. "Where's the fucking stone?"

"I have it." Jillian thrust between them.

"Jillian!" Dante tried to grab her, but she wriggled past, into the room. The only light came from the TV, washed-out and grainy as it broadcast an old black-and-white version of the movie *Frankenstein*. Elliott's friend, Finn, stood a few feet away, his face drawn and leached of color. Across the room, a man wearing a Fiend mask held Elliott with one arm wrapped around his chest, the edge of a knife angled to the boy's throat. Elliott trembled visibly, white as a marble statue.

"Who are you?" The man raked her with a gaze. "Doesn't matter. Give me the stone."

"Let Elliott go, and I will." Jillian's knees felt like they might buckle, but there was something hard and rigid in her, too. She extended her hand and uncurled her fingers to reveal the emerald.

The man snorted. "Fat chance, bitch. Set it over here—" Dragging Elliott backward, he bobbed his head to indicate the nightstand. "Then I'll let the kid go."

Jillian didn't move. "I've already called the police."

"Bullshit."

"If I give you the stone, you'll use Elliott as a shield. How else will you get past us?" She was surprised she could think so clearly when she felt like she moved through a bog. "You're Kirk Porter, aren't you?" Her voice was ice, every muscle in her body strung taut. "Where do you think you're going to go?"

"Please, Jillian. Do what he wants." Tessa's plea was rough with tears. "Give him the stone."

"Yeah, Jillian." The man laughed, the sound muffled by red latex. "Give me the stone."

She folded her fingers over the gem. The only way out was through the door—past her, Dante, and Tessa—the man knew it as well as she did. Why didn't Tessa see? If Jillian stalled long enough, she could keep Elliott safe until the police arrived.

Hoping he understood she'd never let anything happen to him, she shot him a bolstering glance. During the séance, Gabriel's spirit had told her the stone's power could protect or destroy. It was time to see if it would protect Elliott.

"There's nowhere for you to go. Your brother already told the police you killed Boyd Hewitt three years ago."

"Jillian, don't." Dante's tone carried warning.

"You don't know what you're talking about, lady."

Clutched in her palm, the emerald pulsed with sudden heat. "The hell I don't. We just left your brother, Clive, in the back of a squad car. Before he died, he confessed what he did. What *you* did." The balloon of heat grew, glittering like light in her veins, a sun going nova. The deluge was scorching, empowering. "That was my brother-in-law you killed, you bastard. My *sister* you put in a rest home."

"What the hell?" The man ripped off his mask. The motion freed Elliott for the fraction he needed to break away. Ducking under Porter's arm, he bolted for the bottom bunk. The man scrambled to catch him, but Elliot was too quick, popping out the other side. Finn flung a paperweight over his head, and the heavy chunk of glass struck Porter on the brow, dropping him with a grunt.

"Elliott! Finn!" Tessa herded them into the hallway. In a streak, Dante shot past her, catching Porter around the waist. The two hit the floor with a loud crash as Tessa and the boys pounded down the steps. Sirens wailed in the distance, drawing closer, the scintillating heat in Jillian's veins screaming in unison with the tumult. Green light shot through the cracks of her clenched fist, phosphorescent illumination that made her hitch in a breath.

Protect or destroy.

Near the window, Porter slashed out with his knife. Dante reeled backward, blundering into Elliott's telescope. Cat-quick, Porter danced around him and sliced into Dante's arm. Her friend cursed and tried to back away, but Porter had maneuvered him into a corner. One hand clamped on the bloody gash, Dante kept his gaze on Porter's knife. Wildly, Jillian looked for a weapon.

Protect or destroy.

"Porter!" She hated the man. Saw he was hideous inside, twisted with an insatiable darkness like the monsters of Hickory Chapel Cemetery.

Ignoring her, he lunged at Dante. Porter was the shorter of the two, but he had no qualms about killing. He hefted the knife, ready to plunge the blade down on Dante. All Jillian saw was him doing the same to Boyd. Over and over.

In that freeze-frame of time, she stood in her sister's place, watching the man she'd come to care about fight to stave off death. Rather than close herself to terror, she opened her mind to Dante, inviting him to join her as they had in the woods behind Wickham. Resilience flooded her as he gave her his strength. In turn, she poured out her protection, binding them together through the power of the stone.

The room exploded with green light. Porter was flung backward against the closet, then slumped to the floor, his legs corkscrewed at an odd angle. The crack of bone reverberated on the air. Eyes boggling, he screamed and slashed at the nothingness in front of him. Spittle flew from his lips as he yelled and hacked with the knife—tried to drag himself away from something only he could see. His legs hadn't broken in the fall. Couldn't have.

And then Jillian saw them.

Protect or destroy.

Summoned by the power of the stone, they moved in that eerie green light—the monsters of Hickory Chapel Cemetery. If not them, creatures like them—unspeakable things oozing slime and blood. Things that slithered and crawled. That reeked of offal and sulfur. They swarmed over Porter with fangs and stinging tentacles. Tails that thrashed and claws that scored flesh until all that was left was a blood-soaked mass of pulp.

"Jillian." Dante bolted across the lower bunk. Wrapping his arms around her, he dragged her away from the horrific scene. The green light vanished as if someone had thrown a switch, the emerald turning cold in her hand. Kirk Porter sat slumped against the closet, whole and unbroken, not a mark on him.

Without venturing closer, she knew he was dead.

Chapter 17

January 11, 1800

Enoch Crowe stared down at his father's headstone, trying to resurrect some feeling of pity or remorse, but there was none to be found in his heart. His feelings for Atticus had not changed from the night he'd learned of Gabriel's murder. Flipping his collar up against the winter air, he looked from the fancy limestone block marking Atticus's grave—raised more for the sake of Jasper and Dinah than him and Fern—to the unadorned patch of ground behind the church. He'd had a small slab set in the ground as a marker for Gabriel, but it seemed wrong to do more. Vernon Hode had wanted to dig up the grave and give Gabriel a proper burial with a coffin, but Enoch asked him not to. He couldn't bear the thought of his friend being disturbed, of shovels possibly piercing his flesh after he'd already suffered so much.

"Let him rest where he lies," he'd told Vernon. "This cemetery is his now. He doesn't need a marker or a coffin for that."

Enoch drew in a breath and gazed up at the chapel. Clouds massed behind the bell tower, dingy and gray. It would snow before the day was out. He thought of the chores waiting for him at home, of the baby growing in Nellie's belly. If the child was a boy, he'd name him Gabriel after Jasper's friend—his friend. After the man Dinah had loved. Either way, he'd be sure his family never forgot Gabriel. As long as his line continued, one of his descendants would tend to Gabriel's grave.

The crunch of frozen grass beneath boot heels made him glance over his shoulder.

Hands in the pockets of his coat, Vernon Hode stepped to his side. He said nothing for a time, the two of them regarding the tombstone in silence. Finally, he spoke. "Your father's health went downhill quickly."

Enoch nodded. "He was feeble and alone. No one to care for him." Even the friends who'd stood by him the night of Gabriel's death had deserted him. Overcome with grief, Cyrus Herman had hanged himself in his barn a week after the murder. Thaddeus Keel died when a horse he tried to shoe kicked him in the chest. The others who'd taken part in Gabriel's killing gradually drifted away, rarely showing their faces in the village. Sensing something horrific had happened and taking their key from Enoch and Fern, who turned their backs on their father, the townspeople ostracized Atticus.

"He was bitter in the end." Hode's breath plumed in the icy air. "I think he was scared, too."

"Of death?" Enoch's mouth twisted. "He had a right to be, but he's in the ground now—protected by the man he murdered if I'm to believe his inane superstition."

Hode crooked his neck. "You carry no grief for your father?"

"None." Enoch's voice was flat. "There is no room for a man like him in this new century. Let God judge him."

Hode sucked in a breath. Nodded toward the chapel. "With deference to our Lord, do you think we will ever find a man of God to sanctify this holy place?"

Enoch thought of Gabriel, buried in a lonely grave. Of the horror and pain he must have endured before death mercifully claimed him. His eyes misted over, but the tears were not for the brutality of his passing. Rather, for the manner in which he'd lived his life.

"I have no doubt we already have."

* * * *

Present Day

Jillian plucked a piece of cheese from the antipasto platter on the coffee table. Settled several feet away, Blizzard tracked her movement but seemed content to rest with his head between his paws despite the tempting smells wafting from Dante's kitchen.

When he'd asked her out for dinner, Jillian had been prepared to leave the husky at home until Dante insisted differently. "I'm as attached to him as you are. You're forgetting, we spent a lot of time together when you stayed overnight with Madison."

The family room of Dante's house was large but cozy, benefitting from low lighting and candles. He'd kindled a fire in the brick hearth, the warmth inviting Blizzard to lounge nearby. Paintings of riverscapes and cityscapes decorated the walls. She'd seen enough of his work to recognize it now. A single canvas in the corner was propped behind a chair, the image turned away from her.

"Do you need more wine?" Dante appeared in the archway to the kitchen, a tea towel flung over his shoulder, a bottle of Merlot and an empty glass in his hand.

"I'm fine." Jillian shifted to face him. "When you said you wanted to take me out for dinner, I thought you meant to a restaurant."

His expression clouded. "You don't like this?"

"It's lovely." She preferred the quiet evening with just the two of them over a crowded eatery. "But you're doing all the work."

"What work? The lasagna is baking, and the salad is made." Joining her on the sofa, he poured wine into the empty glass, then set the bottle aside. "How about a toast?"

"To what?"

He was silent for a moment as if mulling over the thought before raising his glass. "To Gabriel Vane. He was the catalyst for everything that's happened."

Jillian clicked her glass to his. "I'll drink to that." She sipped her wine. Mention of Gabriel didn't bring the gut-punch of emotion it had before. So much had changed over the last month. Madison was due to be released from rehab in another three days and would be moving in with her. Dante and Tessa had helped her add a fresh coat of paint to her second bedroom—in lavender, Madison's favorite color. Her sister's memories had gradually returned, distance and time providing the necessary filter to keep her sane. Madison was undergoing counseling and would be for months to come. At least Kirk Porter's death had brought a warped kind of closure for both of them.

He'd died without a mark on his body. Not a single broken bone. The coroner concluded he'd suffered a massive shock induced by fright, but Jillian and Dante knew the terror he'd experienced had been real.

To him.

The monsters of Hickory Chapel Cemetery might not have left a physical scratch on his flesh, but they'd butchered him with fangs and claws in the realm of his mind. Slaughter he'd felt. Heard. Breathed. A death he'd believed to be real.

To protect or destroy.

In protecting Dante, Jillian had summoned the power of the stone to destroy the man who'd threatened him. Closing her mind to the memory, she set her wine aside. It was important the emerald be reburied with Gabriel, entombed in the ground so no one could ever use it again.

Leaning forward, she helped herself to the antipasto, putting together a small plate with a sampling of green and black olives, marinated mushrooms, and a few cubes of mozzarella. She used one of the toothpicks Dante had set out to spear a mushroom.

"Sherre told me Gabriel's bones should be released tomorrow. The city is going to stand the cost of reburial."

"That's good news." He picked at a piece of salami, the movement of his right arm stiff. The knife wound had taken stitches, but thankfully, the damage hadn't been extensive. "I want to be there with you when they rebury him."

"Thanks. Tessa and Sherre are planning on attending, too. Even Madison."

In an effort to be supportive of Finn, David Gregg had taken it upon himself to rent a boat and drag the river, eventually recovering the sack containing Gabriel's remains. This time he would have a proper burial with clergy, a coffin, and a marble headstone to offset the date slab that had been his only marker. In addition to the city, the Historical Society of Hode's Hill was contributing funds, and Collin Hode had agreed to cover any excess. Once Maya told him of the situation, he became interested enough to mount a funding project for the preservation of the cemetery and the chapel. With the Hode name attached to the project, the old burial ground and church were sure to see sweeping revitalization.

"I heard Yancy is being questioned about his part in everything." Dante slouched into a corner of the sofa, one arm extended on the backrest, the other over the armrest. "He may still worm his way free given the evidence against him is sketchy. I wonder what will happen to him."

"One thing's for sure. No one will be signing up to be his client at Wickham."

"I hate that damn place." Dante's expression darkened.

"I do, too, now that I understand what happened there." At least Gabriel would finally find peace. His remains had yet to be returned to his burial spot, but after Kirk Porter's death, the rash of accidental deaths had stopped. Almost as if the monsters of Hickory Chapel had been satiated with the Porter brothers' blood. "Did you hear what happened there three nights ago?"

"At Wickham?" He raised a brow. "What?"

"There was a fire. No one seems to know how it started, but it looks like it could have been arson. Sherre picked up the call on her scanner."

Dropping his gaze, Dante swirled the wine in his glass. "Do they have any leads?"

"Absolutely none. There wasn't much damage to the building itself, but the inside was gutted. Sherre said it will likely be condemned and will have to be razed to the ground. It's unlikely anything will ever go there again."

"I can't say I'm sorry."

"I feel the same way." She shook off the gloom. "We should stop dwelling on the negatives and concentrate on the good things that have happened. Tessa told me Detective Gregg was taking her, Elliott, and Finn out for dinner. I'm so thankful the boys haven't suffered any nightmares because of Halloween night."

"Maybe a few, but nothing serious." Dante set his wine aside. "I think Gregg has a soft spot for Tessa and vice versa."

"They look good together."

"He's almost fifteen years older."

"That sounds like the words of a protective cousin."

"Guilty." He shrugged. "Her ex-husband was a jerk. I don't want to see her make another mistake."

"Who says she is?" Jillian laughed. "Besides, they're just going out for dinner. *With Elliott and Finn.*"

"Point taken." A ding sounded from somewhere over his shoulder. "That's the oven. I'm going to check the lasagna. I hope you're hungry."

"Starved." After he left, Jillian strolled closer to study one of the riverscapes, recognizing a point below the North Bridge. Blizzard tracked over, and she bent to rough his fur. Her gaze landed on the canvas propped behind the chair.

Curious, she lifted it to the light.

The building was recognizable in a heartbeat. Dante had painted Wickham with storm clouds massed behind it, but clouds weren't the only embellishment he'd added. Flames shot from the windows and danced on the rooftop, angry red brushstrokes against a night-blackened sky.

"Five more minutes."

His sudden presence as he strolled into the room made her jerk.

The heat of surprise flooded her face. "Dante—"

He walked closer and stared down at the canvas, looking over her shoulder. "You know what's great about having a lot of money?" His tone was conversational, but tension was evident in his jaw. "You can buy real estate for cash, especially when the owner wants to divest quickly."

Tightening her fingers on the canvas, she stared up into his face. "Do you mean—"

"Once you own a building, you can do anything you want with it. Especially when you don't carry insurance."

Jillian swallowed hard and glanced back to the painting. "Like burn it to the ground?" The words slipped from her lips, barely a whisper.

"Wickham took my father. I've evened the score."

She'd never tell a soul.

Some circumstances were best kept secret.

Meet the Author

Mae Clair opened a Pandora's Box of characters when she was a child and never looked back. A member of the Mystery Writers of America and Thriller Writer's International, she loves creating character-driven fiction in settings that blend contemporary and historical time periods.

Wherever her pen takes her, she flavors her stories with mystery, suspense, and a hint of the supernatural. Married to her high school sweetheart, she lives in Pennsylvania and is passionate about urban legends, old photographs, a good Maine lobster tail, and cats.

Discover more about Mae on her website and blog at MaeClair.net.

Acknowledgments

To my critique partners, Staci and Joan, thank you for your insightful feedback and last-minute chapter turnarounds. Your patience in putting up with my scattershot method of writing is greatly appreciated!

To my fabulous editor, Paige Christian, and all of the team at Kensington Publishing/Lyrical Underground—from editing to promo, production and more—I couldn't ask for a better group.

I am so thankful to be part of the Kensington family!

To my readers who continue to support me by purchasing books and leaving reviews, you make it all worthwhile. I am truly grateful you find my novels entertaining. Thank you!

Finally, to my family, friends, and especially my husband, thank you for your unwavering support throughout the years. The writing life is not for the faint of heart, but your belief in me has allowed me to turn a childhood dream into reality.

EVENTIDE

Keep reading for an excerpt from the next Hode's Hill novel,

coming soon from Lyrical Underground.

Learn more about Mae at
http://www.kensingtonbooks.com/author.aspx/29541

Chapter 1

May 15, 1878

One-handed, Hollande Moore twisted the door knob. The room was locked from the inside, the same as all the others she'd tried in the long hallway, leaving her nowhere to hide. Behind her, Sylvia plodded down the corridor, the iron fireplace poker lax at her side, droplets of her son's blood glistening on her face. No rush in her step.

Dear God, how had it come to this?

Hollande sagged against the door, pain from her shattered wrist spiking to her head. Dizziness was a luxury she couldn't afford. A blast of vertigo weakened her knees and made the floor heave beneath her. Perspiration beaded her brow in fat, cold droplets. Gummy with sweat, her palm stuck to the glass knob.

Pat-tap. Pat-tap.

Sylvia's footsteps echoed softly, a harbinger of doom.

Hollande staggered away, every movement sending a fresh jolt of pain through her butchered wrist. At the end of corridor, the door to Darrin's study gaped wide—the single room that had been consistently locked throughout her brief tenure. No matter. Anywhere she could hide was welcome.

Stumbling over the threshold, she fumbled with her good hand to secure the door. The moment her fingers brushed the knob, it came loose in her hand. "No! Please, no!" Someone had battered it repeatedly, making the lock useless.

Hollande fought tears. Had Sylvia planned this killing spree?

Desperate, she swept the room with her gaze, hoping for something— anything—to use as a weapon. The fireplace stood cold and black, both the poker and ash shovel missing. Cobwebs sprouted from lampshades and glommed into corners. Open to the night, the balcony doors sang like a siren, but certain death lay that way.

Her gaze tracked to a cherry desk, thick with dust. Nothing on the top, but the drawers—

She rummaged quickly, relieved when she found a letter opener under a sheaf of papers. The blade was blunt, meant to slice parchment, not flesh. With enough force, it might do the same damage as a knife. In the hallway, the steady tramp of Sylvia's footsteps drew nearer.

Clutching the opener in her good hand, Hollande backed toward the balcony. Even if she managed to clamber over the railing, the drop to the stone veranda was too great, the unyielding surface sure to break bone. Her best chance was to stand and fight.

Pat-tap. Pat-tap.

So close now.

Sweat trickled down her neck. Her heart beat faster and mushroomed into her throat.

Sylvia flung the door wide. She paused on the threshold, hair sweat-matted to her temples, eyes stygian black in the sallow mask of her face. Her fingers twitched on the iron poker.

Hollande forced herself to block the image of Nathaniel—his skull crushed, blood pooling on the floor beneath him. "Please, Sylvia. It doesn't have to end this way. I can help you."

"I don't need help." Her voice was dispassionate, tainted by the cancer of madness. "You never should have come here." She hefted the poker. "I can't change the past, but I can make certain this house becomes your tomb. My son chose you, and so he shall have you—in death!" Without warning, she lurched forward, swinging the rod like a club. A violent displacement of air fanned over Hollande's face.

She hurled herself onto the balcony—

—a step from death on the unforgiving stones below.

* * * *

Present Day

Madison Hewitt stood on the balcony and breathed the air wafting from Yarrow Creek. The heady scent of leafy green plants twined with the sweetness of Spanish bluebells and catmint, warmed by the heat of a late spring day. Elsewhere in Hode's Hill, people took advantage of the long Memorial Day weekend by mowing lawns, opening backyard pools, or gearing up for three days of family cookouts. She'd chosen the stretch to move.

"This one is marked bedroom." Her sister, Jillian, breezed through the doorway carting a cardboard box. She plopped it on the bed, then paused to swipe a strand of hair from her brow. "That's the last of them. Roth left to take the truck back to the rental company."

"Thanks."

Jillian joined her on the balcony. "I love the view."

It was just one of the many things that had attracted Madison to the house. A lot of people would have been bothered by the isolation, tucked eight miles outside of town on a dead-end road. She found it relaxing.

"I noticed there aren't any streetlights, and the nearest house is over a block away." Jillian worried her bottom lip between her teeth. "It's going to get dark at night."

"I'm a big girl. All healed." Madison tried to keep the edge from her voice. "I can take care of myself."

Jillian flushed. "You don't have to say things like that."

"Yes, I do." The stigma of being mentally broken wasn't easily set aside. "Sooner or later, I have to start over."

"You have started over. You're working again."

"Real estate's only part of it." Brushing past her, Madison angled for the bed. Her career had enabled her to learn about the property the moment it came on the market. In search of something small and inexpensive, she'd met one of those goals. The house was far larger than she'd ever need, but the price had been too good to overlook. The previous owner had passed away in a nursing home, her only relative a distant cousin who lived out of state. Wanting to divest of the house quickly, the cousin had been willing to negotiate on many of the furnishings.

"The place is kind of creepy." Jillian scuffed her arms. "Did you see the burial plot in the back?"

"It's only three graves." Madison dug a mint-green sheet from the box. "A lot of people had backyard cemeteries in the eighteen hundreds." She fanned the cover over the bed.

Jillian caught a corner on the other side. "I still think it's creepy."

"Why? We're used to tending graves." Madison tucked a fitted edge around the mattress. "What about Gabriel?"

"That's different. Our ancestors were tasked with that obligation centuries before we were born."

"A person dies three times." Madison recited the oft-quoted lore their mother had taught them. "Once when he dies. Once when he's buried. And once when there's no one left to remember him." The Final Death. Straightening, she reached for the flat sheet. "I'll make sure the people in those graves are never forgotten." The same way she'd carried on the tradition for Gabriel Vane long after his tragic death in 1799.

Jillian frowned. "Grave tending is a serious responsibility. Those people out back are not your concern."

"Maybe I want to make them my concern. I'm sure the woman who lived here before did the same."

"You should let them be." Jillian smoothed the sheet over the bed, the tense line of her mouth telegraphing apprehension. "Sometimes it's best for the departed to embrace Final Death. You don't know anything about those people or the lives they lived."

"I know their names—Darrin and Sylvia Stewart. I think they must have been husband and wife. Their son is buried there, too." In some strange way, the wind-pitted stones had spoken to her. "You worried about me being alone out here, but I'm not."

"Now you're being ridiculous."

Madison quirked a smile. "Says the woman in love with a practicing medium."

"Dante only experiments sometimes."

"Maybe, but when he gets back from his art exhibition, I'd love to get his impression of the house." Madison tossed her a pillowcase. "I've never seen him read a folk memory."

Jillian grimaced as if recalling a particularly painful experience. "Sometimes there aren't any to be found. And sometimes they're better left alone. I have an uneasy feeling about this place."

"No, you have an uneasy feeling about me living by myself after four-and-a-half years under someone's nose."

"True."

Madison huffed out a breath. "Roth asked me to move in with him." Her boyfriend was cut from the same cloth as her sister.

"What?" Jillian's mouth moved soundlessly. She hugged a pillow to her chest. "I didn't know it was that serious."

"It's not. I told him I needed a break."

"You've been together six months. And it's been over four years since Boyd was killed."

"Boyd has nothing to do with it. I need time to myself." She didn't want to talk about it anymore or think of how supportive Roth had been—was still being—by giving her the space she needed. He'd said the "L" word and the prospect terrified her. She was stupid for bringing up the subject when her emotions were caught in a quagmire. Not something you wanted to broadcast when your younger sister possessed empathic abilities. "Let's finish and grab lunch." She reached for the bedspread. "I picked up some chicken salad and mixed fruit."

Jillian nodded as if recognizing the conversation had run its course. After lunch, she helped with more boxes, staying until dusk. By then her dog, Blizzard, who alternately stayed out of the way or followed them room to room, was clearly ready for an overdue dinner.

Madison hugged Jillian goodbye, watched as her sister got the husky settled in the backseat of her Accord then pointed the car down the narrow lane and headed toward Hode's Hill. She waved goodbye from the driveway.

There would be fireworks over the Chinkwe River tonight, something Jillian would catch from the stoop of her brownstone. She'd invited Madison and a few mutual friends to join her, but Madison preferred to spend the first night in her new home alone.

She strolled around the side of the house, where an expansive stone veranda overlooked Yarrow Creek. The second-floor balcony ran the length of the house. From what she'd been able to deduce, that side had once been comprised of two bedrooms. Somewhere in the past, the smaller chamber had been converted into a bath, creating one large master suite.

Not every room had been renovated. Peeling wallpaper, hardwood floors in need of refinishing, and old kitchen cabinets with lopsided shelves were just a few of the problems she'd inherited. But the master suite with its rambling balcony and view of the creek had sold her.

That and the graves.

She followed a trail past the veranda and up an embankment to the rear of the property. The small graveyard—nothing more than a patch surrounded by a knee-high limestone wall—had been situated above flood levels in the event the creek should rise. Grass grew high and spiky at the edges of the stone, a sight that reminded her to invest in a weed trimmer.

Her gaze traveled over the tombstones—three tall, slender slabs dotted with lichen. Darrin had died first, passing in 1863, with Sylvia and their son, Nathaniel, passing fifteen years later. She found it odd they'd both died on the same day. Had there been a fire in the house? An accident?

Thoughts for later.

The air was growing heavy with the musty scent that bloomed around water when dusk settled. She loved the smell and quiet. The feel of a cool breeze wafting from the creek. A few bats flitted between trees and a mourning dove cooed from somewhere among the branches.

As much as she enjoyed being outside, it was time to tackle more boxes. Maybe later she'd relax on the balcony with a glass of wine and watch night settle. Alcohol didn't mix well with meds, but she'd been off her pills long enough. She deserved the treat.

Warmed by the thought, she headed back toward the house. Her sense of serenity was squashed by the sight of a dead squirrel sprawled before the front door.

"Damn." The animal had probably crawled up on the porch and died. Granted, it was an odd place for a wild creature to seek shelter in the waning moments of its life, but the area was infested with small rodents. Maybe the poor thing had tussled with a fox or a raccoon, although she didn't see a mark on it.

Feeling queasy, she headed inside for a trash bag and plastic gloves. When it came time to put the small carcass in the sack, she averted her eyes. The little body was limp in her hand, still faintly warm through the thin layer of her gloves. She bundled the bag shut with a grimace.

The squirrel's body had concealed a single word stenciled in capital letters on the door mat. One that might have been inviting under other circumstances, but now took on a sinister aura.

WELCOME

Madison glanced over her shoulder, the swiftly falling night unsettling. She sprinted across the driveway to the detached garage then dumped the bag in a trash can. Of course, no one was watching her, but it was hard to squash old fears.

How many women survived seeing their husband butchered with a knife? How many people could say they knew what it felt like to be murdered?